COMING CLEAN

CHRISTOPHER MORGAN

Coming Clean

Published by Gate 17 (www.gate17.co.uk)

Cover design: GATE 17

CONTENTS

ACKNOWLEDGEMENTS

Coming Clean took more than seven years to materialize and would not have done so without the support of my family, my father and my wife especially. As always the support of my mother, sister, brothers and step-mother has been fantastic and I'll be grateful forever for their unconditional love, even when I probably was not worthy at times.

Although I doubt they would think much of the subject matter I'd like to think that my grandparents, especially Leeds Grandma would be proud of what this book eventually became. Or more accurately, of what I have eventually become. *Coming Clean* has been a coming of age journey for Dylan Short, for Grace Freeman and by some strange literary osmosis, me, even though my journey has been completely different to theirs. I've been inspired to continue writing and applying what I have learned in *Coming Clean's* difficult and occasionally frustrating birth.

The Chelsea angle to this book is very personal to me. It has been since I started going regularly in the late 80s. So, cheesy as it may sound, I'd like to thank (to name just a small few) Kerry Dixon, Dennis Wise, Roberto Di Matteo, Gianfranco Zola, Roman

Abramovich, John Terry, Frank Lampard and Jose Mourinho for giving me inspiring highs that rank far above anything described in this book. They kept all my fellow Blues and I smiling through tough and not-so-tough times and I believe good writing comes from the same place as the pain and the ecstasy of what we all went through together.

Thank you also to Jon Doyle and my friend Walter Otton for their great advice and encouragement. I'd really like to thank Mark Worrall for chancing a glance at disparate and dirty fragments and seeing the full picture when others (including me) struggled to put it together conceptually.

Lastly also to Stella Mlnekova for her help and feedback, to Don Gibson, John Phillips and Susannah Clay for just being there, to Mirha Mrkaljevic for fixing me, to Mikkel Jacobsen for truly having my back and to Bert for being the best friend anyone could wish for. I miss you every day.

Christopher Morgan
Dubai, July 2015

PROLOGUE

Soundtrack

Bloc Party – 'Like Eating Glass'

The house was silent and cold. Nobody stirred, although the timber floors seemed to echo of the noise from the night before.

A spider ran down his stomach.

Dylan hurtled upright in horror as the scuds of sleep fell away from his eyes. His battered corneas retreated from the light in There was no spider, just a halo of dark sweat across the sheets. Another arachnid droplet scuttled down his flank and onto his thigh. The sun was already cracking the curtains with syrupy light.

Wiping more sweat from his temple with the back of a grubby hand, Dylan swung both feet onto the floor next to his long-ejected duvet, narrowly avoiding an empty fried chicken box. From the night before? Or the night before the night before? The tequila on his breath thudding through his cerebrum would not let him remember.

A hand grasped for his phone half off the bedside table but stopped mid thrust and returned supine to Dylan 's lap.

"...fuck's sake."

The words were just a rasp. There was nobody around to hear it and all the stinking clothes scattered around on the floor were all his. Trying to ignore the taste in his mouth he slipped a hand to a sweaty member and began to rub. Flaccidness turned to semi-rigidity before he began to feel sickly and lightheaded, and stopped.

Even a wank is too difficult. You dismal fucking waste of space.

It was past midday. The noise outside the flat were the usual mid-afternoon sounds. The postman had come and gone and a smattering of what could only be ill tidings of debt lay on the mat, almost luminescent in white from the glass pane. Dylan regarded them for a second or two, debating whether to pad downstairs to pick the letters up.

"No news is good news." Dylan muttered under his breath. The post would wait. It always did.

The large hallway mirror greeted him as he passed, the near-invisible white grains stuck in the corners both calling and castigating him at the same time.

Dylan regarded himself in its tired surface as he passed.

A constant fuck up who actually looked like one: a near-six foot podgy mess.

He would be a large framed man were it not for the consistent lack of definition everywhere but his well-formed man-breasts. His hair was dull and he did not need to sniff his fingers to know it stank. Already it was receding either side of a resolute tuft in the middle. The eyes he knew were too far gone these last few weeks not to be streaked with red and weighed down underneath with sallow bags.

There was a taste in his mouth he was suddenly desperate to mitigate somehow as he lollopped uncertainly into the kitchen, still not fully awake.

No Marmite in the jar.

He held it up to the light and could see daylight through the bottom. It was a sad juxtaposition, he mused.

Dylan cracked a tired smile.

Not a single one of the people he'd been selling drugs to the previous night could even spell the word let alone knew what a juxtaposition was.

How did he get here? It was like hearing the same irritating tune every night, in every bar, its grating synths merciless. Unforgettable but in a bad way. Overfamiliar. What the fuck happened to bring him to this point?

It was rock bottom lasting a month. Over a month now actually. Dylan had lost his proper job two months back.

The late nights and hangdog expressions eventually caught up and the equity he had enjoyed with the company owners extended only so far. One missed train back from Nottingham and one missed morning and it was tea no biscuits in Palmer's office.

It had been a relief in the end. Palmer had been nice enough about it. It was a strange conversation. Palmer knew what Dylan was doing or at least the doing part, maybe also the selling part, maybe not. The raves pushed the weekend out until it was longer in duration than the working week and at the age of 29 Dylan had been finding the alarm calls and comedowns progressively harder to bear. So one day there was a advertising copy writer job, the next a cup of tea, a pat on the back and the drugs.

Kimberley had been surprisingly supportive. He'd sat in Starbucks all day waiting for her to finish work and then she'd come to meet him. He'd told her and she'd just shrugged and observed dryly that the dealing would be a lot easier from then on. He was not sure at the time what she meant by that. Was she sarcastically remarking on Dylan's race to the bottom or was she merely stating facts? Was it really when all was said and done more or less the same thing? Dylan felt a prickle inside as they walked to the pub without talking.

He'd expected her to get angry or at least start pointing the finger in the way she had done so many times predicting that very scenario before. Her lack of anger and apparent unwillingness to say she told him so hurt more than the alternative, yet Dylan had the strange feeling she didn't give a fuck either way. She seemed indifferent. He realised it was not her criticism he missed but his guilt, until that point not given an outlet. She'd bought him a limp Wetherburger and a couple of pints to cheer him up then disappeared into the moistening London night. He stayed in the pub for a few hours drinking alone and telling himself over pint after pint of strong Czech imported lager on special offer, that all would be ok. That it would all work out fine. That these things happened for a reason.

That it was not his fault.

Dylan saw Kimberley again the following night at Rebekah's house party and had been smiling in resignation knowing exactly what was coming and unwilling to fight it even before she laid slender fingers on his arm and gave him a metaphorical cup of tea with no biscuits.

The relationship P45.

It had been huge at the time. A real jawbreaker despite the lack of fight. She had looked great. The best he had ever seen her look. She didn't want to be with him.

Who wants to be with a drug dealer? Aren't drug dealers supposed to drive Ferraris and have loads of guns and country mansions?

The thought had not been far from his mind ever since the party. It returned to him once again.

Dylan gazed aimlessly out of the bay window to the scene of utter greyness outside.

The window was huge. In fact the house was huge. A very large three level Victorian brick town house that despite very much having seen better days was full of character and life. The crumbling brickwork and clattering plumbing added to the feel that the house had character.

Nobody had done anything major to it in probably three or four decades, but forty years' worth of tenants had each left their marks on the house in some way.

It was full of ornaments, drapes, odd items of furniture and plants from the people who used to live there and each wall and ceiling seemed to be painted a different colour. Some walls were painted more than one colour. The items dotted around were all at once alien and random yet seemingly woven into the very stonework of the house. Dylan had no idea who owned most of the clutter. Probably some things belonged to people who had long since died. The house itself seemed old and decrepit but in a charming and homey sort of way. Lightbulbs hung down on ancient browning wires in most of the rooms, apart from the lounge, where someone had fitted some paper lanterns to them for a party in the 70s and nobody had ever bothered to take them down.

The floors were bare wood but not in a stylish modern way: modern floorboards do not have rusty nails sticking out in dark corners and do not let light in or through to the floor below. Huge bay windows dominated the front of the house, and in summer they were open constantly. In the winter the gaps in the brickwork and almost total lack of sealant on some of the windows in the house made it uncomfortably cold in some places, but during those months a hearty log fire seemed to burn of its own accord in the lounge.

The kitchen, despite the huge windows, warmed up quickly, and large dinners of seven or eight people, a normal occurrence throughout the year, soon became close and sweaty occasions with the doors and windows closed.

The house always smelt of something interesting. Some days it would be garlic and herbs from a roast dinner in the kitchen, or maybe wood smoke from the living room. Incense burned often, and all three housemates smoked various things regularly in the house and in the kitchen.

Dylan was one such house member, and had lived there for just over a year.

He shared it with Carla, a legal aide who had the bottom room, and Jason. The latter had the top room. He never really seemed to have a job or do anything even vaguely work related but always seemed to have lots of spare cash and seemed infuriatingly delighted with his lot in life as a result. Jason was always bringing extremely attractive girls back, and Dylan had been introduced to several already that year. He was mostly a considerate and pleasant housemate who had the room over the living room, never cooked, never made a mess and never got drunk and threw up everywhere. But he smoked a lot of dope.

Dylan had the middle room which was a draughty space with very questionable electrics, but he enjoyed it there. Someone had once called the house neglected and unloved but Dylan had set them straight very quickly.

There was a lot of love for the mongrel house in Bounds Green from everyone who had lived there.

Guests either arrived and left quickly, or came over all the time. Some even ended up moving in.

Dylan returned his gaze to the kitchen table.

The tea in his mug was still swirling after the violence of stirring. The grubby-yet—luminous marker laying on the kitchen worktop moist with tea would probably leak eventually. He vaguely recalled it had run out anyway. So maybe it wouldn't. They were not meant to stir tea. But he had not seen a teaspoon in the flat for weeks.

Likely they were all festering in a huddled pack in a half-filled cheesy mug in Carla's room, but he had not seen her for a while either.

The tea was not good. The milk was on the turn; speckles of white curd flecked the surface. Dylan drank it anyway.

The flat was eerily quiet. It stank of stale smoke and something garlicky Carly probably cooked a few days ago. It had to have been her. Jason never cooked, the skinny cunt.

Slick plates covered in yellowy grease, their edges marked with asymmetric chips sat forlornly in the sink and Dylan briefly considered washing them up if purely to do something about the smell. A normal flatmate would have some sort of serious intervention about the state of the place, not entirely Carly's fault admittedly, but Dylan carved an angular, angry FUCKS SAKE into a Post-It note from off the fridge and daintily placed it atop the pile of dishes. He then returned to add a small hyphen - FUCK'S SAKE - to make it grammatically correct.

It got the message across and Dylan was too hungover to be more effuse.

There was fuck-all on the television. Audience sounds and jaunty music sounded tinny and unconvincing. As the ibuprofen began to ease the pain he considered going back to bed.

It had been a big night.

Bar hopping in Soho until midnight, an espresso at Bar Italia to get his edge back and fight off the waves of drunkenness before the actual dealing commenced in earnest. The club was some new place in Brixton.

He recognised a few faces, the usual stuff, drank some more, then Claridge and his group of lads had turned up and gravitated toward him as if they could smell him. Or rather, what was sweating in his pockets and inside his left Nike. The joshing was polite and measured, trying not to attract attention from the door staff while Bean negotiated by screaming in his ear over the din.

It was one of the better club deals he'd done. Claridge and Bean and his mob had taken all his gear, thirty pills and all his Ket. He'd left the packages in the toilet stall and Bean had gone in right after. With the security cameras these days you couldn't be too careful with the big stuff; the big deals.

He'd paced up and down debating to do one more sweep across the heaving, crashing bar area to finish off the last twenty odd of his pills in his pocket. Always better to get rid completely. It was a good almost-policy. Walking the night bus gauntlet with anything in his pocket was a lottery. Taxi queues were the same. Better to get rid completely.

"Anyone need anything?"

"Anything. Party prescriptions. Anyone wanna buy any pills. I have powder."

The voice was low and disjointed, distorted by him not moving his mouth fully open so as not to attract undue attention. Most of his customers were men, some just teenagers. All seemed to want to be his mate. Some were paranoid to the point of something out of a Monty Python sketch. Others were more confident in the mask of relative anonymity afforded by the bubbling mass of dark bodies all around. Money went into his back pocket after every deal, then folded tightly and pushed inside his right Nike.

One more sweep and he was down to a few left less than thirty minutes later, just as the star DJ took the stage. Suddenly stone cold sober and dog tired, Dylan pushed through the throngs for the door, fingering the small hard round lumps in his other pocket.

Seven left.

Claridge was leering at someone at the bar in front and he diverted his course. He was going to dump them outside but better to ingratiate himself further to what passed for a regular and loyal customer these days. Dylan slid in and gave him a hug as if they were actual friends pressing the seven pills into his hand with a mock-tender peck on the City Boy's bacon-like face.

Claridge had whirled around knocking a tumbler flying and bodily picked up all near-six foot of Dylan.

Words were snatched above the screeching noise, fractured sections of the big man's diatribe. Spittle dribbled down Dylan's neck. Dylan agreed with nodding and smiling and pulled for the door, but Claridge was having none of it. His boys were in the corner in a little private alcove, even less well lit than the rest of the club. Sweat dripped off the walls, as the dry ice in the air made it look like the shirted group were actually steaming. Maybe they were.

Hetch, a painfully skinny rat faced junior member of the group tried to feed him two of his pills back and for a second Dylan was tempted. Batting away politely the offer he allowed his tired eyes to close for a second. Just to rest. When he opened them Claridge's huge face and bald head was looming out of the gloom backlit terrifyingly in red club light. Sweat sprayed off his temples as he swooped in, rolled up banknote in hand revelling in the joyous cliché of it all.

The cocaine felt clean. Cool.

It felt everything the club was not and for a second all there was but the taste.

It mischievously reminded him of natural, unfettered and unadulterated things. Of garden centres, post-storm rains and of mown lawns on hot days.

He closed his eyes again as the rush folded over him and the sweat began in earnest. Dylan gave a long exhale, seemingly several seconds long and deafeningly loud, drowning out the klaxons. It was decent gear. It was certainly the best he could routinely get his hands on and for this reason Dylan was in demand for housecalls. Claridge and his boys seemed to approve. Dylan watched him, hands on hips with languid smile as the big guy demolished a huge line of cocaine, double-dropped two pills and then drank one of a herd of Jaagerbombs with such violence that the glass shattered as it was slammed onto the table.

Dylan watched Bean moving up and down, unable to keep still as something began to take the hectic edge off the coke. His eyes all at once seemed to be bulging out of his head, yet screwed shut. Nothing was in time. The music was out of synch somehow.

Dylan realised that the cocaine had been laced with the ketamine he'd sold him.

His eyes lolled. Imaginary hands pulled him back into the seating, stroking his limbs. The last vestiges of sensible thought began to clear out as Dylan recalled the wedge of banknotes secure in his shoe. It had been a successful night. The gear had gone and he felt the danger of it leave his system as the powdered substances coursed through.

The gear was gone, it was just a normal night out now.

Had he done a pill? He could not remember.

“It is. It. IS. It is a night out. A normal one. Normalll niiiiight ouuuuut..." Dylan mumbled to himself over the music trying to smile.

Bean saw him but was too far away to lean in and ask what he said.

The rhythmic breathing in and out. Dylan felt the thudding in his chest and wondered if it was the music or his breathing. The music was disjointed. It seemed to come. And go. As he breathed. Dylan 's eyes eased closed with silken tenderness. In. And Out.

In.

And.

Out.

He doubted Claridge had the skill or judgement but the cut had been well done. There was just enough in it to make his head swim but not enough to blot out the coke. The rapture of the coca plant danced up his cerebrum and Dylan opened his eyes again just to close them again. The lights and music danced in front of his eyes in the darkness, melding into his subconscious behind his eyelids. He saw indeterminate shapes in vivid purples, pinks and reds that flew off into the packed dancefloor to mingle with the heaving mass of bodies when he opened his eyes again. The Amstel tasted strange, yet he did not move his hands to drink from the brown bottle on the table.

In. And. Out.

Had he taken a pill? Dylan couldn't remember but somehow did not care.

The alcove was smaller somehow, he noticed. Smaller. Painted a different colour to how he remembered it a few minutes ago. Had it been made of bricks? Was the club made of bricks? How many bricks?

Bricks from Bedford. They made bricks in Bedford didn't they? Was the club in Bedford? Or London?

Bean threw a meaty arm around him seemingly from the other side of the table. Dylan could not hear him talking but assumed it was about bricks.

In. And. Out.

Bean was proffering something two handed to him, Dylan squinted but could not make it out through screwed shut eyes. His jaw wrenched open and a thick viscous liquid poured in. It tasted vile. Dylan retched but did not vomit. Water streamed from his eyes as the evil tasting potion drained away down his throat. Bean slapped him around the head in a cloud of sweat as he threw the empty shot glass onto the floor.

He was screaming something about "fucking drugs". Dylan smiled and nodded slowly, eliciting another slap from Bean and a thick, emotionless kiss on his sopping forehead.

After a few minutes or longer Dylan began to register a few more details as the music moved back into synch and the group grew. There was tequila. A lot of tequila.

There were taxis and a lift.

And then a large apartment, filled with people he did not know. Unfeasibly huge Margaritas with no salt rim in disposable plastic tumblers with poodle leg thick lines of cocaine chasers he had already sold Bean. Then the sofa.

The doors in the flat looking out over the Thames were wide open and the room was cold even with a throng of people milling about. The cocaine and lager were keeping Dylan warm, but his skin crawled cold. There was a woman. She'd been warm, whatever her name was. She had been warm, with dark blonde hair and lager on her breath.

They came up and then down on a couple of pills each and then someone had produced a lottery ticket of some more ketamine. She was alright looking from he could remember but wore jeans and a top that did nothing for her figure and he could not tell if she'd had a good body or not. It was as if they were both huddled together inside a giant dark duvet cover. The throngs and music seemed so far away.

He was too fucked to care.

They had done bumps off the corner of Dylan's Donor Card without talking much. What words there were melded into tranquilised chaos shortly after. He and the girl moved their mouths together in the most unsexual kiss imaginable, rendered relevant by the drugs and the madding partygoers they could sense rather than see.

There was no memory of the cab ride, of leaving Claridge's flat or of getting undressed and into bed. Whoever the girl was he was sure she would not remember he existed let alone his name.

His attention turned to the then and there. The elderly, labyrinthine house near Bounds Green in the northern extremes of London, in the shadow of Alexandra Palace. Dylan gave an involuntary shiver and regarded his handiwork.

More than five hundred grubby pounds lay sweaty and coiled on the dresser. It had been a good night.

Jason came in and left again without saying hello. Carly came home around four and Dylan listened to her stomp into the kitchen, see the Post-It, stomp out and into her room. She emerged a couple of minutes later and swept into the living room.

"Soz about the kitchen mate."

It was all he was going to get.

Dylan grunted with a dismissive wave of the hand pretending to be engrossed in some antique hunting programme.

Presently he got up and elected after a lot of agonising to go across the road for some food. Unable to find any shoes he went across the road in slippers and a long coat, making him look like some sort of shabby benefit-dodger he realised half way across the road. In the shop, robbed of decisiveness, he settled after further agonies on a moody-looking chicken samosa, a green Pot Noodle, a large packet of crisps, a flapjack and a packet of frozen Findus Crispy Pancakes to do in the toaster as he did throughout university. And six large cans of Stella.

Top night in.

An unfeasibly tiny old woman came into the shop just as he was leaving, seemingly crushed under the weight of her own wig and the knitted tea-cosy she had on top of it.

"Good afternoon Mrs Chaudhury, how are you?" Dylan exclaimed loudly.

The woman looked up at him in a mixture of pity and thankfulness.

"Oh David it so cooled." she blurted out with a thick and barely decipherable Asian accent.

Dylan always smiled at her getting his name wrong. It reminded him of Trigger from Only Fools and Horses.

"Can I help you with your shopping Mrs Chaudhury?"

The old lady gave a sigh of acceptance that for a younger person would convey nonplussedness but in her case carried immense thanks.

Twenty minutes later Dylan walked the old lady back across the road with four carrier bags of shopping on each straining hand. Mrs Choudhury had gone to town glad of his help and bought half the shop. Dylan even contributed a fiver from his own pocket when the tiny old lady came up a little short.

"You are lovely man David. One day you meet lovely wife have lovely chil'ren. Thank you so much for you help."

She was out of breath just crossing the road. Dylan was glad to have made her smile though, even if she had spent much of the 20 minutes shopping scolding him relentlessly on the poor diet choices contained within his own carrier bag.

Jason was in the kitchen when he got back, prone on the floor staring at the ceiling smoking a vast joint.

"Alright cuntface."

"Hullo Jase." Dylan nimbly sidestepped the form of the man on the floor and piled the beers into the fridge, debating dropping on onto Jason's crotch but deciding not to in the end.

Jason being on the floor was the sort of random thing he did completely as if he did them all the time. Him being floorboard angel on the kitchen floor was the most normal fucking thing in the world. Dylan handed him a beer without asking if he wanted one.

"Swap."

The joint was handed up and Dylan settled on the kitchen window frame to draw deeply whilst the kettle boiled. The coughing had more or less subsided by the time it boiled.

Jason kept talking through Dylan's hacking as if it wasn't happening.

"...do you know what i mean though? There's that and then there's actual fucking theft. Its a thin grey line mate. One man's freedom fighter is another man's terrorist they say. One man's thieving fucking scally is another man's Robin Hood. Do you know what I mean."

Dylan had not got the faintest idea what his flatmate was talking about or what link it had to whatever he was staring at on the kitchen ceiling. He stepped over and grasped the hot pot of salt, additives and artificial flavourings.

"Jesus H Fucking Christ Dyl you eat some fucking wrong food sometimes. You're what? 28? 29?"

Dylan was mid-shovel and did not respond.

"Pot Noodle? Most people grow out of that at Uni. Can I have some crisps?"

Dylan emptied the bag into a massive wooden salad bowl with pencil shavings in the bottom and settled down on the kitchen floor with his back against the oven, pot in one hand and fork in the other. Jason passed back the joint and the pot was set down on the floor. More coughing. It searched and scratched at his lungs, seeking another exit than his nose and mouth. The acrid fumes seethed up his nose. Dylan's nose wrinkled. The coughs peaked and the sneeze came out of nowhere. To his horror a piece of dried noodle detritus flew out of his nose and landed with a thud that belied its small weight on Jason's t-shirted chest.

Jason stopped mid-diatribe and craned his neck forward to see.

"Is that a piece of noodle?"

Dylan nodded.

Jason made no move to get rid of it and with heavy limbs Dylan had no inclination to fetch it so it stayed there. The smoking continued and eventually Carla hammered upstairs and started to make a pizza from the fridge. Upon seeing the crisps and the joint arrayed between the two prone men on the floor she consigned the pizza to the Too Hard Basket, fetched her wireless speakers and the last of her Ketamine from the night before and then settled down on the kitchen floor alongside.

"In for a penny in for the pound chaps. Is that a piece of Pot Noodle?"

"I can see up your skirt Carla. Don't move." Jason added helpfully.

"I'm not wearing a skirt you plank. Go back to sleep." Carla laughed.

"Right who wants some fucking horse tranquilliser then?"

Jason raised both arms in a flat zombie pose.

Dylan smiled to himself.

"I'm in."

*****

The Autumn air was chilly.

Dylan's movement down Tufnell Park Road was rapid. He moved with a deftness that belied the poisons his body had yet to fully deal with from Claridge's impromptu house party plus the impromptu smoking session that turned into something deeper and far more random the previous night. The amphetamines in the pills were still wrapped like atheroma around his core making his skin glisten with sweat in the cold night air. Luca's apartment was the downstairs of a very ordinary looking turn-of-last-century semi.

He knocked and Luca's housemate Antonio answered with a trademark scowl and trademark lack of any other kind of communication. Luca was sat in a bathrobe at a dining table scribbling in a bright pink diary. He barely reacted to Dylan as he walked in, slapping his hand against Dylan's in what passed for a greeting handshake.

The room was dark save for the light afforded by a huge flatscreen in the corner, where Antonio was playing a violent and very fast console game up loud. The place stank of damp. It always stank of damp and smoke. Dylan could never figure out how a guy with as much income as Luca obviously had did not do anything about the cloying stench.

"Long time no speak. I hear Rebekah's party was good. Antonio went, he said you guys were having a time." the patter was matter-of-fact. Dylan knew Luca could not give less of a fuck about him or his partying if he tried.

Luca fixed his little nut-like eyes onto Dylan and it was all he could do to maintain the stare. Luca was a cunt. A macho cunt. He liked to intimidate people like he was some sort of big shot crime boss drug kingpin gangster nutter or something. He was a bully. He even had the natty gold tooth to make him look scarier. Dylan had no time for people like Luca normally but this was his living, and he had to eat. So he was the dealer and you had to be polite. You played the game.

"Yeah, was a top night. I was out with Claridge and Bean and the rest the other night too. I went to his place, fucking swish man. What's he do for a living, do you know?" Dylan tried to sound as relaxed as possible.

"Forex broker he told me. What you taking today."

It wasn't really a question. Luca didn't bother to make it sound like one. It was more of an ungentle inducement to hurry things the fuck along.

Dylan straightened his back and ground his teeth, trying to sound cool and not bothered. No matter how many times he bought serious weights of serious drugs that would get him serious time in prison if he ever got seriously caught, it still freaked him. Just slightly. Deep inside he knew it was a good thing. Complacent guys with no fear were the ones who got lifted.

Actually that was nonsense. He didn't know anyone who had been caught, nor did he know anyone who knew anyone. It was more like an urban wisdom based on an urban myth. As he was handing over most of the big wedge of greasy banknotes he had farmed from the night before to Luca's twitching and impatient clutches, it occurred to Dylan that he knew more people who had died on drugs than were doing time in prison because of them.

It was a sobering thought.

Sobering such as one could have such a thought whilst buying more than one hundred speckled pills, twenty grammes of ketamine and a large weight of pristine white cocaine.

The drugs seemed to weigh a tonne in his courier bag. He put an extra spring in his step as he walked away from the house. It was a strange feeling of exhilaration, relief that he had done the deal, and nerves about carrying five years or more of his life very literally in his hand. The front gardens he was passing were every bit the slotted domesticated London that everyone knows but never really sees. A cat eyed him cynically as he came past, sat on top of a wheely-bin. Its gaze seemed to accuse him. It was as if it knew what he had in his bag. Dylan imagined having a conversation with the cat. Telling it to fuck off and mind its own business, and not to be so bloody judgemental.

The cat turned away in disinterest as the thoughts sailed through Dylan's mind.

Yeah you better mind your own business you little furry bastard.

He strutted onwards, as welcome darkness closed in as the autumn grip tightened on London's suburbs.

Bloc Party in his headphones escorted him bravely back to Bounds Green.

To safety. And sleep.

*****

Daydreaming about old black and white cop films, Grace slouched further down into her chair. Her dark blonde hair straggled over the back of the chair like cast off clothes.

The office was, as always, too hot. It stifled her in warm circulated air, drying her skin and making her eyes hurt. Having had a big lunch washed down with two large Pinots at the Spotted Leopard, she was sleepy and listless. The chicken wrap and large potato wedges sat like a bowling ball in the bottom of her stomach, pulling at her eyelids from deep inside. Grace patted her stomach. She was putting weight on and some of her shirts and trousers did not fit as comfortably as they did before.

The day crawled by.

She'd downed a double espresso on her way to her office. The caffeine buzz had carried her through to lunchtime having done all the tasks she was supposed to do, or could be bothered to try and remember anyway. There was probably more bollocks certification stuff Andrew had noted down but it was one email from ages ago and it required a lot of effort to find which she was in no position to expend.

Clambering back up her seat and placing both hands on the desk, she looked out of the office window. The street outside, fourteen floors below, was bathed in that depressing sort of mid-afternoon light. The sort of light where the sun never really got on top of its battle with the thick cloud and was giving up with a chilly surrender a couple of rounds early.

It was almost four PM and would be dark soon. Thursdays were more encouraging than Wednesdays. Tuesdays were not fun, and this past Tuesday had been even worse than usual in a manner of some sad retribution from the weekend's poison consumption.

She had gone out with Abi and Steffen to some bar, met up with Thom who had invited them to a houseparty. It had been really good, despite the fact she had left without her coat. What she could remember of it anyway. They had arrived to Wapping and after some too-ing and fro-ing about outside been buzzed up to a river view apartment overlooking the Thames, belonging to Thom's mate Claridge. It had been way past closing time when they arrived and as usual Grace was lagging having forced the pace early on in Bar Nasty with two for one cocktails.

A blatant-as-you-like keybump of bugle in the back of the cab had taken the edge off, but then Claridge had welcomed them all as they walked in with a pill each on a silver serving plate. She had laughed at the time, making sure even so to appear grateful of his outlandish hospitality.

Who did he think he was? Willy Wonka's sweaty club promoter, porn star shagger brother?

Some parties were like that, weren't they?

You got invited to someone's house and they were a bit older. They reacted to having a house full of international bright younger things by making out it was the last days of fucking disco, like they lived in Studio 54 or the Hacienda or something. All it did was make people more aware that they were probably old enough to have "had it large" way back when drugs were amazing and the music was worth doing. Everyone else hoarded their drugs like life itself and nobody shared with the universally desperate unless they were actually desperate. Sharing with people in such an ostentatious manner was against house party etiquette for people these days, even for hosts. As if everyone at the party was a drug nut.

Grace was on the fringes of her social group. She did not mind the odd line here or there and quite enjoyed a very, very occasional pill but could never be described as a drug nut. A lot of her friends were but it wasn't really a hobby Grace saw much in.

Some of her mates were into drugs like some people are into golf or stamp collecting. The term "drug geek" means nothing to anyone unless they have spent time in London's clubbing and afterparty scene. The seriousness of it all made her laugh every time. Some even had the wine-tasting facial expressions and observational remarks about “finish” and “impact” post-snort. How fucking wanky was that? It was as if the drugs had become an extension of the hipster cool thing she had also never got on with. The cooler-than-thou-better-coke-than-thou sort of thing.

Daft.

Pills usually made her feel really sick for an hour, weed was the same and coke was over-hyped. She did not see the addiction. It was mainly a fleeting and occasional activity she partook in because her peer group did.

It was something you did rarely on a big night out, not a reason to have a night out in the first place, right?

The bath was filled with ice and about twenty different varieties of beer and cider, most from the corner shop over the road. Grace grabbed one, looked around to see if whoever brought them objected and seeing no impediment wandered away, dripping can in hand. The lager tasted hoppy and flat after the coke but she was thirsty and drank it before it got warm. Making sure she took another can of a different batch, she left again looking for someone to talk to just to break the cycle.

As if sensing her solitary unrest Claridge bounded over and man-hugged her again, a huge bearish damp mess of straining muscle. She and he had a stunted conversation with him so close to her face that she could smell his fetid breath. Claridge evidently had no idea what her name was, only that she was a single mate of Abi's and therefore ostensibly wide open and obviously naturally, very keen to blow him out of gratitude for the pill and the party. He got bored very quickly at her recalcitrance and cynically tried to give her another pill. She Graciously took it and put it in her pocket for later.

The music changed as one of Claridge's mates had taken out the CD playing on the decks and was winding up to an energetic if poorly-judged jabbering tech-house set of sorts with no songs she recognised.

Grace had milled about a bit for what felt like twenty minutes. It had to have been longer though as she had come up on the pill, fought off the nausea by pacing up and down grinding her jaw and then chewed some bloke's ear off about foxhunting in the kitchen. Then when Abi and Steffen had disappeared into one of the bedrooms no doubt to fuck and do their coke privately without having to share, she sat on the sofa rubbing her knees. Left on her own as per usual.

Left on my own as per frigging usual.

An averagely tall guy with a ragged comb over that probably looked better in concept than reality had been sat there in silence. He had had tequila on his breath. It was a scene straight out of those park bench scenes in sketch shows. Grace thought for all the world he was about to talk to her about the weather.

He started to talk at her and offered her another pill and then, later, some Ket. She had refused at first but the first pill was a good one. It was hectic and she felt her heart racing as she chewed her gum in time to the music. Feet tapping, knee rubbing and hands floating she accepted a taster of the ketamine on the second offer, making several clear insistences that it was her first time.

The walls and ceiling and partygoers rolled away quietly like scenery at a darkened theatre as she melted into him without really deciding to do so. Decisions came and went. It had been fucking weird. Not good weird and not bad weird but weird weird. She could not remember much of it to say whether she enjoyed it, but the numb emptiness of those couple of hours in memory was not pleasant, in hindsight anyway.

Grace knew with certainty it would be the last time she would try horse tranquiliser recreationally.

Only fools and horses, right?

She remembered very little about the bloke. Declan was it? Dean?

Pushing her bottom lip out she whirled lazily in her chair, narrowly missing trapping her fingers between desk and armrest on the way round. It was the dance of the bored Grace. Debating a cup of tea she picked up her phone to see if she had saved the bloke's number.

Dylan?

Dylan was his name.

He stank. She remembered the smell of beer and cigarettes and sweat on his t-shirt. Funny she could not picture his face but remembered his warmth and his smell. He had been quite chunky hadn't he? Not fat but a little bit fat. Taller.

Grace swept her hair behind her ear and thought hard about what to text him. A phonecall was too intrusive and she was not that bothered anyway, but a text was about right.

But what to say?

Finally she put her phone down with finality. She could barely remember his name so what do you text someone in that situation?

Hi dnt know you but we did drugs together (sort of) at wknd wanna meet 4 a drink? Grace xx

Nope.

Sandra slid up silently behind her. Grace jumped in shock. The woman was like a stealth bomber.

"Grace can we have a quick chat?"

Uh-oh. This doesn't sound good.

*****

Dylan would have missed the text anyway because he was suited and booted in a meeting with a man twice his age.

A recruitment consultant had rung late on Wednesday night to ask him if he was able to come to an interview the following day. He'd agreed on the spot, oddly craving a return to the rat race.

The interview went well. The guy on front of him was a kindly chap. Dylan idly wondered as he watched his mouth move if he dressed up in women's clothes at weekends.

Apparently, his CV was good and they needed someone urgently to cover on the copy desk. The firm was a mid-level agency he had heard of but knew exactly nothing about.

"Can you start on Monday Mr Short? We'd be pleased to have you."

And then there were rushed clammy handshakes and an odd feeling the bloke wanted to hug him. His tea hadn't even cooled down enough for him to drink yet here he was being offered the job. It was less money than the old one but in the same part of The City and an easy commute from Bounds Green. Dylan wondered why they were apparently so keen to have him but figured whatever the reason was it could not possibly be a good one. The main thing was he was back and could start rebuilding his shattered CV. He had not given Palmer's name on his CV as a reference and the guy had not asked so all the better. There was no way his relentlessly unspectacular resume would generate anything other than boredom for most so whatever the reason was, he did not really want to know.

Maybe he could call Kimberley and tell her the good news. The guy was talking to him again and so Dylan flicked his mind back to the then and there. His bottom lip was so wet it looked like he was about to dribble down his white-bearded chin.

"Thank you Mr Atwater, I really appreciate the opportunity and I'd be delighted to join the team. It is a huge privilege." Dylan embellished in his best public-school patter.

The older guy looked like he wanted to hug him again, so Dylan shook hands for a fourth time and moved toward the door. A lift, a flight of stairs, a security gate came and passed and then a blast of cold air kissed him on both cheeks in congratulation as he erupted victorious into the gathering gloom outside.

ONE

Six Months Later

Soundtrack

The Clash – 'Rudie Cant Fail'

Dylan lay in bed, cocooned up in his duvet with the edge of the duvet across his face like a blindfold.

He had woken up some minutes hence, but was unwilling to open his eyes for some Nosferatu-esque fear of the sun. This proved to be completely unfounded as once his eyes were screwed open, he found that the sun was a very long way from his bedroom window in north London.

Dylan had a thick duvet on his bed and the prospect of leaving his warm nest for anything, least of all work, was singularly unappealing.

Dylan's alarm went off at 07:20am, and he snoozed until 07:30am. Eyes resolutely and rebelliously shut, he debated the whys and wherefores of calling in sick (again) and then the whys and wherefores of a furtive self-abuse session into a sock until at least 07:40am.

Better to leave the sickies to when you really need to call one, Dylan. This is not one of those days matey. And you don't have time for a wank either!

Admitting defeat he got up and ran in grubby underwear using grubby towel to hide rapidly diminishing morning glory from Carla who had left the house at least half an hour previously, downstairs to shower. At 07:58am he realised as always that he was running late and bolted out of the door slamming it shut so hard it seemed to shake the whole edifice. He sat down on the train on the last seat available at 08:07am and took stock of what vital lifestyle accoutrement had been left on the dresser that day. There was always one. On that day it was his workpass in its broken holder on grubby lanyard. The train arrived at 08:09am at Alexandra Palace station, whereupon he asked the woman stood in front glaring at him for not immediately offering her his seat, if she did in fact want his seat. She curled up her lip then shot him a look as if he had just stamped on her cat. Naturally she did not make any move at all to accept his gracious offer.

Dylan's train made its way down to Moorgate station, where it pulled in noisily at 08:30am exactly. Every morning he marvelled at the revelation that for a supposed third world rail network, decaying and terminally tardy, his train was never late. Was this the only timely running train in all of the UK? Evidently.

He walked past the stairs and decided as every morning to start going up them tomorrow.

Enchanted by the ever-present smell of bacon sandwiches at 08:32am Dylan spent the whole journey up the escalator weighing up whether he could justify fried dead pig in a sickly, bleached roll this morning for £2.20. He almost never gave in, as much for the money as the health reasons. That morning was no different.

It was like a cut and paste, the timings, the journey, the rigmarole.

The variations on a daily basis tended to be too subtle to truly render his morning commute interesting, but were familiar enough to negate the need for caffeine before leaving the house. Dylan could probably have done the journey in his sleep if he were so inclined.

That morning, having resisted the nasal siren lure of the bacon sandwich, Dylan barrelled past the homeless guy and the dodgy workman café, crinkling his nose. It was the antithesis of the bacon smell from the kiosk near the barriers, the ever-present reek of mountains of melted cheap cooking Cheddar. Outside the wind tugged at him, pushing him and cajoling him with icy pointed fingers for his laziness. Undeterred, Dylan walked briskly onwards, retreating into some Kasabian in his headphones.

The office felt its usual sterile self as he slung his shoulder hard through the double doors and advanced on the desk he had left just nine hours previously like a cowboy slewing into a familiar bar. Nobody greeted him. The metaphorical piano did not start up and none of the dancing girls started cooing his name. Not one single person wished him a good morning or even acknowledged his brave attendance and associated battle-with-bed.

They had no idea what he went though. Every morning.

He arrived at his desk at 08:41am precisely, 11 minutes late, the same as every morning.

The previous night had been a late one with a copy report he was writing, and like many, he found that he got more done in the few hours when everyone had gone home than in the whole of the day that had gone before. In truth, Dylan had very little to do during the day because he did it all at night, and spent his days writing personal emails and surfing the net. In his previous job he had run quite a successful trading business for various things on Ebay from his work desk during the day. The work would always wait until the evening when he could plug in his headphones, order something filthy from the takeaway to be fetched right to his desk by the irate security guard on the reception and concentrate. It was not as if he had anything to go home to.

The pizza box of last night's dinner was still sat there covering up his keyboard, as if imploring him to put the box in the bin before he started work. Taking off his jacket but not choosing to hang it on the coat rack, but instead off the back off his office chair, he settled hard into his chair with a great sigh of an exhaustion not in keeping with the time of day. Placing both palms flat on the table, he looked up for the first time to see who was in the office. Immediately deciding that coffee was required, he switched on his PC monitor, logged in and then walked briskly to the office kitchen to make his morning cup of coffee.

The morning slipped by in a blur of caffeine and pop-up email notifications. He briefly considered a furtive danger-wank in the gents toilets around mid-morning however dodging-work-without-appearing-to and surfing the 'net won the battle for the morning. He enjoyed the immersion therapy of his work. Some people fervently dislike their jobs to the point of physical pain, but Dylan did not mind. The pub conversation where he said he enjoyed his job was, for the most part, a bit of a stretch. There were times of course, but these tended to be workmate social and pub-related more than strictly work per se. Even these had dried up a lot of late.

Dylan was an intelligent, charismatic man who knew his job and was confident in himself and what he could get away with, recent termination notwithstanding. He knew he was something of an old fashioned chancer where work was concerned, even on what had to be, he knew, his last chance at being a professional contributor to society doing anything even vaguely related to his degree.

It was a tag he was looking to shed. It was on his mind. Sadly an outside observer to his rather fragmented daily routine of sloth and emails would probably suggest that precious little will was in evidence from the man himself. The fact that his new superiors were aware of this more or less from day one of his employment may or may not have percolated down into Dylan's consciousness. It was hard to tell. He spent day after day writing rough copy and emails about rough copy whilst other staff members got to go to the conferences and seminars he did not have the slightest interest in going to but was nonetheless hugely put out he was not asked to go on. The copy was solid enough and deadlines hurdled with - just - enough to spare to prevent any major issues. He was more timely than before and although he was calling in sick more often, the weekend's supplementary income and associated lifestyle was not creating too many problems.

He was getting away with it for the time being.

Much of the morning was spent on a Chelsea site forum board chatting with fellow Chelsea fans, some of whom he knew and some he did not. They talked and joked about Adidas trainers, about aways, Arsenal and about aggro.

Lunchtime slipped past, and it was almost 2:00pm before Dylan stood up and resolved to go get something to eat. Pulling on his coat, he minimised the lengthy personal email he was writing to a girl called Nicole so that nobody would see it and headed out. Outside the rain was falling glumly without purpose or intent. The air was clammy. Dylan crossed the road avoiding a mush of wet cardboard on the floor and walked into the sandwich shop that was all but bare of his usual preferences. One enormous chicken and sweetcorn mayo with extra bacon minus the salad bap and £4.90 later, he headed back to the office, cigarette in hand, his mind filled with what to do about Nicole.

She and he had not met but were introduced through an online dating agency of which they were both members. He had told himself that this was the modern metrosexual way of meeting someone and that he found the art of pulling in clubs very hard not least because he was usually pre-occupied with other matters. She had told him he was cute from his pictures; like James Corden. It had taken Dylan a long time to figure out whether that was an insult or not. In the even Dylan decided not to be offended. Corden was funny, and not a bad looking bloke considering he was a dirty West Ham fan…

In truth, Dylan did not pull very often.

It was not a looks thing per se, he just was not the kind of guy women went for based on looks. This is probably the kindest way to describe him. He was not ugly by any means, but at very nearly six feet in shoes and a little under or a little over sixteen stone, he was somewhat overweight which robbed him of his confidence where women were concerned. Women tended to go for looks in clubs, and Dylan could not imagine any woman doing that to him in such a situation and as with so many of the intangibles that depended on confidence, it rarely happened. Dylan stood outside the lift doors waiting to be taken back up to the ninth floor where he worked. His reflection in the mirrored doors looked back at him intently.

Mousy hair in an unintentionally ragged comb over did not mask his rapidly receding hairline but at least it made him feel a little younger.

Perhaps not younger but less old.

His eyes, large and involving, had large bags under them from too many late nights and early-ish mornings. Shifting his footing, he winked at his reflection and smiled a large, yellowy toothy grin stained from too much spicy food and caffeine.

Nobody around seemed to notice.

He pulled his shoulders back and squared up to his reflection. Dylan was a substantial man, but then appearances are sometimes only a fraction of a person. Beneath the rather pale and podgy exterior, there was a lot more to Dylan Short. Substantial, decent and ambitious things that he was desperate to release.

And then to live up to so people could see it.

The online dating thing had worked out acceptably well for him in the past. It was a safe, convenient and interesting way of meeting new people and quite often, getting sex. Indeed, the predator inside Dylan had long ascertained that the women on the dating site were as down in their self-confidence as he was, and that a little bit of silver-tongued flattery went a very long way indeed. If the nightclub was not his habitat, the online dating certainly was where women were concerned.

Dylan felt that he was a smart, if rather cynical and occasionally subversive person who preferred to talk and think his way into and out of things. He had done it enough times to be confident enough for some to have called him arrogant in the past.

In truth, the arrogance, or what confidence in himself passed as such to people, masked a rather insecure young man in some respects. Dylan pressed his chin into his shirted chest and looked at his neck fold over making a double chin.

Sighing, he got into the lift.

TWO

Soundtrack
Editors – 'Blood'

An empty fast food box lay on its side, its brightly coloured hue standing out against the grimy pavement. If someone were asked to picture the colour that comes to mind when you say the word grimy, then London's pavements were most certainly it. The dark grey of the flagstones, cracked and potted triangles and odd wedges spotted with shades of beige chewing gum was a matt colour, unusual for the time of year. Normally the grey streets of London were spattered with reflections of what went on above the streets in the rain, but not today. It had rained the day before and rain was most certainly on the cards, but not yet today.

The naked trees on the park fringes looked sour and disinterested. Even the shopfronts looked wary and paranoid somehow to people, or perhaps because of them. London is a cold, harsh place on those raw grey winter days when it is not raining.

The rain seems sometimes to add a gloss to everything. It is warming in a strange kind of way.

The box skated across an inch or two across the pavement and a piece of lettuce, sticky with some kind of sauce, spilled out. Feet stepped all around the box as it lay prone, inviting the inevitable which arrived but a second later. A dark booted foot on the end of a column of blue denim crushed the box then kicked it across the concrete. It lay lopsided and sad at the foot of some black railings. Beyond lay a four lane crossroads of noisy mayhem like some fast-flowing river. Everywhere there were black cabs, bikes, buses, vans and lots of people. The London traffic was the same as it always was.

London traffic is legendary. There is no uniformity to it. It often resembles pure chaos as a thousand moving objects move in hundred loose streams, while others seem to have no stream and move seemingly at random.

Airliners crammed with hundreds of people bound for Heathrow groaned across the odd shapes of sky visible. Nobody ever looks up at them.

The wind tore down the streets as if mocking the locked traffic below. It kicked up rubbish and pressing it against walls seemingly trying to the show the people how litter-ridden the streets were. The deflated box lay against the railings for some time before being pushed out into the road by another foot and was lost from sight and into oblivion in the slipstream of a red bus.

The bus made painfully slow progress down the road towards the Angel intersection having ground its way up from Stoke Newington.

Its doors opened.

A familiar yet startlingly unfamiliar figure stepped nimbly off the rear exit and skipped onto the pavement.

Grace Freeman. Wrapped in a thick woollen pink overcoat, she moved deftly through the people; her black knee-high boots finding gaps in the cracked concrete spaces. Anyone who knew her would have remarked that she looked somewhat different to six months ago.

She was, in many ways, a completely different person.

She neared the Angel underground station just as a rush of dry air came up the flight of stairs and tugged at her shoulder length hair, pushing it back over her ear. She thought about taking the tube to

Old Street but decided that walking it would be better. Ahead was a mass of people, some headed down towards Farringdon. Others were headed up the hill to King's Cross.

She took in the smell of the throng of people milling outside as she passed.

London had a smell, she decided, as she walked on. Not a specific smell or even food group but a definite mix of stale tube air, fried food, pollution, garlic and cigarettes. And that pub smell, long since separated from the dominance of tobacco.

Like a wine there were layers of it. Sometimes she could detect a generic perfume smell too, like you get when you walk into a lift with lots of well-dressed people. London was like that. It mixed grime and crime, lust, poverty and filth with fine food and opulence found few other places on the planet, and it mixed them so the result was a heady aroma of something socially alien. No matter where in the food chain you were, the smell was always other people. Different is actually a smell, she wondered idly.

Grace was early for her midday meeting.

The wind chapped at her nose and she screwed her face up in the gust of wind as she stood at the pedestrian crossing. All around her were seething masses of people, cars, buses and noise. Above her an unseen low turbofan whistle heralded to absolutely nobody another long-haul arrival making a slow turn towards the west. People walked past in an eerie silence. She was listening to her iPod and could hear nothing of the chaos around her.

Instead, Madonna was singing about her American Pie dream, and that was all that Grace Freeman could hear or wanted to hear.

In a small gap in the traffic she stepped out purposefully. Sidestepping an onrushing black cab she skipped up onto the pavement and walked on down the Angel High Road. The wind was at her back and she quickened her pace down the pavements towards Old Street. In the distance she saw a petrol station with the yellow arches of a McDonald's close by. Madonna had given way to a slower, moody Editors track and Grace became aware that it looked like it may rain but felt detached from it as if the due droplets would not touch her. She loved the serenity and peace that loud music played through headphones can bring. In a city life dominated by interaction or lack of interaction on one level or another the personal choice to shut oneself away from the world and immerse in her own music made a lot of sense.

She was very much a people person. Her job involved a great deal of communication, not all of it particularly sincere. The ability to wrap yourself up in your own private cocoon was important to Grace.

Maybe that was one of the reasons behind the new pink overcoat. But it went deeper.

It was a safety thing as well, she decided. All the bad things that happen on the streets are somehow distanced by it.

Having earphones in meant that she could walk past the ranting homeless crazies with impunity and genuinely not hear them or their angry cries for help. Potential robbers and rapists would try and talk to her, and she could just walk right by and not hear their sugar-coated lures. People who tried to sell things. Useless or irrelevant things. Those Chuggers in the street trying to elicit donated monthly with a fake smile and a step into her path. They could just be dismissed without even having to make eye contact. It was a shame, Grace decided, that she could not wear her earphones when she was with a client.

Grace had been a prostitute for three months.

The post-almost-text chat with Sandra six months ago had been rather more serious than she had expected and she had been asked to leave.

Sandra had been nice about it. She was a wonderful girl to work with but she wasn't performing. They were cutting back. Rationalising. It was nothing personal. She was a lovely girl but they felt that she had come as far as she was going to. That a change would be best for all parties. That she was a great girl but perhaps not culturally suited. That she was sure Grace would find something more suited soon because of what a nice girl she was. That she was really sorry, and that Grace was an awesome girl.

In hindsight it wasn't that much of a surprise although it had been a real shocker at the time. She genuinely had not seen it coming.

Her flatmate had moved out the same week for unrelated reasons. All the trees had been shaken, and all the rocks lifted to see underneath. There were no more metaphorical twenty pound notes down the back of some cosmic sofa somewhere. She had always known she was on the not-especially-attractive side of plain but that the step up to taking financial advantage of the lofty gift of not being ugly was a natural progression for her. She did not mourn any loss of innocence: her carefree years at university and a life of clubbing and afterparties had robbed her of that at least some years hence.

She smiled as she remembered the first night. The decision had more or less taken itself.

She had broken it down into a very simple process. It would be an experiment. If it did not work she would know, and could go temping. Temping was the fallback. Temping was more or less the same thing once you break it down and think about it, right? Doing something temporary for someone who needs it and is paying well for it.

The last of her savings had gone into a four hour session of laser whitening for her teeth and a facial the same afternoon. The endless cups of tea, wine and smoking had taken its toll on her smile and whilst she had not worried too much about it when out socially, it seemed the obvious thing to do. She had started going to the gym three times a week and in the space of only ten days dropped that crucial nine or ten pounds of fat which transformed her rather shapeless and squidgy areas. It was a subtle transformation consisted of a myriad of fronts.

She had started wearing more makeup. She bought herself a new overcoat. She downloaded some porn from Pirate Bay and watched in detail to get some hints and tips. Blowjobs had always been something of an enigma and mystery matched in no small way by her general ambivalence to them as a rule. There was a knack to it, but Fraser never liked them and she had only given a few in her lifetime until that point.

In truth the porn did not give much away, of any usefulness at any rate. It was not the sex she would choose but then it wasn't her choice was it? The porn seemed alien and mechanical. But the message seemed to be: confidence is everything.

And she could fake that, right?

The customers were not supermen or mythical beasts.

Her clients were just men.

Some would push the boundaries of what she meant by "all services" on the little calling cards she would leave in telephone boxes whilst others were sometimes laughably mundane. She started off with a no kissing rule (because that was what hookers did right?) and a no anal rule because that was disgusting. She had tried it once at college and the experience left nothing with her that made her curious to repeat it. Very few even asked for it, and those that did never pressed harder when she politely refused.

Grace had been a normal sexual being before her change in career. Sex was fun. She enjoyed it, but was not overly experienced. The transition to doing it for money was easier than she thought it would be. It was all in the confidence. If she sounded and acted as though it was the most natural thing in the world and she was a skilled pro, then she was. It was a matter of charm and bluster more than crazy skills. That had surprised her at first but she had instantly realised what a blessing it actually was.

From the outside looking in it all seemed as inaccessible and far detached from her own reality as it was sordid and disgraceful. Yet, in the nicest way possible, she had surprised herself as to just how accessible it really was.

She had gone to the newspaper shop across the road that evening and bought some milk, some cat food, some Diet Coke, a copy of Mayfair, a copy of UK Red Hot Amateur Housewives and a disposable sim card. Grace giggled a little inside as she'd handed the cash to the shocked (she imagined) Pakistani woman behind the cash desk and felt a little frisson of something as she walked out.

The sim had gone into a spare mobile phone she'd had in her drawer unused for a couple of months.

The magazines she had spent an hour or so looking for a picture of someone who looked even a little bit like her. After much deliberation and some story-reading she'd picked one. The woman in the picture was wearing an unbelievably tacky red PVC skirt and a lacy red bra. The similarity was hardly what anyone could call striking. The hair and eyes were the same colour roughly, even if Grace probably had larger boobs and less shapely legs.

If she squinted it was ballpark-close.

From a distance.

After a few glasses of wine.

It would do.

She cut out the picture and PrittSticked it to the back of a piece of A6 card, then wrote her disposable mobile number on there.

She poised the nib of the felt tip a fraction of a millimetre from the card, about to write her name, when she stopped.

Grace was a stupid choice of prostitute name. For many reasons.

She giggled out loud at the sort of conversation she had had several times over the years with friends.

If you had to choose a prostitute name, what name would you choose?

The smile faded as Grace realised she could not phone a friend.

Names came and went and she could not decide on one she could say with a straight face. They all sounded like some crackwhore table dancer in the US Mid-West who sucked off truck drivers for fried chicken.

Angel was a terrible name. Brandy made her sick. Montana hopeless. Lucy desperate. Goldie impossible to say out loud. Cinnamon nice for a black woman but not for her. Geri a fucking Spice Girl. Jo had been done. Jordan had some unpleasant parallels. Lucky good for a Bangkok ladyboy but not so good for her purposes.

What were the criteria to adhere to here?

How the fuck are you supposed to choose a fake name to go suck cocks under? How do you even go about doing that?

She had asked her cat but Barney was not much help. Mayfair was next to no help either. Mareska was weird. Lana a total non-starter. Bunny was impossible to say with a straight face. Erika made her sound like a Swedish arm-wrestler. Pussy made her sound like Honor Blackman.

It had made her laugh at first but the complexity soon became frustrating. Angry at her own lack of decisiveness she had switched on the TV and tried to forget about it.

The weather was on and some woman with blowjob lips and a tight blouse was on about high pressure systems...

Nadia.

Nadia the weather girl.

Nadia The Whore.

Grace laughed aloud again. It was perfect. Nobody would ask if it was her real name, nobody would care anyway but it was suggestive enough to pass the dirty test, in her mind anyway.

The fact that the hardest part of become a prostitute had been choosing a fucking name, or a name for fucking, always made her smile when she thought about it.

A week later, the copy and paste cards were up in phoneboxes and very shortly after that the calls started. It was so fucking easy. Or so easy fucking.

Mostly it was harmless.

All that she earned she kept for herself and this was all carefully squirrelled away, kept well away from her bank account lest the tax man start asking uncomfortable questions. She did not have a drug problem and she was not an alcoholic. There was not a hard luck story. Some almost seemed disappointed by that. Sometimes she thought about making one up. The fantasy enthralled her, the power she held as a storyteller of a peculiar type felt unreal somehow.

It was just a job, it just was not nine to five. But that was a good thing, right?

There were some nice guys too. Not many, but a few. Some whom, on another night, in a different town she would like them to buy her a drink in a club. Or something.

However, mostly it was the sad and lonely men, not all old but mostly middle aged, who had nothing else in their lives. Some were in rotting marriages whilst others had nobody and they were the ones that always wanted to know her real name and to ask if they could buy her dinner in addition to her services. Sometimes she said yes and sometimes she said no. Some were tyrannical and some she could tell were fighting the urge to hurt her but she had never had to use the can of pepper spray she kept within reach at all times.

Grace would admit it to her really close friends if she had any whom she trusted enough. She had figured she would come clean straight away. Just bring it up in a lull in conversation over a bottle of SauvBlanc.

But somehow the words never came.

At dinner parties and on nights out the questions about work came and at no point did she get the impression that the inquisitors cared enough to be told her little call girl truth. She had lost a stone in weight, toned up a bit, stopped smoking and wore more makeup. It transformed her from very average and the plain side of plain to actually properly attractive when dressed up and still none of her friends gave any hint of having figured it out. Maybe it was more obvious to her as the main protagonist than to observers.

Or maybe she just wasn't that interesting and they were massively self-absorbed.

Therefore four months on she was still officially working in the office that she had been sacked from, and nobody knew any different. She had not made any friends at Hillman-Benet that she kept in touch with, and anyway none of them knew any of her other personal friends so it was easy. She enjoyed the money those desperate, sad men paid her and the job itself was much easier than people realised.

She was on her way to a flat near Old Street where a middle-aged guy awaited her. He was a regular in so much as this was a (new record) fourth visit, and an odd one. He never wanted sex but paid her to spank him instead. It took all sorts. Grace did not mind.

Ahead, the petrol station was perhaps a hundred yards away. A police car came past with its sirens screeching, audible even over the music in her ears. Grace looked straight ahead, saw the yellow arches and remembered she was hungry, and promised herself to eat something after she had been to see the Old Street guy.

A yellow Ferrari came past and she turned her head to look at it. Grace had always promised herself she would own a nice car one day. After she got enough money for the deposit for a place of her own. First the house then the car. In London there didn't seem much point, but then she wouldn't be here forever would she? Another police car came past. Perhaps thirty seconds later, three fire engines came storming past her, so close that she felt the slipstream of the speeding trucks catch her coat.

Grace walked on some more past the petrol station and just as the smell of petrol was fading from her nostrils, the rain came. It was just a few drops at first, then more, then the whole pavement went dark with the rain. It had a chilly wind behind it. It tugged at her umbrella as she opened it and pulled it close. Quite soon the cars came past with their lights on, and puddles began to form in the pavement. The red of the traffic light ahead sparkled off the puddles on the pavement and had she been at home looking through her window she may have found it soothing to watch. But today she was late.

Today she was cold, wet, miserable, hungry and in a few minutes some sweaty weirdo would be naked across her lap begging to be beaten like a disobedient schoolchild.

She was hardly living the dream was she?

It had hardly been a stellar few months had it?

On days like today, she mused; I have definitely seen better days.

Just then, the battery on her iPod died. She swore loudly but did not take the earphones out. With the music gone the sounds of the street were unwelcome and tinny. Those are the days when the rain in London can seem as ugly and unforgiving as the very worst of its residents.

Two hours later, and with more than £200 in used ten pound banknotes burning a hole in her coat pocket, though in no better a mood, Grace was walking through the windswept streets of Soho looking for a bar. Her arm ached.

What was it called? She stopped on a corner and looked at the text that Abi had sent her.

Tarmac? What kind of name is that?

She looked around, searching for someone who did not look like a nutter to ask if they knew where it was. Nobody made eye contact with her, and for a second she realised that stood there, on a Soho street corner, with her dirty blonde hair, long coat and knee-high boots, she looked like a prostitute. In her own mind at least.

The irony of that wry observation made her laugh aloud, and hearing her laugh, a man looked at her and smiled. Grace asked hopefully over the hubbub if he knew where the Tarmac Bar was, her voice high and shrill. His eyes lit up and for a second she thought the stranger might yell out a helpful direction, but he just looked shocked that she was speaking to him, and by the time he was able to respond the crowd of people stepping across the road as the lights changed had swallowed him up. He mouthed something she could not make out and was gone. Shrugging inside, she walked onwards up Wardour Street.

Tarmac Bar.

Sounds pretentious.

Abi sat alone in one of the huge leather semi-circular pods near the back of the bar. Judging from the glasses in front of her, was down to the ice on her second of whatever it was she was drinking. She looked up and smiled at Grace but did not get up. Grace bent down and kissed her friend warmly on the cheek. She took off her coat, put her bag down, and settled down next her friend. They chatted for a couple of hours over a bottle of slightly under-chilled and scandalously expensive Sancerre. Abi was expressing her nervous excitement about flying off to Venice with Steffen in three weeks.

"You should get a boyfriend Grace, you should. There must be loads where you work. How come you never seem to be dating them?" Abi asked, her voice whiny.

"I'm just picky hon, you know me. As soon as I meet someone I like I will but most of the men I meet at work, in the office, are complete arses. Frankly I'd rather have a night in with some ice cream, a DVD and the Rabbit – much less hassle"

Abi squawked with laughter and made a face that said that this was probably too much information.

God knows how she'd react if she really knew what I do for a living.

"Well even so, I'm sure you'll be happier when you find someone. Men are great you know, they have their uses!" Abi seemed almost like she was preaching to a lost soul, which given the circumstances probably was not far from the truth.

"Yeah… shall we have another bottle?" Grace changed the subject, jauntily waving the empty green bottle of French wine as if to emphasise that it was empty.

"Ok, my turn. No arguments!" Abi had suddenly brightened up, flashing Grace a wide, slightly buck-toothed grin.

"Same again?"

"Whatever is good, you know I'll drink anything" Grace smiled.

"Great. I'll be back in a sec"

Abi turned and headed for the bar. Her slightly podgy bottom was shapeless in an obviously very new pair of Levis, and her pink t-shirt all crinkled at the back where she had been relaxing against the back of the leather sofa. She returned after a while with a Chenin Blanc several pounds cheaper than the Sancerre. Abi was such a spendthrift. She was the type of woman who would ask you what you wanted for Christmas and when you replied that you liked the smell of the new Prada or Vera Wang, she would buy you the shampoo and body wash instead of the actual perfume because it was cheaper. Grace loved that about her. They chatted some more about the weather, about the flight to Venice and whether a bottle of Champagne could go in her hold luggage or would it burst or something because of the pressure. Neither of them knew the answer to that one.

Grace felt every microsecond of the lull in conversation.

By the way, just in case you were wondering, I am a call girl now. Not a prostitute… a call girl. There's a difference you know…

Abi finally asked whether Grace had ever been to Venice. Grace pointed out that she had not, but would one day like to go. The canals and museums were apparently lovely. The thought popped into her head that their conversation was a bit like the advanced learning courses you do when you study another language at night school. "Stilted and unfamiliar" would be the description she would choose. She smiled to herself as she absent-mindedly stroked her fingertips on her pink overcoat. Abi was her best friend there in London, and Grace liked the fact that she was easy to talk to because she was ever so slightly mundane. She liked mundane and easy in her life because of her job. Abi was her best mate and even she had no clue what Grace did to earn all the cash she invariably had on her. Maybe she did know, Grace pondered.

Maybe she knew but was too embarrassed to say anything. Maybe she should tell her.

Don't be stupid, she thought to herself.

What would that achieve?

Chastising herself inside, she turned her thoughts to Amy's last conversation topic.

What were we talking about again?

THREE

Soundtrack

Ryan Adams – 'Wonderwall'

Dylan sat staring into space. It was not a good afternoon. He felt like he had worked all day but had very evidently made very little headway in the copy draft he was writing about a shipping company's new carbon trading scheme. He had done it all last week but deleted the email by accident. It had been several hours work, not all of it memorable sadly. All wasted. Wasted. The word cracked a smile on Dylan's face.

A weekend wasted is never a wasted weekend. Or so the saying goes.

Clicking his neck to one side, he minimised the report window and decided to carry on with the email to Nicole.

Nicole and he, despite having never met, were friends, or so it felt, and Dylan had been chatting to her and making her laugh by email for more than three weeks. The email he was in the middle of was an important one.

How do you ask if she wants to meet up? What is the etiquette here?

He thought of just slipping it into the last few lines of the last paragraph so that she would think it was not a big deal for him. He thought about getting it out of the way in the first line so she would know he was honest about it. He thought about dressing it up in a convoluted way by claiming he had a spare ticket for some show that weekend and his mate had backed out. No – too sneaky. Women can sense a sneak.

Dylan was not a sneaky man. He certainly did not think he was at any rate. He knew how to get what he wanted from a woman. Indeed, he often wondered on why he had slept with probably 90% of the women he had ever kissed, whereas most guys actually go the whole way with just a tiny fraction.

It was not that Dylan was a stud, it was more that he did not get kissed very often. Long ago had he realised that it was his charm and intelligence that attracted women to him, and it was difficult to get that across to women in clubs. This was why online dating suited him. It allowed him to present himself in the best of light, and not look like the slightly downtrodden, overweight, part-time drug dealer he actually was.

After careful consideration he put in the tentative request to meet in a separate paragraph at the end of his email, having already talked about movies he hated, strange places he really wanted to go to, favourite type of domestic pet and his favourite flavour of crisps in an attempt to sound random and cool-nerdy. It was inoffensively worded and he had left all the avenues open for her to decline, as he was almost sure she would.

Yet at the same time he began to format a plan of where to go, what to do, what to eat, and what to wear. He turned over the tombola of thoughts in his head. She was a year older and six months out of a big long-term heartache. An office assistant manager for some stationary firm and pretty, but overweight, although this did not bother Dylan. Would she agree to meet him? Why shouldn't she? Was he her type? 16:00 arrived before he clicked open the unfinished carbon trading copy and resolved to get it out before he went home.

*****

Grace was with her second client of the day.

The painfully thin man with his back to her was her last for today and she was already relaxing on the sofa with her cat, in her head. The man was Latin, maybe Portuguese or Spanish, but definitely not English.

They were in a cheap and rather dowdy hotel box room on the upper floors of one of the cheap hotels not far from Marble Arch. He was a semi-regular in as much as he had seen her once before, and was a decent enough sort but wanted to take her out to dinner the last time, and she had declined. Middle aged, toned, but evidently still an angry young man inside for reasons she could not even guess at, Grace had said no as gently as possible.

This time he had been cold when he opened the door and brushed off her attempts to make light-hearted conversation as he chopped out two lengthy lines of gritty looking cocaine on the wooden sideboard. He had snorted one line with a stomach-churning grunt and hawk in one fluid upwards movement so that when he emerged at the top of the arc, £20 note held pointedly in his left hand and a wild look of adrenalin in the whites of his eyes, he stretched his back and neck up like some neurotic ballet dancer. Rubbing his nose and shaking his head, with a wild grin on his face he offered the note to Grace, but she declined again. With a shrug, the man repeated the bizarre move once more, up the other nostril.

The guy had been quite good the last time she remembered, well endowed, going down on her twice (although that cost extra) and actually making her come, which was fairly rare.

This time though there were no such pleasantries and Grace found herself slightly intimidated by the rushing, straining man whose hands and face were everywhere.

Distracted by her companion's wild-eyed exertions above her, Grace lifted her head and looked towards the large Victorian sash window. The beige curtains had been drawn but the feeble daylight outside was enough to paint the canvas curtains a blotchy orange and yellow as the light shone through. Somewhere close by a vacuum cleaner in another room sounded like it had sucked better days, and Grace smiled to herself.

It isn't the only one.

Her thoughts drifted away to more comfortable times.

When she snapped out of it the guy had just come and was laying back on the bed next to her panting heavily. Grace decided to lay back and make out that she enjoyed what the guy next to her had just done.

He had been harsh, bordering on brutal, hammering soullessly into her like some iron machine from those programmes they had on about the Industrial Revolution sometimes or some God-awful minimal techno record. It had hurt. He had come with a long moan and a vicious thrust that had made her grit her teeth in pain. If she was going to see him again she probably would have said something but the man's demeanour and generally baleful attitude towards her made her mind up on that score long before she had taken her knickers off.

Presently he got up, the sweat glistening off his back and walked into the bathroom and closed the door. Grace could hear him breathing. By the time he emerged, perhaps five minutes later she was dressed and ready to leave, looking out of the window at the rain streaked cars below. At first she thought he was going to say something but instead he walked over and thrust a wedge of money into her hand, with a dismissive wave. He obviously wanted time alone. She said goodbye more cheerfully than she felt and an awful lot more cheerfully than he looked. Then she checked to see if he would be receptive to a goodbye hug, as she tended to do with most of her clients, no matter how vile.

She sometimes wondered if she had missed out on a career in sales and customer support. Sandra had let her go prematurely, that much was obvious.

He had his back to her, sat naked on the edge of the bed, texting in one hand and chopping out some more cocaine with the other. He was muttering something under his breath, and she was sure it was not a thank you and goodbye.

Whatever it was, she left him to it and closed the bedroom door with an emphatic thud after her.

He was not a creepy one or really a dangerous one but she was not short of business and could afford to cherry pick the ones she wanted. The treatment she had just allowed him to give her had left her feeling slightly tender, and this was manifestly a bad thing for a woman in her profession to be. Maybe she would get cystitis or a bruised cervix as sometimes happened. Allowing the thought to drop like a pebble into a puddle, she pushed open the front doors of the hotel and walked into the rainy street.

A few months ago she would have said no pain no gain. But now, with almost no debts and considerable sums of money in the bank this mantra seemed a long way off.

She made her way to a Café Nero and stopped for a long latte before heading home. The coffee was medicinal. It wiped away the imaginary taste of condom lubricant in her mouth and heralded a couple of days where she had nothing on. Three or four appointments a week were all that was needed, although usually she did between five and seven, occasionally as many as ten or twelve. Rebekah was out for a few drinks in Hoxton later on and she had not decided whether she would join.

A few drinks and a night off would do her the power of good Rebekah had informed her, not knowing how right she was.

FOUR

Soundtrack

The Teardrop Explodes – 'Reward'

'You have a new email'

The matter-of-fact pop-up on the right side of Dylan 's screen snapped him out of a deep thought about nothing in particular.

The copy report was not much closer to being done. Grateful of the break in the monotony, he opened the email.

It was from Nicole.

-----Original Message-----

From: Nicole Saunders [mailto: SaundersNic9@GEmail.com]

Sent: Friday 30 March 17:23

To: Short, Dylan

Subject: Re: Hiya

Hi Dylan - Thanks for your email.

I am fine thanks and looking forward to going out with Josie and Annabel tonight for a meal. Glad you are ok not too tired after your late night. First off thank you for your kind thoughts. I do like you but I am not sure I want to be more than friends. I am not really healed properly from Nigel and it is going to take more time. You are a lovely guy and I would like to think a good mate now and I don't want to string you along or hurt you so if we do meet up can it be just as friends? We will have a great time I'm sure but I am not ready for anything else. Really looking forward to meeting you.

I hope you understand,

Nic x

So that was that then.

The awful plunging feeling of rejection in his stomach. Again.

It was the same feeling he had been running away from since his teen years, and in truth, Dylan had become quite adept at pushing the rejection away and pretending it was not down to him.

It was her. She is not ready.

Dylan was glad he found out early and not humiliated himself further by chasing her for a bit longer. Another strikeout. His mind wandered to masochistic feelings of self-deprecating analysis; his scathing opinions of his own belly, yellowy teeth and lack of any meaningful amount of time, money and motivation to do anything about either. He had sent her his picture on Monday and she had not said anything about him but remarked that she liked his tie.

He should have known.

She doesn't fancy me.

The rolling surf of self-loathing and pity rolled back after about five minutes as it always did, and he brightened up a bit as he logged onto website for the pizza company to get another one delivered. The box from the one the night before still sat alone, accusingly on the adjacent desk and he leaned back in his chair to consider it awhile. It sat silently, taunting him.

She did not fancy him, and he was OK with that. It was pretty normal.

Dylan was a nice guy and women felt comfortable talking to him. He had many female friends. This meant that, with regular monotony he developed feelings for women who saw him purely as a friend. He was not churlish enough to suggest that this was necessarily a bad thing in most cases, as his affections were transient and tended to flux. Nicole had not closed the door completely and this was in the back of his mind, but mainly he was angry with himself for misreading her attention and humour in her emails.

All around, his co-workers upped and left, one by one mainly without a sunny goodbye, off to wherever they were headed for the weekend. A load of the others were off to the pub but feeling a little tender and deflated, Dylan made up an excuse and declined. Soon, the floor was empty and all he could hear was the air-con and the cleaners clattering about in the kitchen. The noise seemed a long away off and it had a musical quality to it. The pizza arrived and disappeared in short order, and he finally finished off the copy report just before nine.

Feeling no elation at getting his work finished he shuffled his papers on his desk like the newsreaders do when the credits are rolling but the mics are switched off, and decided to check his email one last time.

Nothing.

It was cold outside, and Dylan was always amazed at how people would go outside in the winter and be amazed at how cold it was.

It was not that surprising really, surely?

That was what happened in the cold seasons wasn't it? You dieted, did not go out much because you were too skint after Christmas and you were cold. Even so the rush of Baltic air took him by surprise as he grunted at the night watchman and walked out of the main doors onto the street. The streets always looked so different at night. Instead of the light, airy backstreets of modern office buildings reflecting daylight those same glass office buildings seemed colder and blacker somehow, with the orange streetlamps streaked across their faces. He looked up at the pink evening sky as the orange lamps had their light shone back off the low cloud.

A gust turned his head as a piece of newspaper flew past his head. It began to rain.

Dylan hurried to the tube station and passed the same homeless guy sat at the base of the steps with the same rather forlorn looking dog in his lap. Twelve hours in the cold.

It would be easy and perhaps a little patronising to say here that Dylan had a moment of pause about the homeless guy and his faithful canine, but in truth it would not be true. It was not that Dylan was heartless or uncaring about homeless people by any means. Indeed, one badly arranged night the previous year had seen him spend the night huddled in a ball in his Parka outside Cannon Street station after he lost his keys and had his wallet stolen whilst out drinking, having let his hair down a little too far on a night when he was not serving up. Dylan learned what it was to be truly hopeless and destitute, if only for eight hours. And what it was to be so cold you were convinced you were freezing to death. But, as a rather sad symptom of modern London life, the stiff memories of that night singularly failed to enter his thoughts and walked past the man, a grubby, ruddy faced guy with a Scottish accent.

Dylan had drunkenly given the guy a chocolate bar about three months ago and not made eye-contact with him since that time lest the homeless man ask him for money, knowing he was a soft touch with a Toffee Crisp. Dylan walked on, past the cheesy café all shuttered up behind a barrier of battered steel and trotted down the stairs.

A gust of tube air swept up the stairs as he walked down them and he caught the smell of the perfume of the woman in front. His thoughts immediately turned to procreation and he watched the woman in front sashay her way ahead, turn sharp right and head off down the platform, all painfully tight black jeans and faded leather. He wondered what she was listening to on the white headphones that spun lazily around her shoulders. He could not see her face and wondered how old she was. Immediately forgetting about her as she was walking away from him, he stared at his feet instead. They rested on the yellow line.

Looking up he glanced down both sides of the platform. A train whooshed past in the other tunnel and stopped. Behind him the noise was of opening doors and people moving into an enclosed space. Somebody laughed loudly at an unheard joke. To his left a couple kissed indiscreetly and to his right a sullen looking businessman sniffed and hawked. Dylan watched him. He clicked his jaw from side to side, shifted his footing and sniffed again. A pudgy pink hand in perpetual motion came up and grasped his rather flat little nose between thumb and forefinger. Another sniff.

That's the Friday night line out with the boys.

Raising his eyebrows in a weary 'that's-not-subtle-you-fucking-idiot' movement, uncaring if the bloke saw him or not, he turned back to the scene in front.

An odd-looking woman with porcelain features and an incredible body was looking sultry but indifferent about him visiting the Dead Sea. She looked at him and Dylan looked back. She genuinely looked as if she was not really bothered whether he came or not. To the Dead Sea or otherwise. Dylan was pondering on why she may well have been a poor, but attractive, choice of person to entice him to go see a very big, very low, salty lake in Israel when the train arrived. It passed just inches from his nose but did not startle him. Dylan watched in fascination as his reflection stared at him and smiled knowingly in the glass windows of the slowing train. The smile faded as the doors caught up. There was that sixteen stone again.

Dylan hoisted his bag onto his back and got onto the train. There was one seat left in the middle of the carriage and the snogging couple showed no inclination to have it given that there was only one and so he ambled forward and sat down. He rummaged in his bag for his iPod as the doors closed and the train set off. He pushed the white headphones into his ears and it took him almost a minute to choose an album to listen to. Then he looked up. There was an attractive blonde sat opposite him. She seemed familiar but he could not place it.

Not familiar enough to say hello at any rate. Was she a customer? No.

Had he sold something to her in a club once? Possibly.

The woman was fairly pretty. Shoulder-length dirty blonde hair going more mousy at the roots and a pink woollen overcoat. She was staring into space over his shoulder and did not notice him looking at her so he lingered some more. She had blue eyes stretched quite far apart across her face, and high, almost regal cheekbones. Her mouth hung very slightly open and he thought he saw a glimpse of some nice white teeth. Looking down, she wore a grey skirt and shiny black knee-high boots that left about an inch of flesh between the tops and the bottom of her skirt. He wondered if she was a prostitute, without any kind of proof or indication that this may be the case. Indeed she looked nothing like one, but the knee high boots induced semi-memories of dirty girls in dirty clothes, even in the thick of winter.

Of course she was not a prostitute, he chided himself.

Her legs were pushed together to the knee but fell open below this; her left foot angled off the floor by a bend in her ankle. The lights shone dully off the leather in her boots, and echoed in the sparkle of small, tasteful earrings that he could not see clearly through her dead straight golden blonde hair. She had lots of foundation on, he noticed. Smiling a stupid, lopsided, sheepish smirk, he continued to look at a poster over her shoulder for some car insurance whilst looking at The Girl In The Pink Overcoat out of the corner of his eye.

*****

He was staring at her. Grace was sure. A chubbyish bloke was sat opposite her on the train, pretending not to look up her skirt.

She smiled at him and made a definite eyes-away movement to make sure he got the idea, but reverting back to his gaze she found him staring at her boots. She glared at him for a fraction of a second in a 'that's-not-subtle-you-fucking-idiot' glance and pretended to rummage in her bag with her iPod, which of course was completely dead having run out of batteries hours earlier.

Amazing that, in her line of work, she should find the concept of men eying her up creepy, she ruminated.

Not a moment too soon, Kings Cross station emerged from the blackness with a roar and she rose gratefully. She shuffled past the tangled weeds of bags and feet to the doors and without really knowing why, she looked back over her pink shoulder at the guy who had been staring at her. He looked sort of familiar. She could not place him though. He certainly wasn't a client. Was he? She would remember wouldn't she? Had there been that many?

Unprepared for him to be looking right at her, she was amazed when he looked her right in the eye and gave her a big, genuine smile, a world away from the disingenuous little smirk he had on his face previously.

It was some distance down the platform when Grace realised she had smiled back at him. Perhaps he was not a creep after all?

Maybe he was just a nice guy?

I guess I'll never know.

FIVE

Soundtrack

The Cult – 'She Sells Sanctuary (Long Version)'

Dylan hated Stoke Newington.

Actually he fucking hated it.

The whole place gave him the creeps. Martin Millfield was a semi-regular customer and long-time fringe member of his clubbing co-operative. Nominally he would be good business for Dylan if it was not for having to go to Stoke Newington. Dylan looked around as he stepped off the overground and the scene was familiar but not any more comforting for it. Graffiti, litter, mess and danger was everywhere. He was not even past the automatic barriers at street level before six tracksuited youths, some on BMXs started eyeballing him. Ignoring them Dylan powered out of the station and turned left, avoiding two piles of reeking dog waste as he did so. The high street was busy with buses and taxis and it seemed like every third car was a lowered high performance saloon with blacked out windows being driven by some Turkish or Armenian wideboy. They seemed to drive slower than the other cars, literally vibrating their way down the street to the sounds of unfeasibly huge basstubes in the rear playing some God-awful noise too loudly to identify. A resprayed aquamarine BMW M3 antique jumped past him, its din drowning out even his own music in his headphones. Dylan chanced a glance at the driver, a fat 30-something who looked as though he could have originated anywhere from Spain to Thailand. Even from twenty feet away Dylan could see the grease and sweat glistening off the man's skin. He was hanging out of the front window of the car, joint in hand, luckily more interested in a group of young white teenagers wearing very little hooting and calling up ahead of him.

Dylan inwardly shook his head as the car exploded into noise, clearly the driver had invested some money in doing horrible things to a perfectly serviceable exhaust system to make it sound like a racing car. Why anyone would want to do that to a 90s era M3, Dylan could not guess at. The noise certainly did little to compel the thought that it was in any way worthwhile. The headphones came out and were put away. There was little point in them now unless Dylan were to elevate the volume from high to ear-damagingly perilous.

Martin hung a head out of a general stores shop up ahead and flashed Dylan the campest wave he had ever seen a straight man give. The goombah in the M3 did not see luckily, because he would certainly have started honking his horn and shouting a lot of homophobic abuse at his friend had he done so. One of the painfully skinny teens up ahead with the tightest pair of jeans he had ever seen said something about Martin being "a battyman", but none of her little band were interested, so focused were they on the attentions of the Bulgarian in the Beemer.

"Alright mate." Martin shook his hand and leant in for a quick and woody man hug.

Dylan flashed a pained expression at his friend and hugged him back.

"Why don't you move mate? Its fucking horrible round here." Dylan asked.

Martin was a couple of inches taller than he was but a solid twenty pounds lighter. Like Dylan he was also facing the prospect of losing his hair into his 30s so was compensating with a scrubby but fashionable neck beard.

The taller man smiled again as they set off up the street.

"It's up and coming Dylan mate. Up and coming. How you doing?"

Dylan shrugged.

"Same old mate, same old. Too many late nights, not enough sex, work is boring, same old."

"Maybe you should move to Stokey. Every day is an adventure here." Martin was only half kidding. Dylan could never envisage moving south east to Stoke Newington, much less paying money for the privilege.

"I fucking hate it round here. I fucking hate it." Dylan complained.

"You're a real ray of sunshine today Dylan old son… I think someone needs to get laid." Martin patronisingly went to tickle him under the chin but Dylan pulled away as they turned let onto a footpath between some brick buildings off the high street.

"I do. That is the truth of it brother." Dylan shook his head. He had not been depressed about his lack of sex until Martin brought it up.

They turned left again down a long and filthy pathway parallel to the train lines below leading back to the train station.

Five grammes of his decent Charlie was two hundred quid. There was nobody about. Dylan plucked the sandwich bag from his pocket. Inside were five National Lottery ticket wraps of his decent coke in an empty packet of Lambert & Butler Lights. Seamlessly, Martin held out a hand and the exchange took place. Both men had checked the alleyway front and back with furtive glances and the coast was clear.

Martin secreted the package on his person with an irritatingly happy smile and then pressed a fast cash deposit into Dylan's hand. The whole transaction had taken two seconds and had employed tradecraft that, Dylan liked to think anyway, MI5 would have been proud of.

The two men exchanged more pleasantries for the last fifty feet of pathway until it opened out at the train station Dylan had only just left. Another hug, another grateful shake of hands and a promise to go for a beer yet again, then Martin was gone. Dylan all but skipped down the stairs to the open train platform relieved to be leaving Stoke Newington, even if he was considerably richer than he had been just a few minutes earlier.

The bad stuff was done.

The rest of the evening would be much more fun. A couple more bits to do at work, a quick change and then meet some friends for a short trip across East London to watch Chelsea away at West Ham. It was almost seven PM by the time he left work. Dylan wisely decided to leave his one remaining gramme of coke in his desk drawer, but did a huge line in the gents before leaving the office. Barging out of the office like a force of nature, he felt reinvigorated. Reenergised. On top of the world.

He almost ran to the train station, where Davis, Mox, Rush, Scottish Mark and Cadgey were waiting. They all but threw one last pint down in less than three minutes in the huge Wetherspoons and then headed underground.

There was always trouble at West Ham – Chelsea.

The Blues always seemed to bring several thousand to the Boleyn Ground and although the atmosphere was nothing like as tense as it had been in the 70s and 80s, the Police presence was still very heavy. The gobby and overconfident amongst the groups of men and boys would use the protection to start mouthing off and shouting but the older lads stayed quietly threatening. The Chelsea fans moved in groups, and groups of groups. Scuffles were immediately stepped on by the police but not before a few got a couple of snide digs in. The air was heavy with hostile tension. West Ham used to be a good team, though Chelsea had been better for many years and the hostility of the locals to Chelsea's dominance was as much out of forlorn hopes of nicking a point than of any real prospect of turning

Chelsea over. They arrived just as the game was kicking off.

The away end, as always, stood up the whole game despite endless protestations from the Upton Park stewards and stadium announcer to get them to sit down. West Ham took the lead in the first half and the home fans had gone crazy. The noise had been impressive, but then impressively shut off dead when Chelsea went right up the other end and scored a breakaway goal. West Ham fancied it in the second half and Dylan was hoarse by halftime singing and shouting in unison with the thousands of other Blues fans.

Pleasingly, Chelsea took the lead early in the second half and scored again late on with a trademark John Terry bullet header as West Ham surged forward for an equaliser.

The rush of emotion having irrefutably tied up the all-important three points was better than any drug Dylan could imagine. West Ham's fans descended into apoplexy, their rage and spittle palpable even from the other side of the ground. Blues Skipper Terry had gone to celebrate the winner in front of their hardcore fans and he was subjected to a deafening barrage of abuse, to which the Chelsea faithful responded in kind.

Dylan could not stop grinning.

*****

The following day, Grace was just leaving the gym before lunchtime when the Batphone rang. It was a regular. City Boy Trevor was having a tough morning at work and needed some relaxation. She informed him she had just left the gym and was by no means looking her best but he did not seem to mind. She got on the tube and headed into the City. Trevor worked just off Bishopsgate in one of the new tall office buildings for some fund manager she had never heard of. He was average height, she remembered, but with unfortunately pockmarked skin telling a story of rampaging and unchecked acne when he was younger. She arrived at his office and waited outside, texting him from the Batphone to come down to meet her.

Almost immediately he appeared from behind the security barriers, sweeping her up in a bear hug which Grace was sure Trevor thought was endearing. He smelt vaguely of spirits, although she could not tell whether it was from the night before or whether he was an early starter.

He ushered her past the security barriers pointing to Grace on the way through to a huge African man on the security desk and proclaiming rather too loudly that she was his personal trainer. Grace looked the part but Trevor certainly did not. Thousand pound suits are wasted on some people and Trevor The Ginger City Boy With The Bad Skin was certainly in this category. Eyes placed altogether too far apart on a rather pancakish face and a nose that looked like it had been broken several times, if it was not for the suit and the stunningly opulent office surroundings he would not look out of place at Smithfield Market, she thought.

Trevor took her hand and escorted into an express lift. He announced to a woman who evidently did not know his name but knew his face that Grace was his personal trainer, and her resultant look of sympathy from the female liftmate to Grace was no surprise.

They arrived onto the 38th floor. Trevor charged out of the lift and headed toward a set of familiar looking toilets marked EXECUTIVE ONLY at the end of the corridor. He jogged on ahead and ducked inside. By the time Grace got close he poked his odd-shaped ginger-topped head round the door with a cheeky smile and gestured for Grace to join him. The toilets were just as she remembered: incredibly nice. The air was filled with the scent of orange blossom from a huge bowl of pot pourri on the immaculate marble counter top. Even the lighting was flattering. Were it not for the line of toilet stalls across the back wall it might have been a smart restaurant or design shop somewhere. Grace had thought to ask Trevor if he was an executive the first and second times she had visited that set of toilets but somehow not got round to it, and decided again on this occasion not to bother to ask. The sneaky smile on his face as he poked it round the door to tell her the coast was clear suggested he was not quite on that exalted rung of the corporate ladder just yet. And asking would likely generate a long and boring diatribe about career prospects she had precisely zero interest in. Better to stay quiet.

Trevor handed her two hundred pounds, shut the toilet lid and began unzipping. A hundred for the blowjob and another hundred to forgo the condom. This was Grace's least favourite activity amongst the myriad she was asked to perform, yet at only a few minutes work was unquestionably her most profitable in terms of time and effort versus financial reward analysis. Briefly she wondered if Trevor was some sort of financial analyst and had a spreadsheet somewhere containing all the ratios.

She smiled, attention dragged back to the here, now and the sex act she had just been paid for.

Trevor was an average sized bloke with a very un-average sized manhood. A matting of bright orange pubic hair formed an undergrowth from which a whole four inches jutted proudly, like a little pale Napoleon. Grace flicked into whore mode.

"There he is… did you miss me?" she wheedled as if actually talking into his cock like a microphone.

It was clean and smelt of shower gel. That was a bonus. Unbeknown to Trevor, Grace had squeezed a little anti-bacterial gel onto her finger tips of her right hand and began to rub it into his manhood. When it was all gone, she shifted to her left hand to get rid of the excess. Within a minute or so it was all gone and she went to work. It tasted of chemicals but it was worth it. Within a short minute or so Trevor began to bend his toes and breathe heavily, and then it was done. She spat out the greasy mess into the toilet as Trevor got to his feet and began to redress. Excusing him to regain his composure in the toilet stall, Grace exited and went to the washbasins. She glugged a huge, burning mouthful of Listerine that took her breath away as it seared away in her mouth. She spat silently into the basin. Last came the familiar anti-bacterial spray and a blue Wrigley's Extra gum pellet. When the heavy-breathing man emerged from the cubicle he was moving slower and had a dopey smile plastered across his unlovely features. The urgency and energy from earlier was utterly gone; flushed down the toilet it seemed. Grace shot him a wink but said nothing in case there was anyone else in any of the other stalls. Trevor made no attempt to walk over to her.

That's my cue. See ya!

Trevor shot out a hand for a massively awkward handshake and Grace almost shook it before thumbing her nose at him with a wink. He seemed to go weak at the knees. She could tell he was deep, head over heels in lust with her, that much was the definition of painfully obvious. Grace gave him a cheery wave and exited the toilet. Trevor did not follow.

Outside the day carried on as normal. She was almost all the way to Liverpool Street station when the Batphone went again. She was surprised to see that it was not Trevor wanting to thank her with dinner but a new number. She answered in her most coquettish way possible.

The man on the other end was youngish, evidently had not done that sort of thing much. He sounded nervous and very pliable. For the second time that day Grace informed a man she had just had a workout and was not looking her best in gym gear, and for the second time that day a man said that was absolutely fine and that she probably looked "fucking banging" in tight gym leggings. They arranged to meet near Bermondsey.

She crossed the road and headed to the bus stop. The Bermondsey bus would take her right to the place she needed to be and was due in six minutes according to the dot matrix information sign on the bus stop. It was enough time to grab a coffee from Nero's and plug in her headphones. The bus arrived and she sat thinking.

Six months ago the events of the previous fifteen minutes had been one of her sexual fantasies. To have a boyfriend who worked in a smart office who would call her to go to his office and secretly give him the best blowjob ever then leave him in bits without anyone ever knowing. Maybe sometimes he would call out of the blue, she would come to him, he would not say anything but make her explode savagely hard by going down on her on his knees as she writhed against the toilet back wall, before leaving her alone with a wink and no words. She reflected that the rendezvous with Trevor had been one of the least sexy episodes in her entire call girl career. Considering it had been one of her sexual fantasies she expected even a slight twinge or rush of blood.

But there had been nothing.

It had not even occurred to her that it had been a fantasy of hers until she had already done it. There were few things that de-sexualised sex for her more than the intrusive taste of anti-bacterial chemicals and the feel of dirty money.

The Bermondsey encounter had, if that were possible, been even less sexual than the one with Trevor The City Boy With The Minute Cock And The Horrible Skin earlier.

She had met him, he had led her to behind an industrial unit off the main road and amongst filth and rotting rubbish piled high everywhere she had crouched down to give her second blowjob of the day, this time blessedly with the condom on. The guy had paid for half and half thus was technically entitled to have full sex with her. However Grace had been so disgusted with the scene around her, as far from the luxury bathrooms on the 38th floor of the offices of Hercules Asset Management as she could possibly imagine, that she put all her energies into a very frantic and rushed blowjob. It was over quickly.

Thank fuck for that.

The man had run off afterwards and Grace had walked back to

the bus stop unable to get the stench of rotting rubbish out of her nostrils and the acrid taste of condom lubricant from her mouth.

Living the dream Gracie. Livin' the dream.

Her mood had brightened only marginally by the time she got back to Liverpool Street. The evening rush hour was a couple of hours away yet, but the traffic everywhere was heavy. As soon as she got off the bus she gargled some more Listerine and spat it in huge relief into a bin. It would be dark soon. While she was there in the City it made sense to do some "promo work" as she liked to call it. There were eight or nine calling cards in her bag and her trusty PrittStick. The City was filled with phoneboxes and she knew their location by heart so the sweep of the area did not take long.

The routine was to take the card from her front bag compartment and PrittStick it inside her bag, then hold it glue side down in her palm, go into the phonebox and place her palm onto a suitable area on the back board above or to the side of the telephone itself, then press hard and pull away. It was a well-lubricated action she had probably done a hundred times before. It was supposed to take no longer than one second.

On reaching Pudding Lane she was about to place her third-to-last card down when she noticed a woman already in the phonebox, pressing up a card with a stunning brunette on it called Paula according to the handwriting. As Grace stared, she turned and looked right at Grace.

Their eyes met. Grace's hand was already half way out of her bag and her intentions sadly obvious. She tried a smile at the woman who just looked blankly at her.

She was an inch shorter than Grace and much skinnier, with a pencil skirt the same length but somehow much sluttier than those all around on officeworker hips. A too-tight crop top revealed a sallow navel suggesting that she had once been or maybe still was a mother. But the hollow look of recognition behind her sunken eyes suggested a drug problem which Grace fervently hoped meant she was not still a mother. The woman's dyed raven-black hair was up in a crude bun, but strands hung down across her ears and on top of large hoop earrings. She wore a very bright crimson lipstick that did not quite manage to eliminate the tightness of her thin lips. Her mouth opened, not to say anything but just to open, and Grace caught sight of irregular, beaten teeth.

Suddenly, Grace nodded at her.

It was a gesture she did not really realise she had made until she had done it.

The woman looked at the card in her hand and then again at Grace's face and curled up a lip in disgust and hostility. Eyes flashing, she barged past Grace and had she not stepped to the side would certainly have shoved her over. Then she was gone into the throngs of people headed to Bank Station.

It was the first proper occasion Grace had met another working girl on equal footing and she had naively expected some sort of sexworker sorority-style sisterhood.

A grin and an offer of a decompression cup of coffee was too much to expect. A wink perhaps, a nod, a wan smile even?

The hostility was hard to take. It was all the more so because there was no angriness. She had not been angry really, just business. Grace flinched at the notion she was somehow a threat to that emaciated, messed up woman who was very evidently in a much darker place than she.

All the way home Grace wondered about the woman. Paula. It sounded like it was her real name. How old had she been? Same age as Grace or younger? Or much older? It was impossible to tell.

Was she on drugs? Real, proper drugs?

Probably. But then again it was not possible to say for sure and Grace felt oddly bad for judging the woman without even knowing her.

She idly wondered which of the calling cards had been hers. Her mind flicked back to Trevor and the Bermondsey man. In a pang of all-too-realistic self-deprecation Grace realised that she was not so different from the street whore she had just met. The dose of reality was almost too much to bear. Sucking cocks and needing to use all that anti-bacterial spray, nonetheless after all just feeling Trevor's spunk violating her mouth? Crouching down amongst rat-infested stinking rubbish, mud and filth for a desperately un-sexy blowjob behind an industrial unit in a fucking horrible part of South East London?

How was she any better?

You know what Gracie. For a woman who isn't really a hooker you certainly do do some nasty fucking things.

Just saying.

SIX

Soundtrack

Above & Beyond – 'Alone Tonight' (Above & Beyond Club Mix)

The pill lay there in the middle of the table.

A marooned red dot with maroon flecks, in an ocean of battered and stained oak. Almost over the horizon sat the huge expanse of the jetsam-filled fruitbowl containing some keys, an elastic band, a pizza menu, a tube of superglue, a leaking luminous marker, some string, a blank CD-R with something undecipherable scrawled on the side, a packet of candles, two cigarette lighters and a broken wine stopper, although noticeably, no fruit. To the east lay the flotsam of an unused tampon in its wrapper, a paperclip, fragments of tobacco and can of beer with condensation dripping down the sides, having just been taken out of the fridge.

That night the house was noisy. Carla was crashing about in the lounge, and Jason was upstairs with another bloke and smashing about getting ready. Dylan flinched and smiled as the huge Welsh dresser next to him, which someone had saw fit to paint a lurid terracotta orange many, many years ago, shuddered as Carla came charging into the kitchen. The whole room shook. It never failed to amaze Dylan how someone so small could make so much noise and shiver the timbers of such a massive house.

Of course this comparison was skewed slightly: the floorboards were so old and worn that a passing milkfloat would probably seem like there was truck racing going on outside.

The energy of the house that evening was lost on Dylan.

He sat at the table in morose resignation. The buzz from Chelsea winning at West Ham midweek had faded a bit. His mind was occupied with the lack of sex, loneliness thing.

He knew Nicole was going to blow him out and still it was not a nice feeling even a couple of days after it had happened. His Thursday and then his Friday at work had blown by with him having accomplished exactly nothing, and there were no plans for the Friday evening, unusually, so he had resolved to do nothing more or less than mooch around the house, maybe smoke some weed and get an early night. He could not even muster up the enthusiasm to go out and sell some drugs to make some money.

He regarded the pill, unsure of what to think. It was tiny.

Perhaps smaller than the nail on someone's little finger, but thick set somehow; almost square. It was either pink with red flecks or badly faded patchy red, he could not decide.

The house was cool, with a pleasant breeze coming in from the kitchen window that was pulled up high.

Smiling to himself, Dylan looked up. Carla who was hammering up the stairs toward the kitchen with a clatter of heels on wood. Upstairs Jason's music stopped abruptly and there was a sound like a cluster bomb attack in the next street as Jason and his mate ran down the stairs.

What was his mate's name again?

Carla flew into the room with Jason and the other man just behind. She looked beautiful. Dylan reached for his beer but was cut short in mid table by Carla, whose voice was full of excitement.

"You aren't changed Dyl! Are you going to sit there and be a boring Mister cunty bollocks all night?"

Dylan laughed louder than probably he meant to, and looked up.

"Seriously Carla, not feeling it today. Seriously."

"BORING!" bellowed Carla and Jason in unison, fingers pointed in mock accusation. Jason and his companion sat down on the bench seat opposite him, laughing. Before Dylan could react, Carla swept past. She flung open the fridge and pulled out three cans of beer, slamming them down on the table so hard that the condensation droplets flew into the air. One narrowly missed the pill. Dylan suddenly felt oddly protective of the tiny little treasure for some reason. In a flash of the naked light on something metal in her earrings and a whiff of a spicy, chocolate scent, Carla moved into his eye line. Her sudden, intense eye contact was like cold water in his face. He recoiled and smiled away, seeking to break eye contact quickly but she would not let him. Undeterred, she began to talk; quieter and more deliberate this time.

"It is going to take us seven minutes thirty seconds to drink these beers and do a line each. Ten past midnight bus. You are going to be on it. Get ready. We'll wait."

She smiled a beguiling grin, with a flash of white teeth and Dylan felt his resistance evaporate.

Forty-five seconds later, Dylan was in the shower. The water was painfully hot, but it felt good against his slightly chilled skin. It had been colder than he realised in the kitchen.

Six minutes and forty-five seconds later, Dylan stood in the kitchen. His jeans were sticking slightly to his not-quite-fully-dry legs, and a droplet of water like an icy spider zigzagged down his neck. Aftershave burned his lips and chin. Almost unbelievably, he had had time to have a quick shave too.

Tugging in his belly as he pulled on his jacket, he watched the table scene. Jason and Drew (Dylan had also had time to remember his name whilst rinsing the Head & Shoulders out) were smoking and draining the last of their beers.

Carla was head down, in the middle of a slow, methodical line.

It was one of those strange things in life, Dylan had noted many times in the past, that a woman who did everything (Everything: the floors were not thick) at one hundred miles per hour, rushing around like the world was going to end, should do a line of coke with such methodical attention. She was so slow as to be almost sedate, regularly stopping mid-line to take another breath. As he watched, she came up and locked eyes on him, her face full of pleasure and her slightly watering eyes full of pupil. That was not her first line of the night and it definitely would not be her last.

Another ice creature down the back of his ear made him shudder. Nobody saw him. Jason was already handing the rolled up note to Drew. Dylan picked up his beer, drained the last of it, and put it in the bin. Drew was face down and making a noise like someone had punctured a high pressure gas line. He could see the tops of his ears go red.

That can't be healthy to snort that hard.

Dylan went to his pocket and pulled out a clear polythene baggy, with perhaps 30 more identical versions of the minute raspberry ripple pills in.

"Ok who wants to buy some pills then?"

SEVEN

Soundtrack

Kate Rogers – 'This Collective'

The pill lay there in the middle of the table.

Grace poked at it with a pen, as it if it were some strange, undiscovered moss or lichen and she were someone who was even remotely interested in such things.

At least the lack of interest part was right.

The pill was a deep greeny-blue, and a rounded rhomboid shape, its surface shiny even in the half light of her gloomy kitchen. It had fallen out of her purse that morning and she had not bothered to put it back. She certainly had not needed it that day and she normally carried enough to make a whole rugby team hard for hours in her bag. Just in case.

Now and again she had a nice quiet Friday night, which she would look forward to all week, perhaps going as far as circling some television she wanted to catch up on in the weekend TV supplements. When it came time to sit down and unwind on a Friday night off, she rarely enjoyed it. These things were rather more fun in theory than in practice. She was just bored, tired, slightly drunk, a little wired on the coffee from earlier and a tiny bit lonely.

With a snort of bored derision, she got up and headed for bed, unzipping her skirt as she walked.

Taking off her bra, leaving only her pants on, Grace moved to the side of her bed, and turned off the light. The unsteadiness from the wine earlier was gone, even so her finger slipped twice off the little black switch and there was a hollow crack as the light went dark. Now all that remained was a bloated, acidic feeling in her stomach and a pounding head. Her flat was silent. There were no noises other than her breathing, and far off the sound of the television from the woman that lived upstairs. Grace had not eaten, and despite the fact that it was an early night by her standards, not even midnight yet, she was extremely tired. She pulled away the duvet and climbed into bed. Her blonde hair cascaded over the pillow and was caught in a shaft of purple streetlight from a gap in her curtains. Screwing up her eyes, she debated getting out of bed to close them, but then thought better of it, and turned her back on the light streak across her pillow.

In her mind, she ran over the images and sounds of the last few days. The surprised look in that guy's eyes when she asked him for directions. Abi's crumpled t-shirt. The weird/nice guy that was staring at her on the tube. The low grunting murmurs of her Old Street client and the overpowering smell of paint stripper in his flat. The look of rapture on Trevor's cratered face earlier that day. The stink of the Bermondsey encounter. The cleansing and solitary coffee afterwards. The several coffees since then. The look from the other hooker, Paula the streetwalker.

Sleep came quickly to her, her mind brushed with quick-drying and fast-fading memories of mothballs, Merlot and Monument station.

*****

Dylan and Jason were stood leaning up against a wall.

The club sound system was almost painfully loud and Dylan could only hear snatched fragments of what Jason was burbling loudly into his left ear. His slathering mouth was just inches from the skin so that he could feel him talk as much as hear him. Jason had swallowed two of the tiny little red pills on the bus down from King's Cross and was starting to come up on them.

Even over the music Dylan could hear his words slurring slightly. Dylan jerked his head round and looked at Jason, who was a good three inches taller than him. His eyes were sluggish and did not react to the dazzling streaks of light that swept across them. He leant into the wall and stooped, craning his neck to speak into Dylan's ear which was of course no longer where he thought it was. His shoulders were swept back somehow, as if he were stood in a windtunnel. Glancing down, Dylan noticed Jason's hands were writhing slowly across the front of his jeans, unsettled, as if he could not find somewhere for them to sit still comfortably.

Dylan leant back against the wall and allowed Jason to chunter on at him. He strained to hear what was being said. Over the deep thudding bass he could make out something plaintive about Carla's mate Anna. Dylan immediately lost interest and let his head rest against the black painted plaster. He looked out over the dancefloor. It was only just gone one in the morning, but the room was packed. Rush Hour. It was almost pitch dark, but flashing lights bounced across the ceiling and periodically flashed into everyone's eyes, meaning nobody ever really got used to the dark in the corners. Everyone who walked past looked dazzled.

The lights flashed and danced across the top of the room reminding Dylan of a thunderstorm he once saw in the Arizona desert.

He had been sat on a hill with a thirty mile view in all directions, watching thousands of thunderflashes scattered across the sky as the cold air dashed in off the Pacific and met the broiled desert air. The lightshow was spectacular and so was the heat. The temperature in the club was almost as stifling. Perhaps two hundred boiling bodies moved in unison in front of him, lit only by the transient flashes of the lights and the harsh green of the lasers. Steam rose off the crowd backlit by the cascading greens and reds. The dancefloor was moving like one animal, with hands raised in places, and the occasional flick of hair or a glass captured like a photograph by the flicker of the light and the strobe.

He could feel the music inside him. The bass rumble resonated in his body cavity and under his feet as the whole room vibrated. He could not see the DJ as he was hidden from view and despite being an occasional DJ himself, and very much into the type of driving, relentless tech-house that was being enthusiastically thrashed out in front of him, he did not recognise a single record. That was normally the way. In younger days he would crowd the DJ box with a pen and paper if a must-have tune came on, but approaching 30, Dylan really was not as bothered as he used to be. Or maybe it was a cool thing: cool people did not crowd DJ boxes looking for a tune and a handshake. Cool people rapidly approaching 30 did not anyway.

Dylan grimaced as the first wave of nausea brushed past his lower stomach. He had swallowed a pill about twenty minutes ago with a mouthful of something bottled and vile that Carla had been furtively drinking, and it was working its way into his system. The line of cocaine he took in before leaving the house had long since faded into the ether and he had not drunk enough to fully relax.

That would be sorted out in a minute.

His mind wandered. Clubbing, drugs and what would no doubt turn out to be a weekend long bender was not what he had in mind when he left the office. Some Friday night E4, a couple of quiet beers and a bifter, probably a late film would have sufficed. He was happy to be out, but in the pre-rush stage of awkwardness and slight nausea he felt sidelined. The notion that he was too old for this drug bender nonsense was just that: nonsense. Carla was at least two years older than he, and Jason older still. The old adage floated into his mind as the sweat appeared on his palms and neck, and the rushes began to whisper in his ear.

You are only as old as you feel.

*****

Grace squeaked loudly and awoke with a start as she hit her duvet at hundreds of miles per hour.

The only noise she could hear was her own panting as she turned onto her back, sat up gingerly, and sniffing slightly, turned on the bedside light. A nightmare. The warm buttery rays of her bedside lamp pushed the gloom away into the shadows and the inky memories of her bad dream were banished along with it.

Sleep did not come again quickly and so bleary-eyed at just after five, she got up and went to make herself a cup of tea. Sighing she opened her fridge, and poured in some milk into a cup. Noticing that the milk had gone off she sighed more deeply and pushed the cup away from her. She did not reach to try to drain it down the sink but merely left it on the kitchen top, not far from the solitary pill.

The house was cold and dark. There was no hint of light yet on the horizon, and from her window, all she could see was a mauve vista of streetlights and blue shadows. Settling down into a chair she considered having a drink to take the edge off and let her sleep but realised she only had tequila in her cupboard, and that it would make her feel worse.

She flicked on her television, and grimaced as she rushed past the shopping TV channels and other such pointless wastes of her subscription fee until she reached Sky News. The next hour was spent looking blankly at the screen and taking nothing in. There was nothing to take in. Some students were rioting in Korea, some guy had died in a mountain climbing accident in Scotland and various politicians were stating how much they disliked some Dictator in some African war-stricken hell hole. She drifted off in her elderly armchair, not watching a music channel full of lurid videos of artists she had never heard of.

The noise of the dustbin lorry outside and its grind of hydraulic rams woke Grace up with a start.

Since fucking when did they start coming on a Saturday?

Light streamed in through the window of her lounge, and she all at once realised how cold she was. The heating had been on all night but she woke up shivering. Swearing out loud, she looked at the clock on the cooker expecting it to say that it was some stage of mid-morning. It was not immediately apparent to her whether the real time, just gone eight in the morning, was good or bad. She rose quickly and made her way into her room and into her bed. The duvet cover was strewn over the top of her bed and the room was stuffy and airless. Her first client was not until midday so she could afford to sleep some more but after climbing into bed and indulging in the feeling of the warm fabric against her skin, she was too awake to sleep so she lay in bed thinking.

She must have gone back to sleep for the unnaturally loud crash of a magazine landing on her mat startled her. It was ten to eleven. Sitting bolt upright in bed she looked over at her cat, who seemed more worried at her startled awakening than with the arrival of Tatler. He looked mournfully at her as if in pity. She liked to imagine what he would say if he could talk.

Sometimes she liked to fabricate whole conversations with him in her mind.

I can sleep anytime I want to and magazines don't scare me. You poor silly human lady.

Grace cracked a smile.

"Good morning Barney you cool customer you… and how are we this morning?" she sang to him with a forced jauntiness that obsequious personal assistants reserve for their Bosses.

Barney looked at her with some interest that he seemed to promptly lose all of, stretched languidly and leapt gracefully off the bed to follow the already departed woman into the kitchen. He walked round the corner to see her picking a tin of something expensive from the cupboard. Turning his head slightly he probably would have raised an eyebrow were he able to, tossed his lengthy black tail into the air and strode purposely over to where his bowl usually was. Arriving at the spot and finding it sadly empty he looked up at Grace still deep in thought towering over him and fixed Grace with a stern look of disappointment, as a business executive might give his dry cleaner were they to hand over a still-marked jacket.

Come on. How hard can this be? You do this every morning and I really do not care whether its tuna or chicken with vegetables, I eat it too fast to fucking taste it anyway, you silly bitch.

Grace looked down at him and apologised out loud, handing the bowl down as she did so. She savoured the feeling of his fur as his head darted past her hand to commence eating long before the bowl hit the slightly grubby tiles.

Hot water streamed across her body and she exhaled luxuriantly as the shower warmed up. Happily, the fears over some bruising or a urine infection from the Latin episode were unfounded. She washed her hair and spent the next half hour getting it dry with a hairdryer. Barney petulantly strutted out of her room at some pace as soon as she picked it up. Her make-up done, dressed in jeans over a different pair of knee-high boots and a little strappy top with some frills round the back, she put on her scarf and her long pink wool coat and walked out.

Murmuring goodbye to an unseen cat, she locked the door and set off under the moody skies down the street.

The midday client was a Muswell Hill type. Spectacled, gangly, not very good looking but with a hipster edge which she did not see very often. Maybe hipsters were too cool to need sex? He had been polite to the point of obsequiousness and his endless apologies soon got boring. She went on top. He screwed his eyes shut so tight she worried he might do his eyes some damage.

He did not move but let her grind away and Grace did so, moaning and making slut noises as best she could whilst retaining an air of believability. She looked down at the man. Who and what was he thinking about with such fervour and determination? In the end he came so subtly that she did not notice and was surprised when he pushed her off and darted for a dark bathroom. It was over in ten minutes. She offered to blow him. He said no. She said thank you. He held the door open. She said thank you again. He said no problem. She hugged him. He nodded and kept the door open. She left.

It was so impersonal.

Grace walked off in some frustration. It was incredibly unsexy. She could not fathom how the client had been able to muster up an orgasm. She very nearly went back to ask him what he had been thinking about, but decided not to bother. Turning up a deep house compilation and popping in a Wrigleys Extra she quickened her pace. Her destination was Westfield to do some shopping.

Dylan was collapsed in the big armchair in the living room back in Bounds Green.

He had got back from the club at six in the morning and had stayed up with Carla and Jason drinking shots of Sallimakki, a strong, herbal green liqueur that tasted just like it looked: toilet cleaner. He had danced and danced at the club, completely losing more than three hours at the front near the DJ box with Jason dancing in front and Carla at his back. The pills had been top class. It had been some time since he had got some in that were this good. Perhaps he would start charging more for them…

The drug dealer thing was something that never sat right with Dylan.

Drug dealers were greasy, untrustworthy people with guns who fed off the misery of addicts. Drug dealers had guns and cars and people to do dirty things for them that needed doing. Drug dealers hurt people and were generally unpleasant people. Dylan was not like that. Over many a conversation at many an afterparty, Dylan had tried to get his point across. Selling a few pills to your mates, plus the odd wrap of coke or Ket here and there did not make him a drug dealer, or so the monologue went. Still, no matter how he tried to convince himself and his close friends who bought the pills from him in the first place, he was still buying large quantities of class A drugs from a guy who was, deliberately, very much an archetypal drug dealer and selling them to his mates.

Dylan started doing it about eighteen months ago as a sort of syndicate thing with another like-minded friend, purely to cover the cost of his own usage.

As his own usage declined, the quantities increased, and soon he was making decent money out of it. The decision to go it alone was forced on him and eventually it became a normal thing. Like being a milkman. It was not a big deal, and he only got through about a couple of hundred pills a month. These went to a hardcore of about six or seven of his friends who tended to buy 20 or 30 at a time and then sold them on to their mates who only wanted three for an evening. Jason and Carla were his oldest and best customers. If they wanted speed, coke, Meow Meow or Ket, then he could get it for them and they were by and large happy to pay the premium Dylan put on the cost price he paid because it was convenient and because Dylan was not a drug dealer.

In his mind.

In his mind, Dylan was not a drug dealer.

The expanse of his small customer base, he liked to think, agreed with his distinction with some enthusiasm which was probably as much to make them feel safer as it was for his own piece of mind.

Dylan had reached his peak of "processing" 400 pills a month in the Summer, but a couple of almost-close shaves convinced him that this was not something he wanted to do with his life. He would make just a couple of hundred quid profit off his monthly buy, which was nowhere near enough to make the risk worthwhile. 200 pills is five years inside, and no matter how he looked at it, the returns were just not worth the risk. It wasn't as if he was saving any money or paying his debts off anything like as fast as he should have been. Every well intentioned month came unstuck, or so it felt, walking past Stone Island or Hugo Boss for shoes, jeans and aftershaves. Was a pair of Armani Jeans with Hugo Boss loafers and a Burberry polo shirt worth the risk?

The risk manifested itself in the physical form of night terrors about tsunami racing inshore boring down on him, or him being chased through a forest by a huge many-eyed spider that seemed to know his name. Of course, to an observer it was painfully obvious that Dylan's drug use which ranged from sparing through moderate to moderately outrageous depending on his mood and financial situation, was having an effect on his mental state.

Dylan did not feel paranoid, but that did not mean he was not.

In truth the daily fear of getting caught was always a problem but recently had become worse. He was scaling things down. Being a little more sensible with his weekends.

Impromptu trips out with Jason and Carla that previous evening notwithstanding, were becoming a rarity.

The plan was to have fewer nights out in clubs serving up, even if the weight of easy deals to the likes of Claridge and his boys made it a quick way to make a considerable sum of cash.

Club night dealing was bad, but it was profitable. Dealing to his mates was less so, but less risky, on the surface of it anyway.

There was not one single reason why Dylan was (trying to be) calming things down, but a variety of reasons that tended to fluctuate in terms of order of priority depending on his mood and financial situation.

Partly it was a concern that he had been lucky and was still in a position where he had not been arrested and convicted of intent to supply class A's.

Quit while you are ahead, Champ.

Then there was the fact that he was getting older, and weekend long benders filled with alcohol, Ecstasy and not much sleep were getting to affect him professionally, especially earlier in the week. He knew he was pushing boundaries with the new job, with near-as-makes-no-difference zero chance of another if he was shown the door again.

Dylan had been doing it for many years before he started dealing properly, and held down a good daytime job the whole time, save for the tea-no-biscuits instance with Palmer.

Even thinking about it made him screw his face up in embarrassment and discomfort. He worked in the city, earned reasonably well considering and had a team working around him that he worked in varying degrees of proximity with.

It was getting harder and harder to keep things together.

The tiredness, the short-term memory loss, the mood swings and the tendency to switch off and just stare into space were more and more prevalent. That was not to say he would ever get caught or that his workmates would figure out what he did with his weekends. They would not, because Dylan would not have let that happen again, as he was too smart for that. Not again.

Nevertheless, it was the effort required to stay on top of things that was tiring him out.

As he got older and wiser, he realised that he himself was changing and that the DJing, partying, socialising and drug taking that dominated his social life for so long, was not what he wanted any more. He had not been out for a big session for some time, barring the clubbing the previous night with Jason and Carla and the impromptu big one with Claridge and his boys. Despite the drug taking, his weight had piled on and of course feeling fat and unattractive meant he was even less likely to want to go out clubbing. Even so, he knew it was time to wind things up. If it was not for the money he would have done it already, he told himself.

Sometimes he would ride on the bus past places like the Tate Modern, National Portrait Gallery, British Museum, posters for Opera and spectacular West End shows, libraries, smart restaurants, and posters for far off places like the Dead Sea, and it would make him think. The assumption was that there would be more time in his life for all that stuff. He was acutely aware that that time was indeed coming. In fact it was here, and had been for some time. Dylan was not burnt out nor disillusioned with his social life but there was something missing.

The internet dating was a tangible admission that the hole in his life was something that needed filling.

Dylan was not an especially unattractive man, but the girlfriends he had had in the last four years or so were all from a clubbing background which meant lots of parties and drug taking as a sort of crazy foreplay. Of course this utterly precluded any and every one of the myriad of suitable girls at work as well. None of the many women he met at the football were any good. The attractive ones were taken and the unattractive ones a unique brand of unattractive that did nothing for Dylan whatsoever. All relationships came from within his clubbing social group. That may have been absolutely fine at eighteen and carefree, but the comedowns and mood swings when staring down the barrel of the big three zero meant that relationships formed outside of casual drug usage were hard for him. The temptation to date within a social comfort zone proved too great for Dylan but he had become more and more involved in each passing relationship, with increasingly catastrophic, not to mention emotionally agonising, results.

The more he put in, the more he got hurt.

It occurred to him the previous summer that the drugs and the lifestyle were probably to blame and that if he wanted someone to see the National Portrait Museum and some spectacular West End show with, that he would have to do it outside his normal social life. The online dating thing had worked out ok for him in the past in that he had met up with a few women, taken them to dinner and ended up sleeping with them. Sadly in every case so far the realities of modern dating and relationship psychology had meant that for a hundred different reasons, none had progressed any further than date three or four. The sex was about as fulfilling as a good line of Bolivian marching powder. Great at the time but fucking miserable without more to follow it up.

But why had the dating not progressed?

Part of it was the internal debate about whether or not to tell any prospective girlfriends about his extra-professional activities and income.

Honesty was always the best policy but then at what stage does it become foolhardy?

How much is too much information?

A girlfriend of any more than casual acquaintance would probably find out anyway so wouldn't he be best off telling her?

Then again, how likely was she to be able to see that despite being a drug dealer, Dylan was not a Drug Dealer, and that his activities were completely harmless?

How did he know she would not freak out and tell the police?

The problem facing Dylan was very obvious.

His gaze focussed on Carla, who was draped over the sofa. Yellow parallelograms of light filled with floating specks of dust moved over her sultry visage and Dylan was filled with a familiar sexual admiration. He had never fancied her really but was certainly an admirer of her curvy lines and porn star lips. She and he had snogged once, but she was so wasted she did not remember and Dylan was so hammered that he could very well have imagined the whole thing. It took him a while to register that she was talking to him.

"...anything like it, but then I guess it happens to us all. It catches up with you. You remember Laura?"

"Yeah" Dylan lied.

"She's having a few drinks out tonight and has invited me and Jase. You should come, you look like you are in the desert. Either too much or not enough last night."

Carla's voice sounded like a searing social critique.

Dylan reasoned that perhaps she was right.

A good night out on the beers with his mates, definitively no drug taking involved, might be just the ticket. The beers would help see off the comedown and help him rehydrate. The alcohol would be medicinal. He had some backlog to clear and a night's work at one of the Vauxhall clubs would probably become a financial necessity before long, but he just could not bring himself to do it that weekend. He felt a bit spaced out and lacking in energy, and when that happened, a few beers and some food was the order of the day.

Part of him wanted to stay at home and watch mindless sci-fi movies but unusually for him he silenced the slothful rebellion as soon as it had risen and responded positively to Carla's invite. She squeaked and threw her arms round him, kissed the top of his ear, and then informed him that he needed a shower.

EIGHT

Soundtrack

Julie McKnight – 'Home' (Knee Deep Club Mix)

Grace stood in the queue at Café Nero's for a cup of coffee. Her shopping expedition had been cut short by an emergency on the Batphone, and her subsequent visit to her London Bridge client had taken somewhat longer than she had wanted it to.

She was thankful for the opportunity to sit down and have a cup of coffee and some food. The suggestively bright afternoon sky had clouded over and rain was coming down softly outside in the pallid afternoon light and the coffee shop was busy. She took her latte and muffin to the corner of the café and daintily stirred in two artificial sweeteners to the frothy drink. She went to take a mouthful but the porcelain mug was too hot to hold so she wisely reasoned that the coffee inside it would likely also be too hot to drink. She yawned and ran the palm of her hand down the point of her chin.

Her iPod was the only sound she could hear, and the calming strains of a Snow Patrol album were a welcome camouflage to the chatter and clatter of the coffee house. A large fat man opposite her left his copy of the Daily Mirror on his seat as he left, and Grace reached over to have a read.

She was not particularly interested in what was in the papers, but it beat reflecting on the not-very enjoyable last three hours of her life. The client had been a strange one, dominating and manhandling her almost to the point where she was going to protest, but that meant losing a lucrative client for whom she did not have to work hard. She had made all the enthusiastic noises and gestures over the two glasses of tepid Krug and the hot-tub that was visibly ready but never got used, but it was the sheer boredom of it all that bothered Grace. She had no moralistic objections to what she did, and sometimes felt rather smug that she was able to make considerable amounts of money off her own back, or on her own back, depending on the point of view.

She was smart enough to know many people who worked much longer hours and who did much more stressful jobs than she did for a fraction of the money.

Maybe there was something else too, she reasoned on occasion. It was, despite the obvious multiplicity of it, a very lonely profession. Some girls worked in groups, or had men looking after or over them but Grace worked alone. The classic definition of a prostitute was a drug-troubled or otherwise hard up young woman who worked for a guy who put her on street corners or a woman who ran a "house of ill repute".

She had nobody she was working for or on behalf of.

She had had occasional problems with other girls and houses taking passive umbrage at her business areas and so tearing up or otherwise removing her cards from phoneboxes, but generally, and perhaps surprisingly, she did not have any contact with other girls at all. Save for the chance encounter in Pudding Lane.

But Grace was not that same as that poor, troubled creature.

Not the same. Not even the same kind of prostitute. In fact not really a prostitute. Not really. Not like that woman was.

Everything she earned she took home and had done for four months. She tended to tell her friends, of which there were not many, that she worked as a document-processing analyst at an office near

Aldgate for a list of customers including the British Library. This stemmed from a one-night stand more than two years ago with a guy she later fondly remembered as the least offensive guy in the world. Alas, he was also one of the most boring people she had ever met, having spent much of the several hours they had in each other's company gushing endlessly about his job at the British Library. They had gone their separate ways the following day with nothing in common but some bodily fluids.

Grace was ok, she knew. She was set up in her rented flat, working a couple of days a week for a couple of hours a day, and making frankly excellent money doing it. No major hassle she could not deal with, and no issues that caused her to lose sleep at night. Not in relation to her job anyway.

It was not uncommon for her to be making her way, still somewhat sheepish after just a few months in the job, home from a hotel or "party" (for two) somewhere and to see the throngs of office workers crowding the tube, bus, and trains on their way to work. She had told herself many times they were just like her, and that their utter, pathetic dependency on the iPod was for the same reason as hers. They all worked for big business and got shafted for a living, it was just that she did things on her terms, was a little more selective about who shafted her, and she in most cases got considerably more money for the privilege.

But there was that thing missing.

Aside from her few social friends, all of whom thought she worked for a bank or something if they had not bothered to ask, or the processing firm or the British Library if they had, and other than Barney the sarcastic cat, she was very alone.

At first she had wanted it that way.

Fraser, her ex-boyfriend had fucked her over badly, and that was one of those hard knocks that everyone thinks other people do not ever go through and could never understand.

Her friends did not pry, she saw them when she wanted to and she was left alone to heal, to regroup, and to get her life back on track. That had been what she had wanted, and now, with more than seventy thousand pounds squirrelled away she was beholden to nobody. She had told herself that she was a loner, but recent months had told her otherwise. She certainly did not want a boyfriend, she knew that much for an absolute fact.

A girlfriend?

No, despite a couple of drunken dalliances at Uni and an occasional fantasy, not worth the hassle.

One morning she realised, watching the workers stream across the very London Bridge she had just been across herself on their way to work in the offices in The City, that it was the daily interaction of a group of workmates she missed.

That afternoon though, Grace's thoughts were not on her loneliness. She was absent-mindedly flicking through the newspaper, listening to a maudlin band sing about chasing parked cars, and eating a very delicious orange and poppy seed muffin, trying very hard not to get the tiny black spheres in her teeth. The headlines floated past like ideas in a dream state. More about the students rioting in Korea. An expose of some Polish guy living in Leicester who was a convicted child killer or something. British troops reportedly doing the country proud in some war-torn place in West Africa. Chelsea to be investigated again by the FA for breaching some rule or other she did not care about. Bored and having not finished her muffin she flicked back to the first page and read back through the newspaper.

An article about teenage abortion rates on the third page caught her attention.

Grace remembered her dream the night before. The nightmares about Fraser and her aborted baby had disappeared some years previously, but this was a different terror. It was a fear that all little girls had. Bad men were coming to try and hurt her. Little girls had Daddies to cuddle them and tell them everything was going to be ok, but there was no such comfort in Grace's life.

Perhaps this was the reason she felt lonely.

Pushing the thoughts to the back of her mind, she pushed the plate with the detritus of her finished muffin away to the edge of the table and drained her coffee. Savouring the comforting warmth inside, she folded the newspaper and placed it back where the fat guy had left it.

Checking her phone for new messages (of which there were none) and changing her music selection to some New York-style soulful house music, she walked out into the street. The air was damp and chilly but not unpleasant, and the feel of the evening London air against her skin after the hot air-conditioned dry heat of the coffee shop felt nice. She had another short-notice client in Baron's Court in an hour and a half, and then a drink with Abi, Louise and some guy they were trying to set her up with in Covent Garden at about nine.

The guy in Baron's Court was a nice one, a "vanilla" client who looked after her, spoke to her with respect, and who never, ever took longer than an hour. He was one of those painfully earnest types who always made sure she was pleasured as well, and that was something Grace found very endearing about him. The hard part of her day was done, and she smiled as she looked forward to her drinks with Lou and Abi later on. The shopping could wait until tomorrow.

*****

Dylan and Jason were stood in the kitchen. Jason had just snorted a monster line of the sort he loved to call "a Widowmaker". He was rattling on about something to do with some savings thing which had matured, and how it meant he would be buying the beers that night. Dylan wasn't really listening. Carla was bent over in front of him and in the middle of one of her methodical lines. Dylan admired her aspect, and the way her legs looked in the pair of shiny leggings she was wearing. Jason did not notice him staring at her. She finished up with all the poise and grace of a ballet dancer, and turned to him, handing the wrap back to Jason.

"Beer?"

"Nice one" muttered Jason, already on the way to the fridge. Dylan watched Carla get her bag and coat ready. He did not fancy her. He wouldn't mind fucking her but he did not fancy her.

Still, nice looking women are always nice to look at, or they wouldn't be called nice looking would they?

Presently they left the house and flagrantly disobeyed the signs on the train telling them not to drink alcohol on public transport. Dylan gazed out of the window, feeling the last of the fuzzy and warm feeling inside his chest rise, wash and pass away. His fingers felt somehow lighter, and his neck felt like he had stimulated all the nerves in it. He had managed to successfully negotiate the cocaine question in the kitchen earlier and was pleased that his coke demons were in retreat. His justification for going on the night out was that there would be no drugs consumed. Last night had been enough for a month of weekends. Oddly Carla seemed to completely understand and did not hassle him about it, although Jason was extremely derisory in his dismissal of Dylan 's attempt at a hypocritical drug free night. It occurred to Dylan all at once that he might have to move out of the big house in Bounds Green if he was serious about getting serious in his life.

Turning to look at Carla and Jason he wondered if he would miss them.

Jason probably less so of the two because he was a mate but not a confidant and not really someone you could rely on. Great bloke to have at a party but not exactly the ideal housemate. Carla he probably would miss, as for all her foibles and occasionally irritating habits, not to mention her proper Habit, she was a proper friend and had been there for him in the past. She was chatting to Jason at one hundred miles per hour, reeling off names and places and who did what to whom and with whom, and a glance into Jason's strained face and darting, coked-up eyes revealed to Dylan that he had not got a clue what she was talking about either.

The bus ground into Tottenham Court Road junction and they piled off so quickly that Dylan was immediately rushing down to catch up with them. The air was freezing cold, but under his coat and scarf Dylan was swelteringly hot, no doubt another throwback from the drugs he had thrown down himself the previous night. He felt lightheaded and vacant, and realised he was walking quickly with his mouth half open, in the way that extremely drunk people do.

It was an eventual relief to get to the bar, but this soon evaporated once they were led inside by Laura, who seemed to be on a mission.

With the authority of a General, she marshalled Jason and Dylan to a space in a corner, where it turned out, Louise and a slightly chubby girl Dylan did not recognise were sat, whilst she headed to the bar. Dylan sat down and was immediately panicked as one of the girls came up and started chatting to him.

Which one is Laura and which is Louise?

By the time Carla returned to the table, Jason had disappeared to the toilets and Dylan was in deep but apparently uncertain conversation with Laura. She handed him a beer and he drained half in one mouthful, inordinately pleased apparently for the break in conversation. Realising her housemate had no short term memory at the best of times, and certainly given the previous night's excesses, Carla made a point of enquiring loudly over the music whether Dylan and Laura had met before.

Dylan winked at her, and went to the bar.

Five rounds later and everyone but Jason was drunk.

Carla was hugging her three girl mates closely and Jason was back in the Gents again for the fourth time, evidently unaffected by the amount of beer he was drinking. Dylan was sat enjoying the view, as hundreds of young and not-so-young Londoners thronged in the lights and darkness of the bar. The music was too loud to hear the girls from across the table and after a valiant 20 minute effort to stay involved in their boring conversation he had given up and taken to watching the women instead. It was obvious that he needed to have sex. The testosterone was building up inside him. Even unattractive women looked attractive to him, and the more he drunk the less he cared that he was being obvious about looking at the women dancing all around.

Dylan lurched up from his seat, noting Jason darting back, hand to nose from the gents, and headed to the bar with a series of nondescript noises and hand-gestures in an attempt to make himself understood to the girls over the pounding music. Swallowing hard he picked his way to the mess of people in front of him, tenderly brushing past the shadowy figures and excusing himself out loud even though they could not hear him.

After just less than half an hour he was bellowing his order to the barman who had to lean across the bar to hear him, despite Dylan's loud yells in his direction.

To his horror, Dylan's movement across the wooden surface to meet the barman roused something inside him, and as the dreadlocked man-mountain leaned in, he burped loudly. It stunk of the Chinese he had enjoyed in vast quantities for late-lunch and the barman visibly recoiled, the order safe but with a look of pure revulsion on his face. Dylan laughed and put his hand to his mouth in a very camp apology. The barman looked as though he might hurt Dylan badly for a few seconds, until he slammed his drinks down, snatched the cash, and moved rapidly onto the woman next to him, who he was sure, was also ignoring him in pure disgust at his noxious emissions. Smiling in amusement, Dylan expertly picked up all five drinks in an elaborate mass of fingers and arms and headed back to the table. Jason was about to take a pill, he could tell that from across the bar,. Carla was lolling back and forwards in mock drunkenness.

He could not tell if she was taking the piss out of him or not, but meeting his gaze, she creased up into shrieks of laughter when she saw he was looking.

Dylan was drunk, and did not care.

"Youth, you know it makes sense...." Jason's voice, above the noise of the music, sounded strained, as if he had been out in the desert too long. Maybe he had. Jason wanted to go to a club.

This was not surprising, given the amount of Class A's he had consumed that night, and yet he still wanted Carla, who had managed to swerve consuming any pills up to that point, to come with him. Dylan remained silent.

"Might as well though, yeah. Better than staying here with these boring bitches"

There he was again.

It was obvious he was not going to let it go.

To be fair, he reasoned, he had a point. None of the women had spoken to him save for a thank-you for the round of drinks, for the last half hour, and it was obvious to him that sex with any of the four was out of the question. Abi was seeing Steffen, and Louise was seeing some black guy. Whilst he was sober enough not to want to seem single minded, he was drunk enough to be pragmatic about his chances with the other two. Jason seemed to read his mind.

"Lots of drunk birds at CoCo Club mate... lets go fuck something eh, yeah?"

Dylan glanced at the girls, still deep in conversation. Carla was on the phone, shouting at someone. He vaguely recalled that one of their party had still to turn up.

Was this likely to change the dynamic?

No.

Nodding at Jason, he lifted from the leather chair, draining his pint as he did so in one fluid movement. The girls did not even glance at him. Behind him, Jason already had his coat on and stood there, towering over him, rushing like a steam train. Dylan made some exaggerated facial expressions and shrugged arms on shrugged shoulders to Jason, and left. Carla made some equally staged facial expressions of great pain, and made a shrug of her own to illustrate that she was unwilling to rise from her sofa seat to give him a hug goodbye. None of the other three girls looked bothered.

Winking at Carla in a way he would never do were he sober, Dylan headed for the door. Jason was several paces in front. Jason was holding the door open, but someone was on their way in, so Dylan stood to one side.

Looking up from the floor, he did not recognise her at first.

*****

Grace was late, but the bar was just on the end of the road.

She doubled her pace as the first drops of thick, heavy rain began to fall and nosed through the doors to bar, as a wave of heat and noise slapped her back. A tall guy in a brown anorak was holding the door open for her, and she caught sight of his eyes, recoiling at their tiny pupils.

Someone is well on it tonight.

A shadow in the doorframe stood to one side to let her pass.

She stepped in, shook the rain from her pink coat, and stopped, the door still held open precariously.

She looked at the figure to gesture thanks for allowing her in.

*****

It took half a second to register.

He knew her, only he did not know her.

The girl from the tube.

The-Girl-In-The-Pink-Overcoat.

Dylan gaped.

*****

He seemed familiar. A client maybe?

No, he was quite cute in a Chris O'Dowdy sort of way and she did not have too many clients like that. She would have remembered. Then, like a tube train emerging into the light in a rush, she realised.

The guy from the train!

Grace, unsure of her reaction, looked at the floor and grinned widely with a definite nod that was executed to be devoid of any meaning. She was certain he recognised her and all of a sudden was filled with an urge to smile at him.

*****

She was smiling at him. Dylan could not believe his eyes. Before he could decide whether to say something, he was outside, blushing in the rain. She was gone.

Dylan kept smiling for the rest of the night.

How bizarre to see her again!

Grace joined Amy, Laura and Louise with hoots of girly enthusiasm and sunk into a familiar rhythm of laughter, gossip and binge drinking.

The guy from the tube was on her mind, and she briefly turned over the incredulity of having seen him again, and recognised him, in a city of ten million people. She thought about mentioning it to her companions, but, in the rapidly descending drunkenness of the group, she did not think they would appreciate it.

It was one of those things you definitely had to be there for.

NINE

Soundtrack

Pet Shop Boys – 'Rent'

The knuckles poised. Floating in mid-air an inch from the dusty surface of the UPVC white plastic.

Grace hesitated.

For a long couple of seconds she listened, taking in all around her. The flat was another utterly unremarkable effort on the second floor of a former-council block near Wapping. Someone was burning something leafy far away, the autumnal smell evoking a full half year in advance or in past. The air was all winter though, Spring some weeks away yet despite the scattering of crocuses poking cautiously out of the unlovely flowerbed on the way in.

Nearby from one of the apartments a substantial dog was barking in alarmed annoyance at something she could not guess at. Cars hissed by on the street outside and ticked quietly in rest in the car port parking area beneath.

Grace exhaled a long breath. She was wearing tight back leggings and another of her mini-collection of knee-high boots, with a tightish white blouse and unusually preppy beige sweater. The pink overcoat masked all but the boots and an inch of legging, yet she felt safely enclosed in its sheepish warmth. The large latte she had taken her time over at Tower Hill station stayed on her tongue with savoury notes not masked by the numbness afforded by the scalding liquid. Remembering to stay professional she pulled out a Wrigley's Extra from a blue packet and chewed quickly to mask it.

Taking a few seconds to masticate thoroughly she turned and glanced long out to the Canary Wharf towers in the distance. The yellow structural supports of the O2 Arena Dome jutted just above the building in the foreground.

As she watched, a large plane swooped low over the buildings alarmingly seeming to head right for the Canary Wharf financial district before sidestepping them and disappearing behind them on its way into London City. Its red and blue tail was distinctive. Grace was reminded of an advert she saw in a magazine. It had been of a very pretty career type woman sleeping soundly with a ridiculously self-satisfied grin on her eyeshaded face in a lie-flat bed on a business class only flight from London City to New York. The romance of it tantalized her. How cool would that be? Just to go, to fly in a luxury bed with bubbly and canapés and everything else from that tiny airport to The Big Apple. Not just for the escapism and novelty but for the comfortable pretence. The eyeshade masquerade that she might play at being a successful executive type who got paid to do such things.

The knuckle hovered again. The juxtaposition was almost too much to bear.

Instead of getting paid to do this.

Swallowing with resolve she rapped hard on the door and within a couple of seconds, to her astonishment, a woman answered the door.

"Come on in."

She was about fifty, plump but not fat, with lines running beyond her years running across the features of a face that, she imagined, was not naturally English. Certainly her features were angular, and the thick jaw suggested she might have been Slavic in descent.

Grace thanked her and came inside.

The woman spoke again and her accent betrayed some more of her eastern European heritage. It was faint and barely noticeable.

"I am Nadej, it is nice to meet you." She shook Grace's hand and the formality of it almost made her laugh.

"You're Polish?" Grace asked with a smile.

The woman made a face as if blushing.

"Yes, from Lodz. I have lived here for 30 years. Would you like cup of tea?"

Grace sat down in a darkish kitchen that smelt faintly of garlic and oven-cleaner. She noticed it was spotlessly clean. Grace guessed Nadej was a cleaner, but clearly a very diligent one.

Grace watched her as she scurried around making tea. She was almost perfectly rectangular with almost no curves. A cheap pair of jeans covered but singularly failed to flatter a backside that was merely there and seemed to have no connection to the rest of her body. A navy blue polo shirt of no specific brand (a uniform perhaps?) encapsulated but did not promote a very moderate sized pair of breasts. Her low-neck length hair was strawlike, rendered brittle and rough by exposure to too many chemicals. The woman's roots betrayed a much darker natural colour. She had wide, pale cheeks and a quite severe hairline, but with greyness in her eyes. Grace imagined that despite her sunny disposition Nadej was probably hard as nails deep inside. She had been expecting a male appointment and Nadej answering the door had thrown her a little.

Still, it was easy money and the idea of it did not disgust her even if the woman in front of her was by no means an object of the very occasional lustful dreams she had had more or less since her teens. It had been a long time. But there was something nice about it. Something that appealed. Grace felt a welcome somersault in her stomach and a tingling lower down. Easy money. Nadej busied making the tea. She wasn't unattractive, for an older Polish lady. Inwardly Grace imagined a huge unruly shock of Polish pubic hair and big knickers…

Lost in her thoughts she did not notice Nadej offering a mug of steaming tea. Stammering an apology and then rapidly scalding her fingers on the mug she accepted as Nadej sat down opposite.

"So."

Grace smiled coquettishly.

Nadej seemed startled into action and with a look of acute embarrassment on her face she rummaged in her jeans pocket and pulled out two hundred pounds, thrusting it at Grace as if desperate for her not to leave.

"I don't normally do women. I don't mention it on the cards, but…" she began, allowing a smile to spread across her features.

Nadej shot up in horror, eyes wide with fear.

"On no! No! Not me! Is for my son! Not for me! I mean you very beautiful but… you know…" She showed Grace a wedding ring as if it gave her some sort of magical exemption from being intimate with a woman.

Grace tilted her head to one side, unsure of what to say next.

"He is disabled you see. Very handsome man, very handsome. But has never seen a woman. He is eighteen now. It is time. It is making him sad."

Disabled? What the fuck? Disabled how?

Grace stayed silent, disappointment etched across her features, and she did not care of Nadej noticed.

"He lost both his legs when he was nine. Meningitis. So sad. He is such good boy."

Before Grace could say anything Nadej was ushering her out of the kitchen, tea untouched, to where she guessed the lounge was. They walked through the door and straight away Grace could see that the lounge space had been converted into a bedroom for her son.

"This is Steven."

A young man was sat on the bed arms by his sides regarding Grace with a mixture of fear and fascination.

The door clicked shut behind. Nadej clearly had no interest in witnessing whatever came next. Grace sat down on the bed and to her surprise the man reached back nimbly and switched on a bright bedside lamp.

"I'm Nadia. Nice to meet you Steven." Grace shot out a hand which the young man took and shook warmly.

"Sorry I'm nervous." His accent was pure East End, nothing like his mother's.

Grace edged up next to him.

"No you aren't, you're Steven." she joked. "No need to be nervous. I'm all yours…"

Steven looked dazzled and Grace was struck by the power of his smile. It could have melted the ice-caps. In fact, he was actually cute in a very innocent boyish sort of way. She imagined but for a speckling of the tail end of some teenage acne he could have been in a boyband. If he had legs.

Taking her cue Grace got to her feet and began to undress slowly.

Steven seemed fascinated, utterly rapt in the sight of her. The boots came off. Then the sweater. Then the blouse, draped over a stripped-down and sporty looking wheelchair idling nearby.

His face was frozen in concentration.

Then the leggings.

Then the bra.

Then the panties.

Steven moved his hand involuntarily and Grace slipped her knickers into his palm. Like a shot he was snuffling in them, kneading them between nose, thumb and forefinger, furtively meeting her gaze with a look of delighted but humourless guilt.

Grace eased off his t-shirt and half way through, still with panties in hand, he raised himself to full height and began to undress. Grace marvelled at his dexterity. His legs were missing just above the knee but he could almost stand up straight on the stumps. Once naked she was surprised to see he had very little body fat and quite an impressive upper body.

She found herself getting quite turned on despite herself.

Ten minutes later it was done. She had lain back and he had gone to work on her missionary style, face full on wonder and stars and sunshine. She was sure she saw his heart break as she got dressed to leave, minus her underwear. She sensed wild horses could not tear them away from the youngster's grasp.

"Can I see you again?" he blurted out.

Your mum's got my number sweetie.

"Any time Steven. Just call me and I'll come for you. In more ways than one..."

TEN

Soundtrack

David Holmes – 'Gritty Shaker'

"This is not right. We can't have this."

Dylan was rooted to the spot in uncertain terror as a diminutive woman with short curly hair snarled at him.

All around the office stopped dead.

"Dylan, this isn't ok!"

Her voice seethed venom. Lucy the HR manager had never liked him and was now in full on dump mode. Dylan pursed his lips in the corner of his mouth in a way he hoped might convey cool non-plussedness but a bit of remorse as well.

Everyone is fucking staring. This is shit.

Lucy beckoned with her forefinger as if he were the home help and spun on her heel before making off for the stairwell at a rate of knots. Dylan shrugged as he imagined the cool kids at school might do on their way to the Head's office, and followed deliberately trying to look like he didn't care. The parallels with being 12 again were so clear it made him smirk, and the smile was returned by a few of his male friends on the way out. It was shut down savagely with a look from Lucy as she poked a chin over a stubby shoulder to check he was following as she smashed through the double doors.

It had started off as a normal day. Dylan had been deeply annoyed about Chelsea's 4-2 capitulation to QPR in the cup the previous evening and arrived to the office metaphorically kicking the dog. The banter started even before he got his coat off.

A Post-It sat on his keyboard stating that "IT IS A SHAME YOU ARE NOT IN THE CUP 4-2 LONG".

Comedians.

Could have been Raja, the fat Indian guy from accounts, or Tony Black from sales.

Had to have been Tony.

As if on cue, (and it probably was) Tony appeared and passed him a cup of tea in a QPR mug.

Very fucking funny.

Dylan went about his preparations to start work and sipped the tea. Tony had, hilariously, dosed it with what had to be a huge quantity of salt. The taste revolted him. He slammed the mug down so hard he nearly cracked it, and spattered tea all over the desk.

Tony, Raja and both the office Rent-A-Scousers roared with laughter behind him.

"Bit hard to swallow is it, you Chelsea mug?" Tony guffawed, clearly enjoying the humiliation.

Dylan thought about taking him to the cleaners. Like most QPR fans he knew, Tony wasn't the brightest and Dylan had no difficulty in out-bantering him to the extent that it got a little bit nasty when he did not react well to being completely served up in front of the office. Still, the game had been a shocker. Chelsea had led one nil at half time, then Matic had been sent off for a nothing foul on the half way line and QPR had scored two quick goals while Chelsea were reorganizing and preparing to take off a winger and bring on someone to replace the big Serb. Chelsea had streamed forward in search of an equalizer and then QPR had sucker punched them twice again on the break in the second half. It was a real low point.

Instead of reacting, Dylan rotated his chair and laid back in it in mock relaxation.

"It is on days like today I am reminded of an ancient proverb thought up by yours truly…"

The room went quiet.

"Chelsea are shit?" Raja offered, to more loud hilarity.

"Following Chelsea is very much like eating oysters. Hideously expensive, absolutely wonderful most of the time but now and again when you have a bad one you want to stay in the toilet and not come out for two days."

The room erupted in laughter, and Tony seemed disappointed at his humility, clearly hoping for more banter.

He walked away shaking his head with a fake grin on his face.

Inwardly a plan formed.

Dylan took an hour or so to get caught up on his emails and for everyone to get back into the work of the day, then slipped quietly out of the office doors and down the stairwell to the ground floor.

It was still there.

The dead cockroach lay on its back in a cartoonish parody of death, legs bolt upright, since its demise a couple of days previously. It was an inch and a half long: one of the largest he had ever seen in the UK. Gingerly Dylan picked it up in a piece of kitchen towel and daintily slipped it into his jacket pocket.

Dylan sat back down at his desk and pulled out some small label stickers from his desk drawer. Picking one rectangular one out, he carefully drew in impressive detail in blue ballpoint some stripes resembling the QPR home jersey, and then wrote "QPR: WEST LONDON IS OURS" in the middle. Peeling back the sticker he touched it to the back of his hand and went to the gents. In the cubicle the sticker was attached to the crispy insect's carapace. Dylan admired his handiwork. It was hilarious.

Will serve this wanker right.

The plan was to put the dead roach on Tony's computer screen but upon entering the kitchen and going for a bottle of water he noticed Tony's lunchbox sitting in the fridge. Quick as a flash he was in it. Tin foil dextrously peeled back. Cheese and tuna sandwich between thumb and forefinger. Then the roach was gone. The foil closed up in a cocoon. The lid clicked shut.

What a fucking result.

Dylan was so pleased with himself he could barely contain himself.

About an hour later he became aware of a confusion at the other end of the office. There were some muffled raised voices. Dylan got up to see what was going on. Wendy Davies, one of the accounts girls rushed past, her tear-streaked face a mask of contorted horror, hands clasped across her mouth.

Oh fuck.

The crowds seemed to divide, drawing him to come near. Wendy's desk was untidy. In the middle lay a large piece of crumpled foil and…

For fuck's sake.

The sandwich.

It lay, deconstructed and discombobulated. Cheese gratings scattered all over the place. Distinctive against the beige plastic of the desk was a brown object, in a couple of pieces. Dylan already knew what it was even before Tony started to cackle behind him.

"You fucking bastard." Laura Standworth said quietly.

"You absolute fucking bastard." She repeated.

Dylan stayed silent.

Laura picked up Wendy's bag and coat and took them away. Dylan guessed Wendy was going home.

The double doors spat open and Lucy the HR manager burst forth, a ball of man-hating, Dylan-despising rage.

On the walk down to her office, Dylan was reminded of a passage in a Roald Dahl autobiography about being sadistically caned at school following a silly prank involving a dead animal, foodstuffs and someone not very likeable. He had the odd feeling that Lucy would indeed love to hurt him very badly. Dylan could not really argue. It was horrible. He would send Wendy some flowers and a hand-written apology and get back at that bellend Tony Black another day.

The bollocking was not fun.

Dylan watched all five foot nothing of Lucy the HR Manager pace around him like an enraged cat, her eyes filled with fury. He imagined her imagining sticking white hot kebab skewers through his knees or scalding the skin off his feet with hot oil. Or taking a blowtorch to his major extremities. It was all too lucid. She hated him. She always had.

About three minutes into the monologue about respect, decency, adult behaviour and the curse of people who do not take responsibility for their actions, Dylan sat up straight. Slouching and looking bored like a teenager would only antagonize her further and this was not a job he could afford to lose. On and on she went. Fists were pounded on the table. Wide sweeping gestures of finality with both arms that would on another day be laughably Napoleonic were not at all funny. Dylan could not get a word in edgeways to apologise.

Eventually she paused for breath and Dylan took his chance before the assault began again.

"Look, Lucy this was a horrible thing to happen. I think you know it was some playful if very stupid banter between Tony Black and myself which I thoughtlessly took too far. I made a mistake. Wendy should never have been involved."

She filled her lungs and was about to have another go.

Better step this up, Dylan lad.

"It was a huge mistake. I take full and unmitigated responsibility. I appreciate I am the last person she wants to see but I will formally apologise to Wendy and to Tony as well because had it gone into his lunch as planned it was still a healthcode violation. A very nasty one at that... He could get all sorts of germs from it and it was a very stupid thing to do. I regretted it as soon as it happened and I still do."

Her lips were pursed. Dylan continued.

"…I wholeheartedly agree with all you have said. I was well out of order, and I need to grow up. I sometimes feel this company doesn't take me seriously, but how can I have any complaints when I do stupid, infantile and dangerous things like this? I mean, really! I take full and absolute responsibility for it and should you feel that it warrants further action, a formal written warning or such, then I accept this fully and with all apologies to all concerned. I recognize it is something that has no place in this office and you may rest assured it cannot and will not ever happen again."

There was a snort of derision but she let him speak further.

"My career here is very important to me and I have been meaning to thank you personally for the time and effort you have put into guiding me in terms of becoming a better professional and more of an asset to this company."

Too much?

"You are aware obviously that I am in the middle of a personal growth phase and it is embarrassing that I needlessly regress to this silliness when I had been making such good advances."

Bingo.

"I know I am a work in progress but I personally take this sad incident as a real wake up call. I think the fact that I am so shocked and horrified with myself as I am, is testament I believe to how far I have come as a person and a professional under the guidance of management here, Mr Atwater obviously but also yourself. I want everyone to be proud of me, not to hate me. This is a major focus."

You sneaky fucker.

"If you allow me I would like to send Wendy a big bunch of flowers and a bottle of something nice to apologise, and I will formally write a letter apologising in full which you can have a copy of for my file. I'd also like to apologise to you Lucy for wasting your time on this. I know how busy you are. You have a lot more important things to be doing I'm sure than dealing with idiots like me."

Genius.

Even Lucy seemed impressed. She agreed not to escalate the matter on the basis that Dylan make all apologies in full as he promised to, and told him any repeat of anything like that would be an instant gross misconduct hearing and almost certain dismissal. Not wanting to push his luck Dylan agreed in full with as much grace as he could and got out of the office as quickly as he could manage.

Carla and Jason found the story hilarious that evening over beers and a spliff. Dylan started the evening determined to skip dinner in the interests of trimming his waistline but the spliff and beer did as it always did and very soon the pizzas were on the way.

ELEVEN

Soundtrack

DJ Shadow – 'This Time (I'm Gonna Try It My Way)'

"One ten…twenty…forty…"

The notes felt cold and impersonal in a way that normal paper could never be. Dylan scanned the count and slipped the notes into his jeans pocket.

Tash, a friend from his clubbing group made a little delighted noise and pushed the bag of pills into a jewellery box by her bedside cabinet. "Friend" was probably overstating it a little, if Dylan was honest.

She was an acquaintance and somebody he had never really had anything much to say to before she learned that he could be a reliable(ish) source of cheap(ish), high-quality(ish) pills.

After that she'd been his best mate for half an hour every month. Dylan did not mind of course, as it was better this way, and Tash knew better than to take advantage of a friendship she had essentially constructed for her own advantage.

"We should definitely meet up one lunchtime for a pint, Old Street is just up the road from me in Holborn you know. Feels like we've not had a proper catch-up for ages."

Her voice was soothing and Dylan would probably have believed it were sincere in years gone by. He smiled widely and fixed the skinny woman with as friendly a cynical look as he could.

"Of course, send me a text one day when you are free and we'll arrange it"

He had already turned his back and was walking out of her room. Downstairs, her Greek Cypriot flatmates were chatting noisily and there was an air of smoke, rosemary and garlic in the air. They would likely not appreciate Dylan's presence were they to guess of his reasons for coming round once a month or so. They were used to him but Dylan always wondered if they suspected, and more importantly whether they knew just what Tash got up to every weekend. She was a trainee Barrister at a well-respected legal firm in the West End, and if ever there was a stereotypical example of someone who "did not look the type" it was her. Diminutive, pale-skinned, and obviously with some kind of eating problem giving that her slightly gaunt, taught look across a face that would otherwise be quite attractive. Now that Dylan came to think about it, she probably did not have anorexia. The two grammes of pungent, butter-like Base and just under one hundred of those raspberry ripple pills was a clue.

She had a group of people Dylan did not know, maybe from her work, who she was selling them to at three for ten pounds. She probably made enough on those pills to pay her coke habit and ten years ago probably would have been able to pay her rent off the proceeds too.

Tash was his only errand that week and with her out of the way, he was relieved.

Closing the door behind him, Dylan set off towards Archway tube station. The warm glow of the pills from a few days ago had gone and so, thankfully, had the miserable numbness of the comedown. Monday and Tuesday had come and gone and Wednesday had been boring with little or nothing to involve him at work. Nicole had not followed up her email, and he had all but forgotten about her. He had spent most of that day on the dating site emailing women whose profile he liked or at least found interesting. More than twenty emails sent out that day, and his Blackberry was not exactly vibrating out of his pocket. He resolved to go to the gym tomorrow.

Sidestepping Carla on his way in, who obviously had one eye on the large Pizza he was carrying, Dylan made his way to his room and ate every cloying morsel of his Pizza and the wedges and the wings. Stuffed and guilty he lay back on his bed, feeling sick.

The next sound he heard was his alarm. Fully clothed and with an ugly garlic sauce stain down his t-shirt, he stumbled to the bathroom more confused than annoyed at having fallen asleep the previous night. Dylan looked at himself in the mirror. Some of his colour had returned after the weekend and he would have looked reasonably healthy were it not for the imprint of his watch in the side of his face and the white tidemark of drool that covered one corner of his mouth.

Belching loudly, then recoiling at the smell of garlic from the pizza he had consumed some ten hours previously, he jumped into the shower and then jumped straight back out again with a yelp. The squint and fuzzy head was gone. He was fully awake now. The water was icy cold. Only then did Dylan notice a piece of torn A4 graph paper with Carla's spidery, all-but-incomprehensible handwriting on it, in red biro. There was no hot water because someone needed to put some money on the gas keycard thing. Dylan did not even know they had one, let alone how much money there was on there. He certainly did not know how anyone went about putting money on it.

An hour later and Dylan was sat at his desk feeling slightly put upon. There were no emails from prospective dates off the website, he was feeling greasy and dirty after not having had a shower, and his Boss had sent him an unpleasant email about his work and how he felt that Dylan really was not showing sufficient drive to improve it. This did not bother Dylan but it probably meant he would not be getting his team bonus next month, which was likely to have been in the region of six hundred pounds. After tax, it would mean a weekend break somewhere nice or his trip to Ibiza paid for. That said, Dylan's trip to Ibiza was a possibility borne more out of assumption on the part of his friends rather than an implicit desire to go on his part.

He was getting too old for that sort of serotonin silliness.

His mates, Carla in particular, had said to him on more than one occasion in the last few months that he always said the same things, and had been getting too old for it for the last five years. Either way, perhaps no trip to Ibiza in the summer would not be the end of the world. The money would have been nice though. Lastly, as a sweetener for the morning, the coffee machine was out of sugar and as a result the coffee was savoury and tasted like it was full of chemicals, which in this case was a bad thing.

Dylan 's day improved from about 15:04. An email dropped soundlessly into his Inbox and a girl called Gemma sounded, judging from the accepting and yet self-deprecating tone of her email, like she might drop soundlessly into his life.

-----Original Message-----------------------------------

From: Gemma Wetherby [mailto: GoodBadWether@danglemail.com]

Sent: Thursday 4th April 15:04

To: Short, Dylan

Subject: Re: Saw Your Profile

Well hello there Dylan.

Thank you very much for your lovely message. It was kind of you to say those nice things. I hate my pictures on the site I think I look like a Muppet, but it was nice of you say. I like the way you write and your pictures are very handsome. I see from your profile we share loads of common interests. I'd like to meet you. Hopefully speak soon. Hugs,

Gemma x

TWELVE

Soundtrack

Deadmau5 – 'Ghosts And Stuff' (feat. Rob Swire)

"One ten…twenty…forty…"

The notes felt cold and impersonal in a way that normal paper could never be.

Grace scanned the count and slipped the notes into her jacket pocket. The client was a new one. His house was nice, but he was obviously married. His tastes were a little left of centre, quite a lot left of centre actually, and it was obvious that he did not get to spend time with his leftfield side too often.

The wife was obviously a ball-breaking bitch and would not indulge him, she thought.

Grace wondered if she even knew what he was into. Most of the time guys got married and had not told their spouse about their little kinks. Most people figured that by the time they were married, it was a little too late to suggest new things, especially new things like what the rather podgy and sallow middle-aged guy stood in front of her was into. If he knew how common such kinks were, he would probably not have such a problem with it. The ashen faced look of pure, absolute shame on his face was nothing to do with his feelings of doing the dirty on his wife, but more the sheer dirtiness of the act itself.

His expression implored her to somehow validate what they had just done, but Grace was careful to offer just a friendly smile and a hug on the way out. Better not to leave a business card. With no more appointments booked, and having done three that day, Grace headed home, picking up a delicious-looking beef and gravy frozen ready meal from Tesco on her way home.

Barney greeted her at the door. He was upset at having to wait well into the evening for his dinner and clearly considered Grace personally culpable for this obvious disservice, despite the fact that she got home late at least twice a week and had done so since Barney had been in her life. She did not take her coat off but went straight to the cupboard and pulled a pouch of something probably putrid out of the cupboard. His plaintive meow was insistent. Normally he would rub around her legs and nuzzle his neck into her hand, but not today. He seemed particularly upset about it today.

For fuck's sake. I'm sick and fucking tired of waiting for you to stop fucking about and get home so I can get fed. Do I fucking look like I'm not hungry to you? Famished, woman, Famished! I cannot believe you'd leave me like this.

The big sunset-coloured eyes regarded her coldly, then disappeared into the bowl. Rather unsettling snorting and grunting noises ensued. Suitably chastised, Grace took off her coat and left Barney to his no doubt very tasty meaty chunks in gravy jelly.

Unzipping and pulling off her boots, she tossed her footwear away to the corner of the room and switched on the television. Some cop show was on one channel, but it was not interesting enough to keep her enthralled so she switched over to a cooking programme on another channel and thought about what she would have with her beef and gravy ready meal.

The next sound she heard was her alarm.

Or, in this case, her black furry alarm squeaking a good morning greeting into her ear. She was fully dressed in her armchair and had drifted off. It was still dark outside but the television was turned off. She had obviously done it subconsciously in the night, but she did not remember. With a yawn and a loud click of her jaw, she looked at her watch. It was just after six, and the debate as regards whether to go to bed properly for another couple of hours or get up and do something went on for some time. There were a number of hours before it was time to go to her midmorning appointment in Vauxhall. In the end, Barney made her mind up and she got up and stretched. She walked to the cupboard and looked down at the bowl. It was squeaky clean.

"Morning gorgeous" she muttered to Barney, who replied with an abrupt meow that could possibly have been telling her to hurry up and stop with the pleasantries. The sun had not yet begun to stream in through the windows and the sky was only now beginning to turn purple from the lights outside and the onset of what would be called an uncertain dawn by a gravely-voiced Hollywood movie trailer voice-over man.

It was one of those days where you just know that absolutely nothing lies ahead before you open those curtains or walk out of the door in the morning. There were no such big budget blockbuster dramas in the offing, that much was clear.

Grace had the aforementioned client at ten, then another at nine in the evening and no other plans. She made herself a cup of very sweet tea with slightly too much milk in and settled down on her sofa. Her mind waded through the backwaters of her day, ruminating on her plans. Both clients were known regulars and neither were too far left of centre-field as far as she knew, and this suited her just fine.

Then, for no reason whatsoever her mind flicked back to The-Guy-On-The-Train. How odd to have bumped into him again.

She remembered the wide, slightly sheepish grin he flashed her like some lighthouse beacon in the rain and she smiled without realising. It occurred to her that he had subconsciously been forgiven for staring at her legs just for having a nice smile. She recalled him like a one-off client from many months ago, remembering his face but little more. For a second it occurred to her again that he may indeed have been a client gone forgotten by her and hence smiling at her more through recognition than whatever his real reasons were, but this was discounted swiftly.

He looked as though he might have been one, as she had a few clients like him; overweight but well dressed and just down on their confidence.

But he wasn't.

As quickly as a client, he washed out of her mind as she got up, yawned and clicked again, and pulled off her sweater and her stockings. Barney stood with his buttocks to her, tail bolt upright in the air like a fairground dodgem car, with his tiny, speckled pink pucker conspicuous against his jet black fur. The tail swayed as he ate, shuddering noisily as the food shovelled into his mouth.

"You really should eat slower you know. Chew your food. You'll get indigestion."

The bench was studded with droplets of rain from the previous night. Grace sat down daintily and waited.

The afternoon was mild. Her three PM appointment, a new one who texted just after lunch, was late, and she was a little skeptical he would show. Her nine PM cancelled.

The public bench was a new one as rendezvous spots went. He had sounded gruff and short on the phone and for this reason Grace had chosen another park bench twenty yards from the actual meeting spot so she could check out the appointment before going over to greet him. Just in case.

It was something she had seen in an episode of Law & Order or something once, a long time ago.

She watched the expanse of London spread out from one periphery to the next from her vantage point near the top of Primrose Hill. It was one of her favourite spots and a happy coincidence the customer had asked to meet there.

The conversation sounded just like in the cop show.

"There are some park benches on top of Primrose Hill on the south side overlooking the hill next to the Zoo. Do you know them?"

Of course I do. I go there all the time to think and be properly alone on my terms.

"Yes of course."

"I'll meet you there at 3PM. I will be wearing a light brown wool coat."

I will be wearing a white carnation!

"See you then."

The cab had dropped her off next to the Zoo and as she liked to do, Grace walked up the hill herself, relishing the warmth and effort. The view was always well worth it.

The clouds were racing across the sky high enough to let the planes pass in full view underneath. It was a busy day in the Capital's skies. Grace watched idly as a huge silver jet banked slowly almost overhead, London glinting in its shiny body and America shining on its tail. It hardly looked like it was moving as its dull whistle changed pitch like the sound of a person blowing across the top of a huge bottle. The soothing noise was drowned out a second later by the urgent clatter of the emergency air ambulance low overhead. It shook Grace out of her entrancement and she realised her customer had arrived. He looked around and did not appear to see her, and sat down on the bench. He did not look like a psycho in so much as anyone can not look dangerous or unstable from that distance.

Grace regarded him with a blank mind for a few seconds and got to her feet.

Time to go to work.

She walked up behind him in his blind spot, fighting the temptation to run away. She wanted to go home, drink wine and coffee, watch some old cop dramas and maybe phone for a Chinese. To count her money and forget just for a night that she was almost a prostitute.

The customer forced the issue as he turned round as she approached and locked eyes with her. There would be no getting out of it.

"Hello, I'm Nadia."

The man rose and bowed slightly, offering a mechanical-feeling hand.

"Hello Nadia."

He did not bother to give his name. Some of them did not want to. Grace did not particularly care.

They hurriedly made their way to a nondescript flat nearby. The man made small talk about enjoying being so close to Camden. Grace politely agreed.

The man's flat was obviously not just his, that is to say, he was obviously not the sole usual occupant. There was even a space in the recessed mantelpiece area where subtle lines of a week's worth of dust suggested a missing photoframe. That he had taken it down suggested either he thought enough of Grace to preserve the lie, or more likely, that he did not want to take any chances with Grace chancing across his wife's face, howsoever seen.

The cash changed hands in the quick, embarrassed way it normally did and then the lights were off, the curtains shielding and the clothes removed. There was no champagne.

He had been fairly average, under-endowed with no particular skill or passion. She drifted off half way and did not hear him the first time he breathlessly whispered that he wanted something. He repeated himself and Grace was almost disappointed. At least the kinks and left field stuff made things interesting. In the end she finished affairs off with a rubbery blowjob. It was over in less than half an hour. His brackish sweat seemed to coat her, catching in her nose, and Grace suddenly yearned for a long hot bath.

Grace wondered whether he would want to make his money go further with a second round to slot into the bottom half of the hour but he seemed disinterested. She threw her clothes on and settled on the edge of the bed. The room was dark and too hot. She sniffed her fingers idly as the guy got dressed in the adjoining bathroom. How strange he should feel awkward about nakedness in front of her given what had just happened.

Presently the man edged out of the bathroom and seemed to usher her toward the door. He was in a hurry. He had not even offered her a glass of water. She noticed he seemed to have a problem with eye-contact in so much as she noticed him not meeting her eye, and had not done before the sex. He hurried them both out of the house with a telltale sideways glance up the street before heading out of the door.

Grace wondered where his wife was.

For no reason she could fathom, the customer had decided to walk her back to the very spot they agreed to meet.

He was a fast walker and Grace had to move fast on the paving stones to keep up. The exertion of the hillside robbed both of the power of easy small talk which neither truly lamented. They arrived at the bench and Grace sidestepped an awkward handshake to plant herself down on the bench to go back to watching the late afternoon vista.

The man stared at her, hand still outstretched in disbelief. Grace smiled as she met his eyes again. He could not comprehend why Grace would want to stick around and seemed unsettled at her wanting to stay, lest possibly someone might see her. Glancing nervously around he darted down onto the seat next to her. Grace could tell he was considering putting the collar of his coat up as if it might help in his subterfuge.

"I...."

Grace smiled and let him struggle.

"I think... I mean... earlier. It was nice. I really enjoyed it."

Grace smiled again.

"You seemed like you needed it. I hope it helped." she lied.

"Oh it did. You are amazing..." the man seemed genuinely bashful.

"Thank you. You aren't so bad yourself. Days like today I really enjoy my job." Grace groaned inwardly as the wan smile flashed across her face. It was so cheesy, the mindless slut routine.

A glance across confirmed it. He was sadly eating the schtick up like bird feed. She knew what was coming even before he opened his mouth.

"So how long have you... you know... been a pro?"

Grace rolled her eyes and fixed a steely gaze to the aluminum clouds out toward the horizon. The lies queued up like the planes shuttling into Heathrow. They were as familiar as the noise they made.

A pang of pride stopped them in her throat. Grace had no idea why but they would not come out. Inside her a truth was straining to be released. Suddenly there was no stopping it.

"I'm not. Not really."

The man looked puzzled but said nothing.

"I'm not a prostitute. I'm saving. For my own place."

The guy was nodding slowly. She could tell even without looking at his face he did not believe her.

"I work at the British Library for a document contractor. This isn't what I do, not really."

It was a different lie. It felt soothing and comfortable.

Grace brought her hands to underneath her chin, her eyes not leaving the horizon. The smell of rubber and spermicide lubricant was strong but she did not recoil. Instead she carried on talking without really thinking.

"I've only done it a couple of times. It's not me, it's not what I am."

"I understand." The condescension in his voice was almost unbearable

"I'm almost there. For the deposit I mean."

"I'm glad to have helped."

The man rose and walked away without a handshake offer.

Grace flicked a look in his direction perhaps hoping for some kind of acknowledgment or approval, and getting none returned back to watching London bustle beneath her.

The lies soothed her as the air around her cooled. Night began to fall and Grace did not leave the bench until it was fully dark and her bones ached with the chill.

The void inside her ached. It was not who she was.

Prostitution did not define who she was.

I'm just a girl who sometimes has sex with guys and they pay me. What has the money got to do with it really?

Am I not just having sex? How is that different to online dating, apart from being less hassle and more certain about the intangibles?

Sex is just a thing. I'm more than that.

THIRTEEN

Soundtrack

Soul II Soul – 'Back To Life (Back To Reality)'

Dylan had printed up the email from Gemma and was reading it on the train. The carriage was all but empty and he was deep in thought.

He wondered what she was like.

Certainly worth an email back, but what to say? The thoughts tailed off hopelessly. Dylan was preoccupied and unwilling to ponder deeply on the contents of the email he had yet to write or send. Making a dismissive gesture with his hand, alone in his personal space, he picked up his iPod and disappeared into his vast playlist for something to listen to.

As the train pulled out of Highbury and Islington station Dylan looked up, caught sight of a pink overcoat for a flash of a second before the wearer disappeared into an exit, and the train was enveloped in tunnel.

His mind snapped back to the The-Girl-In-The-Pink-Overcoat. It obviously was not her, but he remained thinking about her for some time. He felt frustrated. This unknown women had a name and he did not know it. All too soon, when the train was almost at Alexandra Palace the first of the wave of self-deprecating thoughts broached the surface of his mind. She was gorgeous. There was no way he will ever see her again and even if he did, she would go for a million London guys before she went for him. Women who look like that do not go for blokes that look like me, he thought to himself.

Dylan's mood began to darken.

Thudding testily up the stairs he walked down onto the main road and stepped out into the road without looking. There was nothing coming. As he walked a tantalising aroma of Indian food floated past and he considered getting a curry on the way home. In the end he settled for a microwave meal from the cornershop and three cans of warm lager, as this was all the jangling mass of coins in his pockets would afford him. Nodding at a bored-looking Jason on the way in, he walked straight into the kitchen and went about cooking the ready meal in the microwave. The house smelt of cannabis: Carla was downstairs smoking.

His mind flicked back yet again to the The-Girl-In-The-Pink-Overcoat.

Suddenly needy for something he could not quite put his finger on, he picked up his laptop and resolved to write something, anything, to Gemma.

Two cups of tea, ten minutes frantic but hugely fulfilling self-pleasuring into a sock to a dog-earned ancient copy of Asian Babes, no less than seven cheap imitation Jammy Dodger-type biscuits and a few lengthy pulls on Carla's joint, and he had got a fairly ironclad first line-and-a-half, so he thought. It took until well into Friday morning for him to finish the email, and by the end of writing it he was really looking forward to meeting Gemma. The woman had become much more interesting and attractive in absentio in his mind. She was an honest, normal and down-to-earth kind of woman, he decided, and that was the type of woman he needed.

He had not felt he needed a woman that afternoon, but her email had changed that.

Dylan had needed a woman badly for a long time and denying this was him fooling himself in a very real sense. He had his wants and needs tuned to what was available; the sure sign of someone who knows disappointment and is used to getting only what he reasonably could. The irony of someone living in a fantasyland of drugs and dual lives being so painfully pragmatic and bitterly realist was utterly lost on him.

------Original Message------------------
To: Wetherby, Gemma
From: Short, Dylan
Sent: Friday 5th February 00:51
Re: Thanks
Hi Gemma,

Thanks for your email. Pardon the late hour in which I sent this email – I have been to the pub with a couple of friends after work. First let me say that I am truly made up that you emailed me back. This online dating business is a bit of an enigma to me and I spent ages looking through so many profiles before I came to yours. Its hard to figure people out on there but your profile was really nice it gave me a good feeling about you and I was hoping you'd get back to me. You are obviously a smart and intelligent woman and judging by your pic a beautiful one too.

It would be really cool if we could go have a drink and maybe something to eat next week. Your profile says you are based in Sutton, so how about we meet in Balham or Clapham or something? Your call – wherever you feel most comfortable. If next week is too soon for you, that's fine too – we'll do this at whatever pace you need us to. Is there anything you want to know about me? Feel free to ask – anything you like.

Anyway I have to get off to bed as I have an important meeting in the morning!

Hope to speak to you soon.

DS x

Dylan was impressed with his handiwork.

He went to sleep thinking about Gemma and how their date might go. In truth, she was one of twenty or thirty women he had mass-messaged off the site, and had had to refer back to her profile several times during the evening to remind himself. Even so, making a woman feel special was key to his plan with women and he thought it best to start early. Compliments get you everywhere. The thing about being happy to wait and being considerate was actually true: Dylan was a sensitive guy and was not cynical about women in this way, dishonesty about trips to pubs with mates or casual domestic drug abuse notwithstanding.

Friday night was not party night.

FOURTEEN

Soundtrack

Lamb – 'Cottonwool' (Guy Called Gerald Mix)

Grace had always found that Friday nights tended to be her quietest nights. She had not managed to come up with anything like a reasonable notion as to why this peculiarity of the economics of the sex trade was, but it just was.

She was on her way to her second client of the day, a new guy she had spoken to in hushed, rushed tones on the phone. Its ring had given her a start on the bench on top of Primrose Hill, and she had been tempted not to answer it.

But she had and was on her way to meeting him in a cheap, budget hotel room in Battersea. The rain was slow but unremitting, making her mind her step on the slippery pavement in her heels. This was one of those evenings where she could do without it.

A night in with a Chinese which she had been meaning to order for herself for literally months and spending time with Barney was infinitely preferable to the jangled nerves and stilted conversation that a new client always brought. The guy from earlier had been weird enough. Grace hoped above hope that it would not be another weirdo.

He had phoned and not even asked her name but instead got

straight to the point.

He was another spanky type. Quickly demanding to know how much she charged for oral and some hard corrrection of her determination he seemed almost not to hear her reply. She tried to sound sexy and mysterious on the telephone as it was all part of the service. Some guys seemed so tight and tense about the whole thing, almost openly reviled by themselves that it all seemed rather forced, like when the makeup-caked flight attendant asks smiling whether you want the chicken or the fish.

Will that be the oral or the doggy style, Sir? Would you like a glass of wine with that?

The thought that perhaps she should have been a flight attendant made her smile slightly. The cold air rushed past her teeth. She would probably get almost as much sex doing that, but the pay was nothing like as good.

But it is legal.

With a loud cracking round, the door opened. The room was one of those wipe-clean melamine and pastel shade budget affairs with a tiny television on top of a tiny minifridge and with all the fittings such as the desk lamp fixed to its surface to prevent theft. The light was harsh and fluorescent, and her eyes recoiled from it after the gloom of the musty corridor outside. The air-conditioning was on full. The room was swelteringly hot. There was a slight smell of coffee. Sure enough, on the desk there was a plastic cup of coffee obviously made from the room's not-very-generous supply of budget quality freeze-dried instant coffee and little pods of UHT cream. A torn piece of brown paper and a few solitary granules of Demerara lay scattered nearby.

There was no sign of a spoon, but a blue biro lay on top of the welcome pamphlet and the darkening beneath the pen on the picture of what she assumed to be the hotel complex (in full cobalt blue sky and flowers Photoshop glory). This told her that the man stood in front of her cared little for biros that leak in your bag because you stirred your coffee with it.

The man backed off from the shadow so she could see him properly. He was wearing a pair of jeans, some rather worn black shoes and a shapeless, un-ironed grey and black patterned shirt. He was considerably bigger than her and probably in his 30s. He said nothing but gestured for her to come in, stopping in the gap between the two double beds in the twin room.

"You must be Simon…" she said, trying to intone a smoothness in her voice to hide the nervousness.

"Yes I am. Didn't catch your name." His voice was clipped, slightly nasal. She heard a Northern note in it but could not quite place it.

"Nadia" she said almost before he had finished his sentence. She looked right at him. He was shaking visibly, and clearly was not used to doing things like this.

"Well Simon, what was it we spoke about?" the soft, velvetiness was back.

"Oral. That is… I mean… I want to lick you out." he stammered.

Inwardly Grace recoiled again.

She hated that particular turn of phrase.

"Right, so you want to go down on me. And you want me to give you a blow job? And you deserve a spanking? Is that right?" She thought about adding a largely meaningless "honey" on the end to put him at ease, but decided better of it. The man nodded but did not motion towards her.

"That's £150 if you would be so kind" she smiled her best, disarming grin at him and he visibly melted. She noted to her amusement that he was blushing intensely and was obviously very aroused. Regulars got the dubious luxury of paying for the service after it had been given, or a half hour long credit facility as she liked to think of it, but the man in front of her was a new one and was afforded no such liberty.

Grace realised he was holding out a wedge of notes to her and had been since she walked in the door. Smiling, she took the money slowly and with what she hoped was sexual deliberation. Stuffing the (counted) notes into her bag she turned to Simon who was on his knees. In front of her. He was pulling off his belt. This should be amusing, she thought to herself as she took her coat off.

The next few minutes could best be described as workmanlike by Grace. With the oddest grunt she had ever heard in her life he had thrown himself over the end of the bed in front of her. She spanked him, first with her hand and then when that started to hurt her hand she used his belt. She was incredulous to note that he had actually reached orgasm whilst she was hitting him, when he came up all red faced and sweating. He muttered something she did not hear and went to the bathroom.

She sat on the edge of the bed and watched with slight revulsion the messy ribbons of his ejaculate run down the side of the bed next to it and slide like a translucent slug onto the worn grey carpet. By the look of the carpet and the price of the room, this was not the first such mess to hit the carpet.

She absentmindedly wondered what colour it used to be when it was new.

Shaking her head, as if to wake her brain into business mode, she hitched up her skirt and opened her legs, leaning back on her hands and tossing her hair behind her. She plastered her best Miss California smile across her face and waited.

Simon arrived back from the bathroom wearing his glasses and nothing else. He was wiry and very white. There were no arm muscles to speak of and were he a chubby man he would have obvious man-breasts. A cheap Casio digital watch was strapped so tightly to his left arm that she could see it actually push the skin inwards. A thin line of indeterminate coloured hair traced a line from his stomach which was lax and badly formed, down to an unruly shock of brown pubic hair into which his penis was rapidly retreating. She could see red splotches on the side of his thighs.

Preferring not to look at her handiwork she glanced up at his face.

The client certainly was a strange looking man. He had one of those faces that always seemed to be squinting at everything, which was perhaps a harsh observation given the over bright fluorescent lighting in the room. Thick, bushy eyebrows that did not go at all with his short but shapelessly cut hair on his head seemed to rest over the squint, bearing over his tiny dark eyes that looked like brazil nuts. She wondered at his age. At first she thought he was mid-30s, but he could easily have been ten years older or younger. His mouth hung slightly open and a row of crooked, off-white teeth poked out. He was looking right at her but his expression was absolutely unreadable.

For a horrified second, Grace wondered if he did not find her attractive and that she should cover up immediately, but the activity in his pubic region and his sudden, almost frantic wringing of long, bony hands told her otherwise. He took off his glasses, folded them up with a fastidiousness that seemed at odds with his opaque and stony manner, and placed them gently on the desk behind him. He looked like he was about to say something, or that he just could not find the words, and for a second Grace felt a bit sorry for him. She extended a hand to him, which he accepted after a second, and she guided him to his knees by the end of the bed. He was staring at, or straight into, her vagina.

The subsequent few minutes could best be described as bizarre by Grace.

Simon had never been with a woman before and knew absolutely nothing of the mechanics and parts involved.

His technique was rather like a Labrador trying to drain a bowl. She made token moaning noises at first but he seemed so intent on his role that she was sure he would not hear, so she stopped. After that came the most awkward blowjob in the history of oral sex, culminating in an apologetic orgasm. Incredibly, she actually thought she saw tears in his eyes at one point. It occurred to her that most people would or should find such an experience rewarding.

He had put his clothes on very quickly afterwards and sat in the far corner of the bed with his eyes on the floor and his arms folded. She chatted briefly with him and he told her that it was his first time because he had Asperger's Syndrome which was a bit like autism but for adults, he told her in one of the very few moments he was able to make eye contact. Grace then told him in a soothing, rather patronising voice, that she wouldn't mind it at all if perhaps he might want to call her again, which he said he would, but only when he got paid again. Grace could not hazard a guess at what such a man might do for a living but agreed nonetheless. She even ventured that next time they might actually have sex if he wanted to. He seemed bizarrely flummoxed by this revelation and reverted to chewing an imaginary piece of gum and looking at the floor.

Grace watched a bead of perspiration wind its way down his temple, under the steel arm of his glasses which he had placed back on his face in the interim. There was total stillness and the only sound she could hear was the mechanical hiss of the air conditioning unit above her head. Simon then darted, very suddenly, for the remote control from the bedside, alarming her, and turned on the TV.

She saw a Simpsons episode appear out of a snowstorm as a smile appeared across his strange features. Earnestly, Simon demanded to know whether she wanted to watch an episode with him. Grace did actually stay, much to her own amazement, for ten minutes until the episode ended. It was the episode where Bart tries to skate across Springfield Canyon. Simon gleefully informed her without taking his eyes off the screen that this was one of the all-time classics, as if further looking to validate her presence in that stifling room. His breathless laughter was loud and distracting.

Simon seemed overjoyed that she chose to stay, although did not even glance at her or refer to her once during the cartoon. He sat rapt, totally immersed in the slapstick yellow world.

He was on his feet by the time the first credits were rolling and even held the door open for her when she left. She gave him a very cursory and uncertain hug as she did with all her clients, which he returned solidly and with all the feeling of a pine casket. The door hissed closed behind her.

The darkness and cold of the corridor was pleasant after the close confines of the room. As she walked the carpet grated on the soles of her shoes like cheap public building carpet does. Far off she heard Simon laughing again at the television behind the closed door and smiled to herself warmly.

The corridor vented out through two half-open fire doors into a dingy car park. The-Girl-In-The-Pink-Overcoat hastened her step and headed for the main road.

Forty seven minutes later and Barney's insistent mewling was the next sound she registered, having got home entirely on autopilot. Throwing her pink overcoat over the back of her armchair she quizzed the indignant feline about his day. He told her all about it, sparing no grisly detail, until he disappeared into a bowl of something that smelt absolutely vile and remained basically silent save for the usual nauseating grunting, snapping noises that cats make when they are eating. Grace did not need to look in her cupboards: she knew she had nothing in so she made cheese on toast and changed into her sweatpants to settle in for the night.

Sitting down and then leaping up with a lot more energy that she felt, she remembered she had a cold bottle of Pinot Grigio in the fridge.

Barney regarded her with considerable annoyance, as her sudden movement had startled him.

Ah yes. You've remembered about your precious wine. You move fucking fast enough when it's your fucking food and drink don't you? Of course when it's me starving to death on your kitchen floor (which is fucking filthy by the way) you take your own pretty time don't you! You fucking sad excuse for an owner.

Grace beamed at the cat who managed a truly vintage dismissive glance away and sat down. There were no clean glasses so she poured the chilled wine into a chipped cow print mug and started channel hopping, smiling more than she had done all day. Moments of her own, those little pearly indulgences, were not a regular thing for Grace and she was happy to give herself the time off.

That was one of the things she enjoyed about being her own boss.

Take the evening off Gracey because you've done good work today.

FIFTEEN

Soundtrack

PJ Harvey – 'Working For The Man'

Sweating even though it was still early, the man heaved a large box onto the floor. His early morning trip to the Cash And Carry was in its final stage, but the boxes of cans and bottles were heavy and his cousin was nowhere to be seen.

He stepped off the curb away from the open tailgate of his battered minivan and stood with his hands on his ample hips.

Screwing his face up and wiping a stream of sweat off his forehead, he looked down the road. A man was hurrying toward him. Probably a hundred yards off still, but hurrying. The man was not running, as his bag and flailing coat under one arm would not let him. The man half-recognised him: one of the guys who lived at the bottom of the road near the main road. He was obviously late for his train.

No sooner had the realisation that the now rather closer man was hurrying for a train hit Ilhan Bayraktar, owner of the Bosporos Mini Market and Off License, than there was a familiar rushing and clattering sound behind him announcing that the man had missed his train. Ilhan was still smiling in amusement when the man stormed past. He was wearing a suit with creases in the trousers and a shirt that was either beige or a dirty white. A tie flapped limply in the breeze, dangling from his left hand, almost touching the grubby pavement.

Dylan was late. His mobile phone had run out of charge in the middle of the night, and singularly failed to wake him from a blissful rest under his duvet that morning. The birds, did not stir him. The slamming, crashing, stamping and shouting of his flatmates also did not manage to penetrate the layers of sleep. It was almost quarter to nine and he should have been sat at his desk and pouring his first cup of coffee right about that time. The train was not waiting and loitered long enough only for him to be able to see it as he ran up the road before departing with a rather sarcastic blast of its horn.

Dylan arrived at the station sweating, with dark patches spreading across his cream shirt in an ugly stippling effect across his chest. Swearing, he fumbled with his tie, only to find that one end had brushed through the wide muddy puddle by the footbridge and was stained.

By the time he stomped into work, Dylan was in a foul mood. On the short train journey he had convinced himself that Gemma was not going to reply to his message and that his rather patronising email last night had been incredibly ill-advised. He was also fully expecting Atwater to be waiting by his desk wringing his hands desperate to read him the riot act about being so late, or at least having sent a patronising email of his own which was lurking, he was certain, in his email inbox.

It was surprising therefore when there were three emails waiting for him when he, with some trepidation, started up Outlook.

The first was a commendation from the large container company for his work on the green resolution carbon bollocks thingy, which was "quite excellent and absolutely what was required" apparently. Dylan was a little surprised at this. The report could most charitably have been described as lacklustre, the copy was formulaic at very best and yet the container company was from Germany.

Everyone knows they do not have sarcasm in Germany.

Evidently they don't have very good advertising copy writers there either!

The second email was a commendation from Mr Atwater who had been copied into the previous email, who was all wistful comments about Dylan "finally finding focus" and becoming "a more integrated team player" and that "he appeared to be putting recent mishaps firmly in his past".

This actually made Dylan laugh out loud.

Rarely, if ever in his professional career had he been less focussed or more disinterested in his role whilst being confusingly committed to retaining it. Nothing about him coming in very late either, which was good.

The third email was from Gemma.

She wanted to meet him tomorrow.

The tone of her message indicated that she was genuinely flattered by his rather mendacious silver tongue and that she was quite happy to throw caution to the wind and meet him for a drink "etcetera". This last bit was probably her suggesting that dinner might be on the cards, as opposed to her proffering the notion of casual sex on the first date.

Or was she being clever?

Dylan was too pleased to care really. What was left of the morning rushed past in a heady charge of testosterone-fuelled inertia. He was smiling and even got a round of coffees in for his workmates. Ravi, sitting in the next row of desks opined whilst Dylan was swearing good-naturedly at the coffee machine that it was either a new woman or a new job. Imogen, who sat behind him, cynically suggested that given Dylan's rather dishevelled state on rushing into the office that morning, that it had to have been a new woman who was a a dirty nymphomaniac. Both were disappointed Dylan was not in the mood to share.

Dylan could hear them talking but did not care.

*****

Grace was walking down Regents Street. The air was frigid but refreshing somehow and there were few enough people around to make her progress largely unhindered.

The latte she had just drunk had left a metallic taste in her mouth which a piece of chewing gum was unable to shift.

Her first client of the day had been another rather boring one; a pasty white City type who just wanted "half and half". It had not taken long. She had had to listen with feigned interest as he told her all about bonds and futures as if she was a six year old. She played up to it of course, as it was much easier than having to explain to the guy that she had done Economics and Business Studies at University and probably knew more about futures than most mid-class call girls. It would inevitably have led to the "why do you do this then? Out of choice?" conversation which just bored her.

As with so many City types, he paid up front and then tipped her handsomely afterwards, which in this case was accompanied with a toe-curlingly condescending "treat yourself love, you deserve it".

Still, a £80 tip is still an £80 tip and this was the only thing that stopped Grace from saying something suitably crushing in return. She did not have another client until mid-afternoon and another free evening. She was, at the advice of the client, treating herself to various nice-to-haves before her arbitrary trip to the clinic for a no-questions-asked check up to make sure she had not contracted any not-nice-to-haves. She stood at the crossing, waiting for the hectic tide of cabs and buses to subside, as people jostled around her.

Across the road, just for a second, she thought she saw a vaguely familiar face.

*****

Lucky pants.

It was a good luck ritual for Dylan Short and had never, to his mind anyway, let him down. A new pair of designer boxer shorts before a new date. It had taken Dylan less than six seconds to pick out the right pair from the shelf at Armani Exchange and less than three minutes to pay for them. A new shirt which he may or may not wear, (he was undecided) and a bottle of 212 for Men followed swiftly afterwards. There was not much time left of his lunch break before he had to be back in the office so was trotting rapidly towards Tottenham Court Road.

He did not see The-Girl-In-The-Pink-Overcoat looking at him from across the road.

*****

As swiftly as he had come into view, the familiar figure was swallowed up by the mass of people.

Grace was not even sure it was The-Guy-On-The-Train.

It might have been him. Her notions of fate and other such imponderables were plucked from her mind as an Eastern European woman with a face like the bark of a tree poking out from under a dirty shawl dived toward her. She was brandishing a foil-clad piece of rather sad-looking heather in wizened, arthritic hands.

Grace sidestepped deftly, but the woman was not to be denied, thrusting toward her pink overcoat lapels and only pulling away when Grace pushed her away with a rather abrupt East End admonishment. Her pink overcoat remained unsoiled and unblessed, but that was the last Grace thought about The-Guy-On-The-Train that day.

SIXTEEN

Soundtrack
Death In Vegas – 'GBH'

Birds. The sound of birds. No spiders.

Dylan lay in bed, one leg draped seductively over his duvet, with the other end covering his head. He opened his eyes. Light, probably not sunlight, prodded in through the gap between his duvet and the sheets, against which his nose and face were pressed. Dylan's mind struggled to shake off the sticky sheets of sleep and he felt no definitive urge to venture beyond his bed linen right at that moment.

He pressed his nose against the bedding harder, noting for the first time that it probably could do with a wash. He certainly did not remember the last time they were washed. Should the improbable happen that evening, it would be advantageous to have clean bedding, he decided. Picking up a handy sock from the floor, he ventured under the covers for five minutes of self-abuse, fantasising about going down on the redhead from Suits. It was calculated of course. If the impossible should occur that evening, it would be preferable to have it last more than a few minutes, so a precursory preparatory was helpful. All part of the rigmarole. Exhaling with the power of an ejaculation he tossed the sock to a far corner and lay panting for a few seconds, pleased as always with his handiwork.

More noise from the birds. Carla had invited her two closest girl mates over for a curry and a smoke last night and of course they had stayed all night. They had probably not been to bed or indeed left the kitchen.

The floorboards felt warm and rough on his feet as he lurched out of his room, squinting against the shafts of light cascading through the lounge windows. Completely instinctively, a cup of tea was made and then left on the side in the kitchen as there was still no milk. Dylan retreated to the sofa, taking a well-hidden packet of fig rolls and his cup of tea with him. Soccer AM was on, which meant that his morning was written off until gone one in the afternoon.

He lay there happy in his underwear and a very grubby old Chelsea t-shirt commemorating an FA Cup Final appearance in 1997, all greasy skin, orange-peel thighs, matt hair and sweat stains, quaffing biscuits. That day in 1997 had been the best day of his life. The weather, the company, the day had all been perfect.

He had been drunk when he got to the stadium, and almost missed Roberto Di Matteo's wonder strike after 42 seconds to put the Blues ahead.

He remembered the day vividly and the happiness of it always made him smile. Latterly he had begun almost to resent the explosion of joy and lifetimer memories of that day because of how tragic it was to be approaching 30 and having a day out at the football as his single best experience, the single best day of his life. It felt like something a 12 year old might say. Adults always said things like "the day I got married" or "the day I met X for the first time" etc.

It was peculiar that a day as jovial as that with 100,000 fellow Chelsea now felt a little lonely to him because of what it meant to the state of his current life.

It was time for a change. In life.

And practically speaking.

Dylan headed off to start getting ready. The transformation in just a few short hours was quite amazing. Dylan had to hand it to himself:

he scrubbed up well.

He looked at himself in the reflection in the glass of the bar. Smart brown suede slip-ons, dark blue Armani jeans and a slightly edgy Guess short-sleeved shirt hung around his considerable frame. Gemma was five minutes late. He was trying to remember the small and grainy picture of her and had had two false alarms of women who looked nothing like Gemma but were similar enough to warrant a second glance. Butterflies and moths and Daddy-long-legs' were not exactly fluttering around in his stomach, but were certainly present. He imagined dozens of such flying insects sat around lazily inside him, and smiled.

Was he nervous?

He glanced down at the small but (accidentally) well-proportioned bunch of flowers he was carrying and noting a slight twitch, ruminated that maybe he was. Slightly. His mind flicked to the flowers themselves. He realised with amusement that he could not name a single breed in the menagerie.

Do flowers come in breeds? Or is it species?

Those are just big daisies.

Is that what they are called, big daisies?

Daisius Maximus?

Aren't they called the same name as that singer in the 60s? Petulia something?...

"Dylan Short?"

The voice, close by, startled him, and he spun around, smashing the posy of flowers into the glass in a small shower of tiny petals. Gemma was stood just two feet away. She was shorter than he imagined, and with a much bigger nose too. Her hair was neither blonde nor brunette but tied back in a well-proportioned bob and her face, although plain and featureless, was inviting and friendly. Her eyes were almost perfectly rectangular, with a deep darkness only hinted at by the earthy brown in their centre. Unlovely, uneven teeth shone dully back from the edges of her smile and she held her mouth open, as if waiting for something from him.

Her hesitancy caught him off guard.

Her arms were apart from her sides, probably waiting to put themselves around him in a greeting hug. Dylan took his cue and moved forward with more force than he probably intended, enveloping the much-smaller woman in a large, slightly mechanical hug. She mumbled something into his neck and Dylan noticed her perfume. It was one he knew, but had no idea what it was called. It smelled of chocolate and leaves and faintly of roasting coffee. It was deep and brown, like her eyes. Dylan found himself smiling. Still grinning, he forced himself back to look at Gemma again. She was still smiling at him, open mouthed, waiting for him to say something. With a jolt he realised he had not even spoken to the woman in front of him yet.

"Wicked. I'm so glad you came..." was all he could think of.

Internally he cringed.

Now she thinks I go on these things all the time and that the women in question did not usually turn up.

Tit.

To his relief she laughed.

"I had nothing better to do with my afternoon" she giggled, then stopped abruptly. Dylan was sure he saw her cringe. She took the battered posy without looking into his face. Deciding to take the conversation onto the front foot, Dylan made some smalltalk and ushered her along the pavement towards the bar she had suggested.

He looked at her again. She was probably five feet three he guessed, short yes but a little bigger than he had imagined. She wore a pair of plain jeans with a rather plain pair of black shoe/boot things with a zip up one side. She wasn't classically pretty but inoffensively plain with nice teeth and eyes. She was a little chubbier than he was expecting and for some reason that encouraged him.

It was hard to tell from under a thick beige wool coat but she was wearing a grey rollneck sweater. It highlighted her face and Dylan could not resist a surreptitious glance at her boobs, which were of an impressive size for a woman of such small frame. They chatted for a few minutes, walking side-by-side to prevent any eye-contact, whilst both parties regained their confidence.

Two hours later and Dylan was in fine form. They had started drinking almost immediately and were making good progress through their second bottle of wine. Dylan drank wine like beer so was forcing the pace a little and as a result the smaller woman was on the verge of getting quite drunk. Dylan assumed so anyway, as she was laughing loudly at his jokes and openly flirting with him, which he suspected was not a natural activity for Gemma, who was rather a shy woman, it appeared to him. There was some enjoyment on his part of being well in control of proceedings, already dominating the conversation. She seemed more than happy to sit there and let him. Dylan liked that.

The date continued its frenetic pace onwards, and soon they swapped the noisy and close confines of the Clapham bar for the even noisier and more confined closeness of a Japanese noodle bar with long wooden benches. They ate hungrily and Dylan noticed how dainty Gemma was with a set of chopsticks. She moved methodically and with a certain grace about her. Dylan decided that he did fancy her. They talked about the Far East, and both agreed it was somewhere they would like to go one day. Dylan almost felt the need to trivialise the remark in case Gemma thought he was offering her a trip to Japan with him one day in the far distant future, by which time they would probably be married with kids or something, but thought better of it.

They kissed carelessly in a nearby wine bar. She kissed him back when he drunkenly dived in. Her lips were extremely soft. She tasted of wine, noodles, green tea and something else he could not put his finger on. He kissed her with the force of a man who has had too much to drink to properly gauge such things, and she just opened her mouth. She barely moved at all in fact, and this unsettled Dylan slightly.

Undeterred, he kissed her again and then headed to the bar.

*****

He could smell his own breath in the darkness. A stale, chemical smell of beer and wine seeping out through his pores. He lay there in the half-light of a familiar room. Blocks and shapes of shadows and deeper hues of blue and grey lay all around and he closed his eyes. The hangover was building already. Gemma lay next to him, sweat glistening off her forehead, with strands of limp hair glued to it. He could not see her eyes but he knew she was looking at him. He raised himself up to his knees and stretched, and as he did so his erection flopped out in front of him.

Gemma moved to raise herself to her knees and wrapped a clammy hand around him, mewling something he could not hear. They had had breathless, boozy sex when they got in from the pub. Dylan had come quickly which was not in the plan, although he did not care and that was not in the plan either.

She had not let him go down on her, but had made noises which suggested that she had come at least once during the ensuing coupling or at least cared enough to pretend. She seemed to prefer a mundane missionary position but to his dismay did not move with him as he thrust gently into her, no matter what he did. Her arms lay on the bed next to them and she snuffled into his neck as the sweat ran down onto her. He could smell her sweetness and wanted desperately to taste her, so tried again, but she had lifted an arm under his and stopped him once more. There was an air of awkward hurriedness about the sex after that. He came rapidly afterwards, for some reason not caring too much what she thought of him or his sexual prowess.

He was already disappointed and he guessed Gemma could tell.

Now, she was knelt opposite, stroking him. For the life of him,

Dylan could not fathom what she was thinking. It was rather a pleasant surprise then, when she knelt down and put her lips around him. Dylan shrank back concerned he may not taste or smell ideal after the efforts of a couple of hours ago but if she was disgusted she did not show it.

Her mouth was hot, almost painfully so. She ran her tongue along him, in the same way all women who get their blowjob tips from women's lifestyle magazines do, and then plunged him into her mouth completely, like a chocolate bar. She was, amazingly, rough. Her tongue played non-stop and the suction she was imparting was borderline uncomfortable.

In fact… it was uncomfortable.

Dylan shifted in his position and Gemma did likewise, straining her neck.

Dylan mused as to whether her position was as uncomfortable as it looked, and then realised that Gemma was making a noise. It was an odd grunt, like the slap of hot mud. Dylan was bemused. The pressure on his manhood was growing. Now he was certain he could feel teeth. There were definitely teeth grating on either side, although it was hard to tell because of the sucking. She was trying to suck the poison out of him, he decided. Open mouthed, he watched as she began to jerk her head back, eyes screwed shut in obvious discomfort, still making that haunting clicking from somewhere just north of her epiglottis. Dylan wondered if he was still really drunk, and then, pointedly, whether she was.

Then something broke.

In truth he felt it rather than heard it. There was a sharp sensation from beneath. For a fraction of a second he wondered if she had severed his cock with some devilishly sharp implement. For the following second he just gaped. Gemma was still busy on his cock, still very much attached apparently, grunting away. There was just the echo of the snapping sensation, and then oddly little pain at first. Then it grew. Pain welled up around his nether-regions like the blood streaming out of raw chicken. He yelped, and gave an involuntary movement. Gemma raised her head as his cock popped out of her mouth, ugly strings of saliva still attached. He knelt there panting as the girl got to her feet

"You ok?" she said loudly. He could not hear anger in her voice.

His hands swung into view. He saw the blood on them. Psychosomatic pain blossomed. His eyes bulged.

"Fine!"

His voice was shrill, clouded by fear.

Dylan rose stiffly; both hands cupped around his belaboured manhood, and ran to the bathroom, just missing painfully crashing into the doorframe as he did so. The warm, inquisitive light of the bathroom drew a small squeak from Dylan. He stared at his rapidly diminishing member in unbridled horror. Two red grating marks either side of the sad looking tip told him that it was indeed teeth he could feel, molars probably, but that the real trauma was underneath. She had let her bottom teeth touch the underside. She had snapped his string. Dylan debated bursting into tears. It was not particularly painful, but it was the blood and the mess that hurt. A bit like losing your front tooth in a game of rugby when you are thirteen, he recalled. The similarities were striking, now that he came to remember.

There certainly was a lot of blood.

It covered his hands and dripped in great dark crimson streaks down his pasty white legs, matting in the hairs on his thighs. Blood was not flowing, but it was just there. Great silty tidemarks coated his penis, pooling near the end to form a whitish drip hanging lazily off the end. Examining closer, underneath, he saw a definite notch. There was a slice in the string. It went in and then out again, like the battlement on a tiny castle. Dylan was horrified. It was like grievous bodily harm.

Blood dripped onto his foot, and he realised he needed to wash the cut.

Never having cut his penis string before he was unwary of the peril and so was very unprepared for what came next.

With shaking hands, he cupped some cold water from a limescale-covered tap and splashed it in the general direction of the end of his embattled member. Most of it went on the floor but a significant amount went where it was aimed. There was the sudden shock of the cold water, which would probably have taken his breath away. It didn't, because the pain arrived a nanosecond later and he actually screeched out loud.

It was a white hot sting that crackled from the tip of his penis like electric current. It was urgent, acute, sharp and it was coursing through his cock.

Dylan screeched again, a little quieter this time, and gasped for breath. Too late he realised his mistake. Warm saliva is a powerful anaesthetic.

...and cold water is not.

Far from it in fact.

It took him more than ten minutes to debate the merits of a plaster of some kind, then putting some tissue paper on the cuts like men do when they cut themselves shaving. What was the plan when you cut yourself shagging, he wondered?

Finally, he walked into the bedroom, slowly, deliberately, as if it had been his feet or the backs of his knees that had been cut open and saw that Gemma was dressed in his (filthy) Chelsea 1997 FA Cup t-shirt she had evidently found rumpled on the floor, and her knickers. She had obviously been sobbing, but leapt up once Dylan limped in, facing him with obvious concern in her eyes.

"I snapped my string." Dylan mentioned charitably.

Gemma looked at him as if she had idea what a string even was, let alone where on the male body she may find such a thing to snap. Dylan screwed up his face in a valiant effort not to look disdainful, and explained.

"The head comes down… to a… you know. A string… the string

on the bottom. Underneath. It snapped..."

Gemma looked as mortified as if someone had found a string in her Bloody Mary. Dylan thought it best to continue, lest she erupt into tears again.

"Don't worry it happens sometimes. Old tennis injury."

Tennis?

You what?

Inwardly Dylan cringed for the third time that night, but Gemma remained destitute, alone, open mouthed, imploring him for something. Anything. Dylan had a sense that it had been her first blowjob experience in all probability and that the scars would last longer for her than for him.

He turned his back as there was something desperate and wrong about the way she was looking at him, and went to the kitchen for two glasses of tepid tap water.

When he returned Gemma was fully dressed. She spun around at the noise of the door handle just as she was doing up her coat as if horrified she was unable to slip away without him knowing. Her hair was matted, her eyes were bloodshot and she could not hold his gaze. She actually looked in a worse state than he probably did, Dylan thought. In an obvious hurry, she swept past him into the lounge, head down, staring at the floor, as if she had lost something tiny on the floorboards. Dylan was about to ask her where she was going when she opened her mouth.

"I have to go. I'm so sorry..."

Her voice was croaky and strained, as if she was on the verge of tears.

What on earth does she have to fucking cry about? I'm the one with the crippled cock!

Before he could object, stood there without a stitch of clothing, a torn penis and with water for two, she was gone.

A rush of frigid night air from downstairs and the loud noise of an ill-fitting door being closed as quietly as possible were the last signs

Dylan had of Gemma Wetherby in the flesh.

*****

Grace was just a few miles away in a flat just off the Seven Sisters Road.

Simon, the strange Simpsons guy from the other night had been in touch, and she had gone round to his flat without thinking too much. Now she was at his flat, alone in the darkness, and the thoughts were stacking up. Faster than the money.

Simon had welcomed her with a bottle of over-cold Cava and a lingering kiss that she was not totally comfortable with.

His flat was cold but filled with stuff. Everywhere she looked there were piles of stuff. She had no idea what kind of stuff it was, but there were books, CDs, boxes, piles of magazines, little toolboxes, no fewer than seven PC screens sat around in various states of disrepair and things that looked like spaceship parts everywhere. Some she recognised – there was a disk drive on top of a weighty tome about something called Citrix by the bed. This was obviously Simon's bedtime reading of choice.

She could not escape the feeling that the room belonged to a computer student and Simon had acquired it somehow. He was obviously far too old to live like a student like that and yet Grace knew it was his home and his workplace. It smelled of washing powder and old books. He was in the bathroom and had been for almost half an hour she guessed, and a weak light shone from under the bathroom door off the landing where his room was. There was not a sound to be heard.

Grace lay there naked, huddled up under a threadbare but clean duvet, taking stock. Simon had given her five hundred pounds, screwed together in a sweaty, grubby lump of notes, and she had agreed to spend the whole night. Simon had not asked for anything but she had taken the lead, first touching him then letting him go down on her. She had tried to go down on him and he had recoiled sharply, with a look of abject horror on his face. She could not even guess what that was about, but undeterred, laid him down with a smile and some reassuring noises. They had had sex twice. The first time lasted less than a minute and ten minutes later, another three or four. There were no tears this time but he was rigid and mechanical. She wished there was a way she could make him loosen up.

He did not look like he was enjoying it, that was for certain.

As she lay there in the blue chill of his room, staring at the various tiny blue and red lights on the innumerable electrical items that seemed to take up every nook and cranny in the room, Grace began to wonder about the tall, awkward geek. There seemed to be a desperation to him, under the cold and the impenetrable exterior. This was not new of course, she saw desperation in her clients every day, but it was somehow more sad and maybe more ulterior in his case. Men fell in love with her all the time in their minds, or what they thought was love, but it was never as stark and bare as it was with Simon.

She wondered again if he had ever been with a woman before.

He might have done, but the grim determination, the pure and unadulterated requirement of him and his emotions suggested that he had not, to coin a cliché, felt this way before. It was obvious that he was indulging a working fantasy far deeper and more needy than just the immediacy of the sexual contact. She was an object not just of physical desire, but of emotional desire too. Suddenly she felt a wave of pity for him. It was wrong. For the very first time in her professional pro career she felt a sense of moral ambiguity, and an unsettling feeling that she was taking advantage of him somehow. She was. In a very real sense, she decided, and yet she had not the faintest idea how she was supposed to feel about it.

Simon emerged from the bathroom in a pair of navy-blue pyjama bottom-type tracksuit trousers. He saw that she was awake, and that she was looking at him, and looked panicked for a second. Then he flashed her a wide, toothy, and thoroughly uncomfortable grin, showing rows of perfectly formed but rather yellowy teeth.

Grace smiled an equally uncomfortable grin back and regarded him as he made his way out of the darkness of the corridor into the brighter darkness of the room, lit as it was by the streetlights leaking from under the curtains.

He got into bed next to her.

This was the point when she would normally get dressed and leave, but obviously could not as he had paid a nightly rate. Even so, she had to fight off the urge to stretch and go for her clothes, draped carefully over the back of the flimsy-looking computer chair by the desk in the corner. It was not that she was afraid of Simon, but more of his feelings towards her. She felt intimidated by his need of her and wondered what would happen when she did as she had to and had to leave. She had resolved some hours earlier not to accept calls from Simon again but knew that telling him so in person unless absolutely necessary would be cruel and maybe risky. He lay in bed next to her, not touching her, and breathing heavily with his bony hands folded out in front of him.

She realised that he had not spoken to her at all and was just lying there. Was he looking at her? In the gloom it was hard to tell.

She must have fallen asleep against her better judgement because when she woke, Simon was gone. The light from under the curtains was brighter but not yet indicative of full daybreak. Grace sat up quickly and looked around. She half expected Simon to be sat in a chair watching her sleep. She noticed a smell of something savoury in the air which made her hungry. Just then there was a noise of a door opening down the hallway and footsteps on the carpet. Whoever was coming dragged their feet a lot. Simon appeared in a pair of shorts and a Boba Fett t-shirt very suddenly, and she was startled.

"Ah you are awake. I brought you some breakfast."

He was very cheery. His smile caught Grace off guard slightly. In his hands he held a tray. On it was a plate of tinned sausage and beans on toast, with a cup of orange juice and, touchingly, a tiny glass vase, such as you find at pubs in railway stations, with a single red rose in it. He stepped forward to her, and proffered the tray with a wide and very genuine smile on his face. Grace took it and allowed a smile to spread across her features.

"Thank you so much – I'm hungry. You tired me out last night!" Grace lied.

"Really. thanks..." Simon visibly retreated into bashful mode once more.

Before she could lie again he made another of those odd sudden lunging movements towards a hulking television on the bookcase opposite the bed. He did something unseen in the darkness and the screen flashed into brilliant life. Settling back into the pillows, tray carefully positioned across her upper thighs, Grace watched as the half-naked man darted for a remote hidden between two piles of magazines and there flashed up a blue screen she recognised from her satellite television at home. The light from the huge flatscreen hurt her eyes and it was initially hard to focus on the picture. Before she could make out the white writing, the picture changed to a familiar image of bright colours, and the speakers erupted into an equally familiar theme tune, altogether far too loud for that time of the morning.

Grace could swear she saw Simon do a little dance on the spot as The Simpsons opening credits began to roll. No sooner had Homer pulled the control rod of glowing plutonium from his collar, Simon joined her on the bed with a joyful leap of such force that she almost spilt her orange juice.

"You will recognise this one. It's our episode..." he announced proudly.

Inwardly Grace went cold.

SEVENTEEN

Soundtrack

Pink Floyd – 'High Hopes'

Lumps of chicken sat lazily in a heap, surrounded by rice and a pungent smelling curry sauce.

Dylan stared at his plate for a few minutes. An ugly layer of bright orange fat began to seep out of the food and collect like a tidal foam around the edges of the plate. Here and there a tiny piece of some vegetable or other managed to extricate itself from the gloopy confines of the sauce, poking into the air as if gasping for breath. The air itself was thick with the smell, which would normally be appetising to Dylan but somehow not today. Morosely he continued to stare, eventually picking up a fork and picking at the takeaway. It tasted considerably better than it looked and it eventually cheered him up.

He had told Jason and Carla about his night and both had collapsed laughing.

Carla had laughed so hard that tiny strings of whitish mucus began to drip from her nose, in unwitting parody of a mental image branded into his memory of the night before. Dylan had not wanted to tell all at first. They pecked at him like carrion, and it took several minutes to pick him clean. She had doubled up over the kitchen table in paroxysms of coughing and spluttering. Jason sat giggling gently with a leery, shark-like look on his face before rising in mock reverence and going to the fridge to get them both a cold beer with a sympathetic slap on the arm. It was night after the night before and Dylan was feeling rather odd.

On the one hand the injury was not anywhere near as bad as his squeaking and histrionics might have suggested and did not really hurt at all. It certainly wasn't as serious as it looked in the bathroom mirror in the half light. Then there was the feeling of regret about Gemma. She was a nice woman and despite the odd sexual behaviour he had liked her. She dashed off very quickly and only replied to his text that afternoon, explaining in surprisingly abrupt terms that she thought it was best for both of them if they did not see each other again. Dylan had replied with a half-hearted plea to reconsider but inwardly he knew the truth.

She was right.

It occurred to him that she had probably made her decision even before the string-slicing incident and that for all his shock and pain, it had given her a route of escape. Maybe he was being hard on Gemma. What was important for Dylan was that another one had metaphorically bitten the dust, not to mention in more literal terms, his cock.

The damaging part of it for him was that he was firmly in his comfort zone with Gemma. She was, if he was being brutally honest, not as good looking as him nor anywhere near as confident. He was far more charismatic and he did not feel arrogant in feeling that she should have wanted him.

Why didn't she want him?

If he was really as charismatic and good looking as he thought he was by comparison then why would she drop him so quickly and with such clinical firmness. There was not even a "I like you very much but..." or a "you are really great and I had a great night but..." - she had just ended it.

Ended what?

They had exchanged a palm full of emails, shared nothing more significant than a few bottles of wine and some yasai gyoza, and yet Dylan felt a very real sense of loss. Finishing his beer alone in the kitchen, Dylan resolved to get back onto the dating site immediately.

The droplet of water made its halting, staccato way down, hitting and threatening to merge with other droplets sat stationary on the glass. The rain outside seemed to comfort Grace like a friendly pat on her back window. She sat listlessly on her bed in a contemplative mood but not really with the patience to truly think.

She sometimes had days where the enormity of things just numbed her, when her ability to shut out her misgivings about her life in general was sapped. It would be easy to say she had good days and bad days, but she was not depressed and her bad days were more numb days than any real unpleasant period to be agonised about and wished away. She was comfortable with her profession, but it was the fact that it was not just a profession was probably the thing that bothered her.

Bother is a strong term. Some days she did not care a jot that her life was being defined by those abrupt, intense moments of coital profiteering and some days she wished she were one of those sheeple she saw grimly somehow getting to work every morning.

Was it the loneliness of it?

Was it a sense of missing out on life's demands? Was it that she felt she should somehow be contributing something, to someone, somewhere, somehow?

Grace had been living her life in this fashion for almost two years even if the change of career had been much more recent, and her bothered days were in truth more common than perhaps she could realise.

The droplet fell down some more and came smashing into a bigger, fatter one with a microscopic splash. Grace may have mawkishly reflected that even the droplet was no longer alone, were she looking.

Instead, Barney had jumped up on the bed and was regarding her with that wide-eyed honesty that cats sometimes have. She wondered aloud whether the rakish feline were concerned in his own small, selfish way for her quiet solitude. He closed his eyes luxuriantly as her hand tenderly stroked down his neck and across the raised muscles of his back. The tail shot up erect and he moved forward, craning his neck sideways, willing her to touch him in that special place behind his ears, the secret, sensual location that he cherished so. Sensing his need, she opened up her hand to him as he rolled his eyes in pleasure. Her fingers delved into black fur and the quiet dark one responded with a low purring moan of pure indulgence. Smiling, Grace tickled him under the chin for another few seconds and then smiled wider as she noticed that Barney, in his raptures, had poked the tips of his hot pink tongue out of his mouth. The purring was now not so much low and sexy, as rough and like that of a ticking over moped.

"You have got all the moves haven't you, you little charmer?"

Cartoon-like, Barney-the-Lothario opened one eye and regarded the smiling woman with a look that was half pity and half pleasure. He abruptly stood up and stretched, affording Grace yet another wide glimpse of his backside and then swished his tail in the air in triumph, leaping off the bed and looking back at Grace, cross-legged in her sweatpants and an old Scotland rugby jersey that an ex (not Fraser) at Uni had lent her, never to be seen again.

You see, all it took was a little stroke. You are miserable, I cheer you up by letting you stroke me and then showing you my arse. Genius!

Grace watched the smug feline depart. She settled down, laying on her back, hands by her sides, regarding the new stain on her ceiling. She wondered if it was spreading. The shadow inching insidiously across her pristine white roof made her think again of her own life, and whether a spoiling watermark of her very own was making its damp presence felt. With Barney gone, she suddenly felt very alone. Like a torrent of falling rainwater, she was all at once caught up in a very real feeling that it was her loneliness that was causing her to feel so unsettled.

Sure, Barney was a life companion in the way that she knew no human could ever be, but wonderful as he was, he was not a human.

For someone who got all too much feeling of the touch of another human being in her life, she certainly did miss it.

Companionship.

Wasn't that what old people said? When the sex stopped being important, all there was was companionship. In a bizarre way, she reasoned, she was in the same boat. Sex was a non-issue. What she craved was companionship. Her few friends were pushed away by her in terror of them finding out, or her being daft enough to tell them, and that suited Grace. The hole in her life was far more personal and far nearer to home. Not since Fraser had there been anyone serious, The-Least-Satisfying-One-Night-Stand-With-The-Least-Offensive-Man-In-The-World (in public) notwithstanding, and her experiences at the hands and mind of Fraser haunted her still in the small hours of the morning where all is quiet and the brain sometimes cannot cope with the stillness.

Perhaps the prostitution was a way of empowering herself after the emotional, mental and occasional physical, abuse, she mused.

But was it deeper than that?

Did a little piece of her want to be a prostitute?

Initially it had been a necessity. Something to keep at arm's length. The nastiness and cynicism of it was almost a comfort, allowing her pigeonhole it all and to not have to commit to it emotionally.

The snap-fingers quick initial answer was no – she did not enjoy it. No, she did not want to be doing it.

But latterly in the dark times when sleep would not come and the thoughts would not go quietly into the night, something had become more and more apparent.

A tiny, dark place inside her liked it. Not in the way that she might tell a customer that she loved her job. Not in that slutty superficial way at any rate.

Deeper than that.

So deep inside she could barely reach it.

The bored part, the disappointed and disjointed part. The part where she needed to be needed, needed to do something.

Anything.

The drudgery and the rigmarole engendered a need to be doing something. To consume time and energy.

Was there such a thing as emotional and spiritual boredom?

Grace now realised that there was.

It had occurred to her mid-session a month or so back in a moment of clarity where the bubbly was just enough but not not quite enough.

It was actually the perfect metaphor for sex itself. Dirty ilicit, furtive sex. Where you know you should not do it but you do because a little part of you is not to be denied when the alcohol or lust is too much but not too much. When something inside you craves something you cannot question or shut away and the booze gives you an excuse.

The prostitution was merely her scratching that itch for some people, whilst scratching the same itch for herself in a different way.

Wasn't that what it was all about? All of it? Life, money, sex, relationships, work, everything. Getting what you want one way or the other.

The customers got what they wanted and so did she, on a couple of levels. Part of it was money. On another level it was about security. On another level it was about empowerment and about taking control of her life, doing things on her terms. On the deepest level of all it was the minute fraction of a percentage of herself that wanted it, and needed it. She craved it. Not the sex but actual act of doing something significant away from the rat race. On her terms.

The sex was exactly as meaningless as she intended it to be. As utterly insignificant as it had to be.

The more she thought about it the clearer it became. The deeper The Whorehole got.

How ironic. How fitting.

How tragic she had, in a way, become the very thing she was doing. Becoming what you do. Of being defined by your actions.

A woman who is a prostitute.

It was a depressing realisation. Not the least because it involved, for the first time, an acceptance on levels other than flippant superficiality that she was in fact a prostitute. Call girls are still prostitutes.

I am a prostitute. I'm not just having sex with guys and getting paid for it like that is a different thing.

I am a prostitute. With all that entails and engenders, for good or for worse, I am a prostitute.

As soon as this thought emerged from her rain-sodden mind, so too did the jolting revelation that she no longer needed empowerment. It all fell into place, and the waters cleared. She had done her time.

Hands by her sides, remaining perfectly still, Grace Freeman began to wonder, to allow herself to dare to wonder, where she was supposed to go from here.

Hours later and after a robotic, anaemic encounter with a faceless punter she barely recognised as human, Grace was still deep in thought.

Her musings turned to Simon and her horror at his emotional requirement. This horror was matched or even exceeded by her own sincere, honest and genuine heartbreak for the man. Despite his oddness he was obviously very alone and floundering out of his depth in a pool that in all likelihood, he would probably never be able to swim successfully in. They both knew he was out of his depth with Grace and yet the fantasy of it, the innocence of him daring to dream it was the thing that made her throat tighten and her eyes prickle if she dallied too long over the thought of him. He was just lonely.

Loneliness made her sad. People do things when they are lonely.

The funny thing, she realised, was they could have met at any one of the many parties and afterparties she had been to over the years in Ali and Steffen's little social group and they would likely barely have spoken.

She could have snogged him whilst out of her box on God knows what at any stage and not remember.

She felt sure without a hint of positivity that Simon would certainly remember.

Grace realised that she and the gangly man with the glasses were very much closer than appearances may have suggested. She had texted him to say that she was taking a break and that she was not seeing any clients for a couple of months, and he had got back to her inside 20 seconds with a searingly ambiguous two letter acceptance.

She wondered if he realised how lonely she was.

With a stab of empathy somewhere deep and unloved inside she hoped not, for many reasons. Japanese noodles she had thoughtlessly consumed after her client visit boiled balefully inside of her. The view across London from the top of Primrose Hill was always spectacular but that night Grace was all at once captivated by it, and at the same time surveying a different landscape in her head.

The course of the day had wordlessly, relentlessly, reminded her that her easier-than-expected few months as a prostitute was coming to an end as it was, and that all the things she had wanted were now either hers or immaterial but that the process itself and the time involved had set her new desires and needs. It was becoming clearer and clearer that it was time to move on.

Not physically, but emotionally.

She stared at the orange buildings, glittering in the fine haze of the evening rain, and knew.

It was time to join the land of those who lived.

*****

In the mass of orange buildings, Dylan was drunk. A night out with Jason and Andy had turned into a session he had no appetite for so rather than make his excuses and leave, for they would surely be derided and rebuffed, Dylan chose his favourite tactic.

Just slip out.

Nobody noticed he was gone. They were off to a strip club and he just could not face it. Nor indeed, could he afford it.

Drunk but with that steely if slightly unfocussed clarity that some drinkers have only occasionally when they drink, Dylan strode resolutely through the puddle strewn streets. Green Park tube station was some way off and the rain was not so much coming down as filling the air with a nonchalant fine mist. Despite the apparent disinterest of the rainfall, Dylan was wet through. His thin cotton jacket lagged across his shoulders darkened and heavy. Three bars, one curry house and a swanky gastropub that barely survived one round had come and gone. Jason had been making calls about getting some coke in as bizarrely nobody amongst them actually had any on them and Andy had swerved their evening in the direction of Parker's; a Holborn lap-dancing club.

Dylan was glad he had decided to bail out on them. He hated the way Jason made a point of calling men about dogs and cocaine right in front of him, as if rubbing his nose in the fact that he was not the best drug dealer he knew.

What was loyalty when it came to gear anyway?

It wasn't as if Dylan would say yes. He was out for the night and not carrying or serving. Jason would have not given a second thought to Dylan having to head back to the house to pick some up and then come back. It wouldn't even have registered, Dylan knew.

As long as you have a good night out. Don't mind me, you cunt.

Dylan smiled at his own negativity.

The rain was refreshing. He savoured the chill of the air on his lips and the moisture on his cheeks as he powered on. Twice he had plucked up the confidence to speak to women, both of them early in the evening and the immediate setbacks to his evening that followed through polite but terse exchanges and no eye contact had left him chasing himself for the rest of the night. In truth the lads had not helped.

If they knew of his sadness and rising desperation to remedy himself it did not show in their remorseless piss-taking.

Dylan willed silently, for just a fraction of a second, for his phone to vibrate in his hand in his pocket. Maybe Andy or Steffen to call to find out if he was alright. That thought soon went away. Inwardly he chided himself for his self-indulgence. He did not need his drug friends and their raucous laughing.

Not tonight.

Frankly, not for a long time before.

He did not hate them or blame them but the night he had just had was a stark reminder that there are mates and friends, and that sometimes the gap between the two is a big one. The chasm had never been so wide.

As if on cue, Dylan yawned, clicking his jaw painlesssly, sending the click of popping gristle echoing through his head, every bit as loud as the grinding house music he had been unable to hear anything the girls had said over. Shifting stride, he walked on.

Get back on the dating site. Apply yourself to it and do it properly, he almost mouthed to himself as he walked, repeating a mantra started the night before.

The whole messy business with Gemma had both encouraged him and devastated him. On the one hand, the underlying rejection of him, for whatever reason had hit home with an all-too familiar thud, but on the other, Gemma had been a nice girl, well adjusted, seemingly fairly decent girlfriend material, and it was probably not his fault if she was not ready or that she could not deal with something about him.

Casting his mind back, he admitted sagely to himself that Gemma

Wetherby had been something of a rarity. Most of the nice ones he had met online had not fancied him.

That was a little too much truth for him so Dylan took his chance and dived into a dingy but expensive 24 hour pizza slice seller, seeking refuge from more than the rain outside.

*****

The following day dawned clear, young, as if the skies were embarrassed at the limpid performance of the night just gone. On one side of North London, Dylan was a growling, snorting lump under a clean, thick duvet. On the other, Grace was up and about. No client until midday so unable to sleep again although thankfully not because of a return of the night terrors, she had risen and was just putting the finishing touches to the epic cleaning of her kitchen. The cupboards had been emptied (this had not taken very long) then scrubbed. Her oven would probably not belch out noxious, stinging black fumes when she turned it on, now that she had first dabbed, then scraped, then scrubbed, then rinsed the burnt food detritus off the bottom of it.

Even Barney looked impressed, she fancied.

Well, kind of. He looked at her with those foglamp amber eyes which should have been full of wonder at her sudden bout of cleaning conscientiousness, but for some reason she could not read him. No sarcastic comment from him popped into her head. He was sat there looking at her. Blowing him an imaginary kiss, she turned and flopped into her armchair with a can of Diet Coke. Then she reached for her laptop.

Having decided better of bombarding London's unsuspecting single hopefuls on the dating site with his rather pickled lines, Dylan had gone home full of pizza and hope that the following day would bring him what he craved, or rather, put upon him things that he did not realise he wanted.

He woke up with a vigour, and stayed in bed for ten minutes whilst he fantasised about a woman he had not yet met. Already he needed a pressure release. Gemma had been a matter of days before and yet he already felt that urgency. Sex, he knew, was like Diet Coke, cocaine, Thai food or football. The more you got the more you needed.

The woman would not want to know his name but usher him as fast as her heels would carry her to a hotel. There they would scarcely have time to undress before they were having hot, pressure-release grubby sex. She would strip and be wearing nothing under her coat but a pair of stockings and suspenders. She would beg him to fuck her. She would be dripping wet in anticipation of him, so incredibly turned on was she at the sight of Dylan straining against his underwear. Mid-sex, she would leap off him and gasping ruddy faced she would beg him to fuck her like he hated her, thrusting her bottom toward him, pleading…

Stars danced in front of his eyes as he opened his screwed up eyes post-ejaculation, breathing hard and with a smugness of familiar satisfaction. The damp sock was laid gingerly on the bedside table.

In this case, Dylan was grateful of the focus. His life had been focussed for too long on the drugs and the fear and loathing that went with it. This was a healthy, lusty pursuit with definable goals and a chance of success and fulfilment however temporary, which the drugs could or would not provide.

The day was dull and grey but dry, with the low clouds insulating what warmth the day provided making it feel mild outside. Spring was definitely not in the air but neither was winter and that was good enough. He ambled in to work deep in thought and with a clarity afforded only when he left his iPod on the dresser, as he did so that morning. He had made a decision that his profile needed sprucing up. Carla texted him to get her some pills for Friday, and he did not respond. This more than his bacon sandwich from the cafe in the station, or indeed the huge, sweaty piece of carrot cake he bought with it, in fact more than anything else that morning, made Dylan feel good.

It was a good, solid, progressive, positive feeling. Like going to the gym.

Carla would have to wait.

The drugs would have to wait, on the backburner.

EIGHTEEN

Soundtrack
Vibrasphere – 'Manzanilla'

Grace was closely scrutinising a desk.

She was with an older guy, perhaps 50-ish, who liked to dominate his women. Grace imagined there had been a long line of submissive girlfriends and possibly wives too, but in their absence, or possibly not, Grace was a surrogate. She had been ordered to "perform a sex act" on him, as the Sunday tabloids might smirkingly write and was now unceremoniously bent over a scratched and scored computer desk whilst he toiled away behind her. He was more thorough than rough but she knew what noises to make and when to make them. When she finally felt him strain and grunt like some pale and washed out old steer, she gave a long, luxuriant moan which he acknowledged with a vastly patronising pat on her rump.

"You are amazing – none of my clients know how to fuck me like you do" she murmured, her voice low and almost feline. The lies dripped out of her.

"Years of practice." he boomed in clipped, public school tones from behind her, still in the same position and showing no signs of extricating himself from her or thus allowing her to straighten up.

She nudged and he pulled away.

Wiping a bead of sweat off her lower back, wondering whether it was hers or his, she turned slowly to see the man disappear into the bathroom.

Why did men always do that? Grace wondered.

You have sex with them and they can't get closer to you, they are all over you, and then as soon as they shoot their load they high tail it into the bathroom to hide...

To her amusement he began to whistle, perhaps conscious of her silence and solitude. She rummaged through her mental stock cupboard for suitable small talk while the man got dressed. She was singularly unable to find anything, and so was relieved when he emerged from the still-dark bathroom with a tatty blue and white striped dressing gown on. She thought he looked like a man from a toothpaste advert but resisted the urge to smile, putting on instead a sultry, lopsided look which she hoped told him that she had been well fucked, that he was a stud, and that she fancied him.

All it was really meant to do was to butter him up in case he felt like tipping. He advanced across the carpet towards her and thrust a pair of red banknotes into her hand – a pair of fifties.

"You are the most beautiful woman I've ever seen. You deserve this." He said matter of factly.

Grace knew not to feel condescended upon by such high-handed gestures, and smiled at him broadly as if the extra hundred pounds would change her life. Inwardly, she noted the room and the furniture of a worn but excellent quality and his suit which was likewise. She guessed that his intimations that she was the most beautiful woman he had ever seen was patently untrue. The well-oiled process of call and visit suggested he did this a lot, and that he was slumming it a little with her, an untried call girl who still put notes in phoneboxes. Grace knew she was not Belgravia escort material. On her best days she probably could have been able to hold her own in the lower echelons in such lofty and exalted strata had she had the contacts, but as it was it did not seem like an option for her. And that was a different life, a different thing.

Was that the pinnacle of her profession? Was it the equivalent of a boardroom position for people who led "normal" lives? Grace was not sure.

The man ushered her out of his flat with as much politeness as he could, and suddenly she was stood in a street in West London, looking at a row of parked cars. She put her hand in her coat pocket and thumbed the hundred pounds he had given her, and the roll of twenties underneath that that he had given her before she had even got into his room.

Two hundred and eighty pounds for less than two hours work.

Not bad.

*****

Dylan was well into his afternoon at work, having not even opened up the programme in which he wrote his copy and analysis reports.

Despite his (slouching) presence in the quiet office, work was not on the agenda. Instead, he was laying back in his chair totally immersed in re-writing his profile. He had been on an honesty mission that morning; being painfully honest in his self-appraisal almost as if it were something to do with work. Which it really was not. Having drafted a not-at-all boring 476-word review of himself, he pasted it onto the website only to realise that the page now resembled a blog, and that he had obviously put a lot of effort into the writing. It was clipped, witty, funny (to him), and flowed well like a good piece of writing should. The problem was of course that he did not want to look like he had put a lot of effort into it.

This made him look desperate and desperation is not a good look on a dating site. It did not matter that everyone on the site was desperate. He had to look anything but, so he deleted great swathes of his morning's work. The second incarnation made him sound incredibly arrogant and self-centred.

He deleted much of this as well.

By early afternoon he had come round to the honesty thing, having decided that political spin was something he disliked and that if he was honest about his motives he was more likely to meet a woman who was likewise. By the time he finally published it, the profile was a positively svelte 219 words and he was pleased with it. It occurred to him only after he logged off the site, opened up a work window (and left it so anyone looking would think he had been doing work all morning), and stepped out of the office, that brevity was probably a good policy. Women did not have time to read through profiles and giving too much away about himself merely eroded an almost non-existent sense of mystery about him anyway which was, it was clear, manifestly a bad thing.

He spent the afternoon looking through profiles of the other men on the site to see what they had written. It was a bit like being at school, he remembered, when you weren't sure what the teacher was asking you to do, so you looked at everyone else's work to see if you had got it right. Indeed, much like being at school, Dylan was tempted to laugh at some of the earnest and not-so-earnest submissions of those who obviously did not get what the teacher wanted at all. Not even slightly. Not even a teeny tiny bit. There were a couple of non-clichéd lines which being non-clichéd were eminently more valuable than the throwaway ones he was not entirely immune from using. It even occurred to him to write some of the better ones down.

By the time home time came, Dylan was absolutely satisfied that his profile was a nailed on certainty. A guaranteed home run. A Grand National Favourite. Didier Drogba in the Munich Final stepping up to take a penalty. A win.

He was ready.

But there was an errand to run first.

The visit to Crabby had taken just a few minutes.

Crabby's decrepit place on the way up the hill was very much in a similar mould as Dylan's ramshackle home. Dylan had gone in and been surrounded as he always was by cats. Two greeted him as he walked through the door, another stood indefatigable on the stairs as he passed. A fourth was lying outside the lounge room door and at least three more were dotted around the lounge area when he entered, squinting into the dimness.

Crabby was slumped in his armchair, fully awake but with little mind to rise and embrace Dylan or even so much as shake his hand. Dylan moved over to him to see that Crabby was holding a tiny kitten in a cradling arm. The juxtaposition between gnarled, wizened old raver, complete with straggly grey beard and grubby off-grey matted hair streaked with dreadlocks and the tiny black and white kitten was stark even in the dark.

"She's only four weeks old. The Polish woman downstairs left her when she moved out, just rubbish, cat shit and this little treasure." Crabby's deep, ancient tones seemed to come from within him as he barely moved his mouth when he spoke. The gloom in the cosy front room merely enhanced the illusion. Dylan decided not to shake his hand.

"How many of these are yours?" Dylan asked with genuine interest. How strange to have two cat people in one house, even if one had apparently dropped off the face of the Earth.

"Agnelli, Nelson… think you saw Skydive on the stairs. Over there you have Pants, Corset and Ayla. Six. Her downstairs left the tabby in the kitchen, plus this little one. Haven't named them yet but they fitted right in."

Dylan blinked in incredulity.

"…you have eight cats?"

Crabby laughed, jutting a chin at the tiny ball of fluff asleep in his arms.

"More like seven and a half. This little scraplet barely qualifies as a half."

Dylan smiled. It was impossible not to be touched by the old man's love of his feline friends. Crabby had been on the fringes of their clubbing scene since long before Dylan got involved. He had retired at 40 for reasons unknown owning outright his own place and lived off his pension and the rental income from the flat below. Dylan often wondered what could have happened to him to drop out of the rat race at such a young age. He never talked about his life before. He'd discovered The Age Of Love in the 90s at raves at fields and in warehouses. Had he been a hippy before then? Dylan did not know but guessed that he had.

Crabby had a little circle of raverhippy mates who he bought drugs for and they could be found anywhere there was a rave, especially outside. Crabby was easily the oldest of his group and tended to enjoy the afterparty much more than the raving itself now. Dylan did not sell him his weed (although it was clear to all that Crabby smoked a lot of it) and in fact sometimes bought small amounts from Crabby rather than buy it from Luca. Dylan supplied the pills, Ketamine, Meow Meow and acid.

Crabby was exactly the sort of customer Dylan liked. He did not ask too many questions, always had the money in cash, never asked for credit, never quibbled about weights and was very careful. He always gave Dylan plenty of notice, always offered him a cup of tea and treated him with respect but was not obsequious as some of his customers were. The only thing Dylan did not like about it was the fact that he had to go on a mission down to Brixton Hill to go see him for a housecall.

Dylan looked around. The room was very warm and welcoming if a bit untidy. It may be expected that with 7.5 cats wandering around the place would smell but Dylan was always impressed at how it never did. An incense stick burned silently on the mantelpiece. Dylan could not see a TV, he guessed Crabby did not want one. Instead some deep and melodic psy-trance was playing down low from a sound-system he could not see. Dylan recognised it.

"Vibrasphere?"

"Yeah, I need to give you the CD back actually thanks for the loaner."

"Keep it mate, I've got another copy." Dylan smiled.

Crabby got to his feet slowly and with all the care of a bomb-disposal expert trying to diffuse a huge device. The kitten stirred as it was gently placed on the cushion on the chair but did not wake.

"You're a gentleman and a scholar Dylan. How much was it?" Crabby moved over and shook his hand in a belated greeting. Dylan knew he was not talking about the Vibrasphere CD.

"Two hundred please Crabby mate. You'll like these, no speed in them I don't think, lots of MDMA, nice buzz, quite strong."

"Can't wait, sounds perfect. You fancy doing one now?" Crabby looked up hopefully as he pressed a roll of notes into Dylan's hand.

"I'd love to mate but I've got to get back. Another time though yeah?" Dylan actually meant it. He found Crabby very interesting and enlightening company whenever they met up and was one of a very tiny group of customers he would be prepared to sit and have a speculative discussion pill with.

Crabby looked slightly disappointed. "So you don't want a tea either?"

"Sorry fella I need to get back." Dylan regretted not having a cup of tea at least. He looked over at Crabby who was already engrossed in one of the white and tabby cats curled gracefully on the far sofa, muttering platitudes he evidently was not supposed to hear.

"So I'll see you later, yeah?"

Crabby came back to him and gave him a long hug.

"Really appreciate it Dylan. An absolute pleasure as always. Let's have that night in soon."

"I'd like that" Dylan smiled and shook his hand.

The white and grey cat was still stood on his step as he passed. Dylan flashed him a look as he opened the front door. The cat's gaze was hard to place but almost seemed caustic, judging him for selling Class A's to a 68 year old man.

Dylan did not respond to the cat but closed the door discreetly behind him.

Tears for Fears in his headphones accompanied his on his walk back down the hill toward the tube station.

Shout. Let it out. Talking about things he could do without, walking down the street to Brixton High Street.

The music was rich and deep in the headphones pressed deep inside Dylan's ears. The words echoed in his head. It was as if the universe was trying to speak to him, to get him to exorcise demons that slithered in the shadows of the dark places inside him. Brixton bustled around him in the blackness as the hill opened onto a huge crossroads; a mass of lights and noise audible even over the loud music.

The satchel seemed to weigh heavily despite having almost nothing in it as he moved quickly down the pavement. There was no reason for it to, the drugs he had been carrying were gone.

Dylan smiled as he thought about Crabby. The crusty old guy was so content, surrounded by the cats and hippy trance he loved so much. The cats were not pets but genuine life companions and usually followers of his need for stillness and calm. Dylan had heard him preach about the timeless wisdom he claimed he saw in their eyes more than once. It was hard not to think the enlightenment cliché had something in it, for Crabby at least. Crabby was incredibly wise for someone who had done as much drugs as he had, for more than two decades. Some people blow their mind on drugs, and some carry on blowing it until the money runs out before the brain cells. Some never seemed to suffer any ill effect.

Did Dylan feel bad about selling drugs to him?

Dylan searched his soul.

No.

Not really. He was not a proper drug dealer and by Crabby buying his reliable and not-dangerously cut mind-expanding substances from him, he was not having to go metaphorically and literally down the hill into Brixton to buy from some Yardie loon who would probably one day cut his throat for £40 whilst strung out on crack and drain cleaner. That was proper drugs and proper drug dealing. Dangerous shit that Dylan wanted no part of.

Much better he should buy from Dylan instead of a proper drug dealer.

With that, his thoughts flicked back to the online dating, and his nailed-on star profile.

Dylan stopped on the way home for a packet of tortilla chips and a glass jar of something grim looking that he took from the cursory illustration on the lid that he was supposed to dip the broken fragments of chip into, a bar of chocolate, and a large packet of HobNobs. It was going to be a long night!

It reminded him of being at college, pulling an all-night revision session the night before an exam and the comparison became even more stark when he charged into his room, slammed the door and threw his coat and scarf on the floor.

The selection of his much-treasured Leftfield album, which also hailed from his college days, only served to reinforce the feeling.

Smiling, he logged on to the site. The screen filled with thumbnail pics of women.

"Solid effort Dylan old son… solid effort!" he muttered under his breath. A long night indeed!

*****

Barney was staring at her. His big amber eyes bored into her from her periphery as she studied the screen of her laptop. She was, to use a phrase normally associated with tests at school, stuck.

For someone who spends her life talking to men about sex, you are useless at this. Give up. Come and pay attention to me, or if not, at least stop making that daft face. You look like a fucking idiot.

Ignoring the cat, she screwed up her face even tighter and

redoubled her concentration.

"I'm stuck" she said out loud, folding her arms across her chest and sticking her chin out in the way she used to do as a child.

She glanced at the cat sat across from her directly as if imploring him to tell her what to write on her dating profile. Barney looked unmoved by her apparent plight and did not move. Sighing dramatically, Grace looked at what she had written and then read it out loud to nobody in particular.

"Hi! My name is Grace and I am an easy-going..." she trailed off.

"Is there a hyphen between easy and going do you reckon?" she asked Barney, tipping her head to one side. Barney gave no indication that he knew what a hyphen was, or that he cared at all about her possibly erroneous use of one. Remembering this, Grace glared at the cat who remained unmoved. Deciding that she did not care whether there was supposed to be one and thus any potential men off the site would be unlikely to either, she continued.

"I am an easy going twenty-something..."

Another hyphen. This one looked like it ought to be there, so she left it in.

"...who is looking for someone to have a laugh with. I am new to this, so be nice!"

She liked that bit. As might be expected, Barney was nonplussed.

"I have a good sense of humour and I enjoy life. I'd like to meet someone who does the same."

That doesn't sound right.

"How can you "do" a sense of humour?" she muttered testily.

Deciding against reading the last two lines out loud she glanced at Barney, who, insultingly, had closed his eyes and appeared to be asleep. So much for an interesting profile!

She laboured away for another twenty minutes before finally conceding that it really was not that big of a deal and that as pointless wastes of time in her life went, this was pretty pointless. Grace had convinced herself that nobody would reply to her ad anyway and even if they did they would be too old, married, hideously obese or an axe murderer. Or worse, a former customer. Leaving her profile finished but unpolished she published it to the site with an old picture of herself from four years previously, closed the laptop down and gave it no thought for the rest of the day.

Her afternoon client was the older guy from Old Street who liked to be spanked.

A bread and butter client and easy money.

She spent the tube journey home moving her aching wrists wondering whether she was not right all along, and that her profession was what she was supposed to be doing. Maybe she was being too hard on herself, and maybe it was not the profession that was a problem. Two hundred quid for less than an hour's work with no ill effects save for a slightly tired arm from giving a hugely grateful old man a hiding was not bad by any stretch.

There are million worse things to be doing, she thought to herself.

NINETEEN

Soundtrack

Nuyorican Soul – 'I Am The Black Gold Of The Sun'

Dylan was also pondering his choice of employment. Both of them, in fact.

Laying on his bed, staring at a crack that snaked across the ceiling like those big rivers you could see from space, he wondered about his capacity for decision-making.

He had days where, in painfully self-critical mode, he reviewed and castigated every bad decision he had ever made. Looking around at the shabby and dusty room with the cracks in the ceiling and the poorly fitted windows that whistled with the wind, he reflected yet again, that there had to be more to his life than what he was getting out of it. In true Negative Day fashion, he reminded himself that logging into the dating site and revamping his profile, or indeed the abortive run around the block he had attempted that morning, hardly constituted positive remedial action.

Wishing to take his mind of such solipsistic wallowing, he raised himself off the bed and walked across dusty floorboards to go and see what Jason and Carla were destroying in the kitchen.

The air changed smell and temperature dramatically in the short twenty-foot walk down the corridor to the kitchen. Carla was peeling potatoes and Jason was laying in the windowframe looking very bohemian in tight jeans and a waistcoat, smoking a huge joint that looked for all the world like a whitish carrot.

Even with the window open by a good foot, the kitchen was very hot. Steam (and despite Jason's efforts, smoke) collected in the high ceiling area and then dripped in inky streaks down the walls as if the house itself was perspiring. Jason nodded at him as he walked in and made a nasal sound that probably might have been a greeting, and Dylan nodded back, clicking his tongue and winking. He looked over at Carla, her pans on the stove and the oven light on. There were a multitude of packets and jars of spices and herbs and preserves out on the side.

Having taken it all in, Dylan was absolutely none the wiser as to what she was actually cooking and in fairness to him the smell was giving nothing away. Helping himself to a can of Jason’s strong Belgian lager from the fridge he glanced at the pile of washing up that rose above the sink rim. Halfway down he noted a plate covered in orange fragments of rice, washed across the plate with great smudges and tidemarks of bright orange grease. It was the plate for his curry he had eaten three days ago. He was about to complain to Carla about it when she finally noticed him and threw a piece of potato peel at him.

“alright mate...” was all he could manage by way of retaliation.

“You look like shit” reported Carla in a matter of fact tone, as if she were stating that there was no milk in the fridge or that the postman had not been yet.

Dylan chose to ignore this comment lest he be drawn into a discussion as to why he looked like shit and all the various topics which would surely come spilling out after that.

Instead he chose to make another of his non-committal noises and pulled the ring pull on the can in a theatrical way, complete with exhalation on breath to match the jet of pressured beer gas from the can, in an attempt to steer the conversation towards beer or something else comfortable. Jason proffered a hand and Dylan took the joint, walking to the window, taking a deep pull, and wiping the condensation off the other window with his other hand. As expected, nothing to see out in the garden whatsoever.

Two attempts with each housemate to engage in something topical yet not in any way related to Dylan came and failed as Carla was too busy and Jason was too stoned. Dylan was about to make his excuses and slope off to bed when Carla rounded on him in that suddenly urgent way she did sometimes.

"We are off out for some drinks in Shoreditch after work on Friday... uh tomorrow – me, Abi, Steffen, Louise, Antonio, Hetch, Dooley and a few others. Come along mate it will be fun."

Her sunny, singsong turn of phrase and jaunty manner was completely at odds with her forceful body language and slight frown. Dylan was initially taken aback.

Before he could argue he found himself agreeing, downing his beer in some insecure show of masculinity borne out of the aggression of Carla's frontal assault and swept out of the kitchen, like so much dust from a broom. Jason did not look up from his megajoint as he left, and Carla was chattering on her mobile, with a baking tray in her other hand. Still none the more aware about anything, Dylan paused in the lounge, unwilling for some reason to return to his room, as if retreating there was a sign of weakness.

He switched on the television and immediately began to think. It was incredible, he realised, that he could only really think clearly when he had the television or some music on in the background. Some people did their thinking on the toilet or in the bath, but he could do it anywhere, as long as there was noise.

No wonder I'm a city boy.

TWENTY

Soundtrack

Anthony White – 'Love Me Tonight' (Gomez House Mix)

The following day defined itself largely by his occasional lapses from steadfast doing nothing into some semblance of serious work.

A yoghurt company in Mortlake wanted to do some online advertising for some new probiotic shit. The creative guys had sent some buzzword heavy collection-of-adjectives shit-on-paper and he had to meld it together into cohesive shit.

Even so, by the time he finally lost interest and went back to his fantasy football team in preparation for the weekend's coming fixtures, he was buoyed with an unfamiliar sense of accomplishment. It was the positive feeling you get when you have just been to the gym for the first time in ages. You know full well that you have done yourself little real good, and yet the mere act of going, of doing something positive, represents some good of its own.

He headed downstairs to the gents toilet to wash and brush up, recoiling at the odd aroma of a myriad of aftershaves and deodorants of all his fellow workers all doing the same thing, mixing with the stale urine, underlying hint of faecal matter and industrial cleaners of a busy office toilet.

Next to him at the washbasins was a guy he recognised but did not know by name. He was putting what seemed like a whole can of pungent-smelling designer anti-perspirant under each arm, while the brown hairs around his armpits turned white and frosty, as if he were sleeping rough outside in the cold. He was considerably fatter than he was, and this made him feel better about taking his own shirt off and going through the same rigmarole, only with somewhat less damage to the ozone layer. He had decided to risk the new shirt he bought for the date with The String Butcher, a different pair of the veritable mountain of dark blue denim jeans, and another pair from his stack of once-shiny brown slip-ons. Putting some maximum hold gel in a rather futile gesture to the comb over effort in his prematurely thinning hairline, he splashed on some Valentino and regarded himself in the mirror, free to do so now the hulking great deodorant monster next to him had left. Like a pilot doing a pre-flight check he went through his checklist, baring his teeth, clicking his neck from side to side and craning his neck upwards and back, his eyes never leaving his own in the mirror.

This was as good as he was going to look on that particular Friday night.

Smiling to himself, he left the toilet.

Dylan quite liked Old Street as a place. It had a certain charm to it, which was rather in spite of the not-very-dapper denizens of the place as opposed to because of them.

Here, boozed up office workers in high street suits mixed with the bizarrely dressed meedjah or arty types of all ages, who seemed to dress as though they wanted people not to know what sex they were. Many wore painfully tight denim, huge, improbably lacquered hair, makeup and ripped t-shirts whilst the women did the same but with more colour, even bigger, back combed hair and even more makeup.

Dylan had visited the gents to relieve himself of the three pints of Fosters he had consumed in the first forty five minutes of being in the bar, and the two guys stood next to him at the urinal trough were discussing how great they thought Tangerine Dream were.

Neither looked a day older than 16. He wondered if either had actually heard any of their stuff, or whether they were just parroting conversations heard in pubs full of older arty types, and were trying to be artier-than-thou.

Both disappeared into a cubicle for what Dylan assumed was a furtive blowjob or a line or three of Bolivia's favourite export. Maybe both. Dylan had just begun to wonder whether Carla had any on her, when he saw her.

*****

Grace was stood at the bar, having made a cupped hand to mouth gesture to Carla to moment she spotted her when she walked in, to which she had responded in a flurry of nods and smiles, even though she had almost a whole pint of lager in front of her. She had just seen her last of three clients that day, and was looking forward to a night out that did not involve having sex for money.

The last guy had pulled off the condom whilst she was bringing him off with her hand and although she did not stop, the vile sticky goo that he had deposited on her hand but a few seconds afterwards had been less than well received.

Occupational hazard or not, it seemed to burn into her skin and she felt dirty. The client had not cared but given her a big tip as if that made up for forcing his bodily fluids onto her naked flesh in an unspeakable intrusion of her personal space.

How telling that in her line of work, personal space could be measured by the thickness of a Durex Elite.

Reaching for her newly-poured glass of Sancerre, she let go an ejaculative breath loudly like a builder who had just spent the day humping wood and had just downed a frosty tankard of ale or whatever they drank these days. Over her shoulder a man pushed in close to the bar and she moved up to accommodate him.

Turning to nod at him, she looked straight into the face of the

Man-from-the-Tube.

*****

Dylan was struggling. Badly.

It was not so much the approaching the woman that was the problem as moving to the bar had just about accomplished this nicely, but what to say to her. Should he ignore her? Should he speak to her? If so, how do you introduce yourself? What to say?

Dylan was stuck. The more he tried to think of something witty or even intelligent, the more he just went completely blank.

Jason would just slope up and say the exact perfect thing and be really cool and stuff. The cunt.

Inside his head, sand dunes rolled off into nothingness on the horizon. He was very stuck in the sand, aware only of how his pulse was racing as if he had just done a huge line of coke, and how his mouth was dry. His mouth was dry as the Gobi. All he could see in his mind was miles and miles of sand. Why did he have to come steaming over?

What the fuck was he supposed to say to her?

Sand. Lots of sand.

Far off Dylan heard a man's voice.

"Hi. I've seen you around"

Oh Holy Fuck.

Please God no.

Please, please let me not have just said that.

Please, please let her not have heard me.

Please, please let her not have recognised me. Please let her not think I am a weirdo.

Please.

Please.

Fuck.

Fuck.

Fuck.

Oh fuck she is looking at me. She is going to say something. Something like “Fuck off weirdo”.

She is going to say it.

Grace craned her head to one side, grimaced slightly, then....

....burst into a wide, toothy genuine grin.

“Have you indeed? Your face looks familiar. Have we met?”

Her voice was low and soothing, like the voice-over women on TV try to sound. She was suggesting to Dylan with her words that she did not recognise him. But the mirth in her eyes and the smile that revealed those perfect, perfect teeth insinuated that she was being coy.

Once again without any actual impulse to do so, Dylan opened his mouth again.

“I think so. But I can’t remember where.” Dylan lied matter-of-factly.

Pressing home the moment, he decided that it might not be best to dwell on how he knew her, even though he was certain she knew that he knew, because if she did not know how he knew her, she might suspect he was some kind of stalker person. This naturally was a bad thing as far as Dylan was concerned.

This is complicated.

“Do you fancy a drink?” Dylan asked hopefully.

Grace glanced at her wine glass. The old “I've got one thanks” excuse would not work here, as she was down to droplets. Would she use the “I'm driving thanks” or the “I was just leaving” lines? Grace could not decide.

“Ok, that would be nice”

Dylan looked stunned, and as he looked right into Grace's eyes (trying not to look too closely in some crazed stalker sort of way), he was sure he saw that she was surprised too.

Perhaps she did not want a drink but had agreed to one anyway?

*****

Grace could not quite put her finger on it.

The-man-from-the-Tube was definitely the very same one stood in front of her who had just spent seven pounds eighty five on a large glass, nay a bucket, of Pinot Grigio for her, and yet he looked more familiar still. You did not meet people on the tube and you certainly did not meet them just by looking at them. Did you? Was that what this was?

All of a sudden she had the chorus of "It started with a kiss" by Hot Chocolate in her head, only the words were "It started with a stare".

Dylan was still stunned and amazed. Inwardly he cursed himself for his almost fifteen years of experience of talking to women not standing him in any kind of stead whatsoever, and him being about as suave and sophisticated as a jelly mould since meeting her.

She was plain yes, but attractive plain and had a great body by the looks of it. Dylan morosely admitted to himself that she was so far out of his league it was sad and he knew full well that he had just wasted seven pounds and eighty five pence on a rather unnecessarily large glass of wine for her. She was going to walk off in a minute and leave him alone. In the train of consciousness way that drunk or even semi-drunk people think, Dylan reminded himself that he did not want to be alone. Not any more.

He looked at her as she chatted about her job at the British Library. Her eyes were cartoonishly huge, accentuated by heavy eye makeup. They were a deep greyish blue, sparkling in the harsh bar neons and fluorescents like the jewellery on home shopping channels. Curls and locks of her layered hair fell scattered about her shoulders, and across her eyeline as she talked. Her subtly painted lips were in a nude hue, neither too full nor too thin, covering immaculately set teeth that betrayed only the slightest fondness for coffee and red wine.

Her skin was not perfect, but had enough foundation on to look as close to perfect as Dylan had seen for some time. The girls he met in his social group and out clubbing never wore makeup like that. All it did was run down faces and blot onto other people's shirts in the hectic humidity of the clubs. And no makeup in the world could make a woman look good after a night on it taking all sorts and dreading sunrise at some afterparty.

As Grace turned her head, Dylan noticed that she had the scars of more ear piercings in her left ear, since replaced with what he imagined would be a set of inoffensive, unremarkable but classy earrings, were she actually to wear a set. He looked down to see her pink woollen overcoat draped suggestively over the back of the bar stool.

The-Girl-In-The-Pink-Overcoat.

What were the chances of that?

*****

Grace had nervously drunk most of her vat of wine quite quickly and it was rapidly going to her head.

Carla and her mates had been over to say hi, semi-astounded to find out that Dylan had already introduced himself. They had retreated to the big table in the corner where she was sat down next to Dylan on the sofa.

They were chatting to a tall and largely uninteresting guy across the table, whom Dylan appeared to live with. Dylan was involving her in every aspect of the conversation and evidently felt as if he would prefer to be talking just to Grace. But proximity to the other members of the group made this difficult.

Though Dylan was giving it a valiant effort, she had to admit.

Another vat of wine appeared courtesy of Carla so Grace resolved maturely to drink this one much slower.

She thought the tall uninteresting guy might have been the one

Carla and Louise were trying to set her up with a few weeks ago at that bar in Covent Garden. Either way, he was as disinterested in her as she was in him and contributing only to the conversation in snorts of laughter and the occasional bang of a fist on the battered wood tables. Dylan was shepherding her through the conversation and she found herself laughing at his quirky and sarcastic sense of humour.

He was clearly more intelligent than he looked.

He was not particularly attractive but large framed and he smelt nice. Dylan's dress sense was average at best and the shirt he was wearing would not be one she would ever have picked out for him.

Picking out clothes for the bloke already and you have barely even met him. Steady on Grace!

She watched him in side profile as the wine further fuzzied the edges.

He probably used to have bad skin when he was younger, she observed from the landscape around his nose. His eyes were red around the edges from too many late nights but he had long, attractive eyelashes. The teeth were yellowy and not the straightest. Dylan's hair was scruffy but not in a cool hipster way but all the more endearing for it. His familiarity seemed to extend further back from the time he was staring at her on the Tube but he could not place it as it was too far away in the ether of memory.

He was funny. Grace liked sarcastic guys. He had a self-deprecating charisma and charm to him.

Grace found herself enjoying Dylan's company. It was a rare and refreshing thing to enjoy the company of a guy, also for there to be no pressure and no financial transaction. Grace found herself drawn as much to the circumstance as to the slightly podgy, funny, charming guy sat next to her.

Carla was on fine form and it was not long before a tray of sambucas appeared, and then disappeared in due order. Pretty soon her and the big guy, Jason, were disappearing into the corners or the toilets for what was obviously a powder job, although neither offered

Grace any. She would have said no anyway.

Interestingly, they did not offer Dylan a line at any stage either, and that made Grace happy for reasons she could not quite understand right at that moment. Dylan was full of beans as it was; happy, laughing, joking and not fawning over her the way that some men did. She liked men who were funny not fawny. Not Funny Men, but men who were funny. And who did not fawn.

Dylan was, judging from his jokes and stories, actually very funny indeed. She found herself laughing out loud on more than one occasion and whether it was the alcohol, the stress relief of her day's activities being over, or something else, she let herself slip into the warmth of the occasion and joined in heartily with the conversation. Dylan was a nice guy, she decided.

Experience brought up other questions leading from this revelation.

Dylan was finally doing fine. The sambucas had helped and he was in his comfort zone, telling jokes, drinking, impersonating and generally having a good time. Grace seemed content to sit next to him and join in and he felt no compulsion to interrogate her further. Something told him that this would not be appreciated. She had got up to go to the toilet earlier and had put her hand on his arm. What did that mean?

His mind bottomed out and began to form something out of the ether. A minute wonder. Some sort of wistful, tiny hope or gaze to some future eventuality, but he did not dare bring it to the surface lest his hands begin to shake and his blushing return.

Pressing down the beginnings of something like a tender hope, he carried on drinking and telling jokes.

Carla and Jason had trumpeted that they were off to a club, and everyone apart from Grace and Dylan had loudly stated their desire to carry on the evening's libations. Claridge, Bean and his boys were going to be there apparently.

Well that’s a real incentive. Not.

Dylan did not fancy Fabric, but looked to Grace who looked underwhelmed by the possibility of a night out clubbing. Dylan noted for the first time that she was actually quite drunk.

"I don't fancy it. I'm going to head home now, got an early start in the morning..." she said to Dylan as she rose to put her coat on.

"Those books won't catalogue themselves!" said Dylan with a grin.

You are going to have to ask this woman out Dylan.

Fuck.

Dylan's heart dropped in terror.

Fuck.

Grace noted his teeth again were not great. It would possibly have been more of an issue for any prospective boyfriend in the past. But for obvious reasons her own sensibilities had been diminished somewhat in the last few months.

Prospective boyfriend...?

Mind you, Fraser had had perfect teeth, and what a complete fucking arsehole he had turned out to be.

Dylan moved in to give her a hug, and surprised at this unexpected turn of emotional events, she just froze. Dylan resolutely hugged her stiff form anyway with all the feeling of a straw bale but did linger long enough to say... something.

What was he trying to tell her?

She looked right into his eyes to see, and saw that Dylan was, under the haze of the alcohol, wide-eyed and apparently very nervous.

What could he possibly be nervous about?

"Listen, umm..." he mumbled, unable to hold her gaze.

"Would you, like, I mean, sometime, if you are bored and fancy a night out maybe? With, like, me? Dinner? Or a drink sometime? Maybe? With me, like?......." his stuttered voice tailed off.

You have got to be kidding.

For fuck's sake.

You are a fucking twat, Dylan Short.

He looked at her more in hope than faith. Her eyes moved away. Dylan stared at the floor in flushed mortification.

The seconds ticked past.

TWENTY-ONE

Soundtrack

Shapeshifters – 'Lola's Theme' (Original Mix)

Dylan was sprinting.

He had not sprinted anywhere for years. Hot breath surged out of his sticky, oily lungs and great globs of hoppy spittle flew out in front as he clattered through the damp Spring night.

Grace had said yes.

His grin seemed to stretch up to his ears. Uncaring, he bellowed into the sky.

"Yeeeeeeessssssss!"

Grace had said yes. She was massively out of his league but she wanted to go on a date with him! When did that ever happen?

Dylan was delighted. The sheer joy of it overwhelmed him. He had no idea where he was running to, or why, but the jolt of adrenalin coursing through him demanded it. Fist-pumping and grinning in delight he presently came to a stop, heart pounding. He stopped windmilling his arms.

Blood thundered through his temples. The hammering on the tarmac stung the soles of his feet though his shoes and the exercise made him feel oddly nauseous. With hands on thighs doubled over but still smiling, Dylan let his breath return.

"Fucking.... yes."

*****

Grace was trotting down the stairs of the Underground station. Warm air tugged at her hair and flattened her pink coat against her sides as the tube train pushed though the tunnels beneath. People milled about, moving more languidly than on week days. A lack of purpose made people act differently. It was strange to see. Grace reckoned they didn't even realise they were doing it.

She pulled out her headphones to progress a little further through an anthology of The Rolling Stones she had downloaded from iTunes. They were a band she had never had much regard for but she was tired of the same house and trance mix CDs, or of the 80s bands she'd grown up with. In an effort to broaden her horizons, The Rolling Stones seemed as good a place to start as any.

At the very least she'd have something to discuss about music with some of her older customers.

As the opening strains of Gimme Shelter came clear in her ears, her smile returned.

Dylan had asked her out and when she'd said yes had been clearly, evidently delighted. Grace liked that. It was so lovely to have someone want to see her for a date where there was no money and no cynicism involved. Dylan liked her and nobody had cared for a while. It was refreshing.

Smiling, she stepped onto the train, the doors hissing shut behind her. Ahead a couple were sat together, close. Both were engrossed in their phones and despite the proximity of each other seemed barely to realise the other was there. Grace shook her head. That was not how a relationship would be. Not for her. Not for them.

She tried to imagine the wordless, perfunctory, polite sex they would probably have when they got to where they were going. Then they would lie in bed smoking and tweeting or playing Candy Crush or something. He would go down on her. She would either get bored at his lack of effort and fake it or actually come, then he would fuck her like a piston missionary style for about three minutes before filling the condom with a self-satified jerk and then they would turn out the light and go to sleep.

Hardly wild wanking material was it?

Grace let a wisp of wistfulness pass her features as the train eased into the darkness of the tunnel. She knew it because Fraser aside, all her ex-boyfriends had been like that. She had been accepting of the comfort and familiarity because it was safe and she did not have the confidence to indulge herself.

It was something the young and the plain went through. Grace was more familiar than most.

You have hopes and dreams. You have no idea really how to go about making them happen so you take what it is in front of you. You go through the motions. You meet a guy, you know he isn't the one, you don't even like him that much but he doesn't offend you or smell bad so you date him. He eventually fucks off like the emotional retard he almost universally is and you do it all again with someone slightly better, or sometimes, slightly worse. In between are periods of working hard, of focusing on career and personal development. This means almost universally going out and getting fucked, doing drugs, drinking too much, seeing DJs and bands you love but without anyone to fully appreciate them with you. Hence you do more drugs and you drink more than usual.

Right?

It was only once Grace lost her job and became a sex worker (as she laughingly referred to herself as, in the tabloid sense) that these things became defined enough to see clearly.

The prolonged period of alone time that accompanied being with several different men in the biblical sense per week saw various things change in Grace's view of herself change.

Confidence bred a more coloured view on one's self, she had

mused. Self-assurance was temporary and a shell at most, but the sense of self-awareness was never clearer.

Her third "date" had been the eye-opener for her. The guy had been all smiles and niceties then they had sex. She had got on all fours and he had been hammering away behind. Right before he was about to come he had pulled out, grabbed the back of her head, snapped the condom off and masturbated himself to a thudding, dramatic climax. Hot ribbons of bleachy ejaculate rained down on her.

He shouted. Grace remembered the words, dripping with disdain.

"Have… have this you whore!"

Head released and with ugly drips down her torso she tiptoed to the bathroom. He had gone while she was getting changed. Not so much as a goodbye, although she didn't care about the thank you.

She felt used. Abused somehow even though it had been a financially profitable encounter and one done (mostly) on her terms. He had just wanted a multimedia Dolby Surround High Definition 3D wank. She was merely the receptacle. The cum disposal unit.

That took some getting used to. It dehumanised the most human of acts and made Grace feel very alone. It took a couple of days to get over.

The train pulled in and Grace alighted, utterly on autopilot.

On one hand she felt a warm happiness inside Dylan had asked her out. But on the other hand straightaway there was a doubt.

What would he think if he knew?

And what possible future could they have if she had to lie to him, yet could not tell him?

TWENTY-TWO

Soundtrack

Electronic – 'Getting Away With It'

Dylan had come home empty-handed. He'd gone as far as walking through the door of the Pizza place but then turned on his heel smugly and walked out, much to the surprise of the Turkish guys behind the counter who already knew what he was going order.

Grinning to himself Dylan walked down the street toward the house. He did not need a pizza. Pizza made him fat and a fat Dylan would turn off Grace quickly. He needed to start looking after himself if he had any chance of looking after her.

Thoughts flashed through his mind. Where would he take her for the date?

There was nobody home and Dylan made himself a cup of tea. He planted himself down in the kitchen chair with a self-satisfied groan.

A packet of four pills lay in No Man's Land in the middle of the pockmarked kitchen table.

An unfamiliar plunging sensation dropped Dylan's stomach.

He would have to stop the gear. He would have to stop dealing. That was for sure.

But how could he support a lifestyle that included dating on what he earned from his 9/5 job?

What were the chances of a promotion and a major payrise from Atwater to soak up the difference?

Slimmer than you, Dylan old son.

*****

He'd gone to sleep alone and hungry out of choice. The alcohol brought rest to him quickly but it was short-lived.

Dylan was walking up a beach sluggish with the effects of a few Thai beers. The sand was studded with rocks. It was dusk but the sun was still high in the pink sky. The air was warm and Dylan could feel droplets of sweat running off him.

There was a sense of knowing something was going to happen before it did. Almost a self-conjuring, a self-determined event. Dylan stared out to sea as if he knew what was going to happen.

The horizon out to sea darkened as flocks of birds erupted out of the jungle in alarm. The darkening was accompanied by a far off whistling. Like a great wind. The rushing noise grew in volume and deepened in pitch as Dylan watched.

A great wave was coming.

Dylan swung his neck round mechanically like the turret of some machine to look for someone. Anyone. There was nobody about although Dylan could hear laughter and music from the resort behind him. He tried to scream and point at the horizon but could not make enough noise somehow.

The wave was huge. Its rolling face was webbed with white foam, the water underneath a dark and malevolent greyish blue that darkened all the time as Dylan stared. It captivated him.

It was many miles off but already loomed large over the spit of land jutting out below the hills either side of the bay. A sickening gurgling sound like a billion bathtubs draining at his feet dropped Dylan's gaze. The water was retreating under his feet, taking the sand, and in fact the whole beach, with it.

It melted under his footing.

Dying fish flapped around in the sand as Dylan's panic set in and he began to clamber up the slipping sands toward high ground. It shifted and voided below his footfalls and his legs began to burn with the effort. He had only gone a few metres when the fatalistic urge to look came again and he could not resist it somehow.

The wave seemed impossibly close now. It had to be dozens of metres high and was rising all the time as the seabed got shallower. It seemed to be heading right for him, right at the piece of beach he was attempting to flee from. The animalistic sound was now so deeply pitched he could barely hear it. It seemed to be roaring at him, roaring inside him. Cold air rushed across his cheeks as the wave pushed toward the beach, splintering the palm trees on the archipelago and hurling them aside like matchsticks. Yachts and boats in the bay were annihilated as the wall of water zeroed in. He could not run.

He could not escape.

This was his destiny, to die alone and helpless on this beach.

Smashed to pieces by a force of nature that hated him and judged him but somehow knew who he was and all the things he had done. The sun and starlight ceased like a light going out as the black juggernaut bore down, blotting out light with as much ease as it blotted out the hills and trees and boats and hotels. His clothes began to pull toward the wave as the sand beneath his feet threatened to drop him to the shifting surface to die on his knees. It sucked him towards his end.

A sharp pain.

Blackness.

Sweat, sheets sticking to him.

It took Dylan a few moments to realise where he was.

The bedroom air was cool but he was hot. The bedclothes lay in damp disarray around his legs and droplets of sweat trickled off his head. Raising himself weakly onto his elbows, he tried to slow his breathing. Something salty tainted his mouth. He had bitten his tongue again.

It never got any easier.

Dylan had started having the dream a couple of years ago and had it a couple of times over the course of the period before he lost his job, but several times since. The wave never hit him but it was just a matter of time. He knew this deep inside on a level he could not quite explain. He did not need a psychologist to figure out what it was about.

Fractured pieces of hot and listless sleep were all that would come afterwards and Dylan was actually in early for work after uncharacteristically giving up on the prospect of more sleep as the sunrise began to taint the tops of his curtains. The day at work went by in a slow-motion blur. A chocolate company was trying to market a new hazelnut bar and the creative types had been more obtuse than usual so Dylan was glad of the distraction.

Tired, with Grace surprisingly far from his mind, he got the train home after work, stopping for a medicinal chicken, avocado and bacon ciabatta with French fries on the way home.

Almost one hundred pills and several grams of various powders secreted themselves seemingly all by themselves on his person and in a flurry of professional phonecalls Dylan was up and out again by 9pm. 214 Bar in Whitechapel then LoveBean at Bass Factory. Tiredness tugged at his eyes.

The usual pre-club pints did little to wake him from his torpor and all a Red Bull and vodka managed to accomplish was revisit a metallic tang on his breath. The powders disappeared in short order in the bar as was always the way, and a lot of the pills went too.

He did not have the energy to do sweeps as was the normal modus operandi, so having found a CCTV blackspot with enough shadows to render reasonable doubt behind, Dylan stayed there and relied on people he knew. It was a good turnout as he knew it would be and regulars plus friends and associates of regulars were enough to keep things ticking over nicely. Dylan had hoped to drop all the pills before having to go to the club so he could have an early night and for a while it looked promising but as midnight approached more than thirty remained. Too many to dump, and far too many to take home.

Dylan made his way into the club alone and feeling oddly detached from everything. Bean came over to say hi. Claridge was away in Switzerland, Hetch lurked in the background. Shortly after Bean came back to ask if he had any pills. The transaction went smoothly. Thirteen left.

Dylan looked away to secrete the cash away in his zip pocket. He turned his head back.

Bean was peering into his cupped hand. Two of the pills were sat here, being poked and examined like some tiny creature. Dylan all at once realised Bean was much more drunk than he first appeared. His head was lolling and his movements exaggerated. A podgy forefinger continued to probe.

The smile dropped from Dylan's face.

They were far enough back from the front of the bar queue for the bar staff not to be able to see, though anyone stood nearby would be in absolutely no doubt. Worse, the lights for the dancefloor were right above, and every few seconds dazzling bright white light illuminated Bean and Dylan as the lights moved in time with the thunderous music.

Bean was muttering something vaguely enthusiastic but Dylan could not hear and felt no compulsion to lean in to find out. Suddenly changing his mind, Dylan stepped between Bean and the bar to make sure and got his body between the drunk man and the lights above. He was trying to close off Bean's impromptu drug examination session from public viewing. Bean was grinning inanely. He evidently recognised the pattern or logo stamp and had enjoyed the last dalliance with this specific batch. Dylan wondered whether the last one Bean had had and so clearly enjoyed had come from him.

It was hard to say. Luca was one of several wholesalers serving up these pills to hundreds of dealers like Dylan, made by the million in Europe, and it was not uncommon for people to ask if he had a specific type in his pocket.

Distracted, Dylan chanced a look around.

His breath was stolen from his chest.

A doorman was thirty feet away and staring right at him from the balcony above.

He felt the colour drain from his face. An icy bowling ball materialised in his gut.

He had to have seen him.

He surely must have seen him!

Pure, uncut terror gripped him. The bouncer had to have seen him. Dylan chanced a sideways look again. The bouncer was gone. This was either a good thing or a very very bad thing.

But he had to have seen him.

This had not happened to Dylan before and rational planning of eventualities never even registered. He knew he had to get out. But if he dropped the pills the bouncer could very easily find them, and his fingerprints were all over the baggy.

No, they have to be flushed. Bag and all.

Dylan drifted away from Bean without saying anything to him. Bean had just double dropped the pills in his hands and did not seem to notice him leaving. Hetch stepped in front and tried to say something but Dylan pretended not to see him and pushed past. The crowd swallowed him up before he could object.

The luminous sign for the toilets was like a blinding beacon. It was all Dylan could see. The throngs around seemed darker somehow, the disco lights washed out and irrelevant.

Walking as fast as he could without drawing more attention to himself he picked his way through the crowd of people. Dylan's mouth was dry. His sweaty fingers grasped for the baggy in his pocket.

Only another twenty feet.

It would be a fluid motion. Into the nearest open stall, shut the door, drop, flush, walk out, head for the exit and leave.

Ten feet.

He pulled the baggy into his palm, ready to drop.

Two feet.

Like a blind-siding truck the doorman stepped right out of his periphery. The force was enough to knock him sideways almost tripping but somehow staying upright. Another huge presence shunted hard from the back. Gaping, he felt two thick arms pin his own upwards from underneath. He pushed back but there was no movement. His hands were clasped together so tightly he wondered if his wrists might snap.

The looming, thundering guy from behind bodily lifted him up, his breath hot in the icy nape of Dylan's neck.

An enormous wave of pure, utter horror crashed over him. It crushed the air from his lungs as he was pressed hard under the water, his mouth flopping uselessly as he struggled for breath. His lungs were bursting. His heart was hammering so hard he was sure he would collapse. The doorman had him in a hold from behind and the other had prized apart his fingers and retrieved the baggy.

It was over.

He was done.

He was dead.

The doorman let him go from behind and they stood over him. He began gabbling. They ushered him roughly to a side room just a few feet away. The door closed behind and the sound seemed to stop. It was freezing, Dylan could almost see his breath. Then their hands were everywhere, in every crevice and pocket, patting and probing.

Shaking violently, Dylan did not resist.

A woman came in from another door. The bouncers pressed what they found into her hands and she placed them all into a red plastic tray, and gestured for Dylan to sit. He did so, not taking his eyes off the woman, but noticing for the first time the row of screens behind him, the sound management equipment, the PC and the water cooler. A huge gunmetal safe hulked in the corner.

Scrabbling from the tray yanked his gaze back. She was picking through his drugs. Dylan doubled over, hands on his knees and was about to retch when the woman passed him a bottle of mineral water.

"You alright mate?"

Her voice was calm and almost kindly in a way. It was too much for Dylan. The kindliness in her voice just too divisive and unexpected. He felt a huge pressure in his throat as the tears came. He was finished.

He kept his hands on his knees, crushed under the enormity and the enormous significance of what had just happened. A dry retch came up in his throat as the tears began to fall. Like a spring shower, a couple at first then he could not stop. The woman gently guided him to a torn office chair and proffered the water again. Realising he was shaking too much to accept it she placed it carefully on the tabletop.

Dylan was sobbing loudly, offering apology after futile apology as the woman went back to counting the contents of the tray. There were several baggies there though Dylan could not remember how much was there. The wedge of notes sat accusingly next to both his phones next to the tray. He was every inch the drug dealer she thought he was. Unmistakably so.

She asked him if he had any more drugs on him. Dylan made a show of searching all his pockets and coming up empty.

"its… I swear its.. personal I swear its personal…" he managed between deep racking sobs.

"Fucking big night for you then." She laughed.

It took Dylan a while to realize what she meant. Almost two dozen pills, a joint and a gramme of Charlie. That was, he had to admit, a very big night. The emotions shook him and he surprised himself by laughing long and hard, hysterically at the idea of one person doing that many pills in one night.

She laughed with him.

The laughter seemed to fortify him a little so he went for the water and sipped. The doors were locked. She was going to call the police. She has a job to do. Dylan saw no sense in being a cunt about things.

"I swear honest to God its all for me and my girlfriend she's not here yet." Dylan lied, spilling water down his top as he did so.

"Are you a member here mate?" she asked pleasantly.

Dylan passed her the laminated membership card with his photo and name on without thinking. She accepted and studied it closely. Two CCTV cameras in the ceiling scrutinised Dylan the whole time.

"So Dylan Short… not seen you here before, you are a semi-regular I guess, right?"

Dylan froze. He suddenly realized he would have to be very careful what he said to her as she would tell the Old Bill everything.

Yet at the same time, cooperation seemed like a very sensible strategy.

"My ex was one of the originals, this is only the third or fourth time I've been here. I swear to God I'm not a dealer…."

The woman gave nothing away but nodded slowly, still closely regarding the card.

"Two phones, a shitload of drugs, a shitload of notes and a missus who may or may not exist…" she ruminated out loud cynically.

Dylan felt his heart drop again. Despite the water his mouth was dry as the Sahara. He looked around. There were only two doors, the one behind was locked and in any case the bouncers would be on him in a minute flat if he could bolt for it. The door behind may have been locked, maybe it was not.

But where did it go?

He would have to get past the woman. She was not much older than him, plain but reasonably attractive. She was smaller than him and if he needed to he could probably knock her out.

For fuck's sake mate. You don't fucking hit girls. Since when did you start fucking doing that, you lowlife cunt. They have cameras anyway. You want to get another six months on top for beating up a woman? Prick.

She seemed oblivious to the fight and flight monologue going on inside Dylan's frantic subconscious.

Raising her eyes to his, she smiled disarmingly. She was just about to phone the Police, Dylan knew with absolute certainty. Maybe one of the doormen already had and the only thing waiting for him behind door number two was handcuffs, a ride in a police car and a life utterly at an end. Panic racked him again. He grimly realized he'd have no chance of knocking her out with hands shaking as much as his were, and that a rush for the door on legs that probably wouldn't hold him would be unlikely to end well. Desperate, he tried the last card he had.

"Look, I'm so so so so fucking sorry." He said for the thirtieth time.

"I swear to the Good Lord Almighty I am not a drug dealer. Please please can you arrange for your boys to give me a battering and I'll fuck off I swear.. I'll never come back and you'll never see me again and I'mnotadrugedealeriswearplease…"

She raised a hand to pacify him. Dylan stopped begging.

"We have a thirteen pill rule here Mister Dylan Short. That means…"

There it was.

He was done.

He was dead.

Dylan felt his bladder start to weaken.

"…that we're going to confiscate the gear and you cannot be here tonight. You can't be here, I'm sorry. We need you to leave."

Dylan flashed his eyes open in stunned shock.

She was holding out his phones, his wallet and the reams of cash.

He gaped.

She smiled reassuringly, obviously embarrassed at his utter and complete lack of dignity.

Still gaping, he wordlessly took his possessions. She rose and opened the second door via the locking bar. It slid open and beyond it was sky and streetlights.

Dare he hope?

Dare he?

He moved toward the light, toward his redemption. Still not daring to believe. Dylan could almost hear the sirens and the bootfalls of the coppers running toward the door to arrest him.

"Dylan?" she was calling him. About to break into a run, he turned and stopped.

Incredibly, unbelievably, she was holding out his membership card.

"Take care of yourself ok?" She said kindly.

*****

Dylan was sprinting.

Sprinting faster than he had ever done before. The streets and cars and rubbish streaked past. It was almost as if he was trying to outrun his own breath. The streets hurtled past in a blur of relief. He did not stop for four streets, until finally he broke down panting, sobbing, laughing and swearing. His legs gave way and his sprawled on the floor.

How the fuck had he got away with that?

When did that happen? Most clubs had a four or six pill rule and were obliged under their licensing laws to inform the police. He had heard of people who had heard of people getting arrested and charged with possession of a Class A substance for one pill in their pocket. He would have been charged with intent to supply, no doubt about it at all.

If she had phoned the police as she had to do, as she must do, but as she somehow did not do, he would have been charged and found guilty of intent to supply. That many pills, coke and a joint would certainly had led to them searching his room and there was enough there to ensure he would do years not months. Life, ended. Gone. Finito. Bust. Disintegration.

Dylan ran his tongue along his teeth. They were all there. He was still there. His life was still alive!

Shaking his head he got to his feet.

"I cannot believe it. I cannot fucking believe it. I cannot. Believe. It."

The words were discombobulated somehow. It sounded like someone stood next to him saying it. His eyes seemed glassy somehow, the vista of the dirty streets of London replete with sheen of rain, clothes of litter and inhabitants of the night seemed beautiful. It had a fuzziness to it like when film producers put filters over camera lenses sometimes to make things look prettier.

He walked quickly and with purpose to the tube station, savouring the smell of dry air and track grease as he got down to the platform. The whole time he was muttering under his breath.

I fucking cannot fucking believe it.

“Fucking….. yes.”

Carla was in when he got home. For some reason he elected not to tell her of the night's happenings and instead sat with her on the sofa watching Californication. They got through a bottle of Jack Daniels between the two of them, drinking it neat and without ice like actors do in the movies.

Carla was already drunk when he got there and seemed to know something major had happened to him, regarding him with care and concern with wet, tired eyes. They laughed at the TV together in that loud, off-kilter way drunk people do, and when Carla fell asleep she snuggled into his side like a little sister.

Dylan turned off the TV and stared at the screen still luminescing slightly in the darkness as it cooled down. He swept away the last two inches of whiskey slowly with deliberation. He was determined to savour it, to make the day last. For it to have more meaning somehow.

Was it just an eerie coincidence that he had had the dream then had the nightmare, so to speak?

Did it mean anything? Was it a sign? Was it merely the universe telling him what he already knew?

The monolithic trauma of the experience still laid raw across him. He relieved the breathless existential terror, momentarily halted his breath as he recalled it. It had been the single scariest experience of his life. He had never experienced anything like it, pure horror. It made him feel emotional and the Jack Daniels broke down enough barriers for tears to form again. This time he was unable to beat them back in the darkness with Carla breathing noisily against him.

A decision began to form the moment he moved desperately through the club exit door and had been hardening like concrete ever since. The decision was made. He could not go through that again. He honestly did not think he had it in him. The dealing had to stop.

I fucking mean it this time.

TWENTY-THREE

Soundtrack

Crowded House – 'The Private Universe'

The door had fingerprints in grease on it.

Grace had knocked softly twice and there was no answer. The door was a huge wood effort in a very smart corridor. The block was a smart one down from London Bridge not far from Borough Market. The customer was a new guy. He had been terse and distracted when he phoned, as if he was trying to keep the conversation private, which was entirely understandable under the circumstances. She had a phial of pepper spray in her coat pocket and another in her handbag for visits like these.

She was about to knock again when she became aware of a movement on the other side of the huge door and at once a clicking and ratcheting as the door was unlocked.

It swung open and Grace was reminded of one of those old over-dramatised films about Transylvania and Frankenstein's monster. She was smiling, expecting the man beyond to be Uncle Fester.

It was dark, she stepped in. He was average build, average size and turned his back on her before she could greet him. Shaking her head, she shut the door behind her. The flat was dark. Up ahead the man was beckoning her to follow.

They passed a couple of closed doors and into a dimly lit bedroom at the end of the hallway.

He ushered in past, fussing after her, holding out hands to take her coat. In the light she saw he was perhaps fifty, with strained features across a slightly pinched face. He was not a good looking man but not ugly either. He looked like a civil servant, she decided. They sat down together on the bed and at last he spoke to her. His voice was low and guarded.

"Hello Nadia. You can call me Mike. Please keep your voice down."

Grace shook her head in befuddlement but said nothing, tipping her head to one side arching an eyebrow.

"My wife is asleep in the room next door. She is bed-ridden, a stroke last year."

Grace had to wipe away the disbelief on her face to replace with a mask of sympathy and actually genuine concern.

"I'm really sorry..." was all she could conjure up.

"Mike isn't my real name you understand."

Grace almost laughed out loud but nodded slowly.

"She's bed ridden and sleeps for 15 hours a day. Hence why I called you." The voice was barely a whisper.

Before Grace could argue he thrust a wedge of notes in embarrassment toward her, unable to meet her gaze. With as much grace as possible she accepted it and secreted it in her handbag. When she looked up he was heading for the door. At first Grace thought he might leave the room but instead he silently made sure the door was locked and then to her amazement switched the dimmed overhead light off.

The room was very dark. Her eyes too a second or two to get used to the deeper gloom. Amber streetlights outside the window afforded only the barest of illumination.

Mike stood in front of her, getting undressed, texting at the same time. His features were underlit by the screen of his phone. He snapped it shut and Grace could not make out his features in the half light. In her imagination he was leering at her and she fought off a wave of panic. For the first time it occurred to her that she was out of her element and potentially in some danger.

Then her phone vibrated.

"Get that." he ordered quietly.

Puzzled, she picked her phone out from the bottom of her bag as it nestled next to her pepper spray.

Sure enough, she had a text.

It was from Mike.

What the actual fuck....?

Nadia, I am very nervous so do not want to ask in person. There is a vibrator under the pillow and I want you to penetrate me with it. Please put two fingers inside yourself and rub them under my nose before you do. As I stated please keep the noise down as my wife is sleeping and she must not wake up. Thank you, Mike.

Grace snapped into action. It all made sense now.

She got down to her underwear and gestured for Mike to get onto the bed. He did so stiffly and hesitantly. She spent a few minutes running her hands over his back and shoulders eliciting not the slightest reaction from him. She reached under the pillow and sure enough a contoured, girthy seven inch dildo lay there expectantly. When she turned back to Mike he was on all fours, pointing his rear end toward her.

There was no lubricant to hand so she spat softly in her hand, caressing his buttock with her other, and then rubbed it over the end of the vibrator. She twisted the end and it sprang to life in her hand. She could have sworn she felt Mike shudder as she did so. It sounded horrifically loud in the darkness and for a second she wondered whether it was too loud and perhaps Mike's wife might hear it from the other room. Mike shuffled up the bed a little and began nuzzling a pillow.

Remembering her instructions Grace slipped two fingers inside the elastic of her knickers.

The situation could not have been less sexual for her and she allowed herself a long, luxuriant few seconds of up and down touching to bring about any degree of wetness below. Very gently one then the other fingers slipped inside and she allowed another few seconds as if trying to soak up the moisture.

Vibrator in one hand, fingers forth in the other she moved in behind Mike who was nuzzling and whimpering softly in the darkness. Leaning over she thrust the fingers in front of his nose, wiping the moisture across his top lip. Mike responded by emitting the strangest high-pitched whine she had ever heard, muffled by the pillow. Shaking her head smiling broadly in the darkness at the sheer silent lunacy of it, she nudged the tip of the vibrator against the darkest of dark areas in front of her. The whining got higher and more insistent as she played harder and harder.

He moved both hands in front and began to violently rub himself, almost hitting himself as he did so.

Mike mumbled something and Grace asked to repeat it as the punching and swiping gathered pace and ferocity up front. He muttered something snatched away by the force of the whisper and he almost snarled in desperation as he repeated himself a third time.

"SPIT ON ME!!!"

What? Seriously?

He was going to come. She reached forward again to rub her fingers over his nose and was alarmed as he took them both into his mouth, wheedling and suckling like a piglet.

His breathing was getting ragged. He was not far away. Taking her cue from the pounding he was giving himself up front she gathered pace and thrust at the back. Mike's pitchy whining was lost in the pillow as he ground his face hard into the down, saliva and sweat making the material face wet and sticky.

He arched his back up as if on strings, backing hard into her driving right hand.

The whining again. It rose in pitch, constantly this time. Grace was fighting back giggles as Mike shook and shuddered. A messy, painful orgasm was just a few seconds away.

You've got to be fucking kidding me mate...seriously?

Getting creative, Grace indulged him and spat as disdainfully and dismissively as she could. The crescendo when it arrived soon after was silently spectacular, like the peak of some epic last record at a silent disco. He came with a squeak that very much sat with her piglet observation of earlier. She stood up and put her hands on her hips.

Mike was crying quietly into his pillow. Her spit was glistening in the streetlights, rolling lazily off his stomach and onto the sticky mess of the duvet below.

The vibrator hummed away uselessly, jutting out of Mike's rear end like the remnants of some weird train crash.

Grace stifled a giggle. She patted him affectionately on the buttock expecting him to get up or do something at least, but the sobs continued and he showed no signs of moving.

Nodding in amused acceptance Grace put on her clothes and left. The whole thing had taken less than seven minutes.

The guffaws of laughter could not be stopped as she headed out into the rain. She chuckled to herself all the way to the tube station and when she settled into her seat on the train pulled out her phone. A pang of sadness came over her, stopping the giggles as she realised she could not share what had just happened with any of her friends. All of a sudden she felt very lonely.

Laying shirtless on his bed, Dylan was in contemplative mood. The text had come out of the blue.

Carla heard through the grapevine that Crabby was gone.

He had been travelling back from a rave in Northampton with two other guys they did not know. The car had apparently been hit head on by another car and all three had died instantly. The driver of the other car had also died. Four people snuffed out in an instant. It was almost too huge to process.

Dylan was numb. It was a strange sadness. He found himself filled with regret. As much for not having had that last pill and cup of tea with the old man as for anything.

The old man had lived a long and happy life. It was maybe a better death than a slow lingering spectre of cancer or the agony of a massive heart attack, but there was a suddenness to it that had a savagery of its own. He was a proud man. He would not be robbed of his clarity and vision by Parkinson's or Alzheimers. The drugs would not get him.

But the loss was keen nonetheless. Dylan remembered his eight cats. Carla did not know what would become of them. He found himself short of breath and with eyes running with salty tears as he imagined them alone.

He fervently hoped they would be taken care of. Carla had come to sit on his bed and he had hopefully talked about adopting one or maybe two, but Carla and Jason were apparently not in favour.

The afternoon dragged on. Scrutiny of the ceiling, eating HobNobs and the very lacklustre singing along to the choruses of rock classics was largely a blocking tactic, as any meaningful thought on what was on his mind would engender that restlessness where music and food had no appeal.

Dylan made an informed decision to try to put Crabby out of his mind, but never to forget about him.

There were other things that required his attention.

The metaphorical elephants in the room were the memory of his recent trauma alongside the prospect of his date the following evening, and although he was looking forward to it, the nerves threatened to rob him of the bitter-sweet anticipation. He had rushed his date proposal to Grace and blushed his way though a strange goodbye after that. She had taken his number but the look in her eyes was one of pity and he could tell that she was not going to call him. Never in a million years.

It came as something of a shocker therefore when, the following day, at a polite hour just before midday, Grace had sent a short but unequivocal offer to take him up on the offer of another drink by text. Resisting the urge to go charging into the kitchen to tell Carla and Jason, he stood up instinctively, clutching his phone so tight that his fingers went white, then sat down again breathing hard on the end of his bed, staring blankly at the screen.

She actually called him. Well fuck me.

*****

Grace hurried through the rain. The wind prodded at her overcoat and sought to get inside her protective layer like some hostile sex offender. Her hair was tied back in a ponytail because anything else would be futile in this wind. She had a tight transfer across London after her mid-afternoon client had overrun by no fewer than three hours. Although he had tipped her extremely handsomely she was subsequently in a rush to make her nine o'clock in Canning Town.

The afternoon guy had been generous with the champagne and at first she was lightheaded and mirthful, but now that she was battling the freezing wind and lashing rain outside, the onset of a headache had begun to manifest itself. She felt the three glasses of Veuve boil and bubble inside her, without any food to calm her down, and wondered if maybe she should try and be sick before the next client so her mind would be clear and not focussed on her loudly, she imagined, rumbling stomach. As there was no time, she resorted to her emergency Snickers bar that had been at the bottom of her Tardis-like handbag for a considerable period of time.

Once on board the DLR train the Snickers bar disappeared in short order and her mind flicked to the client to come.

She had only met him once before, several months ago, and she strained to remember what his "thing" was. Every bloke had a "thing" - even if it was just vanilla-style missionary, although only a very tiny and timid minority of her customers preferred that. Most had rather deeper and more rangy aspects of their sexual character in which she was able to allow them to indulge themselves. His vanilla-ness was a perfect juxtaposition from the dark, silent weirdness from the night before. It relieved her somehow. But a little tiny part of her was bored. The weird shit amused her. Last night had not been the first time she had giggled her way home.

Nowt so queer as folk.

Some girls referred to themselves as Practical Sex Therapists and Grace had some sympathy for that point of view.

The straight-laced populace, struggling to reconcile their tastes and needs to their social requirement had always been belabouring under a veil of secrecy in terms of what went on behind closed doors. It was the great cliché of British society not just in the 21st century but down through the ages.

British men have always been repressed in terms of their sexuality and sexual needs, but Grace had become aware over the last few months that it was what was not going on behind closed doors that was most notable. Most of her clients asked for things they would never ask their wives, spouses, partners or girlfriends for.

Most, Creepy Simon notwithstanding, had at least one significant other, and came to her more for relief than anything else. To be able to indulge themselves fully everyone participating seems to fully understand that the veil of secrecy had to come down. Men only liked to do that when they had paid for it. Money changing hands meant they were in control and genuinely did not care whether Grace judged them or not.

The fact that Grace made a point of marking what went on with a touch of tenderness, not to mention approval from some well-timed sexual moaning and the odd squeal, was what made her good at her job. If she was honest the duality and the subversiveness of it all appealed to her almost as much as the money and the self-reliance thing. It merely was a reflection her own life and she had long been of the opinion that everyone had secrets, and everyone has a side that never sees daylight.

In her case this aspect was true at that moment as the night was pitch black. The lights of the DLR stations were painfully bright against the sopping, howling darkness.

Orange and gold droplets of water specked the windows of the driver-less train as it rattled and jolted its way to Canning Town. All around her the scattering of people in the same carriage looked like characters out of a modernist painting depicting a rainstorm night in East London. Thick coats, scarves, hats and the like formed odd 3D shapes rather than people, with a watery blur of flesh at the front, and a wash of colour of shopping bags on one side. Nobody looked up. They preferred to stare dejectedly at the grubby floor slick with rainwater reflecting the bright fluorescent lights in the carriage. The shapes moved in passive reaction to the bumps of the train, silent except for the tinny clicking of a youth sat in the corner seat across two chairs listening to his music at ear-damagingly high volume.

It was as if he was wishing that the gangster RnB might chase the cold and misery of London away and instil some California sunshine and solidarity, instead of the rather lonely vigil he alone was making aboard a late DLR to Mudchute.

There was nothing glorious or song-worthy about that, Grace mused, as her station flickered into view through the streaked windows and she rose. Ten minutes later she was stood outside a nondescript flat in Canning Town ringing a buzzer. For a horrible moment she wondered if the client might have gotten annoyed with her lateness and gone out instead, as the buzzer went unanswered for two presses. On the third, a low male voice snapped out a greeting and the door hummed into life, opening for her using two out-of-sight electric motors.

Another ten minutes and Grace was sat in one of her most drearily familiar poses, sitting on the edge of an unfamiliar bed waiting for the client to come out of the bathroom. She had given him oral sex, and with a £100 extra charge, had agreed to do so without the use of a condom. This was something she ordinarily did not like doing but at £100 it made good business sense for something that she was going to do anyway. It took half the time. And it wasn't as if (well washed beforehand) cock tasted much worse than rubber and spermicide anyway, she reasoned. She had a small vial of anti-bacterial spray which she discreetly discharged into her mouth before she went down and this should, she reasoned with zero basis in scientific fact, be enough to fend off any fleeting encounter with anything nasty he might be able to give her by mouth.

The client had come inside one minute and almost choked her when he gave an involuntary surge right at the point of climax. She had closed her mouth and let the stalagmites of pearly ejaculate drip down her chin and onto her breasts, which was something the clients tended to like, and was infinitely preferable to having to swallow.

Some things money cannot buy, and that was one of a very short list as far as Grace was concerned.

She had darted off to the toilet to rinse off the still-warm goo while the breathless client, full of platitudes and implausible statements riven solely from a mind still racing from a sexual encounter, had gone to fix her a glass of wine and put some music on. By the time she had emerged from the bathroom, he was stood there with two glasses of wine, one in each hand, with a thin string of come moving slowly towards the expensive-looking carpet from the tip of his still erect member. Stifling a laugh at the incongruity of the scene, she took the wine and told him jokingly to get cleaned up.

She was away and into the night inside the hour with a massive wedge of scruffy notes as he had paid in a series of aged tenners and fivers, as if he had just raided the back of his sofa. Either way, cash is cash and money is good, or so the saying went, and spraying her little anti-bacterial mouth spray as she went, her mind flickered. Another working day was done, now to think about more comforting things.

Dylan. The guy off the tube. He was a nice guy, she could tell.

Up front. And yet with a darker, secretive side to him that

appealed to her and made her distrustful at the same time. He was rather bigger than she would normally go for, and the teeth were something she was initially rather taken aback by, but still, there was something about the man which, despite her cautious nature, she liked. He was fat. This was inescapable. He was likely beyond fixing up in the gym either, in the short-term anyway. Although he carried it well across broad shoulders and she had an odd fixation with his arms which were large and tattoo-free. She liked men with no tattoos.

She had made a decision that she would let him down gently at the end of the night when they first met as it was obvious that he liked her and yet when it came to do the letting down gently part, the words would not come. Instead of cutting it off there and then, she had taken his number and given him hope. And yet, still, as a resolution not to text came and went, then a positive resolution to text to let down gently also came and went, she found herself oddly compelled to just go for a drink. Where was the harm?

She liked him, and he was a nice guy. She knew all too well that there were almost none of those around.

Stepping onto the same DLR platform she vacated just over an hour previously, she turned over the strange man in her head, ruminating on what she liked about him for about the fiftieth time since they met in the bar a couple of days ago. He was funny in a funny way, serious in a funny way as well, and had an air of confidence about him that was belied by his rather self-deprecating humour and obvious attempt at irony in his shambolic attempt to actually ask her out.

He was an interesting guy who asked questions which she was able to answer truthfully and not too many where she had to lie. Most of all he seemed keen on her as a person and if he was interested in her body, he had kept any lecherous gazing largely stealthy, and she appreciated that. She also appreciated that he let her walk first, opened doors, gave her drinks before everyone else and was generally a gentleman in his manners. How rare that was!

Grace was not a feminist, nor was she one of those women who writes into the free London Papers bemoaning the death of chivalry in general and the fact that nobody would stand up for her or her pregnant mate on the tube every day. A cursory glance as a soiled copy of the London Lite on the empty seat next to her reminded her again. She did like to be treated like a lady though, and she had always felt that deep down only the most bitter of wounded females do not like the same thing.

What occasionally amused her was how clients tried to treat her like they thought a lady should, but get it all wrong because the lady was a tramp.

Champagne and poured-honey compliments are all well and good but the odd opened door here and there never went amiss.

It rarely happened with her clients. Perhaps it was a subconscious thing. Where the whore is in control and she does not need a door opened for her. Or maybe it was a case of the whore being in control and that he needs to be first through the door to assert some kind of passive dominance over a proceedings in which he could never hope to be the true governing force. That was number two on the aforementioned very short list of things according to Grace Freeman, which money could not buy. Dylan was, it seemed, almost the opposite. Submissive and respectful in his actions but retaining an unspoken, barely-hinted at dominance which manifested itself very rarely but was always there, in her mind anyway. That excited her.

It would be easy to say that Grace decided to text Dylan to go for a drink after seeing an arthouse picture of two people kissing in the rain, or that she saw an advert for a couples resort in the Caribbean. Prone though she was to occasional bouts of couply brooding, it really was just a whim. She was at home, chatting to Barney as was often the case, and was texting Carol, another of her Uni friends, to say congratulations on her Masters degree when she flicked past Dylan's number and just texted him. Right in the middle of a plate of scrambled egg on toast.

It was rather un-Grace, and that excited her too.

Remembering the curt, rather surgical text she sent Dylan, right there in the DLR carriage, she opened her phone to read it again.

DRINK SOUNDS GREAT. HAD GREAT TIME LAST NIGHT AND WAS GOOD TO SEE YOU. HOW DOES NEXT WEDNESDAY SOUND. Grace . X

She cringed.

Who forgets to put in question-marks? And the use of the word "great" twice in three words. Badly written but it got the point across, she conceded.

After the nonsense with the online dating thing, she tended to feel that the less time spent on writing things to attract or otherwise communicate with members of the opposite sex, the better. The more she thought about it the worse it got. She snapped shut her phone with a smile, got it half way to a damp coat pocket when she suddenly moved it back up to her eyeline, flicking open the phone as she went, thumb already pressing the menu button to see the reply Dylan sent her. It had arrived about two hours after she had texted him, and she wondered if it was that his phone was in his jacket pocket and he was in a meeting or something, or that he was keen but did not want to appear overly so.

The reply read rather better than hers, she had to admit.

Excellent. I had a top night as well and it was so lovely to speak to you. Amazing that you are mates with Carla and Lou! What a mad coincidence! Drinks next week sounds cool. I'm looking forward to it already. Have a great weekend if I don't speak to you and I'll call you next week to organise. D x

Grace wondered briefly, perhaps cynically, if his reference to "great weekend" was him mocking her poor use of English in her text, then dismissed it. She smiled at his enthusiastic reply, reading it for about the fiftieth time since she had received it.

She had a date.

With a man.

Who was not paying for her company (but would be paying for dinner probably). That excited her too.

TWENTY-FOUR

Soundtrack

Deep Dish feat. Tracey Thorn – 'Future Of The Future (Stay Gold)'

Dylan was on his way back into London after a long and completely forgettable Monday trip to Glasgow for a work seminar. He had risen before the sun with a creaking walk to the bathroom. He was barely conscious until the first cup of coffee of the day at Heathrow Terminal Five and felt something like normal by the time the British Airways Airbus touched down in Scotland an hour later.

The seminar was lengthy and extremely boring, with the room hot and close. He nearly fell asleep several times that afternoon. Hands shaken and cards exchanged with toothy and completely false promises of further communication, Dylan got back to the airport early and spent more than an hour idly watching the planes from the window, already unable to remember the finer and more useful aspects of the seminar.

The flight home was just as forgettable, the highlight being him offering his tuna mayonnaise sandwich to an elderly lady next to him who had absolutely inhaled hers and looked like she had not eaten in a week. Despite her initial refusal, she eventually relented and Dylan was gratified to see her inhale his sandwich as well. Dylan did not eat tuna and it would have ended up in the bin which was a sad waste of such a magnificent fish, Dylan considered. He had spent the rest of the flight forcing the old lady to help him out with a packet of butter toffees in his bag, enjoying the smiling and the gratitude.

Grace was on his mind, and he was forming a plan of attack in terms of venue and strategy of how best to maximise the potential of his short allotted time for drinks with The-Girl-In-The-Pink-Overcoat.

Breezing past the arrivals halls stopping only to hail a fortuitously passing black cab, Dylan began to unwind from his day. The traffic was quite heavy as always and Dylan slumped in the back of the noisy taxi taking in the scenes and trying to relax. London always fascinated him but it was funny: you have to leave the city and come back in order to recognise it. He had lived there for some time and actually grew up not far away, but it was a fascination for him nonetheless. Dylan retreated further into the seat and closed his eyes. His own aftershave caught his nostrils and he luxuriated in the deep, citrus and sandalwood smell of something expensive from Liberty in Regents Street.

Dylan always liked to smell nice. He wanted the nice suits, the nice cars, the nice watch, expensive meals, and exotic holidays, but these things were badly defined dreams and ideals for him and all indicative of a wider need for acceptance and love. Still, Dylan liked to have the nice things in life, and this was one of the reasons he took up drug dealing in the first place. He had a nice(ish) watch, the designer jeans, the few pairs of deadstock Adidas trainers and the nice mobile phone. One of the things that annoyed him about life was those obviously highly materialistic people who swore blind that they wanted for none of these things.

Some of them claimed the ultimate cliché: that love was all they needed. Dylan was never a big fan of the Beatles.

The cab made its staccato way up into West London, into the main arteries of the city, and he unconsciously sat up in his seat and straightened his coat. The cab swerved hard into a bus lane and came to a halt. With a click the doors unlocked and Dylan stuffed some notes and some coins into the driver's palm, which were swapped with a scrawled receipt in red pen bizarrely reminiscent of Carla's incomprehensible scrawl. Almost forgetting his laptop case, he got out of the cab in front of Earl's Court, the neon lights bright and clear in the wet darkness. He cast a smiling glimpse over in the direction of Stamford Bridge stadium as he passed down the stairs and into the sublevel underground system. He surfaced again in North London, having travelled a long way to Tufnell Park.

Nonchalantly, Dylan tapped his Oystercard on top of the barriers and stepped out into the rain. It was one of those days when you sensed it didn't really want to rain but it had a quota to keep up and was sort of apologetic about it.

The walk up the residential street took a few short minutes. Dylan knocked and rang the bell. A police car screeched past, and he wondered if Luca or Antonio had heard his bell over the din.

Antonio cracked the door and waved him in.

Luca was sat in his underwear on the sofa, eating a bowl of Frosties. He did not rise to embrace Dylan but gestured for him to sit down as the shook his hand. Pleasantries were exchanged and seemed warmer somehow given that Antonio was out of the room. Luca almost looked like a normal guy. Apart from the gold teeth.

Dylan regarded him with the usual mix of cynicism and a little bit of fear. He noticed Luca had skinned knuckles and considered making a comment but came up short in the bravery stakes.

"Where you off out to tonight then?" Luca asked, being as conversational as Dylan had noted him for a while. It was unnerving.

Dylan smiled. "Carla and Jase are off out but I've got a date tomorrow so I'm at home doing some work and chilling. Quite fancy a night in. They are off to see Steve Lawler tonight… he was fucking awesome, you remember last time we saw him…when was that?" his voice tailed off.

"I was with you, we went back to Ollie's…" Luca's voice sounded far away and cautious, as if he did not remember.

Dylan remembered the state everyone was in at Oliver's house after that night, perhaps two years ago and winced inside. It was probably the last time Luca had been out on a proper night out with them and had been the first and last time Dylan had tried GHB.

That was a different time and he wanted different things now. The Battlestar Galactica box set at home was unopened still and perhaps he needed time to think, to take stock. He needed to think about Grace, and about their date. Where would he take her? How should he play it?

His mind drifted away again.

"…never, not really anyway, just enough to keep it going like, just enough. You know what I mean?" Luca laughed mirthlessly, rapping his knuckles on the TV remote.

"Totally mate, just enough, yeah" Dylan lied.

That happened a lot these days. He would slip off into a dreamworld, remembering how things used to be and how things ought to be and keep chiselling away at resolutions of what to do with his life. These were towering decisions and took a long time of sustained thought and consideration to weigh up. These great convoys of thoughts like the road train trucks in the Australian outback tended to have a catalyst. His date with Grace was most certainly that.

Endless questions.

Luca had turned his back on him, still chatting away to him.

Dylan did not have a clue what Luca was talking about. He stopped listening all at once and switched off again, as the near-naked gangster wannabe man in front of him mumbled away about something. His concentration slipped again and he paused to glance around the flat. Luca was probably high. Weed always made him chattier than normal (although this was not exactly difficult) and it would certainly explain the Frosties.

Dylan took in his surroundings and sure enough, an ashtray with a pipe laying in it sat in the shadows by the sofa foot.

Imminently after the natural end of the pleasantries, Luca saw him to the door.

Just as it was about to open, he felt a large hand on his upper arm. Luca's face was just a few inches from his, and his eyes gleaming in the half-light. His demeanour was completely different.

"Little birds telling me you had some trouble at Bass Factory. Anything you want to fucking tell me about?"

His voice was little more than a whisper, dripping malice. There was no implication about it; Luca was very serious.

Dylan was taken aback and lost his cool. He stammered and then tried a forced laugh to show he was not bothered. It came out pathetically fake and desperate.

"You heard about that? Fucking harsh man. Fucking Bean picking over the goods in the open, got intercepted on the way to the Gents and got lifted. Didn't have much on me but still. Got kicked out with a kicking and a warning. Lucky really but there you go..."

Luca didn’t say anything, just kept on regarding him in the darkness. He was getting really good at this scary drug dealer schtick, Dylan had to admit.

Finally he spoke.

"Ya have to be more careful Dylan. Lucky lucky lucky..."

His accent was almost impenetrable. The eventual smile was sharkish, all teeth with a flash of gold. There was no humour. It was all threat. Luca had every right to be worried. Had Dylan been arrested he would certainly have rolled on Luca in an attempt to avoid prison, and Luca knew this as well as Dylan did. Dylan had considered it for endless dark hours since. What did they do on those cop shows? Make him wear a wire and admit to conspiracy to traffic? Testify in court? Even if he had a tougher time associating these dramatic Americanisms with London’s (other) Finest boys (and girls) in blue, he was very clear in his mind that he would have done anything they had asked.

Dylan started right into Luca's dark eyes.

He knew it.

Wordlessly, blessedly, the door swung open and Luca softly closed it behind him as he walked out into the dank London evening. The rain was still coming down. Luca's words echoed in his head and he cursed himself for not thinking that Luca might find out. He did not blame Luca for being worried, sinister doorstep shit notwithstanding. Hopefully Luca would forget about it now.

He was right, to be fair to the wanker. Lucky indeed. Dylan still could not quite believe it.

Uncomfortable with the rehash of his dodged bullet, Dylan felt in need of escapism. With still shaking hands he plugged in his headphones and selected some uplifting house to listen to on his journey home.

House music. Curry. Travelling. Cooking. Gregariousness in everything that he did. Spending time with people he liked and who liked him. As the rain came down, slicking the pavement, Dylan took in his surroundings. Rows of locked and alarmed parked cars lined up around the corner on one side, with locked and alarmed shutters and sturdy doors on the other, Dylan remembered how important these things were to him.

The bag of drugs in his suit jacket pocket burned against his shirt as if it were glowing.

It seemed to glow hotter and less comfortably in light of recent events and in harsher light of Luca's words.

The dealing put all the things he loved at risk, as and that was why he wanted to stop, but why should he not enjoy himself?

These were days that he knew he would never repeat. These were days to earn money and enjoy himself. Young, streetwise, smart, self-educated and not short of money, it was a time in his life where all things took a back seat to his primary mission, which was to take life and enjoy it for what it was. The man walking down those rainy streets totally immersed in his own private pool of jabbing, percussive house music was not stupid. Even if he often thought he was.

Those days could never last forever but the endgame, the final twists and turns of this stage of his life were to be welcomed. And at that moment he felt no fear of the change that was coming. Like a dance record that builds and builds, his mind was filled with anticipation of what was to come. In many ways, he realised, his life was similar to the song he was listening to. The song builds from percussive, simplistic, easy-to-understand beginnings and matures as it grows.

The breaks come. The breaks come, again, and again, and it loses something by natural process, and when you used to it and stop listening to the song, then its time to change the record.

But that evening, there in the wet and cold streets of a dark North London, amongst the cars, the shutters and the bus shelters there was at least one tired soul still reaching for the lights and smiling inside.

The song began to mix out and a new record started to come in. The time for a new record was at hand. With that, his mind flicked back to The-Girl-In-The-Pink-Overcoat.

Dylan wondered, as he descended into the harsh lights of the underground station whether he would ever stop referring to her as that, or moreover, if he would ever tell her that was what he called her.

She'll probably think I'm mental.

*****

There was a movement, of some kind of presence in her coat pocket. Numbed hands darted for the woollen flap and pulled out the warm phone inside.

Hi there hope you are well. Just wanted to check that you were still on for tonight. Looking forward to seeing you again – is seven PM at The Brewers Arms in Angel ok with you? See you later on. Dx

Grace spent two long, listless minutes staring at the text.

It dawned on her not that she was meeting Dylan, but that she was meeting a guy not for work. A date. Not work. An actual date. A personal liaison.

Suddenly terrified that she would have to tell him the truth she got half way through a cancellation text before she thought better of it.

She was on the way to a lunchtime client. Her mind was a jumbled mess of indecision and unanswered questions as she stepped off the bus at Angel, glancing obliquely at the aforementioned pub across the road, and headed into the underground station, followed by a bitter winter wind. The tube journey was a relief, and gave her time to think about the date. She had felt happy and almost excited at the prospect of a date with Dylan previously but his text had brought the reality home to her, and dredged up a muddy sediment of feelings and worries.

With a jolt just as the train slammed into Redbridge station she realised again, for the thirtieth time that she liked Dylan because he was honest and that in order for them to have anything she would have to lie to him.

Wouldn't she? Did she know that?

Was it certain? Could she lie to him?

Was she prepared to do that, and did she care enough about Dylan or what she could have if things might, against all fighting odds work out with him, and what was she expecting anyway?

She did not ever remember making a conscious observation that Dylan might amount to something more than the casual, if amusing, encounter in the bar the other night. A date was a date but when did the prospect of a relationship raise its head? She marvelled at how far she could progress in terms of thinking and ruminating on a issue without actually thinking about it directly. It had sneaked up on her, she realised with a wry grin.

So was she going to meet him or not? It took her a while to figure it out, but eventually she came to a decision because she could not make one outright, and so decided to postpone the decision. Decisions were supposed to be decisive. Feeling oddly indecisive, she resolved out of curiosity and an inability to cancel in coherent English to meet him anyway and see how things went. She texted him back as she walked up the client's driveway in a suburban line of detached and semi-detached houses in the far north east of London.

Tonight great. Looking forward to seeing you. I'll be in the pub from six. Hugs. Grace x

There is that "great" thing again. I fucking overuse that word! I sound like a twat.

*****

The client was a middle-aged, angular man named Leo with an indeterminate accent from somewhere east of Canterbury. She was buzzed up to his flat and shown into the lounge. She was all smiles.

Leo was undressed quick as a flash as soon as money had changed hands and seemed disinterested in her so much as taking her coat off. He almost threw a condom at her and lay back on the bed. To her astonishment, a woman emerged from the bathroom with a quizzical look of something that might have been malice on her face.

"Ignore her. That's my wife. She's been a naughty little bitch and so needs to watch me fuck you like she fucked Nigel Staplehurst."

Grace stopped dead.

The woman eyed her coldly and she held eye-contact for a few seconds.

"Do you want more money?" she asked finally.

"No…. erm its ok." Grace stammered.

The woman's gaze unsettled her and all at once Grace realised the gaze was not one of anger or resentment but of extreme sexual arousal.

Grace stepped out of her skirt and deftly unclipped her bra. The condom snapped on and she went to work with her mouth, making sure the woman sat in the dressing chair behind had a good look at her from behind as she did so.

The woman sat behind her started to moan and Grace chanced a quick glance behind. She was firmly pleasuring herself with a substantial sex toy of some sort as she viewed her husband's infidelity on the bed in front. Leo below pushed her off and rolled away. Before she could react Grace was on all fours and the heaving, snuffling mess behind was nudging against her sex. Then it came, softly and surprisingly tenderly at first then harder. Soon he was thrusting with all his might as his wife's moans and screamed reached a crescendo behind. He grabbed her shoulder savagely battering in and out. Grace squeaked a warning but it was too late – Leo was climaxing and by the sounds of it so was his wife.

"You fucking BITCH!" he yelled.

Grace was unsure which of the women Leo was referring the pejorative insult to but did not really care. Ten minutes later she was fully clothed and walking down the street toward the tube station, money in one pocket, phone in the other.

I'd better reply to Dylan.

*****

His phone vibrated so loudly on the hard surface of his desk it made his heart leap almost out of his chest as if in some cartoon parody of love itself. With a dry mouth and shy fingers Dylan read the text from Grace.

She is looking forward to seeing me. That is a good sign.

Tonight great. Looking forward to seeing you. I'll be in the pub from six. Hugs. Grace x

The rest of his day passed by in super-speeded up slow motion. Dylan was riding high on some kind of personal validation wave. It reminded him of when he was a twelve year old at school and his Mother had bought him a pair of nice shiny Doc Marten's shoes to wear. For about a week, he, the usual antithesis of all that was fashionable or fashionably expensive, rode tall (literally, as the soles were so thick) in the glory of owning a pair of shoes that all the other kids wanted.

Most of it was in his mind of course, as most of the other kids had a pair, or even two, but the feeling was one of personal gratification in the mere act of fitting in, and of other kids wanting what he had.

Not that his bored and miserable clichés of office workmates wanted what he had, but the personal gratification was there and so was the feeling of something a little like pride that was putting something like a spring in his expensive Loake slip on's with the big heels.

Extreme happiness and raw nerves added a blast of adrenalin to his day which meant the hazelnut copy nonsense passed by without even a second thought and he even skipped lunch.

Five came and went and Dylan rose from his seat to go down to the men's toilet on the floor beneath. After a long and nervous evacuation of his bowels he emerged from the cubicle to find, to his amusement, the same huge fat guy with the predilection towards too much deodorant at the basins, shirt off, exactly the same as the time before. Dylan nodded to him in the mirror and the man grunted an acknowledgement, which may also have been the cough of half a can of Lynx catching in his fat-covered throat.

Dylan waited until he was gone to apply his own deodorant, spray on some Very Valentino (the only one of his dozen or so bottles of expensively assembled sprays he was sure she liked) and then brush his teeth and rinse with a travel bottle of Listerine he had bought at Glasgow Airport. The teeth and mouthwash thing was a new addition to his pre-date rigmarole, and the thinking behind it when packing his bag the previous night was to safely negotiate the thorny issue of the breath effects of the sandwich he probably would eat at lunchtime. The fact that he did not eat at all all day mattered not a bit, and Dylan scrubbed as if there were indeed insidious pieces of sandwich stuck in his teeth and scraped as if the whitish deposit on his tongue was down to something other than the three cups of coffee and a single Diet Coke he had consumed all day. Shirt on, jeans pulled up, hair pushed across with a reasonable degree of tidiness. Nice smells assured, he stood back and studied himself in the washroom mirror, not smiling but not frowning either. He reprised the glance in the lift doors, and again in the mirrored walls in the lift, taking care not to look up lest he be reminded by the mirrored ceiling of his retreating hairline and the spot on top where the retreat was now a full-scale withdrawal.

Striding purposefully out of the building with a nod and debut night wink to the Indian security guard, Dylan smiled and headed for Angel.

*****

Grace had not intended to take any clients that day. In her mind, it was inappropriate. Maybe she worried for tell-tale signs, maybe she just felt wrong, but she did not intend to take any clients that Wednesday. The battering she took in the morning left no lasting damage.

But somehow it felt wrong. That she was having sex – for money – with strangers on a day where she was meeting Dylan. It did not occur to her at first, but it had snuck up on her again. In her mind, even though she was just going for an exploratory drink with a guy who, in theory at least, she did not find attractive, she was already making allowances for sleeping with him.

As it turned out, she answered her "work" mobile in Pret a Manger and found herself on her way to a post-lunchtime liaison with a regular in Shepherd's Bush very much against her better judgement. She went through the motions of her trade with just enough gusto to entertain the client's requirement that she enjoy what he was doing to her, and made just enough noise to convince him, or rather suspend his disbelief.

The client was a good tipper and as vanilla a regular as she could think of – needing only oral and then to fuck her with all the precision and might of a prize bull as she offered herself up on all fours, squeaking (for the second time that day) in all the right places. It was, as always, over quickly and she politely declined the offer of a drink. Then she declined even more politely the offer expensive lunch at a nearby restaurant of which the client, (who actually resembled a ruddy-faced bull now that she came to think about it), was the owner and head chef. He tipped her with the customary friendly slap of her backside as she walked past and out of the door. He winked at her obviously aroused and disgusted in equal measure at what he thought was her reason for cutting their lunchtime session off before it became an afternoon and evening session.

Grinning with genuine amusement at the sheer boorish ignorance of the man, she walked swiftly to the lifts in his block of flats and headed for the tube station.

Sat at home, the empowered confidence was completely gone. Grace sat on her bed with tears of worry and frustration threatening to break down her cheeks. Barney was sat ramrod straight on her pillow and regarded her coldly.

You silly bitch. Leo the fucking weirdo and then Chef Nino fucked the daylights out of you and he'll smell it on you. You know he will. Besides, how fucking wrong are you to go out and fuck guys the same day, nay, just a couple of hours, before you meet a guy for a date? Is your fanny sore? Is it a bit tender? You are a silly woman. He'll know. Of course he'll know. You better fucking not bring the poor cunt back here either, because I'll fucking tell him. You're a disgrace. Whore. Harlot. Tart!

"Fuck off." ...escaped Grace with less venom than perhaps the cat deserved, in her head anyway. She looked up and could have sworn she saw the cat smirk as he looked away and closed his eyes.

It took Grace quite a long time and the best part of a whole bottle of Chablis from the fridge for her to choose an outfit and do her make-up. Incredulous that such a mundane thing as a drink with a guy who she didn't really fancy anyway could get her in such a state, she grew in confidence as she told herself that she/Barney was wrong.

Fucking clients the day of a date would have to be something she would have to get used to if she wanted to start dating properly, and anyway, how would he know? She was being paranoid and she knew it. Even so, although her mind and fears were making it a far more painful and stressful experience than it needed to be, she found some odd enjoyment from the sheer act of getting dressed up in something nice for a guy and not for client. She had not done that for a long, long time, and the change felt good, like a cold shower on a roasting hot day. Revelling in the happy drama and positive trauma and yet confused by the mood swings she was experiencing, she felt herself soar inside as she rose from her bedside.

Presently, Barney came back in, looking rather mournful and full of eyes imploring her to do her owner duty and feed him.

I am sorry. I didn't mean it. You look lovely by the way.

"Thanks Mister. Let's get you some dinner shall we?" She was so full of nervous happiness that her voice nearly broke and the corners of her eyes tinged. Barney answered with a deep, long noise that was too strong and purposeful to be called a squeak and leapt off the bed as if showing her the way to the kitchen.

"Can you believe these mood swings? One minute I'm up, the next minute I'm down. I bet this is what it's like to be on drugs." She offered to the black form on her kitchen floor, now face down in a bowl of something stinky.

Give me a minute here, Lady. Little busy.

Picking up her pink overcoat, draped over one arm, and her bag, Grace grinned affectionately at Barney and closed the door behind her.

TWENTY-FIVE

Soundtrack

Big Muff – 'My Funny Valentine' (Stephane Mix)

Sometimes it is just teasing you. When the sky goes dark and close, and you feel the spot of rain but then it decides not to.

Dylan ruminated on his own solipsistic brand of that most British of conversation topics in his head as he walked up the road, up the hill. Angel glittered in the distance more out of it being his destination as opposed to being any more lit up than the streetlights around him.

Inevitably, his mind switched back to Grace and he wondered if she would wear her Pink-Overcoat.

Normally, Dylan would get the tube everywhere but given the immediate lack of proper rain and the fact that the London Underground system had a unique ability to make him clammy and sweaty even in the depths of mid-Winter, he had decided to walk. Of course, had it decided to rain then his shoes might have become spotted and what gel in what he had left of his hair would have been rendered a gelly mess, but Dylan Short felt lucky.

Nervous, but lucky.

Very nervous actually.

In actuality he was sick to his stomach in anticipation of seeing

Grace again. He realised that she had snuck up on him, (as opposed to him stalking her) and that what had started as, at least in name, a casual drink with someone who may or may not fancy him, had turned into the possibility of Everything, in every possible connotation of the word. It reminded him of the long walk from the metro station in Munich and glimpsing the Bayern Munich stadium for the first time on the day of the Champions League final a few years ago. The nerves and churning terror were the same.

She's just a fucking girl.

Why are you getting all out of shape about a girl? Twat.

Cursing and castigating himself for the tenth time that day for his softness in even thinking about something other or more than the possibility of getting her into bed, he crumpled his forehead as another droplet landed there. Since when had she become his One?

Whoa. Hold on there Tiger.

"Dont be a twat." he muttered out loud, the words lost instantly over the rush of the evening traffic.

That was good advice, now that he came to think about it. He had innumerable memories of dates and other nearlies where the simple act of him saying, doing, suggesting or otherwise acting in a twattish way had screwed things up, or rather not screwed, if the pun were intentional. Suddenly, like the splash of a puddle from a passing bus across his train of thought, several people at once all started to taking to him. His father. Carla. Crabby. His sister. Jason. His mate Mike. Frank Lampard. His uncle Andy. All giving him the pre-match pep talk, just like they all had on past dates at one time or another.

Best behaviour. She isn't your One, but it never hurt to keep your options open. Don't be a twat. Be yourself but don't be a twat. Filter the twat aspects of your personality. Engage Twatfilter. Think, listen, pay for dinner, be yourself and don't be a twat.

Got it?

*****

The pub was as laughably unsuitable for a date as any she could imagine. Grace laughed out loud as simultaneously a Slade record came on the speakers above her at ear-splitting volume and the red-nosed drunkard at the bar in front of her ate a pickled egg whole, his bristly face screwed up into what was either pure ecstasy or excruciating heatburn.

A bored-looking Pole swept past with a plate of chips that looked like they had been refried several times, and what was surely the world's saddest looking piece of plaice. The toxic looking bright green fluid in the pot she assumed was supposed to be the mushy peas. As the tray came past the lights reflected a film of grease over the sides of the plate, pooling in the middle to form a puddle, almost as if the poor plaice was not quite done swimming. The smell hit her. It was pure grease. No tender aromas of freshly line caught fish battered in light beer and herb batter, or even of the fresh, rainy garden smell of peas pureed.

And she hated Slade.

Shaking her head, she wondered if old man pubs like the Brewers Arms still existed in London, and indeed, whether Dylan was attempting to be funny or ironic.

The cocaine surged through him, belying the scale of the tiny bump he had flourished up his nose before he left work. It was not enough to blow his pupils or make him sweat but it was, hopefully, enough to make him less of a twat.

Coke normally makes people more of a twat you silly sausage.

Dylan stopped dead in his tracks on his way to the table in the pub. He was taken aback by two things.

One, that Grace was early.

Two, that she did not look remotely impressed at his choice of pub.

In fact, having taken a quick glance around at the dark corners, silent re-runs of Spanish football and small band of hardy drunkard regulars dotted in the dark and uninviting corners, and inhaled the stench of stale beer, overflowing urinals and hot fat, he could see what she was unimpressed about. It was just before six on a Wednesday night in Angel. The pub should have been busy but it was not. He realised with a plunging certainty like a kick to the stomach that the Brewers Arms in Angel was as ludicrously unsuitable a venue for a date as it was possible to imagine anywhere in Central London, and also that Grace had seen him and was walking over.

"What the fuck is this pub about?" He burst out laughing, slightly too loudly, in the way that only the very tense or the mentally ill do. Grace may not have heard him over the deafening Brummie rock in the background, but she understood his meaning, and they all but flew out of the pub door and into the gathering London night, laughing as they went.

"Please tell me you haven't been there before!" Grace giggled.

"Never. It is just really well known and easy to find. Easier that's all"

Dylan was all smiles. The ice had been broken, and they had been saved from the Slade.

"That's really thoughtful, but don't do it again!" Grace looked right into Dylan's eyes and stopped him in his tracks.

Again? She wants to see me again. Result.

"I'm hungry. Can we go for something to eat? And I don't fancy two week old fish and chips in a grease jus!" Dylan laughed at her sarcasm, hugely gratified to see Grace stop in her stride just as he did, so much so that it elicited a swear word from a hurrying man in a leather jacket who was pushing past.

"Do I trust you to choose a venue though? You aren't exactly on a run of form Dylan." she laughed again. Dylan decided that she had an extremely attractive laugh.

Now is the time to be positive. Be decisive Dylan.

"Cliché, but there's this little place I know..."

"Bring it on!" she answered immediately, in the abrupt way that either the impatient or the mentally ill do sometimes.

"There's a great place not far from here, serves the most wonderful, succulent chicken lightly fried and coated with a herb crust. You have it with potato julienne and a bean and tomato tagine… Service is very fast indeed and the prices reasonable"

Dylan arched his eyes in the way that he did when he was being sarcastic. Grace did not read it and made a noise that indicated that the food sounded delicious. Dylan placed his hand on the door of the fast food restaurant they were walking past and turned to Grace, just failing to keep a straight face.

"Plus they give you a free Vienetta with every value bucket!" Dylan cackled.

Grace instantly looked mortified, then disbelieving, then she melted into laughter.

"You had me going then, you really did. Arsehole! I'm a classy bird me – at least make it a Burger King!"

She gave him a playful punch on his upper arm. Dylan just winked and indicated for her to follow him up a side road. They walked for about five minutes, chatting and laughing and getting on well, until they arrived at a rather dark looking glass fronted restaurant with tinted windows and rather forgettable signage. Sensing Grace's dubiousness, Dylan leaned in close to her and whispered for her to trust him. Inside was a dark but very warm Thai restaurant with minimal interior design and luxuriant wafts of richness and culinary beauty from the kitchen.

Each table was lit by a small but brilliantly polished naphtha lamp, set on tablecloths of brilliant white. Dylan took her Pink-Overcoat and hung it up by the door, rather stealing the thunder of the pretty Thai waitress who just appeared from nowhere to stand by the table. She bowed to them both, and sensing he was on a roll, Dylan ordered a bottle of Sancerre.

Grace was at once impressed and slightly put off. The restaurant was dowdy but nice and quite evidently the exact opposite of the pub they had just left, and she was impressed with his assurance to bring her there, but less so at his ordering of the wine without asking her. She felt slightly railroaded. What if she did not like Sancerre or Thai food?

"You mentioned you liked it the other day" Dylan stated matter-of-factly as if reading her thoughts.

"What, Sancerre or Thai food?" she shot back gamely.

"Sancerre." Dylan raised his eyebrows.

"Did I? Must have been more pissed than I thought. Top marks for observation though!" Her laughter diffused her own tension. Dylan looked relieved.

"Do you not like Thai food then?" Dylan enquired with a concerned look on his face as a basket of crackers arrived.

"Not really had it too much to be honest. More of a Chinese kind of girl really, but it's always nice to have something new" She almost sounded apologetic.

"Cool." Dylan smiled.

They ordered and talked. Grace was grateful for the crackers and then the rice and noodles to give her something inside to combat the white wine which was slipping down rapidly. The duck curry was something she had never seen before let alone tasted, and Dylan was delighted to note that she seemed to genuinely enjoy it. They chatted about the weather, about Carla, about Jason, about Grace having been previously set up with Jason and how he was not interested, and how both of them had always wanted to visit South East Asia. A second bottle of Sancerre arrived as the restaurant began to fill up and their conversation rose in volume as both tables on either side of them were successively occupied.

Dylan was in no man's land again. He sensed that Grace was opening up and their conversation was rattling along nicely. They were getting on really well, in fact. He could not read her though, and was becoming increasingly aware that when he talked to women in this friendly, disjointed, accordial way, that the women in question invariably went on to become good friends. That was something that Dylan was strenuously hoping to better, as "avoid" was rather an ungrateful expression.

"Friendzone" isn't going to happen. Be positive.

He looked across the table at The-Girl-Who-Wears-The-Pink-Overcoat and marvelled. Her hair hung down across her shoulders, masking all but the tips of her ears, and reflecting the golden light of the lamp in the middle of the table. He marvelled at her cheekbones, her neckline, her beautifully proportioned nose and her wide, earnest eyes, which shone in the half-light and seemed to light up all of their own accord when he said something funny.

Even over the odour of the food he could sense her smell, a perfume. She wore a fitted white top and blue jeans, and his eye feasted across the curves of her upper body, and down the nude curves of her neck. It was intoxicating.

The urge, the need, to kiss her neck was so keen it felt like it was sat on his chest, making him breath shallower. He just could not believe how such an attractive woman would even consider a date with him. Not that he believed in such things, but Jason might say she was so far out of his league it was not funny. Well, no he probably would not, based on his past performance.

Grace was easily the best-looking woman he had ever dated.

Then the paranoia returned and it all unravelled in his mind, falling away until he was her go-to guy for a shoulder and some advice when she got fucked over by some good looking cunt who did not respect her and was probably fucking call girls behind her back.

Anger flared like a lit match inside him, only to fade into the tension and paranoia.

This is going too well. She wants to be your mate. She is too good for you. This is going far too well.

Grace watched Dylan from across the table. He was intriguing to study, as his expressive face seemed to go through all the range of emotions as she talked to him. She could not work out if he was distracted or so painfully focussed on what she was saying that it made him look uncomfortable. Normally such behaviour was not good, but in the tubby-ish, slightly perspiring man sat opposite her who smelt of too much aftershave, she found his vulnerability endearing. How could he be so confident and easy going and yet be so obviously vulnerable and unsure of himself?

Grace had a good sense for when men were not being themselves and when they were playing a game and she got a real and evident sense from her dinner companion that Dylan was very much being himself. Games were seemingly a long way from his mind.

Strangely, she became aware of a kindling attraction to him.

She used to listen to a chillout CD at Uni which had a track on it called 'My Funny Valentine', where a woman was singing low and sultry about a man who was so unattractive that he was attractive. It fitted Dylan perfectly, if a little harshly.

Yes, he was overweight, and no, his teeth were definitely not good but nonetheless he had a certain attraction. He had deep and serious eyes with a light in them that made him easy to read. She knew at once he could never lie to her because his eyes would betray him.

On some level that was very comforting. Reading guys had never been a talent of Grace's.

His eyes, his solid jaw and broad, powerful shoulders, bull-like and yet a million miles from the chef earlier on in the day. His confidence, his humour, his vulnerability and his obvious intelligence were intoxicating indeed. Or maybe it was the wine. Either way she realised that the real or imagined youthful, slightly lecherous advances were gone in favour of something more tangible. Dylan had grown on her and along with him the thoughts and wonders of what he may become to her with him. Grace wondered to what extent her mental image and feeling of him and what he meant could be reconciled to the chubby but amusing man sat in front of her.

As if on cue, Dylan wrinkled his nose up, and she realised he was struggling to contain a drippy nose. The slices of chillis in the curry and the noodles had obviously taken their fiery toll. Whether he was trying to be macho or not was unclear, but he had eaten all the chillis and all the ones she had studiously picked out of her food as well and was now probably regretting it. His cheeks were blossoms of red and flecks of light speckled his wide forehead.

They visited an All Bar One after the meal and progressed onto the third bottle of wine for the night. Conversation flashed and darted, neither one wanting to let a lull in to give the other an excuse to pack it in and call it a night.

*****

Dylan was battling an onset of nerves.

Grace was out of his league. Not massively. Not overwhelmingly. But discernibly. She smiled and laughed at his jokes from across the table, flushed in the warmth of the pub as the wine showed up in her cheeks. Grace was one of those women who had expressive eyes that laughed with her mouth and face. He found himself staring at her. She was confident enough to meet his gaze and Dylan found himself compelled to look away. There was something about her eyes and the way it made him feel. The layers peeled back from him in his mind as she stripped them away.

The drugs thing was a huge fucking problem. Looking into her eyes he knew. It would not be possible to lie to her. Not for long anyway.

If she found out it would be over. That was obvious. She was a great girl. A great woman. A real actual woman with a proper job who had her shit together and was going places. If he was going to date her, however fleetingly, he had to close the averages. That meant dressing better. Losing weight. Going to the gym. It meant eating better. It meant saving cash. It would soon mean getting his own place to rent. And it meant knocking the pills and powder on the head. Not just the serving up but the actual doing them as well.

The cash situation was decent and he could probably afford his own flat if he did not have any debts to pay off. In typical Dylan style though he had paid very little off what he owed from the wedges of cash he had brought in over the months and months of dealing. A large slice of the profits had been wasted on getting wasted.

The dealing had to stop, but getting his own place meant he probably needed to carry on another month or two if he put all his earnings into paying off his personal loans.

The prospect of another trip to Luca's or a stressful night pushing his luck as well as his gear in some sweaty nightclub was uniquely unappealing. The thought of getting caught again held a particular horror. Ice formed in his internal cavities as he remembered getting lifted at Bass Factory. If he got busted again Grace would be history. There was no way she would understand and there was no way he would get away with it again. It had been nothing short of a miracle. A bolt of lightning from above, enough almost to make him believe in something more than his mortal existence.

Lightning never struck twice. Wasn't that what they said?

The universe had granted him a reprieve and he could not hope to be as lucky again.

So yes. The dealing had to stop. Actually with or without Grace in his life the dealing had to end. It was time.

No time for that wallowing now. Start being charming and funny and hope she doesn't see you shitting your pants in fear behind those glassy eyes of yours you utter fucking fat mess.

*****

Grace found herself enjoying the conversation with Dylan and soaking up his companionship. He was funny. The jokes and sarcasm seemed to roll out of him with a confident ease. It was like he wasn't even trying, he was just naturally funny. Or she found him funny anyway. A blend of slightly edgy opinions and sarcastic observations and the sort of childish silliness she had always found funny. The alcohol loosened him up and Grace found herself flirting with him: she was attracted to him but could not put her finger on why.

She watched his face as he talked. He had earlier seemed a little detached, as if worried about something. Probably first date nerves.

He was only distracted a few minutes but it was enough time for Grace to realise Dylan had something on his mind and for Dylan to worry that Grace could see something was bothering him. Batting it away, Dylan countered. The conversation rebounded and Grace began to laugh all over again.

Spending time with him was very easy. She felt nothing for him yet but in her case this was a good thing. He would be an easy person to develop feelings for. Might he be boyfriend material?

Grace cursed herself for being soppy.

Far too early for that you lame bitch.

But maybe.

Just maybe. He hadn't offended her or made her feel inadequate or uncomfortable. He made her feel special in as much as someone could who she had only been on one date with. She remembered back to when she thought he was some creep staring at her. She was sure he was not like that. That was about as good as it got in terms of starting blocks for something, or anything really.

The lights in the bar came on. They had missed the last call for alcohol. Finishing up with no sense of finality in the air Dylan held the door open for her and she followed him to the tube station. Dylan leaned over and hugged her warmly, lingering just long enough to convey something other than friendship but not long enough to suggest any counting of chickens.

He kissed her on the cheek and pulled away. Grace did want to kiss properly but said nothing. Dylan took both her hands and spoke quietly and earnestly, eyes wide open.

"I really like you. I'd really like to see you again. If that's ok with you?"

It was almost the perfect line, she thought.

Even though she wanted to kiss him long and indiscreetly in the street she admired and valued the fact that he was being a gentleman and letting her dictate the pace of things in the old fashioned way. He could not know how well judged it had been.

"I'd love to. I like you a lot as well." she mumbled in response.

You daft fucking bitch. Who the fuck says things like that???

Dylan smiled widely in obvious relief.

Heart in mouth, Grace raised her hand to his lapel and gently moved him closer, before closing her eyes.

It took a second before anything happened.

She was just about to open an eye to see if she had been left hanging, all puckered up and with nowhere to go, when he kissed her very gently.

His lips were warm and soft.

The beer smell coming off him did not offend her and she hoped the wine coming off her did not offend him. The kiss lingered a second and a half, but felt longer. It was tender and laden with as much meaning as any first date kiss either had ever had. Hearts in mouths they pulled apart and opened their eyes.

Grace was touched to see Dylan looked absolutely terrified. His eyes were wide and she saw him shaking visibly. It was her first real kiss for months and it had been lovely.

Just.... lovely.

*****

Dylan thought he was going to throw up.

Blood pounded in his temples as the bile churned in his stomach, threatening to release in panic.

The nerves had been building inside him all evening and although the final lines he had to some extent rehearsed in his head earlier, the kiss was unexpected and scared him to death. He was convinced she would recoil in horror at the brewery fumes and the garlic seeping out of him. That she hadn't, he was sure, was down to politeness. He loved that she was too polite to say anything about what had to have been evil bad breath and a full on rabbit in the headlights surprise of a kiss.

She had agreed to see him again though!

Success!

Grace had gone on one line and disappeared with a smile and wave down the escalators. Dylan pulled out some headphones and disappeared down the other as the last few of the Piccadilly Line trains of the day ran through below him.

A successful date.

It was massive. He was a little bit relieved but also a little bit surprised. She was discernibly out of his league. She would have been perfectly within her rights to tell him to fuck off. And he would have been perfectly within his bracket to accept it. That she did not, he was sure, was down to luck and a degree of poor judgement on her part. Whatever he had done, she'd appreciated it.

Now he had to figure out where to take her for the second date. Questions rattled though his head keeping pace with the tube train. Where would he take her? It was too early to ask her over for dinner so he could cook for her, right? Did she like sushi? Maybe sushi and movie?

Or maybe he should stop being so boring and think of something original?

*****

Barney greeted her at the door.

Alright. How'd it go then?

Grace locked the door and daintily hung up her coat.

"Went very well Barney thank you for asking." she sang to him.

He went to stand by the fridge, evidently having heard enough.

"Very well indeed in fact. I'm going to see him again I think." she continued as she forked out something far more unpleasant in real life than on the picture on the tin, into a bowl for the expectant feline.

That gives you a fucking problem then doesn't it?

"Yes it does Barney. Very true indeed. I'm afraid it does give me a problem. "

TWENTY-SIX

Soundtrack

New Order – 'The Perfect Kiss'

Dylan closed his eyes.

The Friday morning air was fresh and cold. He opened them again.

Walking to the station he had decided for the first time in many months to take his sunglasses to work with him. It was one of those stunning spring mornings everyone thinks of in the dark winter months.

Upwards was brilliant cobalt blue sky with a chill in the air belying the bright sunshine. There is a period either side of the sticky, heady summer months in London where it is too cold not to take a coat out of the house but too bright not to take sunglasses also. London seems to wake from a slumber as the clouds are swept away and dreams turn optimistically to summertime.

The walk up the street was a little slower than usual because Dylan was taking his time, wondering idly whether crime statistics showed that people really were in a better mood when the sun came out. Were there fewer rapes and assaults in London when the weather was nice? Might this be something he could Google at work in lieu of actual work tasks perhaps?

The trance playlist in his headphones seemed bigger somehow; more in tune with his surroundings. The trip to work went without a hitch and work itself eased by with no catches. The copy flowed uninhibited and crime statistics remained un-Googled as the trance continued.

At about four Carla texted him asking whether he wanted to go with her and Jason to an all-night rave. Grace was apparently away seeing her parents in Eastbourne so he agreed. It would do him good, a dance, a few drinks and maybe the chance to shift some of the backlog of party prescriptions massing in his bedroom as if preparing for an all-out assault on a neighbouring room.

He left early, ate on the way home and got in at the same time as Carla. She ribbed him gently about his date with Grace and they sat smoking and drinking for several hours until after eleven when she abruptly leapt to her feet and charged off to get changed. The whole house shook as her bedroom door slammed in its hinges. Jason bumped into him as he left the upstairs bathroom.

"Alright youth."

"Hullo mate. Good day?" Dylan enquired.

"Not so bad. You coming with us to this rave ting later?"

"Didn't have a choice. Carls was particularly insistent on this one." Dylan laughed.

Jason poked his head round the bathroom door again. "How'd it go with Grace the other night? She shuffled you off yet?"

Dylan laughed dryly.

"Not yet. Only had one date though. Give it a week."

Jason's trademark nasal cackle echoed from the bathroom as the stairs shook behind him. Carla was ready. She already had a rolled up £20 note in her hand and was rushing for the kitchen table. Dylan threw some clothes on and joined in. Carla had racked up three perfectly proportioned lines and made one magically disappear as he watched. Dylan bent over and did his, then immediately did Jason's up the other nostril.

It was great fucking gear. Even though he said so himself.

Carla was about to interject about the shameless purloining of Jason's fair share when Dylan pulled out a baggy with three grammes of his personal in it. It was like the gear he sold to Carla but uncut. The words stopped in Carla's throat as she moved in close to watch him rack up. A huge smile crept across her features. Dylan could smell her perfume. Or was it her bodyspray? It was hypnotic. He closed his eyes and breathed her in, just a few inches from him. The breath seemed to expand inside him. Heart hammering, eyes shut, Dylan felt his limbs go light and his fingers go cold. The shakes began in earnest as he opened his mind's eye. Carla was grinning at him, entirely too close for friendly comfort. Dylan imagined her in glorious coked up Cocavision peeling her sopping underwear down, pressing his head down as she laid back pressing herself into his mouth, needing his tongue. How she would taste as he went down on her. Breathing her in. Her grinding against his face, coming hard...

"Good gear. Jolly good show Dyls auld bean."

Carla nodded at him with purse lips in mock reverence.

Dylan opened his eyes. Carla was laughing, yet shot him a knowing look as if she knew exactly what he had been thinking about.

Suddenly lightheaded and dizzy, Dylan stood up and put his hands on his head, exhaling deeply. His mind was racing at a hundred miles an hour and he could not stop it. A wave of nausea came and went breathlessly. Carla laughed loudly again at his lack of response.

"I'll take that as the tacit agreement it was meant to be!"

The rolled up £20 fell soundlessly to earth from dumb fingers as Carla began to rack up another three. Far away Jason had turned off his music and was banging around on his way down to the kitchen.

Heart beating out his chest, Dylan went down on one knee to retrieve the banknote from the grubby floorboards. Carla was only a few inches away from his head. He could almost smell her...

"...while you're down there..." she muttered mischievously, not taking her eyes off the delicate concentration of cocaine arrangement in front.

Dylan laughed. There would never be anything between them. He did not really fancy her and she definitely did not fancy him despite the sexual tension. Coke always did that. As he was coming up on it he always got incredibly turned on as the blood rushed to his extremities. Fingers. Toes. Cock. Prostate.

Awkwardly, Dylan backed away headed for the toilet as sudden onset "coke poo" was another feature of his favourite type of drug abuse. He would probably masturbate too, he knew. Although it would be unlikely he could come.

Never stopped him trying before, he thought as he smiled to himself.

"Stopped what before?" Jason enquired.

He'd been talking out loud.

Dylan shook his head and loped out of the kitchen as the sounds of delicate snorting accompanied his short walk to the bathroom.

Eyes closed, sat on the toilet Dylan allowed himself to relax. The vigour of the cocaine was passing and the breath was returning to him. Great slugs of the drug dripped off the back of his throat and slithered deeper down inside. His mouth tasted of chemicals and was drying out fast. Finished on the toilet he decided against the self-pleasuring and washed his hands. Nose twitching he walked back to the kitchen where Jason and Carla were already onto round two and preparing for round three of his personal coke stash. If he were not so fucked he might have said something but already the powder was calling him to return again even as the near-panic had only just subsided. The warmth was back. The energy was back. Dylan clicked his teeth together. He felt on top of the world.

The next huge line was always the best. Its concept sang to him even as Carla began to arrange the little white tramlines.

The smack in the mouth first poodle leg was always hectic. But the widowmaker after was just pure pleasure, a last unadulterated complete thrill before the laws of diminishing returns kicked in. He luxuriated in it, all fears and worries about drugs, dealing or anything else a million miles from his mind.

A beer came and went in an ice-cold savoury rush and then they were outside in the cold and the darkness, almost jogging to keep warm. Conversation was turbocharged, relentless barely allowing his breath time to escape steaming into the dark purple skies.

The train stopped at Finsbury Park and they piled out as London seemed to open up before them. The closed streets and peering buildings thrown wide somehow. Dylan knew it was the cocaine but the scale of it all spread apart like some epic movie set took his breath away.

So many dazzling lights!

The cab flitted through the traffic sprinting from red light to red light and sitting back in the seat Dylan began to sweat. It was uncomfortably hot in the taxi and the movement made him feel a bit queasy. Queasy turned to nauseous turned to outright pukey very fast. He was about to open a window when the cab rattled up and stopped. Carla all but threw some banknotes at the driver and they piled out.

Dylan took great precious lungful's of the cold air as he felt the colour visibly return to his face. Jason held a monologue with him about West Ham staying up as Carla paced up and down interrogating someone on her phone. Then they were off, striding through the evening. Dylan looked around. They were in some deserted side street near Willesden. The vast expanse of railway tracks spread out in front of them. The streetlights twinkled off the young shiny ones, whilst brushes of weeds grew up from the older, duller ones. Dylan knew better than to ask Carla where they were going. Suddenly she was off again, darting up a pathway between a canal and the fence for the marshalling yard.

Far away Dylan became aware of something over the drone of Jason's plaintive feelings on not having properly bought a decent striker in January.

A presence.

A happening.

At first he put it down to the coke, but as they walked up the path it became clearer. There were lights emanating weakly from inside a woody copse, hidden in a depression between the railway and the canal. You couldn't see it from the road. Silhouettes of people were moving around inside the trees. A lot of people in fact. As they walked a bulky shape moved down the path in the almost complete darkness and warmly embraced Carla. Jason and Dylan were introduced to a huge black man called Forrester, made even more huge by the improbably large puffa jacket he was poking out of. Right away Forrester was into Dylan, shaking his hand and being overly welcoming as if he was a long-lost brother.

Dylan knew the patter by now.

Carla had told him Dylan was serving up and it being Forrester's rave (in the forest, no less) Forrester was trying to square him onside to ensure he could be counted on. Or he just wanted to buy the drugs. They quickly came to a solid agreement. Dylan kept a few pills and a gramme each of the Ket and the good coke back and sold everything else to the colossal lump bobbing alongside of them before they even got to the treeline. A very solid night's work. Dylan collected a fiver from Carla and Jason and handed them a pair of pills each. The trees and brambles gave way like bouncers stepping aside to a set of two clearings almost in a figure eight. An unfeasibly large sound system complete with lights and a DJ stand dominated the back of the larger clearing, with a portable generator clattering almost unheard over the thudding bass. Grinding acid house was being laid down with considerable enthusiasm by the hooded DJ, and already perhaps three dozen people milled around bobbing uncertainly to the music. A large camping table was set up nearby from which two women were selling cans of lager for two quid and bottles of water for a pound.

Dylan was mightily impressed. He wondered if Crabby was there. It was definitely his sort of night. The idea of seeing the old guy again and getting to finally have that pill and a few beers with him appealed greatly.

Just for a second he forgot that Crabby had gone.

Then the memory of his loss shot him in the stomach again.

Shaking his head and fighting back a wave of sadness and regret, Dylan resolved in Panavision technicolour to get absolutely, completely, profoundly, utterly fucking fucked.

Have one for Crabby.

He spent a couple of hours wandering round chatting to randoms. Jason came back from out of the trees having apparently sold a gramme of his ketamine to a friend of Forrester's for a snatched and evidently not that impressive blowjob. He matter-of-factly went back to complaining about West Ham's lack of width and Dylan settled into the evening not really minding his company.

They were joined by two women and Jason made no effort whatsoever to stop talking about football. Dylan laughed inside. He didn't care, did he?

It turned out one of the women, a freezing skinny rake of a girl with dodgy skin and slack greasy hair had been the one Jason had just transacted the transfer with and he obviously could not remember her name. She knew it and wasn't going to tell him either. The conversation stopped and she stepped in close to Dylan. Cider (he hoped) added a sour note to her breath as she tried to look up at him coquettishly.

She wanted some gear.

Fucking Jason told her I have some fucking coke.

Dylan scowled at Jason with a look of pure venom and his flatmate began to laugh hard.

"So Jase here tells me you have some gear. Can I buy a line off you mate?"

Then she fluttered her eyelashes in a move straight out of a

Looney Tunes cartoon and Dylan began to chuckle. It was pathetic but funny at the same time. Tragic and hilarious.

Dylan made some muttered excuses and the woman leaned in closer.

"I give a fucking top blowy. Give us some of your gear and I'll nosh you right off. Does that sound good?" she was speaking in low sultry tones trying to sound sexier than she was.

Dylan found himself agreeing without really thinking about it. Unable to believe his own lack of standards and self-control, he allowed her to take his hand. She led him off into the bushes as Jason watched incredulous. They moved round the copse and behind some thick bushes where, obligingly, there was a fallen log. The woman pulled Dylan over by the hips and suddenly her hands were inside his jeans and probing inside his boxer shorts. He felt himself get hard. Her cold fingers felt fantastic. Remembering she had just a few minutes ago had Jason's manhood in her mouth, Dylan warned her off a blowjob and instead let her use her hands. She seemed to get into it and he soon felt a tightening and a sense of urgency. He was close. She suddenly stopped and hitched up her skirt, leaning back on the log.

"Go down on me and I'll finish you off after." Her voice was urgent and desperate. All thoughts of gear were long gone.

Before he could believe it, agape and shaking his own head in disbelief he was kneeling between her thighs. She was obviously very turned on and he found himself... not reviled.

Not disgusted at himself and disappointed at his lack of control but revelling in her not-unpleasant slippery musky heat. She started yelping like a seal as she ground against him, her cries in his head not coming from an unemployed former hairdresser called Donna but from Grace and at the same time evoking his coke-addled mini-daydream about Carla earlier. She came quickly and disappeared without asking for any cocaine or finishing him off as she promised. Dylan wondered whether she had a boyfriend.

Poor fucker.

Adjusting his jeans he walked slowly to the clearing he joined Jason and Carla drinking out of a bottle of red wine. Jason was stifling howls of laughter while Carla seemed blessedly ignorant. Dylan shot Jason a wink and a nod in her direction in the hope he would let it drop and not mention it, and he seemed to get the message.

Dylan headed to the bar table and brought back a half litre bottle of cheap supermarket vodka and three beers. They were handed out and they agreed to double drop their two pills each.

Uncomfortably, Dylan was a little close to having a reality moment.

He could still hear Grace and Carla over the music only now they were disgusted with him.

Their judgement weighed heavily on him on his head.

Who the hell does horrible fucking skanky shit like that?

When did you start doing screwed up nasty things like that? That's so wrong. On so many levels. What the fucking fuck is fucking wrong with you, you fucking dirty fucking cunt?

Dylan was furious with himself.

"Fuck's sake."

Dylan downed his beer in desperation, trying to blot out the judgement and recrimination. The worst part of it was it had turned him on. He should have been horrified but it had excited him. All at once Dylan wanted to find the skinny, tragic woman and apologise to her.

He spent the next half hour wandering from clearing to clearing until he finally found her. He apologised and pressed his remaining cocaine into her hand. She did not seem to recognise him at all, or if she did she did not want to acknowledge him. Dylan could well understand that. He did not blame her at all. Who knows he wondered, maybe she really didn't recognise him? The ketamine was obviously in full effect and she was sluggish and out of synch somehow. She did not take the baggy from him but regarded it in puzzlement in her hand. She did not appear to recognise it or him. A selfish apology would mean fuck all now.

And neither would the gear.

She's not a fucking prozzie you twat. Nice tribute to Crabby as well, you horrible bastard.

Suddenly ashamed and reminded of recent events, Dylan plucked up the baggy in haste not wanting to pay the woman for her sexual services for reasons he could not quite comprehend. She did not react to him in any way as he walked off.

Relieved and saddened at the same time he re-joined the others. Jason was almost unable to open his eyes and deeply entranced by the music.

Very shortly afterwards he came up like a freight train on the pills he'd double dropped earlier with Jason and Carla. The shame dropped off him like scales from his eyes.

Crabby seemed to be in his thoughts, comforting him and telling him everything was ok. He was in a happier place now. He could even hear his voice over the thudding acid techno. It was deep and ageless.

It's ok. What you're doing. Its ok you know. It is good that you are ashamed of the stuff you are ashamed of as it shows you have a heart and a soul. That's the measure of the man. Of the life. Of the Being. It's why I've always rated you. But don't take it too seriously Dylan. Everyone does things they don't want to remember, you aren't any different mate, I promise you. You're ok. You're a gentleman and a scholar and I'm glad to have known you. Always rated you Dylan. Life's too short.

What's important is the here and the now. The drugs, the music, the life and the soul. Be all you can be and love as much as you can.

You're alright Dylan.

Life's too short mate.

Have one for me young man.

It occurred to him that he was just projecting his own fears and heartache onto Crabby's memory. And yet somehow he knew that was what the old guy would have said to him. The shame would engulf him later. That was part of the comedown process.

Briefly in clarity before the amphetamines washed over him and pulled him under he marvelled at the capacity of drug taking to make you escape bitter realities and harsh truths.

Dylan had a favourite statistic. At its peak in late 90s and most of the 00s, more than six million ecstasy pills were consumed in the UK on average every weekend.

That's a lot of pain and heartbreak. So much shame and dissatisfaction.

TWENTY-SEVEN

Soundtrack

Kristine W. – 'Land Of The Living'

Grace was at the moment on her way to a late night rendezvous.

The phrase made her laugh every time. It evoked those black and white French filmes noir where the impossibly beautiful raven-haired seductress would lay on the bed completely naked smoking unfiltered Gauloises and taking about Sartre to the tortured yet manly protagonist who was weighed down with secrets he could not tell. Her with not a hair out of place and him with a warm soul but cold eyes...

Come to think of it she had never actually seen a film anything like that. It was a sort of cinematic cliché. They all were weren't they? The idea that romance trumped sex and that love was the most important thing in the world. It was ok if you were beautiful.

The guy on the phone was a new one. She tried to imagine him as the taxi pulled up outside a painfully suburban house in Sidcup. It was probably the furthest outside central London she'd ever ventured for a call and would normally have said no but was out anyway and he'd sounded very genuine on the phone.

As if that was any gauge.

The guy opened the door and he looked almost exactly as she

imagined he would. Similar to the actor who played King Edward Longshanks in Braveheart, only more downtrodden and less powerful. A half crown of wispy white hair ringed a long-bare pate topping a palish moon face with stress lines and skin that alluded to never having been a smoker or much of a drinker.

She'd sat down on the sofa in the front room and he'd disappeared to make her a cup of tea.

It was something that amazed her. She would not have imagined anyone offering a hooker a cup of tea instead of say, a vodka or a glass of wine, but so many of her customers did. Maybe it was British thing. Maybe it never happened in other countries. Maybe they got offered espresso in Italy, green tea in China and a Coke in America.

Maybe it was her. The-Girl-Next-Door-In-The-Pink-Overcoat. Maybe customers wanted to make her feel at home, comfortable. Maybe they would offer her the same thing if she was from the gas board or going round fixing people's cable TV boxes or something.

Grace snapped back to the here and now as the guy, cringingly, dimmed the lights and took his cup of tea to the armchair opposite. It was one of the least sexually charged scenes she could imagine. Even going round fixing cable boxes in porn films had more erotic substance than this. She stifled a smile.

"Hello Nadia. My name is Peter. I'm sixty two years old and I come from Sidcup."

Grace laughed out loud. It was like that old dating game show Cilla Black used to present. What was it called...?

Grace played along.

"I'm Nadia, I'm 24 and I'm from London." It was all she could do not to emphasise the word London, perhaps with fist pump to get an audience reaction.

Peter smiled bashfully.

"I'm sorry. I've… never done this before. I'm sorry to call you out so late. Past bedtime for normal folk isn’t it?"

Grace looked at her watch. Almost two.

"Not at all Peter. Now what was it we spoke about?" Grace let her voice go low and seductive.

The guy opposite visibly flinched.

"Errm. Well... I'd very much like to make love to you. Its... well... its been a while you see? I'd just love to know what it feels like again you know?"

Grace melted a little inside.

"Well I'd very much like you to make love to me Peter. Do you have the cash we talked about?"

Peter leapt off the chair like a salmon and almost threw the notes at her in clear embarrassment.

"Its all there. I think. You can count it. If you want to... erm.... yes."

Grace stood up and took her coat off, draping it suggestively across the arm of his rather worn sofa.

"Would you like me to strip for you Peter?" she asked as sexily as she could.

"Only if you want to Nadia. I mean, I... if..." he seemed to be having trouble retaining his composure.

Grace took her clothes off and Peter led her to a dark bedroom that smelt of bodyspray and faintly of mothballs. It was pitch dark and she could barely seem him. Grace suggested a light but Peter declined.

The sex was strange. Grace had a real sense he was revisiting something from years ago. Maybe his wife left him? She decided against asking how long it had been. He had not put a condom on for a very long time either and got exasperated with it so Grace had to help.

He kept repeating how beautiful she was and how he was really sorry. About what, Grace could only guess at.

He had seemed horrified at the idea of her going down on him so she lay back and let him go on top. He came quickly with a regretful but almost relieved series of whimpers and she lay back exaggerating her breathing in the hope it might seem more dramatic to him. More significant somehow.

He apologised haplessly again and darted for the shelter of the bedroom.

He began chatting her through the door, apparently relieved to have a thin plywood barrier to his obvious shame. His wife had walked out on him seven years hence and the internet dating was not going well. The finality in the manner he told her wanted to have sex one last time suggested something more dramatic and sinister happenings under the surface but if something was awry he was gracious enough not to tell her.

He poked his head round the door looking happier and offered her another cup of tea. Grace knew she shouldn't but it would not do any harm while her cab arrived.

They went downstairs and she reverted to being just another person. Peter was actually a really nice bloke. A kindly older guy with the sort of East End accent you didn't really hear any more and a slight paunch that could have come from a lifetime of pie, mash and jellied eels. He had been working for the big sugar importer in Silvertown all his life and was going to retire soon, having never been out of Europe and not so much as used his passport since 1998. He was a nice bloke. Very caring, very easy to be with.

And he made a fucking superb cup of tea.

Grace could tell he was desperate to ask so she sweetly asked if he wanted to see her again.

Peter seemed delighted, reassuring her he would pay, obviously.

Grace batted her eyelids. Obviously.

They chatted about the weather until the stroke of three when her taxi turned up. Peter helped her with her overcoat like a gentleman and ushered her with deference toward his front door.

She turned and kissed him tenderly on the cheek as she crossed the threshold and for a second she looked right into the older man's eyes...

BANG.

It was like an claw hammer to the intestines.

What she saw there rocked her to her core. The most violent of looks of emotion imaginable. It was savage.

Pity.

Worry.

Sympathy.

Desperately scrabbling to regain a lost composure she hurried to the car and slammed the door behind her. Out of the corner of a bubbling eye she saw Cup-Of-Tea-Peter waving from his doorstep.

The cab driver hurried through the streets. Grace slumped back into the seat and leaned her head against the upright, looking out of the fogging windows. It had gone three in the morning and there was a surprising amount of traffic on the roads still. Ignoring the normally-impressive fact that the driver knew exactly where her road was, she handed over three purple notes fresh from Cup-Of-Tea-Peter's ownership and went inside.

Her coat was thrown over the table. Her boots left where they laid.

Grace slumped into her chair, bottom lip trembling.

Barney approached her with more caution than might be expected given that she had not been home since the early afternoon which was almost like a lifetime in hungry cat years.

Presently he daintily leapt up onto the arm of the chair and sat down facing her.

Don't worry about it. He is just a kind bloke who thinks you live a life of pimps and abuse. He's just worried about you, that's all.

Grace could not get past the feeling that Peter's concern was very much as real as the look in his eye. He felt sorry for her. The most tragic customer she could imagine, an old guy with no prospects for retirement but a slow and lonely twilight. Forced to pay money just to feel human warmth again. A dried up bald bloke who knew his own decline all too viscerally.

And he felt sorry for her.

It was almost too much to bear.

It was different to the usual diatribe of questions she got most of the time. Everyone wanted to know what made her choose to do what she did. It was part of the patter. Part of prostitute patois. They all wanted to know how much she enjoyed her job, how she got paid to have orgasms and how she was saving for a car. Or a holiday. Or a law degree. She had the fantasy and the answers down perfectly. It was not because they were interested in her it was to assuage guilt for some and to reassure that she enjoyed fucking them for others. Not a single one of them gave two fucks about her. Zero fucks given by all. Too busy fucking to care.

But Cup-Of-Tea-Peter's sympathy was like a stiletto between the ribs, puncturing. Drawing the breath out of her. It was pain. He felt pain at her plight. Her situation. The suffering she must be going through to be doing what she had to do. He was guessing at some terrible run of misfortune, of addiction, pain, loneliness and neglect that came to pass to see her selling herself for money. Grace imagined him alone in his house crucifying himself for contributing to her misery but reassuring somehow at every turn that he had done some good.

That she had needed that chat and those cups of tea.

Maybe she had.

The thoughts came like a series of tired kicks after that. Her life had to change. The hooking was a means to an end. She'd saved up almost enough to pay off her student loan, credit cards, personal loan and still had a couple of thousand in the bank to start off a savings account for a deposit on her own place soon. She would probably have enough in a couple of months if she kept it tidy and her spending very much in check. After that she could return to the land of the living.

Unable or unwilling to go to bed as the stimulants from the cups of tea still coursed through her, Grace put a CD on and sat in silence in her chair as Barney kept her company seemingly as lost in a mess of his own emotions as she was.

The first track on the progressive trance compilation she had chosen was a perennial favourite since her college days, all through university and ever since. It was about her surviving. Living in the land of the living.

Grace listened to the words, mouthing them as she did so.

It felt like a decision had been taken by circumstance many weeks ago and only now was she waking up to the reality that her time as a prostitute was coming to an end. She would need to get a proper job. It took some effort to visualise and get her head around even though the decision was more or less made for her. Lying to Dylan that she was away seeing her parents in Eastbourne so she had a weekend to work solidly was just the start, she knew. The lies would get harder and so too would the effort needed to stay committed. Eventually she would make her excuses and end it with him just because she didn't want to carry on lying. And that would be a shame.

Dylan popped back into her head for the dozenth time that night. She thought about texting him but did not want to wake him. Barney butted her hand gently asking for strokes on his head and she obliged so he stepped carefully onto her lap and allowed her to pleasure him.

She woke up with Barney still dozing contentedly on her lap. Sunlight streamed back into the room from a promising-looking day outside. She looked at her watch. She and Barney had been asleep in her chair for almost five hours. He did not wake immediately but as she stirred he opened an eye, immediately registering what Grace took to mean a hearty good morning greeting of care and consideration but was more likely to have been a complaint about a lack of dinner the previous evening.

He leapt off her lap and walked up to his squeaky clean food bowl and turned to face her, meows becoming more and more insistent. Grace fed him and went back to bed.

TWENTY-EIGHT

Soundtrack

Iio – 'Rapture' (Armin Van Buuren Mix)

Dylan cracked open an eye.

He was in a room he did not recognise.

He'd apparently fallen asleep in a lounge chair fully clothed but had no memory of going to whoever's house it was after the forest rave thing. A scattering of other people were dotted around also fully clothed, some asleep or passed out and others clustered around a small table at the other end of the room with a couple of bottles of spirits and a mirror. They were talking in hushed tones. Some Massive Attack was seeping out quietly from somewhere, not tinny enough to be someone's phone but not loud enough to be a major sound system. Dylan realised it was coming from the next room. After scanning for Jason and Carla and coming up empty, he rose stiffly and walked out.

The room next door was a little more lively. Jason, Carla, Forrester and several others he did not recognise were huddled around a huge baroque mirror. The curtains were resolutely screwed shut but the overhead lights burned as if keeping the party alive.

"Alright mate." Forrester cheerily offered. Jason and Carla ignored him, too busy with a pile of something pink and powdery he could not identify.

Someone nudged him from behind. A black woman in her 50s had a tray with cups of tea on it and smiling easily she offered him one. Dylan took one without truly expressing the depth of the gratitude he felt and leaned against the doorframe watching Jason hoover up small matchstick sized lines of the pink powder.

Dylan thought about asking whose house it was or at least attempting to make conversation with the actually-very-amiable-in-real-life Forrester. Deciding against it, he stayed quiet for a few seconds.

His jeans were dirty and having slept in them felt as if they were stiff with a layer of his greasy sweat. His t-shirt stuck to him. He could smell his own stink. It made him crave warm running water and fresh clothes.

"What's that?" he asked nobody in particular as they busied themselves with the pink dust.

Forrester pointed to the mirror.

"CK. Your coke, my coke and all the Ket all mixed in. Want a blast?" Dylan still did not understand where the pinkness came from but declined the invitation anyway.

Next thing he realised he was kneeling over the mirror, drinking straw in hand. A smallish line disappeared with more effort that usual. It seemed hard to summon up the suction.

Straight away Dylan wished he hadn't.

He stood up curling his toes up and rubbing his nose.

"Fuck's sake. Fuck..... fuck's sake" he muttered resignedly.

Bright eyed and bushy tailed, Forrester pointed at another one magically lined up.

"All yours when you want it fella. Don't ask just do it. Epic bad boy pills by the way. Fucking epic. Love your bad self bruv."

Dylan nodded at him in acceptance which was all he could manage.

Right then a large presence next to him made him turn round. It was Bean. He picked up Dylan in both arms with a violence completely at odds with how he felt and when he set him down Dylan felt totally overwhelmed. The line was starting to take effect. He would not be able to stand much longer, so nodded and made sounds at Bean (who thought it was all hilarious) while he went to sit by the radiator.

The room changed. Bean managed to safely guide a credit card corner with a bump of pink CK on it from across the room and seemed to visibly shovel it up Dylan's nose.

The room compacted and darkened. Colours changed, walls wheeled away and Bean melded into a still and soundless part of the chair he was learning against. The music got deeper and more visceral. His consciousness opened wide in the act of tranquillised closing up and actions became reflexes in slow-motion. The drugs coursed through him, running down his still limbs as if he was stretching them after a year's sleep.

"Time to go Dyls. Time to go mate."

Someone he knew was speaking to him but he could not make the connection. He could see her stood over him but she was many metres away still and he could not place her name. Her voice was mixing with the music and he could not tell what she was saying.

Dylan peered finally over the lip of his hole. Carla and Jason were stood over him. Nobody else was around. The Massive Attack was still playing but it was quieter.

"Party's ooooover mate." Jason informed him.

Dylan couldn't tell if Jason was slurring his words or whether it was in his head.

"Time to go." Dylan managed, trying to sound more together than he felt.

"Cab's here." Carla was already heading to the door.

Outside the sun was shining but offered no reassurance to Dylan. Jason helped him into the cab and then they were gone. The cab rumbled through the streets. Dylan listened to the different bumps from behind closed eyes.

It was almost rhythmic.

Thud. Thud. Thud.

The radio was talking. Or was it in his head?

...As if maybe someone could sample the noises and turn them into a techno track with the bumps and the rolls and the grinds like cattle grids but they did not have cattle in London so there were no cattle grids but they had them in St James' Park didn't they? Neenor.Neeenor. Because there were horses and cattle in the parks they did not want them escaping into the streets because cattle don't like grids and they can't open doors or put petrol into cars but they like sugar and sugarlumps and horses don't like house music no house for horses no house for horses just CK and truth and Crabby in raver heaven with his brains and his spirit and his energy and his brains and truth… grind grind thud thud thud bump bump bump grind grind neenor neenor. Bump.

Thud.

A familiar sounding door pulled shut. Dylan did not open his eyes but felt unimaginably warm and comfortable in his duvet, sinking further and further into the bed away from the light and the noise.

*****

"Tea is the fucking daddy. It is the best fucking thing in the fucking universe."

Carla was offering him a mug. It was his chipped and faded but much-beloved Chelsea mug commemorating the 1994 Cup Final appearance. He remembered the day as if it were yesterday, not more than two decades in the past. He had been caught up with the optimism of the day like everyone else. They had already beaten United home and away 1-0 and had the measure of Alex Ferguson's men. The first half had been all Chelsea, Gavin Peacock had hit the bar and they were all over United at the break. Then the rain came and with it two dodgy penalties and a crushing 4-0 battering. The soggy walk back down a funereal Wembley Way was etched into the minds of every Chelsea fan who had been there. It was desperate.

The comedown from the weekend was similarly jarring. Dylan had spent the whole day staring blankly at the TV then listening to trance classics completely at a loss to know what to do with himself. The ketamine had long since faded but the sticky amphetamines resided still in his hands, toes and powdery jaw.

Dylan winced a thank you to Carla and shifted over to allow her to sit down on the end of the sofa.

He collapsed back and closed his eyes. In the background Nadia Ali's sultry tones over the Armin mix of Iio's 'Rapture' touched him deep inside, closing his eyes from the inside, telling him that all was going to be ok. Making him want to cry.

The warmth of the mug snapped him out of his reverie and Dylan opened his eyes to place the mug on the floor.

"How you feeling?" he asked, already knowing the answer.

"I'm ok. Had a top time, no ill effects. You look like shit though..."

Her honesty was not as refreshing as it ought to have been.

"Big session. Not had one that big for a while. Going to be feeling this for a few days I think."

"You going to meet up with Grace again?"

"Probably this week yeah she said she was going to text me." Dylan said.

"You should text her." Carla informed him in that matter-of-fact way she had of expressing opinion as truth.

Dylan gulped. The idea of meeting up with Grace with half his faculties missing-in-action was not working for him.

"I'll be lucky if I can remember her fucking name mate. I'm going to be a space cadet until at least Wednesday."

"So meet her on Wednesday then." Dylan could not tell if Grace was being short or not.

Dylan stayed quiet. After a couple of minutes Carla had another go.

"You went down on that fucking wrongun didn't you?"

The truth of it made Dylan screw his face up.

"Leave it out mate."

Carla cackled at him from across the sofa.

"You are the fucking wrongun Dylan mate. Dirty fucker! What would Grace think?"

"Well I'm not going to fucking tell her am I?" Dylan parried.

"There's a lot you aren't telling her." It was the definition of a loaded comment. The open-endedness of it hung in the air, demanding of him.

Dylan shrugged.

"How do you know I've not told her about the dealing?" he asked, becoming a little exasperated at her line of questioning.

"Because you are dating her and it doesn't exactly come up in conversation over a bowl of pasta does it? She would never speak to you again." Carla told him as if this was news.

"Would she though? I mean, it's just a little bit of gear, a few pills and such. It's not proper dealing. What's so bad about that?" Even Dylan knew he was not being truthful.

Carla shot him a look that told him all he needed to know about her views on the subject.

Jason joined in from behind them, neither realising he was even there.

"Its your choice mate. We're not criticising." he explained, clearly trying to prevent an argument.

Dylan gestured toward Carla who now sat facing him, arms folded and eyes ablaze. It was very clear he felt Carla was criticising.

"That bullshit at the Bass Factory the other week?" she accused.

Dylan visibly wilted, feeling more emotional at the memory of it than he should have done. Dylan instantly regretted opening up to her about the horrors of that night.

"That was a mistake..."

Jason butted in again, unexpectedly.

"By rights you should be doing a fucking two stretch right now mate. Carla told me. Fuck's sake mate…"

Dylan unfolded his arms in a gesture of surrender. They were both right. He looked up at Carla who was staring at him with worry and concern in her big eyes.

He decided against answering.

They were absolutely right of course. First he nearly got busted then Luca nearly beat the shit out of him, and then there was the litany of poor choices from the previous night. It was like a fuckup smorgasbord.

It would be easier to criticise, he knew, if it had not been fun in parts and had it not come so easily to him. The mere fact he was in recovery mode, a well-oiled and time honoured process of rest, relaxation and restoration across the early part of the week post-session, was truth enough. That he had a recovery mode at all was damning in itself. It was not something he needed even to think about now, it just came naturally. Ease borne solely out of repetition.

You don't get good at dealing without being a proper dealer. You don't get good at recovering from drug-fuelled binges without loving doing the drugs in the first place.

As if reading his mind, Jason piped up again.

"Its too bloody simplistic to say you are knocking it on the fucking head Dyl. You been saying it for fucking ages. Feels like you've been saying you are done with it and you want out since before you were even dealing."

Hearing one of his friends call him a drug dealer specifically jarred him all over again. There was a difference between Monday comedown talk and the existential conversation they were having. Dylan could see that easily.

Carla took his hand.

"You've been saying it for ages mate."

Dylan nodded with a rather forced fake laugh.

"What is this, some kind of intervention?"

Carla and Jason did not laugh with him.

"Not at all mate. It's your life. But it just feels like it is all getting a bit Guillermo Del Toro for you at the moment. You know?" Jason added calmly.

"Del who?" Carla asked, trying to add a bit of much-needed levity.

"Spanish film producer. Fucking dark. Really dark-as-fuck mainstream horror films." Dylan offered, glad of the opportunity to swerve the conversation.

"Dark is about right. Just as you meet a top bird. Would be a shame if you let it all come on top... you know." Carla was shaking her head at Dylan.

It was not so much reproachful as regretful.

Dylan found himself blushing in spite of himself, embarrassed again at the dim memory of the sex acts performed whilst on drugs in a random piece of forest in North West London in the middle of the night.

He had to admit it was dark.

There was a long pause. 'Rapture' was still playing, approaching its melodic climax. Nobody said a word as the track came to an end.

The orchestral strains of 'Set in Stone' by Bedrock floated up next. Dylan closed his eyes, trying desperately not be in the room having that conversation.

The silence over the cathedral trance was so heavy it almost stopped Dylan's breathing. It seemed to crush him. His eyes opened again. He had to face them. The trance moment would wait.

Carla looked worried, perhaps that Dylan may burst into very awkward tears.

"Next time you want to go down on someone…"

There was a long pause.

"…call Grace for fuck's sake!" Carla laughed loudly, obviously keen to push things along.

Or you…

"...not judging you like, you know." she added.

Dylan thought about protesting at their judgement of him given that Jason had gotten an equally personal sex act performed on him from the same random just a few minutes prior, or even that he had categorically not gone into the bushes specifically to go down on her etc. In the end he just cracked a smile, thinking about Grace.

"I wish."

Jason punched him in the arm in his own levity attempt. "Sloppy seconds. You filfy cunt."

Carla glared at him.

"So you reckon I should tell her?" Dylan asked.

"About the sket in the forest, no mate." Jason laughed. "I'd leave that one out if I was you pal."

Carla was still glaring at Jason.

"You're a dirty cunt as well Jase for fuck's sake.. he means about the dealing you prick."

Jason stopped laughing and immediately went serious. His face fell so fast Dylan wondered how much of the previous mirth had been genuine.

There was a stony silence.

Carla turned her head sideways in the way dogs do sometimes when they do not understand something. Lips pursed, she offered nothing but an exaggerated sigh.

Dylan glanced at Jason. He was stood behind them hands on hips showing no signs of expressing an opinion.

In the end Dylan aborted the pregnant pause.

"Well I'm going to extricate myself from the dealing next few weeks, sell what's left and square things with Luca and Antonio and then all we're talking about is occasional light recreational drug use. 100% manageable."

Carla and Jason both laughed long and hard at his understatement in light of the state he had been in just 12 hours previously. The deafening release of humour seemed to press the tension out of the air like a thunderstorm finally breaking after hours of stifling pressure.

"Cutting back then!" Carla snorted, tea coming out of her nose.

Dylan was hurt all over again but tried not to show it.

Jason hammered him on the shoulder again.

"Cutting back!" he repeated.

"What are you, a fucking parrot?" Dylan spat, defensively.

"Twat…" Jason shook his head.

Carla shot him a toxic glance. "Shut up ballbag."

She gently placed both hands on top of Dylan's in his lap.

"Cutting down will happen naturally if you don't have a shoe box full of drugs in your room. And if you are seeing more of Grace. So we believe in you mate."

"It's not a fucking heroin addiction Carla."

Dylan was still exasperated at what a big deal his housemates were making about his life. They both probably did at least as much gear as he did and irritatingly neither seemed to suffer anything like the ill effects he had to put up with. Carla if anything loved coke even more than Dylan did. And he'd never met anyone who smoked as much dope as Jason. So them having some soppy fucking intervention-over-tea was a bit off, he mused.

"Look, fuck's sake man. We do as much or more as you do, it's not a fucking judgement. I just think Grace is a great bird and she's perfect for you. I'd just fucking hate to see you fucking… …mug yourself off over something as daft as the fucking gear. Its bollocks honey." Carla stated, articulately. It was like she could read his mind. Dylan repressed a smile about what would happen if that were really true.

There were more pressing things to worry about.

"So you do think I've got a problem." Dylan wasn't really asking because he did not really want to know the answer.

"No, but you will have if you let it create problems for you, bird-wise, you know?" Jason offered.

Carla nodded in agreement. "Agree."

"Can't help but agree with you both. Like I said I'm going to knock the dealing on the head and..."

Dylan's phone buzzed.

He glanced down. It was a text from Grace.

By the time he'd finished reading it twice, Jason had sloped off and Carla was back engrossed in the ancient trance compilation muttering about how much she fucking loved this tune.

Grace wanted to meet up tomorrow for coffee.

Fuck.

*****

Grace was in the back of a taxi heading back to North London.

Her midday appointment had not shown up. She had waited in the pub for more than an hour. Eyes everywhere had bored into her subconsciously. In her mind every other person in the pub had been her customer. He'd taken one look at her and not fancied her. Maybe it was a group of lads, calling her on a wind-up. Maybe they were laughing at her.

In the end she'd texted the number back a terse "Do not call me again." and left the pub. Not in the mood for a full-view public Underground trip she'd chosen to get a cab, suddenly feeling very alone. She'd drafted the text to Dylan and sent it really before properly thinking about it. But she was glad she had.

Her thoughts moved from discomfort to warm places as she remembered the slightly podgy funny man with the great sense of humour and soft lips.

Lies about Eastbourne and work be fucked. I'm looking forward to seeing him again.

*****

Dylan had texted a short reply to her almost immediately, in no mood to play games. He was a definite proponent of lengthy and verbose texts but his bruised mind was not feeling charismatic enough to take any chances on being funny. Not today.

He'd gone into his room and pulled out the ornate wooden mini-chest from under his bed. It was hardly an original hiding place but he reasoned that if he were ever raided by the police no amount of furniture subterfuge would stop the sniffer dogs. Thus, anything other than ease of access was a waste of time.

The box had been a present from an uncle way back when from a visit somewhere in Indonesia. It was decoratively carved in rich dark hardwood and solidly built. The sort of thing you might find in the sand washed up on a tropical island filled with timeless treasures, or so the boyhood daydreams went.

Inside now though was cursed treasure of the modern age. He had more than two hundred pills, nine grammes of cut coke to sell, a large bag of indeterminate weight of uncut coke for personal use, four tabs of ancient blotter acid with faded pictures of little purple flowers on that would likely never get used, and seven grammes of ketamine. Two small and battered pink 2CI pills sat in the bottom, also never likely to see the light of day - with Dylan anyway. Lastly there was an Olbas inhaler, three grubby and splitting Marlboro Lights, two half-filled Poppers bottles that made him shudder involuntarily whenever he smelt their distinctive amyl nitrate reek, and a threadbare, barely-smokable joint. The dust and detritus from everything that had been in the box over the years lay in the corners like the after remnants of a large dinner. He had joked more than once that someone could get higher than a kite just by burning the box on the fire in the front room, so many myriad chemicals and agents had it contained over the years.

In a side section were some laminated photo souvenirs from past nights out, none very recent. Some dated back to before he had left university. He did not want to be reminded of how skinny and hirsute he had been back in the day so left the reminiscing for another day.

All the drugs laid out before him on his duvet.

It was quite the horde, he had to admit. It was a lot more than he realised he had.

Ah well, more to shift. More money when I do.

On a whim, Dylan phoned Claridge to see if he needed anything. It turned out in one of those weird drug coincidences that Claridge was having another of his quarterly house parties the following weekend and had been about to get in touch with Dylan anyway to source the gear for it. He was after six grammes of the coke and a hundred and twenty of the pills.

A very good start.

*****

Grace arrived home and ignored Barney's mewing as she barrelled through the door in a mixed mood. The anger from the no-show was still fresh but it was not the first time it had happened to her and she knew it was just one of those things.

Some men are gutless time-wasting pricks. Fact of life.

In other news, the sun comes up and the music keeps on playing all night long.

The coffee date with Dylan had been accepted very quickly and the very rapid response was gratifying. Dylan was an honest guy, who did not play games or get involved in all that boy-meets-girl-politics shit.

Dylan was not a gutless time-wasting prick.

This is good news.

No sooner had she taken her coat off and pressed play on her favourite Basement Jaxx album on her stereo when her work mobile cheeped again.

It was Spanky Dave from Old Street. He informed her he had bought her a tribute gift and that he also had a special surprise.

They set a 3pm meeting the following day, and it worked out well in one of those weird sex industry coincidences that her coffee date with Dylan in very nearby Liverpool Street was at half five.

All good news. Plenty of time for her final appointment of the day at half past nine in Dalston.

She signed off the text by informing with as much ominous authority as she could muster that Old Street Dave would "be dealt with in a most severe manner" the following day. She imagined the horror-meets-sexual-pinnacle look on the old guy's face when he read it.

TWENTY-NINE

Soundtrack

Bedrock – 'Set In Stone'

The vomit would not come.

His eyes burned as the sweat seemed to run down his face seeking them out. His breath rattled in his chest and hands on knees, Dylan dry-heaved once more.

The gym session had been a good idea in theory.

A punishment session. Brutal, agonising discipline.

Sweat out some of the toxins, focus the mind, thrash away some of the cobwebs. Maybe lose some weight.

The reality had been sadly different. The half hour run he had planned was cut short by a light-headed coughing fit around the fifteen minute stage. In a fit of pique he'd clambered off the treadmill as if he'd meant to do only fifteen minutes and uncertainly mounted a futuristic-looking cross-trainer. Shamefully less than fifteen minutes later and the wheezing and dizziness had reached crisis proportions and he had half-fallen off the device utterly insensible. The whole experience had been more torture than catharsis and seemed very much to have done more harm than it had done good.

Eyes locked on the floor Dylan headed for the showers convinced everyone in the gym were laughing and mocking his pathetic, purple-headed efforts. He could almost hear them giggling.

After going through the final indignity of having to dress in front of the scattering of huge-cocked fitness freaks in the changing room, Dylan walked out keen to get as far away from the Fitness First chamber of horrors as he could. A trainer he had spoken to after joining almost a year ago about taking his free (and to-date still unused) personal training hour session tried to corner him on the way out.

"Great session? Got a top gym buzz I bet?" He was all perfect dazzling white teeth and bronzed Aussie twattishness.

"Fuck off." Dylan said, only in his mind.

"Errr. yeah... cosmic mate, yeah." was all he could manage.

"My name's Trent. We need to talk about some training there big guy!"

Big guy?

Oh do fuck off mate.

With your cunty name and your cunty smile with your cunty teeth and your cunty long hair and your cunty fucking abs and your cunty arms and your cunty fucking trainers with little cunty toes on them.

Cunt.

"I'll be in next week. " Dylan lied apologetically.

"Then I'll see ya later mate. Have a great day!" Dylan was dazzled by the flashing white teeth.

Then the doors opened and he was gone. Free.

The sweat was still running like a tap as he walked down the street towards work. Maybe tomorrow he would be proud that he had managed to go to the gym before work and had uncharacteristically eschewed an extra hour or so in bed.

His mind flicked back to the large amount of illegal drugs in his bag. It turned the sweat on his face to ice straightaway. Carrying large quantities like that around the City always made him nervous.

*****

Grace was stood in Old Street Spanky Dave's front room less than a quarter of a mile away from Dylan's afternoon in the office.

Dave had let her in and then closed the front room door behind him. It was a weird thing. He loved the roleplay aspect so he asked if she would make him wait outside until it was time for his punishment. Grace was not in a hurry so made him wait a few minutes. It all added to the theatre for him she supposed.

"David, come in here please." she boomed. Grace had added a headmistress tone to her voice, complete with over-pronunciation and a flowery traditional upper class accent.

The door opened and a very sheepish-looking older guy walked in. He walked over to her and handed her a daintily-wrapped gift.

As it happened it was two gifts in one. The first was a surprisingly lovely pair of Tiffany silver earrings in a tiny aquamarine box. The second was a rigid cardboard box containing a fearsome looking dark leather strap.

"Its an Loch original..." he seemed delighted to inform her. If he was disappointed that she very obviously had never heard of such a device or had any concept of what determined an Original (acquired for what was likely to be an extravagant sum), he did not show it.

"...you can keep it and then bring to our meetings... uh sessions... err.. If you want to, that is." he added.

"I see." said Grace with a little too much extravagance, suddenly evoking over-acted school plays from years ago.

"Come here please."

*****

Bag-o'-drugs slung over his shoulder, Dylan had finished work and was walking just a shade too fast to Cafe Nero at Liverpool Street. Realising his mistake he arrived sweating again, only to find Grace already there. He was about to do a slow loop outside to cool off when she spotted him. She was sat inside half way through a large latte.

They greeted each other warmly with a kiss and a lingering embrace although neither knew of the other's reason to treasure the closeness of comfort.

"So how was your weekend?" she started.

Dylan felt himself flush again as the lies poured out.

"Quiet one mainly, night out with Carla and Jase on Friday, chilled out rest of the time didn't really do much. What about you?"

"Same. Went to Eastbourne, saw the folks. Sunday night I stayed in, glass of wine, West Wing box set. Boring really."

"Cool, sounds nice." Dylan said politely.

"Not really, just saving money you know?" Dylan thought it cute that she felt the need to justify being boring, when being boring sounded just about the most attractive thing in the world at that point.

"You look gorgeous." Dylan blurted out.

Grace blushed coquettishly.

"You didn't have to get dressed up just for me you know" he said seriously.

Grace laughed, mind racing.

"Neither did you!" she fired back.

Dylan looked down at his shirt and tie.

"This is work gear but glad you like it."

Twat!

"So what you doing later?" Grace asked, trying to get away from any more potentially-awkward questions about her attire.

"Nothing much, got to go drop off some wine to a mate of mine later then off home. Got a gym session early tomorrow before work so going to keep it an early one. You?"

You lying shitbag!

"Same really." Grace idly responded, all at once wishing she'd gone into more detail with the lie.

"D'you fancy a pint?" Dylan asked suddenly, hoping his dynamism and decision-making would impress his radiant companion.

Grace laughed.

Dylan watched her laugh. She was beautiful. He noted again the little dimples she had when she laughed loudly. She'd thrown her hair back and placed both hands on the table. They were perfectly smooth. Dylan decided they were easily the best looking pair of hands he had ever seen.

"Are you saying I'm boring?" she giggled.

Horrified at the insinuation Dylan hunted for the right words.

"You.... ....have got beautiful hands."

You have got to be fucking kidding me. Seriously? What, does she think you're some freak with a finger fetish now? Great. Nice one. Prick.

Grace stopped laughing and turned her head to one side at the randomness of his remark. Dylan thought he might stop breathing if he stopped smiling. As it was the smile stayed and she almost seemed happy at his hapless attempt at flirting.

"Thanks."

They left the coffee shop. Grace made a move towards the large ornate Wetherspoons in the station. Dylan realised the last time he had been in there had been when Kimberley bought him dinner to cheer him up about losing his job, knowing full well the whole time she was going to dump him at Rebekah's party just a couple of a days afterwards.

The snidey, cynical fucking disloyal bitch!

Dylan gently suggested Dirty Dicks across the road and took her arm without really thinking about it. Grace was different league to Kimberley. She made him feel completely differently, about so many things. Kimberley obviously never really gave a shit about him or his feelings but Grace was at once well out of his league yet interested in him. She listened to him, she laughed with him. He had a real sense that if he were upset or hurt about something he could tell her, or that she would know if something was on his mind. That captivated as well as terrified him.

One pint turned into two. Dylan loved the fact that Grace, pretty though she was and far daintier than he, drank them just as he did. Kimberley had strictly been a white wine spritzer sort of girl. Sad really, he mused.

"I love that you like good pubs and good beer and you drink it properly." he told her.

Grace nodded.

"I'm actually a bit of a Tom-boy really. I used to be a bit bigger than this. My brother used to run beer festivals back in the day and I used to help him. Always liked a nice beer. I like wine as well but depends who i'm with. If i'm out with the girls I drink wine but my preference is whiskey or beer. I'll drink anything really."

Dylan tried to imagine Grace a stone and a half heavier, thicker set and wearing jeans and sweatshirts and could not quite picture it.

"Same here. Apart from cherry brandy. And Baileys." Dylan gave an exaggerated shudder.

"Let me guess, misspent teenage years right?" Grace smiled.

"Correctamundo. On both counts. Never been so sick in all my puff." Dylan shook his head, trying to look traumatised.

Grace pursed her lips.

"I'm like that about tequila and raki. But those are from bad nights more recent than my teenage years."

Dylan nodded sagely.

"I don't mind a margarita, but I can't be doing with shots of tequila. Ruinous."

Grace nodded in agreement.

"Sambuca" they said in unison.

Grace yelped with laughter and Dylan stared into her face.

"Snap!"

"Well that's it. It's done. We're meant to be together. That alone is the basis for you to marry me and have all my kids and stuff...

Sambuca forever more." Dylan's tone reassured Grace he was joking.

Before Grace could follow up Dylan had ordered two sambucas and all but thrown the banknote at the barman.

He rounded on her with much more apparent confidence than he felt.

"I'm really glad I met you Grace." He decided against telling her he had referred to her for a couple of near-meets as The-Girl-In-The-Pink-Overcoat.

Grace melted a little inside. He was actually into her!

And she wasn't at all creeped out!

This was good news.

"I'm glad we finally got to meet too Dylan. You are a really nice bloke. I've been looking forward to seeing you again."

"Ditto. Do you want to go see a film this week?" Dylan blurted out. He had not planned this. The words had just come out.

Grace nodded a little too emphatically. "There's that film on, you know the one with matey boy? Him, whatshisname? With the thing, was in that other film... oh fuck what's it called?"

Dylan had a strange frisson of sexual excitement just for a fraction of a second. Good looking women who use bad language...

"Can't do this week but next is good. Say next Thursday? Maybe?" Grace was willing him to say yes.

Dylan scooped up his shot and threw his other arm round Grace.

"I propose a toast. To whatshiname in that thing that neither of us can remember!"

Grace laughed loudly again, lifting her shot with mock apology.

"To whatshisfeatures!"

Dylan did not remove his arm straightaway, but let it a second longer than would be casually acceptable. Grace did not mind. He had big arms. Not muscular really but big. Powerful.

It had been a long time since anyone had put an arm round her to protect and comfort her. The raw emotion of the chain of thought stopped the breath in her throat and for a second she wondered if she might tear up as her cheeks reddened.

Dylan noticed her flush and ordered them two more pints.

"...Takes the taste away. Always makes me go Farmer Giles in the cheeks..." Dylan informed her.

Grace laughed and nodded but said nothing, still worried her voice may crack. She desperately fought back the huge sheets of emotion as they draped over her. She felt comfortable and safe with Dylan. He was a nice, honest, trustworthy bloke who she fancied and would look after her. He made her laugh, he could read her, he was sensitive and he had a good job. And he was someone she could tell anything to.

It had been so long since she had let anyone into her life like that. Being a prostitute made you have to put boundaries up. Safeguards. She had not been nor was she still prepared for how desolately lonely it was to have other people pay her to be with them in the closest physical way one person can be with another.

It shocked her how lonely the company of another person could be.

The warmth of Dylan's company defrosted her somehow. She imagined her insides frozen solid with solitude crackling and pulsing as the ice retreated like one of those time-lapse films of the icecaps.

"You ok?" Dylan asked.

Grace smiled and nodded. "Sorry, I'm knackered. What were we talking about?"

"I was saying how I'd love to go on holiday somewhere. Feels like it's been years, Well, it has actually." Dylan continued.

"I'm well overdue for a break as well." There seemed a sadness dripping out of Grace's observation that even Dylan could register.

They finished the last two pints and Grace refused a third. Grace took the lead and embraced Dylan warmly before they had left the pub, leaning in close. Dylan was not to be taken by surprise and accepted the opportunity of the kiss. Her lips were impossibly soft. Never really one for kissing much, Dylan found himself wanting to kiss her endlessly.

"I love kissing you," he whispered into her ear.

Grace didn't respond but redoubled the kiss. Dylan took a chance and moved a hand to the side of her face, gently cupping her ear and running his thumb through the hair behind it. He was absolutely certain he felt her break a little inside.

In a good way.

Yes, in a nice way.

It was, he understood, the sound and feel of ice melting or barriers being broken down. At that moment he knew he needed to know everything about her.

Retaining his cool and not wishing to get carried away lest the tightening in his boxer shorts become an issue, he ended the kiss with a huge, endearing smile.

Grace withdrew and opened her eyes to see Dylan grinning sweetly like a moron. The incongruity of it made her laugh. She darted in for one quick peck on the lips and erupted into a grin of her own.

"I'll see you Thursday week."

"Can't wait."

Then she was gone. Just like that.

Sluggish after the beer and sambuca Dylan moved to the wall of the pub and pulled out his headphones. It would take half an hour to get to Claridge's to drop off the gear. He got on the bus from outside the station in a near-trance, unable to get Grace out of his mind. Objectively, when he first saw her he thought she was a bit plain. The plainness was gone now. The smile she had dazzled him with after the kiss had been a show-stopper. It was like one of those movie posters where whatshername the actress smiles for the cameras. Just perfect.

He had never believed in those cheesy movie moments where the film goes slow-mo, the music goes soppy and the leading lady and the leading man go as fuzzy as the camera work. That didn't happen. Not in dirty London with its dirty people and all their dirty little secrets.

Well here's a dirty little secret for you Dylan old son…

Dylan realised his heart was still beating out of his chest. It was thudding so hard he could barely catch his breath.

He held out a hand. It was shaking like a leaf.

THIRTY

Soundtrack

Massive Attack – 'Attack'

Grace was on time for her evening appointment but had she been late she would not have cared.

Quite unprepared for the emotion of such a small gesture, she had been taken aback. The kiss had been perfect. She had wanted to continue. Had she not had a customer that evening she might have suggested a couple more drinks and she knew it was likely to have ended up back at his or hers. It was strange, he was not a conventionally attractive bloke and the teeth again were not good, yet he was a great kisser. It added a sexual note to the companionship tower that dominated her thoughts of him. She found herself wanting to go there with him. It was a thought as surprising as it was welcome. Wasn't I supposed to be off shagging? Busman's holiday or something?

It was not like what she had been selling. It was about wanting to be with him, to experience him.

She cursed herself at the Mills & Boon style clichés. In those books she would think about giving herself to him, to allow him to have her, a giving in, a duty and a weird fixation with love.

Grace was modern enough to be realistic. She had started off not fancying Dylan. Then she did. It wasn't the switch of a light, it was a bit like coming up on a pill. Nervy and a bit discomforting at first then soft, then softer and then BAM!

Lady love is ticking your cortexes and running her digits across your oblongata, writing the letters L O V and E across it.

Then she fancied him a lot, now she wanted to fuck him. Her stomach did knots just thinking about it.

How lovely it is to feel something good, something clean about the act of sex with another person! So nice!

So how was it different to what she was going to do with the guy she was going to meet? Or for any of them for that matter?

She honestly could not say.

Shortly afterwards she was on all fours, eyes closed with a customer behind her. He was muttering to himself and she tried not to listen. Nothing the sweaty mess could possibly be saying would make her feel good. She imagined it was Dylan. It fell apart as the customer was malcoórdinated and was trying to make up for an apparent lack of something with considerable power and grunting effort. She moaned loudly and it did the trick, she felt him jerking his endgame away behind her. Feeling slightly tender and a little manhandled she picked up the cash in her normal charming manner, got dressed and left.

The cab wound its way back to North London, and exhausted Grace sank into the back seats. She felt dirty and used. It was not a new feeling but manifestly one brought into sharper relief by the earlier date with Dylan and her revelations about The Welcome Return Of The Actual Honest Fanny Flutter.

Was there a degree of guilt there?

THIRTY-ONE

Soundtrack

The Jam – 'Going Underground'

It was one of those mornings where it would be easy to imagine videographers taking time lapse film of the sun rising and dismissing the epic sky of clouds on its rise to its zenith. London's buildings gleamed in the Spring light set against a startling blue sky of pure cobalt.

Dylan had risen before nine and gone for a radish-faced and slightly-too-short run up to Alexandra Palace with only one thing on his mind.

Grace was dominating his days in the same way she dominated his day and night dreams. Suddenly acutely aware of his own embarrassingly dilapidated body and health he resolved yet again win some alacrity to do something about it. As was usual with Dylan, it was all or nothing. Feast or famine. Not a man to do things by half measures, he had not eaten a square meal for a couple of days, assuming (and he did) that quinoa pots and raw Japanese seaweed salads did not count. The run was too brief to do any real good but as always, the benefit was solely one of confidence. He found her eyes an uncomfortable place when he was unhappy about his body and although there was no real change physically, the mere knowledge of doing something about it was change enough.

He fell through the front door of the house in a paroxysm of coughing and wheezing. Lightheaded, he stumbled up the stairs. Jason walked past completely naked carrying two pizza boxes.

"Morning." he remarked casually as he swayed past, clearly entertaining in his room some very lucky young lady who liked pizza and high grade green weed.

Dylan said nothing but carried on toward his bathroom.

Jason looked round and shot him a thumbs-up which under any other circumstances would be hugely patronising. But Dylan just smiled. He knew what Jason meant.

It was going to be a good weekend. Jason had already got laid several times in all likelihood, joints and a pizza for breakfast with a cocaine chaser was not a bad start to a Saturday for him. Certainly Jase seemed to think so judging by the languid grin on his boatrace.

Dylan was off to watch Chelsea play Leicester at 3pm and then was going to meet up with Jason and a couple of mutual friends for a house party, hopefully to make some money at.

Grace texted him while he was out running. He replied that he had gone out for a long run, and she sounded about as impressed as someone can via SMS. There had been two "XX"s at the end of her messages. It was a good morning, he told himself again.

The clothes fell to the floor in a stinking damp heap as Dylan's breathing returned to normal. He downed a pint of water on his dresser from the night before and belched loudly as he reached for a CD.

Too early for trance.

Too late or too late for acid jazz or Leftfield.

Too many people listening for something from his 80s collection.

Ah.

That was it. Perfect.

The Jam.

The volume went up and Dylan danced naked to the bathroom,

passing a disgusted and highly indignant Carla on the way. Her stream of invective and threats to "fucking walk out and not come back you dirty fucking cunt mess, inconsiderate wanker" barely registered over the deafening noise of Going Underground.

Dylan bellowed the words out, aware that the world could see his naked body through the full length sash windows and not caring in the slightest.

Inwardly he glowed. The singing wouldn't win any awards but fuck it felt good. Goosebumps swarmed across his skin.

Tears prickled the corner of his eyes. It was just such a glorious song. A song about fucking off the status quo, about taking back your life from the every day and the evils of society. It was about standing up for himself, Dylan felt.

I fucking love Paul Weller. Its like he wrote me a song about knocking off the drugs and the bolloclks and the all that shit and just taking back my life.

Half an hour later Dylan marvelled at the skyline of London as the train rattled toward its terminus. Was there a finer place to live in the world on stunning clear cold days like this? Dylan could not think of one.

The thought that he had precious little to compare it to by way of places travelled to depressed him for a moment but then Grace came soaring back into his thoughts like the sun coming up over Silvertown. Who better to see the world and all the amazing things it has to offer with than Grace? Inwardly he chided himself in brutal, self-deprecating terms not to get too far ahead of himself. She barely knew him and would undoubtedly send him on his way soon. That was almost certain. But what if??? The thoughts tantalised him with exotic promise.

The beers disappeared in short order, as if on another time-lapse film. The boys were on rare form amongst themselves and singularly disinterested in Dylan or his presence much past bear hugs and hooting when he arrived and furtive loaded handshakes when he dished up. It suited Dylan. Being the centre of attention was not top what he had in mind. The jokes came and went, the banter crackled but Dylan remained comfortably on the peripheries. Beating Leicester and daydreaming about Grace was it. The cocaine felt like a reassuring arm around him as he screwed up his nose on his way out the gents in the pub. It coated his throat and kissed his cerebrum, telling him that all was going to be fine. He was sound. He was a great guy. She would see that.

*****

In the blink of an eye Dylan was stood swaying in the Shed Lower away from his usual season ticket seat. Had he drunk more than he thought? From far away the sums fell together in his head. He had little memory it but the lads had been drinking with him in the pub for three hours and he had been keeping to his usual three pint per hour speed. Eight? Nine pints? How did that happen? The cocaine reassured him again even as his vision swam. Dylan struggled to concentrate on the game. The crowd bristled like a flock of birds. The ball broke to the tall Serbian who looked up and played an inch-perfect pass into the path of the rampaging Spaniard playing up front. The 'Keeper moved across Dylan's vision. The Spaniard looked up. The 'Keeper was still coming across to close off the angle.

He wasn't going to get there was he?

THIRTY-TWO

Soundtrack

Depeche Mode – 'Policy Of Truth'

He did not get there. Stamford Bridge erupted in roaring release.

It turned out to be the first of two goals from the swarthy Spaniard that afternoon as Leicester went down 2-0. Their fans had nothing to say after the game and oddly neither did Dylan. Mox was bodily pulling him toward the pub but he had little compulsion to join. Making his excuses about needing to go to Jason's house party to a chorus of catcalls he walked off uncertainly down the street. The beers were fading and so was the coke but something was missing.

It wasn't food, the coke made sure of that for now at least. There was an odd longing for something and it took Dylan half an hour of wandering and a bus ride before he realised what it was. He was lonely. Grace continued to dominate his thoughts all afternoon and despite previous musings the score that afternoon at the football scarcely seemed as thought it mattered less. Dylan found himself at Liverpool Street station instead of Moorgate to get the train back to Bounds Green so decided to wander round some more. Walking was slimming right? The house party wasn't on the cards, besides Jason had not texted him so he probably wasn't going either.

Walking was good. Walking was slimming.

And slimming was what was needed, he knew.

None of the food looked very appealing at Spitalfields. Couples zigzagged between the puddles holding hands seemingly all round him. The loneliness pounded inside him like a second lost heart. Brick Lane. More couples.

Suddenly a woman stepped out in front of him as he walked down a side street.

"You looking for some business?" she cooed.

Dylan was so lost in his thoughts he almost didn't hear so gaped like an idiot until she repeated herself. He found himself staring at her as his cheeks flushed in embarrassment.

"Uh… ummm" The words would not come.

"I only live around the corner, hundred quid for half an' half, full hour." She offered hopefully.

Dylan stared. She was skinny, with black hair in a straggly ponytail and a battered-looking leather jacket. Her skinny stonewash jeans gave her an odd 80s look, and Dylan was at once reminded of the older one from Birds Of A Feather, even though the woman stood a few feet in front of was scarcely older than 30, he guessed. She had an off-white smiled but bright eyes which suggested she probably wasn't a smackhead. She did not have a Romanian accent, or any accent at all for that matter. Dylan stayed silent and continued to stare and silently assess and judge. He was astonished to feel her take a step toward him and take his hand.

"You're a lively one. Come on, I'm only over there."

She led him wordlessly to a house on the other side of the corner and a dark alleyway between the two houses. It led out onto a small courtyard and she led him firmly through a door and into a living room. It stank of cigarettes and stale booze. A television set in the corner was showing some gameshow but the sound was on so low as to make him need to strain to make it out. Clearly there were other people in the house but Dylan could see nobody else. The woman rounded on him.

"You have got the cash right?" she seemed suddenly wary.

Dylan snapped out of his trance.

"Ummm…. yeah course I do."

He rummaged in his pocket and pulled out a wedge of stinking and faded fivers and tenners. He counted out a hundred pounds and was left with one fiver and the half wrap of cocaine.

The woman's snatched the bank notes and with a renewed brightness in her eyes led Dylan again by the hand up some very dark and narrow carpeted stairs. They shuffled into a basic bedroom with a bare lightbulb hanging from a cracked ceiling. A wardrobe hulked in the corner and the bed looked as though it had seen better days. Some folded clothes sat on a melamine chair in the corner, and a rolled up sleeping bag and some carrier bags of something he could only guess at sat under it.

Did she live here?

"Is this is your room?" he asked.

"Fuck me, it speaks" the woman laughed. "I'm Paula."

Dylan cracked into a smile.

"Hello Paula. I'm Dylan. Would you like a livener?"

"Oooh you little charmer." she was already going for a mirror on the wall.

Dylan realised what he was doing as he began to chop out the gritty powder.

"We don't have to fuck if you don't want to."

The words came out as he just mentioned like it had just occurred to him, absent-mindedly.

"Christ you are the proper fucking romantic aren't you?" Paula laughed. Her laugh was as gritty as the coke.

"Well… you know…." Dylan found himself blushing.

She slid a slender hand inside his jeans, almost putting him off his portion control.

Like a photograph flash going off, when his vision cleared into consciousness he was naked, daintily clutching a rolled up tenner, whilst Paula was giving him a warm and very proficient blow job. The cocaine would put paid to any possibility of him coming but…

How the fuck did I get here? Fucking hell Dylan you don't half get yourself into a pickle sometimes.

"Let me see your fanny." he muttered.

Paula obliged, already casting greedy eyes at the mirror laid on the threadbare carpet floor.

"That's the most romantic thing anyone has ever said to me…".

If Dylan heard her he gave no sign of having done so.

Dylan was filled with an urge to go down on her, to get her to want him, to need him, to make her feel something. He wanted to do something for her. A small mercy of tenderness and intimacy that was more for his benefit than hers.

He was about to push down on his elbows to do so when reality hit him. Performing oral sex on a prostitute was probably a recipe for some very unpleasant things, none of which would clear up in the four days he had until the date with Grace, he realized. Hookers are like walking petri dishes of vile infections.

"I have to go."

Paula propped herself up in disbelief.

"Are you alright?"

"Yeah…. I just…. Don't feel very well. Keep the money, I'm really sorry."

Paula giggled at the idea that she should be disappointed that this handsome specimen should end up not fucking her for what in his mind was basically a glorified wank.

Keeping as straight a face as she could, feigning concern, Paula stood up and watched Dylan get dressed.

"I'm sorry." He repeated.

All at once she felt a little sorry for him. He was overweight, drunk and looked very lonely. Resisting the urge to offer him a compensatory cup of tea she closed the door behind him and went back to bed. He had not even taken his wrap of coke.

"What a result…" she muttered out loud.

*****

Dylan sat on the side of the Thames in the darkness watching the lights play across the startled surface of the river. Grey and brown during the day, the Thames only really shone at night; a lustrous deep jet black flecked with reflections. Dylan imagined he saw himself reflected.

…A fat fucking lonely miserable pathetic mess who fucks brasses because he is so scared some bird way out of his league on a sympathy trip will see sense and fuck him off for someone who isn't a loser drug dealer dirty scumbag.

Right?

He did not realize at first that the first of the tears that welled in his eyes had set off down his cheek. His throat was tight as if someone was grabbing it.

For two long hours he sat on the bench watching the water and wishing he was someone else. Grace's innocence and goodness juxtaposed with the images burned into his brain from the events of the evening. The bare lightbulb. The coke. The darker coloured skin and stubble surrounding Paula's intimate places. The rolled up tenner. The threadbare carpet.

Hookers are a new fucking low for you, Dylan Short. Apart from that one time in Prague but that is different. Banging brasses because you are worried that Grace is going to see through you is daft. So is spunking your money you made on the coke and not even shagging her. You are pathetic. She is going to see it in you, she's going to smell it on you and she's going to throw you away like the human trash you are. You almost get lifted for a three stretch for serving up and now you are fucking dirty prozzies and going down on skanky birds for no reason now? Deary me.

Hardly living La Vida Fucking Loca are you?

"Shut up." Dylan said to himself. The man on the bench next to him cast a worried glance over then went back to his texting.

*****

The weekdays sank into routine and Dylan lurched from self-loathing to dawning confidence and back. Before he knew it he was back at Claridge's, it was the weekend and there was business to be finalised.

Claridge had taken the pills and gear and offered Dylan a beer. Bean was on the sofa texting his girlfriend and not saying much. He looked as if he was in a worse comedown state than Dylan.

He had noted with relief on the bus to Wapping that he did not feel too bad all things considered.

Birds can do that to you.

Claridge was his usual ebullient self, all bear hugs and bacon-faced platitudes.

"So I hear you got onto some bovver out in Whitechapel the other night?"

It had been too much to expect Bean to keep his miserable trap shut.

"Nothing I couldn't handle old son, you know me. Fucking Bean counting the fuckers out in his fucking hand in the club like a retard..." Dylan joked, holding out his hand in front of him, pretending to count invisible pills.

"Sorry youth." Bean actually sounded genuinely sorry.

"Bean loves his beans Dylan mate, that's a fact o' life." Claridge observed as if it was some hugely insightful universal truth.

"I was fucked geezer. Per-ropperly fackin' cuntfaced. Good gear by the way Dyls."

Yeah like I spent hours slaving over a hot stove for you, cooking them up for your tasting pleasure you cunt. Fuck off.

Bean may have thought his compliments on the standard of the drugs he had sold him may make up for the fact that he almost got

Dylan a lengthy prison sentence. The mindlessness and lack of care Dylan recalled made him flush with anger all over again.

"Idiot." Claridge said finally.

"Are these lot the same pills?" asked Bean hopefully.

"Yep. I've got a hundred or so more at home as well." Dylan responded, equally hopefully.

Bean joined them sat at the coffee table.

"Top gear youth. Serious. Bang up gear." Bean was shaking his hand in some weird form of show of respect.

Dylan accepted the clammy hand and shook it, wondering if it was Bean's way of apologising again.

"You should have been here Saturday fella." Claridge was speaking. Little gobbets of spittle flew out of his mouth as he did so.

"...me and Finchy and a couple of his boys from Millwall came over and brought so much fucking nose honestly you've never fucking seen it mate you should have been here and then he calls some brasses fucking four of them knock up and Finchy's cunted right off cos he can't get a woody ‘cos of the gack so i got one of ‘em to nosh me off while I did a line out of the messy fucking fanny of the other one then the miserable cunt fucked off on Sunday morning with his gear and me and Beano had to pay for fucking brasses fucking moody fucking.... Barnet cunts they was."

Dylan regarded him as he spoke, not pausing for breath and apparently someone who had no concept of sentences beginning or ending. The thick London accent and course choice of vocabulary made him sound pig ignorant. He was pig ignorant. And yet he worked in forex broking for one of the huge banks in Canary Wharf and owned the beautiful flat overlooking the Thames. Dylan felt envious and a little wronged that Claridge, a man superficially nowhere near as smart or charismatic as he was, with no obvious gifts save for a talent for using the word “cunt” in every single sentence, should have such luck when he could not get a break. He had no talent. He had no charm. He was a big boorish mess, an ignorant no mark who was only someone because he had money and was six foot four or something. It grated on Dylan. For the first time he realised, right as he was looking into Claridge's face, that he disliked him a great deal.

The idea that the drugs had forced them into a relationship, even if it was a profitable one, made Dylan sad all over again.

If it wasn't for the drugs I wouldn't even give this dickhead the time of day. What do i want human trash like that in my life for?

Still, business was business even if it was the last time. Claridge was his best customer and he had made a great deal of money over the years on his various illegal proclivities. Dylan glanced around the flat again as Bacon Face was still chuntering on.

Maybe I should be charging Claridge more, if its such good fucking gear.

"Should have been here youth..." Bean agreed.

"Gutted I missed it boys. Sounds like a top night out." Dylan managed to sound like he was not being sarcastic.

Claridge high-fived him with enough force to make his hand sting.

"Too fucking right. Will bell you next time deffo. Been too long Dylan me old matey. You're sound."

"Cheers boys." Dylan shook hands with them both.

"Well its been lovely but I've got to dash off. Hope you don't mind..."

Claridge snatched his hand out of thin air and fixed him with a wilting stare.

"You coming on the weekend though, yeah?"

Dylan had the uncomfortable feeling Claridge would not take a negative answer well.

"Got some things I have to do mate, birds to shag and bugle to smash you know how it is…"

Too much Dylan. Wind it in.

"… but I'll be able to pop in I'm sure. Will be great to have a proper catch up and a few beers."

Claridge was already ushering him toward the door. "Bring the gear mate."

THIRTY-THREE

Soundtrack

The Cure – 'Just Like Heaven'

Friday came about seemingly by accident. Dylan had muddled through the week in an absolute state. The proper comedown had hit in earnest late on Tuesday. He had been on the train home fairly early by his standards and Brothers In Arms had come on in his headphones, a by-product of a shuffle function of well over a hundred gigabytes of music.

Dylan did not see the danger coming and listened to the words as the train emerged into the London night from the tunnel by Arsenal's ground. A wave of emotion broke over him as the words resonated.

They reminded him of a life he could have chosen in the past, by going into the Army or Navy or Air Force. It would have made him. He could see that now. He allowed himself to wonder what a fuckup he would not have turned out to be had he taken that route. How much prouder his parents and relatives would have been had he actually tried to make something of himself. He felt his throat tighten. The tears would come soon if he did not stop it. But the mawkishness would not be denied.

It grabbed at him from the shadows.

It was not the first time he had cried himself to sleep after a big session at the weekend and he knew exactly what the reason was, chemically speaking. He had pressed all the serotonin out of his system like squeezed orange juice and without it the body and mind was chemically imbalanced. Emotions took on twists. Moods bloated and would not shift. It was painful because it was so familiar. And because it was so painful, Dylan allowed himself to concede to it. To let it happen.

Wednesday was better. His appetite was back with a vengeance and as the poor diet choices came and went so too were his poor recreational choices from the previous weekend wiped away. There were few things in the world that helped with serotonin production and chasing the shadow moods away but soul food was one of the more reliable methods.

Wednesday's soul food consisted of a lamb tikka masala, large chips, a spinach paneer and a whole carton of Ben n' Jerry's. His body did not complain after the cloying feast but already he could feel his emotions start to balance themselves. Thursday was an unusually productive day at the office, and a speculative gym session in the evening more listless and uncertain than painful or traumatic.

Listless and uncertain. I'll take that.

Friday dawned with the skies of London reflecting his mood. The cloud and chills from earlier in the week was replaced with clarity and optimistic blue. His day at work dragged by in a blur. Finally he left the office with a spring in his step.

Grace was waiting outside the cinema in Leicester Square but she did not see him approach. Dylan slowed to stow his headphones and regarded her in the mass of people eddying round her a like a pink stone in a fast-moving stream.

Fuck.

Dylan fought back the old familiar panic. She was perfect.

The pink overcoat seemed like a beacon, like in those arthouse films where they film it in black and white and then only highlight one colour. It captivated. It drew the eye. She was unmissable in so many ways.

Grace was expressionless, staring out into the throng of people. Her hair was straightened. She was wearing jeans and boots. Dylan could not help but stare at her figure. The denim highlighted and the boots represented. With an involuntary tightening in his groin, Dylan picked his way through and tapped her on the shoulder.

Grace's face melted into a warm and welcoming smile which Dylan found it impossible to stop himself from reciprocating. She threw her arms round his neck and amazingly, leant in for a lingering kiss. He had not expected it but was delighted nonetheless.

Grace almost giggled out loud at his obvious lack of preparedness. She had taken him by surprise and she found that factoid wonderfully comforting.

The movie was very average. Grace seemed to enjoy it and laughed most of the way through, but there were a few too few helicopters and explosions for Dylan's liking. Even so, she had chosen it and he made a point of expressing satisfaction at her choice as they left the theatre.

It was a few short steps to a nearby All Bar One and then a bottle of wine appeared. Relieved of the opportunity to talk again after more than two hours of forced silence both were relaxed and the conversation flowed easily.

"So where are you from originally then, I mean where did you grow up?" Grace asked.

"I grew up in Milton Keynes and Southampton. Was pretty boring all told. My folks live in Buckinghamshire. Well my Dad does, my Mum lives on the Isle Of Man."

"Blimey, what does she do there?" Grace seemed impressed.

"She was teaching in Douglas and ended up settled down there. She's met a guy quite recently, need to go back and see her really."

"Do you not see them much then?"

"Nah, not as much as I'd like to. I see more of my Dad as he comes to the football with me sometimes but I only see my Mum about once a year really... what about you?"

Grace shrugged.

"Not much to tell really. I grew up in Kings Lynn and moved to Banbury when I was thirteen. Couldn't wait to get out so I went to Kingston College and have stayed here ever since. I don't see much of my folks apart from the odd run down to Eastbourne when I can. Moved in with a guy when I left uni. Met him at uni. Didn't turn out well, been on my own since then..."

"...obviously I've had boyfriends and stuff!" she added quickly.

"I live in Bounds Green. You know Carla and Jase, right?" Dylan asked.

"Sort of. Carla is a mate of Abi and Rebekah's, I've met her a few times out and about. She's really nice."

Dylan loved that Grace was trying to be nice about his housemates.

"Yeah, it's cool. I like sharing but I want my own place now you know?"

Grace nodded in agreement.

"I've got my own place in so much as I'm the only one who lives in my flat apart from Barney and the landlord hasn't rented out the other room. But I want somewhere of my own."

"Who's Barney?" Dylan seemed baffled.

"He's my cat. I got him when he was a kitten when I was living with Fraser and when he fucked off I kept the mog. He's a sweetie… you two should definitely meet."

Dylan liked where this was going.

"I love cats. My parents are both allergic so I was never allowed one when I was a kid."

"Yeah, I'm weird lives-on-her-own-cat-lady..." Grace laughed.

Dylan saw an opportunity and dived in.

"Listen, don't worry if you don't want to. But I can get you a ticket for tomorrow as my Dad's away in Cyprus. D'you fancy it?"

Grace pushed her lower lip to one side in a cartoonish gesture of puzzlement.

"Why, what's happening tomorrow?"

"Oh yeah, I forgot. You hate football..." Dylan sounded genuinely regretful.

"I don't hate it!" said Grace hurriedly.

"...its just that my ex was a Tottenham fan."

Dylan laughed and made a gesture that implied a great mystery of the universe had just unraveled before his eyes.

"That explains it then. Was doomed. Let me guess, complete arsehole, right?" he laughed.

Grace smiled knowingly. "Something like that."

Dylan could not resist it so carried on.

"I'm a Chelsea fan you see. Totally different. We're all gentlemen."

Grace had a stabbing memory of Fraser and her aborted baby she was struggling to shut away so could not engage Dylan fully.

"I see."

"So do you want to go?"

Grace had a sense that it would mean a great deal to Dylan if she accepted. It was true. She did hate football. She hated the boorishness of it. The beered-up lager boys all singing vile songs and beating each other up. That was what they did wasn't it?

And Chelsea. Aren't they all racists? Nazi national front thug moron types? It did not sound fun at all. Fraser popped into her head again. She recalled how much he hated Chelsea. How angry he had been that night after going to White Hart Lane to see them play his beloved Spurs. Chelsea had beaten them. How he had argued with her then sent her sprawling across the kitchen with a savage backhand.

Well if that arsehole hated Chelsea then it might not be all bad.

"Yeah why not. It will be fun." Grace tried to look more cheerful at the prospect than she actually was. Dylan looked absolutely delighted.

The wine disappeared in short order after that. Dylan was about to order another bottle when Grace knocked him sprawling with a smiling, softly-spoken question.

"I hope you won't think I'm too forward but would you like to come back to mine? To meet Barney. I have a bottle in the fridge that needs drinking you see..."

Dylan was speechless.

Grace had a weird feeling she had made a mistake. Dylan looked shell-shocked. She panicked. Had she moved things on too fast? Had she scared him off?

Right at the point where the smile drops and the horror sets in, Dylan accepted and a wave of reassurance hit Grace. She could not disguise it, breathing out in a very obvious sign of welcome relief.

"Well... obviously yeah. I'd love to like... you know."

Grace saw the fear etched into Dylan's face. He could barely string a sentence together! That he was nervous but massively keen to accept her offer was very sweet. The large man with the funny teeth and the great sense of humour was anything but a player.

"State of us two." Grace laughed.

Dylan shook his head.

"Not being funny but… look."

He held out a hand. It was shaking visibly.

Grace let out a relieved laugh.

"That's so sweet!"

*****

They had been kissing passionately before the front door to Grace's place had even opened. She ushered them quickly to her bedroom before Dylan could say hello to Barney and he was a little shocked at her insistence.

He was surprised at how she moved. Dylan was used to drunk fumbling and awkwardness but Grace seemed fully relaxed and at ease. The way she moved suggested it came naturally to her. Dylan was utterly spellbound.

She was kissing him hard. There was a need there. He responded by wrapping his arms around her shoulders as she undid her jeans. There was a moan on happiness from Grace who redoubled the kissing. Suddenly her hands were at his waist, expertly undoing his belt one-handed and easing down his jeans whilst running her other hand under his shirt, up his back.

Just go with it mate.

She's amazing.

Just go with it.

Dylan's thoughts counselled him. He had a real sense of something to prove. That he would only get one shot, so to speak. It had to be made to count.

Grace was certainly into it.

She lay back on the bed up on her elbows in the half-light and for a second he did not follow, just wanting to stand and see her. Her skin was pale. A darkish Royal blue bra and knickers set provided the perfect contrast. Dylan wanted to remark on the good choice of colour but somehow the words would not come. She took her bra off, gesturing for him to join her on the bed, brushing dark blonde hair from her face.

He stood there a chubby, hairy fat mess in badly fitted Calvin Kleins with his mouth open and a grotesque straining in his underwear. With his heart beating so loud he was sure Grace would hear it Dylan wondered as he stared at her whether he had ever been so turned on in his life.

She is perfect.

Grace's curves screamed at him from across the room. The gentle curves of her thighs. The subtle tones of her legs. Her flattish stomach and belly button piercing glinting. The sinews of her upper torso. The perfection of her breasts. The curves of her feet. A tattoo on her shoulder he knew nothing about.

He cursed himself under his breath for the Mills & Boon daftness.

"Come on." Grace reassured him.

Panic rose in Dylan again. His breath stopped in his throat.

What if he was not good enough? What if she was disappointed?

What if she saw him now for what he really was, an average bloke with no right whatsoever to be in the same league as her?

A dirty fat drug dealer loser who goes down on people because he wants them to need him?

Grace propped herself up on her elbows. The room was cool and the air across her breasts made her nipples harden. She watched Dylan intently. He could not take his eyes off her. It should have been creepy. It should have been weird, she thought.

But it was not.

He was bigger than she imagined. He had not looked that big and powerful when he had started at her that time on the Tube, or bumped into her coming out of that bar. In the flesh he was a somewhat different proposition.

Nearly six feet tall and bulky with it. Even with his arms at his sides she could see they were chunky. Grace wanted more than anything else in the world for him to put them around her and not let go.

She looked down at his legs. They were like tree trunks. She wondered if he might have played rugby in younger and fitter days. For a chunkier guy they retained a lot of shape. There seemed to be almost no fat below his waist. The black briefs he was wearing utterly betrayed him, and the primal simplistic need to know what was inside rose in her.

Finally he spoke.

"You're perfect. You are absolutely perfect."

Dylan could not have known. There was no way, she knew. But it was just about the perfect thing to say right then. Another piece of ice inside crashed down and melted.

"Thank you," she said softly.

Dylan was rooted to the spot.

She had not told him to fuck off.

It was unbelievable!

How could she not have told him thanks but no thanks? Why was he still stood there?

A dawning acceptance began to form. He was actually about to have sex with Grace.

Actual sex. With her.

In that bed!

She fixed him with a soft and easy smile. Maybe she could tell how deeply terrified he was.

Maybe she can see I am absolutely in bits?

One foot in front of the other Dylan old son. One foot.

That's it.

He began to shuffle toward the bed, gait somewhat stiffened by the straining pressure in his underwear.

One foot in front of the other.

You got this. She likes you. She wants you.

Just try to relax. If you fuck this up you won't get another chance. Relax.

She likes you. Try to remember that she likes you.

He went to her. The worries and over-thinking had retreated as instinct took over. She wrapped herself around him and sensing how much she wanted him helped Dylan enormously. He found himself dictating the pace, not wanting it to end too quickly.

I wish I'd had a fucking wank this morning.

The thought elicited a smile lost between them.

Her mouth was everywhere, kissing and touching. The urgency surprised Dylan. He could not resist any more and shuffled down to her, slipping off her knickers. Before diving in he glanced upwards.

Grace was biting her lip, eyes screwed shut. Her arms were gripping the back of her bed. She wanted this. She was perfect.

The idea of her getting so turned on by him forced something deep inside. He took his time, listening to her moans and allowing them to guide him. She had, Dylan had to admit, the single greatest vagina he had ever seen let alone had the privilege and dumb luck to get anywhere near. It was perfect in every way. Her heat and wetness made the straining in his underwear almost unbearable. He could feel himself flushing. He had never been that turned on going down on anyone ever. The thought of the random in the forest at the week evaporated like a burst balloon.

Another smile drifted across Dylan's lips, again lost between them.

Very quickly it mounted up. She began to breath like she was finishing a marathon and he could feel a tremendous pressure in her building. She yelped and moaned long.

Something exploded.

Stars flashed across Dylan's face. He gave a long groan. It was a rush like no other. No pill or powder could ever get near...

Fuck.

A realisation smashed Dylan in the face.

He had come.

Right at the same moment she had.

Eyes bulging and mouth agape he leant back. Already he could feel slippery wetness dripping down his thigh. Unable to hide it he just gaped.

Grace let go of the bed and wiping her forehead with the back of her hand she sat up. It was obvious what had happened.

Grace laughed.

Dylan looked mortified.

"Oh don’t worry, I love that you got that turned on!" She reassured him in a low sultry voice quite different from her normal sunny one. Dylan stared, open-mouthed and with eyes bulging. Grace to her credit did actually look as if she loved the fact that he had gotten so turned on.

"But..."

Grace could see how devastated he was so knelt forward and hugged him. They kissed for several minutes. At first Dylan could not get into it, so traumatised had he been at the premature ending to proceedings. But after a minute or so the heat returned. Grace was by any measure of the imagination a wonderful and enthusiastic kisser. She ran her fingers through his hair.

Dylan pulled away.

"That's never happened before." he said guiltily.

Grace was about to respond when he darted back in.

"...i'll be ok in a minute or two, just need to... you know..."

Grace giggled as he jerkily pulled down his soiled underwear, wiping as he did so.

His manhood had shortened somewhat and no sooner had he extricated himself from his damp Calvins then Grace was kissing him again, pushing him back onto the bad. Then her mouth was there. Impossibly hot. Impossibly soft.

Dylan's breath stopped in his throat again.

How many times had he imagined this? How many times had he dreamed of getting a blowjob from The-Girl-In-The-Pink-Overcoat?

"Job done." Grace informed him.

Dylan looked down through half shut eyes. She was right. He was ready to go again. That had not happened since he was a teenager. She rummaged in a drawer for a second and then deftly put a condom on him. Dylan was too starstruck to marvel at her two finger technique.

Then they had sex.

THIRTY-FOUR

Soundtrack

INXS – 'Mystify'

Grace was delighted.

They had sex for a solid twenty minutes. He was gentle and considerate. His much-larger frame dominated her in a quiet and safe and respectful way. His big hands were everywhere. He was not amazing in bed but definitely no slouch. And there was no hint of the breathless violence of her secret profession. His lack of coordination was compensated by the languid slowness to everything, despite his very rapid premature problem from earlier. He seemed to want to take her all in, to know every inch of her. She allowed a dismissive smile to flash between them as the antique flowery prose came and went to her mind.

His cock was really nice. If she pressed down she could press herself against him and knew she would be able to come that way with a little prompting from her side to his.

He was not a shouter or a moaner. He was not much for eye-contact either but then neither was she, she realised.

The overwhelming feature of the encounter was that it was such a happy and fulfilling thing to actually have sex again. It had been so long since she had actually had sex with someone. The physical act of intercourse-for-hire did not constitute sex. Not in her mind and most certainly not in her body.

It had been the first time since she had begun the sex work and the fears and terrors had been unfounded. She had been so worried that it might feel wrong somehow. Dirty. That the guilt she pressed away into the dark recesses of her professional mind might spurt out and ruin everything.

She had surprised herself at her desire. Dylan was hardly Channing Tatum, yet she had breathlessly driven him to bed. There was a need.

Or a need to know, maybe.

The happiness inside was just like being 18 again. Butterflies and all. Dylan lay soundlessly behind her, big arms wrapped around her, keeping her close to him.

It was ok.

It would all be ok.

THIRTY-FIVE

Soundtrack

GTR – 'Mistral' (Original Mix)

Dylan could not believe his luck.

He had been sure the setback earlier would rob him of his chance. That she would start cackling at him for being such a pathetic loser.

And yet it had not bothered her. She had evidently been determined to have sex with him and he had joyously been able to oblige. She had tried to control the pace and he found himself trying to slow things down lest he embarrass himself still further. Yet the more he tried to slow things down the more turned on she had become.

Images had flashed vividly in his head in the darkness, so bright he had to screw his eyes shut. The bouncer at Bass Factory. The woman who had let him go. The woman who had let him go down on her. Forrester. Tasha. Carla. Luca. Hetch. Bean. Jason. Claridge.

Crabby and all of his cats.

The memory of the old man made him want to cry again but the visions flashed by before his mind would let him. The visions got darker. The drugs. The box under his bed. Gemma. Kimberley. They passed so fast he could barely recognise them.

He almost had to slap himself in the face to bring himself back to the then and there. Dylan was suddenly panicking that he was floating away without a mooring line, he scrambled back.

He looked down. He pressed his face into the side of Grace's. Her smell made him giddy and lightheaded.

He noted that she had been pressing down on him, driving herself onto the top of his cock. If he could make her come that way...

In the end he'd been unable to stop himself.

She was all reassurances and seemed delighted he had come again. Dylan hoped fervently her world had just moved off its axis as it had for him.

Afterwards she had snuggled back into him so his manhood pressed hard against her backside threatening to kick things off again. There would be time for that later.

Dylan had never been much into snuggling. It was not in the Dylan Short playbook. Yet something deep inside told him it was very much a Grace Freeman thing and that she wanted to be held.

So he held her.

It had been quiet at first. After ten minutes or so she started to talk and then she got up and made them both a cup of tea.

She got up stark naked again and Dylan was again struck by how easy and comfortable she was with nakedness.

That's fucking hot to be fair. Mind you if I had a banging body like that I'd be walking round naked too.

A shadow darkened the doorway.

The shadow turned into a substantial cat. He walked in, eyes fastened on Dylan. He did not seem afraid of him and approached the bed, still staring at him.

"You must be Barney." Dylan said out loud.

"Well remembered!" Grace shouted from the kitchen.

The cat turned toward the noise and then fixed Dylan once more with huge amber eyes. Dylan was taken aback. He was a very handsome cat. Dylan imagined him talking to him.

Alright cunt face?

"How's it going big guy?" Dylan asked the cat, feeling a little stupid at having to try to make conversation.

Let's get one thing straight. She's into you.

…(long intense pause)…

I have not made a final decision yet but for the time being I shall give you the benefit of the doubt. For now. In the interests of diplomacy I shall also try to forget that you just did filthy dirty filthy disgusting things to her, you horrible little man. Don't think I don't know!

But understand this.

You fucking hurt her and I'll cut you.

...got it?

Dylan read his expression perfectly, oddly reminded of Nelson, Crabby's stalwart cat who always stared him out on his stairs whenever he went to visit the old guy.

Such a shame.

By the time Grace emerged into the bedroom carrying two mugs, Barney was lying on his side on the bed and Dylan was gently stroking the top of his head.

"I see you two are getting along..." Grace grinned.

THIRTY-SIX

Soundtrack

Headstrong Feat. Tiff Lacey – 'The Truth' (David West Progressive Mix)

Saturday morning came and almost went. Grace and Dylan slept in until late morning. Tea cups were swapped with filled ones and Grace set about making a round of toast.

"I don't normally let guys stay over you know." She smiled without a hint of irony.

"I'm not asking for a drawer, don't worry!" Dylan reassured her.

"Yet." Said Grace mischievously.

Dylan tried to ignore the remark that was like a ray of sunshine deep inside him.

It made him want to dance around the room.

"Listen I'm going to head back to mine and get changed, put on some wearable pants as I don't think the colour of these ones…" He held up his stained and part-starched Calvins from the night before.

"…. how about we meet at The Bridge at one?"

"What Bridge?" she asked.

"Stamford Bridge. The stadium!" Dylan nodded emphatically.

"Sounds good to me. I don't have to wear a bloody football shirt do I?" Grace moaned.

*****

At exactly one in the afternoon Dylan was still at South Kensington. Texts were refusing to send. It was hot on the tube and packed with Chelsea fans already.

Dylan could not stop obsessing over Grace. She dominated every thought. He barely even remembered who Chelsea were playing. It occurred to him several times to call Grace and go back to hers just to be with her again. Like that. Just to be with her. The train made agonisingly slow progress.

Fuck's sake mate. What's she done to you?

Dylan blew out a breath.

It was true. Dylan was someone who developed feelings for people quickly but he could sense already a major build up of feelings for The-Girl-In-The-Pink-Overcoat-Who-Doesn't-Mind-Him-Coming-Prematurely. She wanted him. That was what really got into his head. He was used to women not being into him, but seeing for circumstantial reasons. Kimberley never wanted him really, he was just someone to shag when she felt like it. Poor Gemma. She did not want him either.

What right did he have for a woman of that obvious calibre and class to have any interest in him? Let alone want him? Let alone just need him like she did the night before.

How do you process that?

I'm massively fucking into this woman. I'm far far far more into her than I should be at this stage. She's the absolute business and I'm a lying scumbag lazy useless fat ugly fuckup drug dealer.

He longed to come clean with her, but dared not contemplate the results if he did.

I want to be better. I want to start living. I'm done being scared and fucked all the time. She is my life, now in person but in what she could be to me as well. She represents everything I want, everything I need. She is the walking embodiment of a better life, of doing better and being better – of being a fucking man for once… and I think I love her.

Fuck's sake mate. What's she done to you?

The thoughts would not leave. All around him the close crowd in the carriage jostled and pushed and Dylan did not move.

Fuck's sake mate.

What's she done to you?

He was almost half an hour late when he sprinted down the sidestreet to emerge onto the Fulham Road. It was a mass of thousands of people. Dylan allowed himself a quick indulgence of a lungful of the smells of a matchday. Fried onions from the burger van. Diesel smoke from the generator. Horse shit. Hamburgers. Thousands of people. Cigarette smoke.

Grace was texting when he reached her.

"Sorry I'm late. Fucking tube was worse than usual. You alright?"

Grace smiled. "It's ok. Where we headed?"

They walked up the street to find a pub. She may not be a football fan but she got the dress spot on, Dylan noted. She had chosen a pair of tightish black jeans and a different but no less sexy knee high boots and a royal blue Ralph Lauren rugby top sort of effort. The pink overcoat was noticeably absent.

Dylan was in his best Diesel jeans, pride and joy pair of blue Adidas Muenchen's with the yellow flashes and a pale blue Stone Island polo shirt. Unseen, there was a pleasantly pristine pair of Hugo Boss briefs that just showed above the waistband of the jeans. An optimistic pair of Prada Wayfarer-type sunglasses sat delicately atop his combover. She looked him up and down in the pub.

"You are a bit of a dresser aren't you Dylan?" she giggled.

Trying his best to carry off false modesty, Dylan retorted with a blasé,

"I try."

The pub was heaving. Dylan stopped and introduced Grace to a couple of people none of whom she could remember the names of. It was weird. Everyone either had a nickname or went by their second name. Shorty. Big Chris. Rocky. Irish Keith. Cadgey. Chidgey. Beck. Nilesy. Stinky Paul. Little Dave. Kitty. Bisto. John The Taxi Driver. Davis. Jak Riley. Casual Callum. Walter Who Hates Tube Trains. Gypsy Paulie. Bermondsey Phil. Streaky Tom. Greeny. Tweeds. Wino Gaz. Beansy. Arab Tim. Tim Rolls. Mark from Gate 17. Amanda P. Fountains. The procession seemed endless. Dylan seemed to know most of the people in the pub either by wink and a handshake or by actual name. Grace stopped trying to remember names after the first couple.

The atmosphere was filled with laughter and banter. Songs flashed back and forth. Everyone was having a good time and Grace wondered idly when the fighting and racist stuff happened. She had to admit, it seemed incongruous. The evening news bulletins and screaming sirens felt a million miles from the sunny and very relaxed atmosphere in the pub. Even so, large groups of men made her nervous.

What if I meet a fucking customer? Fuck.

Grace stood in Dylan's shadow and nursed her drink.

Two pints came and disappeared in short order before seemingly en masse the whole pub put down their glasses and filed for the exit. It reminded Grace of one of those mass migration films you see sometimes on the natural discovery channels.

The blue steelwork of the stadium jutted out into the sky above the houses and Grace tried to sound impressed as they walked up to it. The crowds were thicker and with only ten minutes to go until kick-off everyone was in more of a rush.

Without thinking, Dylan took Grace's hand. The surprise of it shocked her but she did not let go.

They hurried to the West Stand and got into a queue to get in. Grace watched Dylan's face. He seemed so comfortable and happy, and she felt obliged to enjoy it so his feelings were not hurt. The couple of pints roiled inside her and she needed to take a detour via a stinking, massive toilet before they got to their seats. As she walked up the stairs the stadium folded out in front of her. It was much larger than she was expecting.

Dylan looked at Grace's face.

She seemed impressed. Of course she was. She had taken his hand again as they walked through the concourse.

Chelsea, as so often in Dylan's life were a bit of a disappointment. A player she had heard Dylan talk about before the game had scored first late in the first half, and Dylan had scooped up Grace in the wild and deafening celebration rush and given her a hugely uncomfortable bear hug. She laughed it off. The sheer unbridled joy on Dylan's face was a picture to behold. She found herself smiling and laughing, high fiving the guys sat behind them, pleased because of how pleased it made Dylan.

In the second half as the sky clouded over the game tempo dropped. Grace found herself watching the planes grind over the patch of sky overhead and wondering where they were coming from. Aston Villa equalised with a scrappy goal after an hour had been played and the smiles and laughter faded all around them. The away fans opposite went absolutely wild. Even from across the pitch she could see them throwing themselves about and leaping into the air. Chelsea were not able to get another goal and they filed out under a sense of anti-climax.

Grace knew not to say it was just a game. Dylan looked very disappointed.

They got outside onto the main road and the crowd was solid as far as she could see.

"What now?" he asked, his words almost lost in the noise.

"Pub?" she suggested with a shrug.

"Deal." Dylan grabbed her hand and they crossed the heaving river, bumping and apologising as they went.

A mile or so up the Kings Road they went into a large pub not far from the old cinema. It was not as busy as she thought it was going to be. Dylan gestured for her to go sit down and he went to the bar.

Just as she was sat down she realised her handbag was vibrating.

The batphone.

She had taken a call earlier when Dylan was late.

It was her Baron's Court regular wanting a date for the evening. She had texted him to apologise and proposed a meet up on Monday night. Whilst they were at the football he had texted her back twice, unable to wait. Now he was following up the unanswered texts with a plaintive and begging phone call. She rejected the call and began to text him when she realised Dylan was stood just a foot or so away staring right at her.

Fuck.

Dylan brought back the pints to the table to find Grace engrossed in a text on a cheap Nokia, not the iPhone she normally used.

"I thought you had an iPhone?" he asked as he put the pints on the table.

"Work phone." Grace replied tersely.

"On a Saturday. Harsh." Dylan observed.

"Harsh indeed." Grace agreed as she pressed send and put the phone back in her bag.

Grace seemed inordinately interested in engaging Dylan about the football. He could see she was not interested in it really but appreciated her taking an interest.

The truth of it was that Grace was desperately trying to steer the conversation away from the subject of work, and specifically work mobiles. She had almost panicked when he had silently moved up next to her. Had he read the text? Evidently not.

But it had been a bloody close call. Too close.

The superficiality of what had been a lovely date, an amazing evening, wonderful sex and a nice if slightly un-stimulating day out at the football hit home. Hard.

At what point does omission of truth become outright lying?

With a plunging feeling inside Grace realised that that exact moment, the first proper lie (weekend in Eastbourne excepted) she had told him, that road marker had gone breezing past.

The point of no return was coming up fast.

Grace cradled her pint and watched Dylan chat animatedly about some kid Chelsea had playing for them who was completely two footed. Didn't everyone have two feet though?

She decided against asking what she felt sure had to be the definition of a stupid question and carried on watching him talk. He was absolutely in his element, absolutely delighted just to be having a drink with her. She wondered whether he may be able to relate to her loneliness from before better than he was letting on.

No, he was a funny bloke. He had loads of friends. Everyone liked him, he was always going to parties and such. People like that are never lonely.

Are they?

She idly imagined his fleshy head growing, blowing up as if inflated. Bigger and bigger it grew with every little lie she told. The lies got bigger and so did his head. Soon it would be too much and his head would explode. Then there would be no going back.

She imagined telling him.

She pictured the words rising in her throat. Just letting them go. Releasing them into the ether, never to be contained ever again. Then in devastating clarity she pictured the horror and disgust that would surely follow. Dylan's pain and hurt at her deception and filthy other life. The idea of hurting him like that after last night was too painful to bear. Biting her lip she blinked back a tear and forced a smile.

"I really enjoyed today. Thank you so much for taking me. It was not as boring as I thought it would be." she lied.

Dylan did not look like he fully believed her. His reassurances that it was much more fun when they win and play a decent team and a few other things she didn't fully understand suggested he felt the fault was Chelsea's not with her for not being the football type.

Dylan drained his pint. He rose and headed to the bar, just as his phone began to ring. He picked it up and made childish gestures about answering a boring phonecall and doing it at the bar and would she like another one and was it the same again and he would only be a minute and he was really sorry etc etc. Then he was gone, leaving Grace to reflect on a near thing and a rapidly growing lie.

Dylan answered his phone on the way to the bar and immediately wished with all his heart he had not.

Claridge was already drunk by the sound of it. He was over-pronouncing his words and yelling them over some undetermined background noise Dylan could not identify.

He bellowed that he wanted Dylan to come to his party and he wanted to buy another hundred pills. And did he have any of that nice coke left?

For fuck's sake.

He was yelling so loudly the people clustered around him waiting at the bar could probably hear what he was shouting. Dylan panicked and cupped a hand to the bottom of his phone.

"Claridge son I can’t do it, I've got something...."

"Can’t do it buddy."

"Mate I’m out of the...."

"GEEZER! I'm telling you mate I can’t do it! I'm away!"

Claridge did not seem to be getting the message as clearly as Dylan wanted so he hung up and switched off his phone. He brought two more Heinekens back to the table.

Grace looked up. "Can’t do what?"

Dylan froze.

Fuck.

She heard.

He put the pints down and scratched his head. "Mate wants me to lend him my CDJs. I told him to do one."

"You're what’s?" Grace asked, seemingly quite interested.

"CD Decks. I sometimes DJ a bit in my spare time."

Top response son.

"Cool. They are quite expensive aren't they?"

"Exactly." Dylan nodded as he handed her a pint.

"Cheers."

Grace accepted the lie seamlessly. It was almost the perfect thing to say right at that moment. She talked to Dylan a bit about various hobbies and pastimes she and her friends had and Dylan allowed himself to join in as the panic faded and he regrouped.

That was a big lie.

A proper lie.

He had been leaving things out up until that point but that was a full on telling of an untruth.

He did not feel as guilty as he should have done but an ominous feeling manifested in his stomach as he began to fully realise the implications of the lies and where they would inevitably lead.

The sooner he was done with the dealing the better. Like an addiction his mind flashed back to Claridge's bawling orders on the mobile. Shifting the last of his powder and the last of the little fellas would bring things to a nice conclusion. He could probably bin the rest and then it would be done.

The idea of being done with it was intoxicating.

They chatted and downed another pint before Grace laid a delicate hand on Dylan's arm.

"Listen, I have a headache and I've got an early start. Do you want to go out for dinner during the week?" Grace asked suddenly.

Dylan's mind raced.

"Sure. Sounds good. Do you want to go out?" he asked uncertainly.

"Yeah, why not? I know a nice place nearby me?" the intonement tailed off just enough to suggest the proximity to her place may mean a second round of what happened last night. Dylan felt an involuntary tensing in his groin.

"Ideal. Sounds great. Are you ok?" Dylan looked concerned.

"I'll be ok, just don't think I can drink anymore and maybe not had enough water. Need a bath and an early night. Hope you don't mind?" She leant in and kissed him long and luxuriantly.

Dylan's worries evaporated.

They walked outside and Dylan hailed her a cab. She snogged him passionately and grabbed his backside as she did so.

"Looking forward to dinner already!" she winked at him with a disarming smile.

"Me too." Dylan agreed.

The cab door closed and she waved at Dylan as he receded into the distance.

"Where to, sweetheart?"

"Baron's Court please."

Dylan watched the cab roar off into the darkening evening. Her rather abrupt departure was a concern but she was still into him and had made all the moves about meeting up during the week, leaving him under no illusions that sex was very much on the cards. She was still into him. She was still interested and it was obviously just a headache.

So it was all good, right?

More or less.

Suddenly very alone, Dylan pulled out his phone and switched it on, pressing his thumb against the big button. It sprang into life. A panoramic photo of the very stadium he and Grace had visited that afternoon was partly obscured on the bright screen by App icons.

He looked the last calls and then pressed the number.

It picked up on the second ring.

"Claridge. Change of plan mate. You still on for later yeah?" Dylan asked in his best Danny Dyer patter.

"Sweet. Catch you later youth."

Then he hung up.

THIRTY-SEVEN

Soundtrack

Chemical Brothers – 'In Dust We Trust'

The room was dark and cold. The house was empty and he did not know where Jason and Carla were.

Dylan was stood paused for thought next to his bed. He regarded the box with a mixture of relief and trepidation. It was now just an ornate wooden shell; a husk of memories most of which he had little interest in preserving. The good ones were written in his memory indelibly, and the box was just a dark piece of wood to remind him of the dark side to those memories. He could not bring himself to smash it, burn it or ceremonially catharsise it from his life.

It was empty. He had secreted everything into his bag, put on a new polo shirt and was ready to head to Claridge's. Aqua di Parma filled the air.

He bent down and sniffed the box. It smelt strongly of sandalwood, tobacco and stale marijuana. The smell felt like an end to an era.

Dylan imagined it filled in years to come with trinkets of foreign holidays. Keepsakes and mementoes from a new life without the threat hanging over him. And above all, nice things from doing nice things with someone nice.

Dylan did not feel alone. Grace dominated his thought.

One more job. One more night. He had to press Grace from his thoughts one more time and get it done.

He should get a cab. He knew he should get a cab.

The train, tube and bus journey to Claridge's would take an hour and via King's Cross and London Bridge. There was often sniffer dog teams working by the exit barriers at both those stations and the amount of drugs he was carrying would be unmissable. Then it was the years behind bars long feared by Dylan. That was obvious.

But wasn't he trying to save money?

A cab to Wapping would be fifty notes, easy. That cut sharply into the margins for the evening, and even a minicab would likely be over forty.

Risk.

Reward.

*****

Grace was sat on the bed.

Baron's Court Regular Richie had been delighted to receive her. It was clear from his demeanour that he had no intention of calling another girl and his disappointment of earlier having been almost forced to had been palpable.

Grace imagined telling him that she was about to quit. How would he react?

He was a nice bloke. She imagined him shaking her hand, patting her on the back, congratulating her.

The flat was nice. He was a record producer or something and in the lounge various musical memorabilia adorned the walls in studiously dusted and polished glass frames. He'd obviously never made anything major but seemed to have done ok. He was a good tipper, her best in fact.

The concept of tipping always amused her. As if she was a

waitress or something. You paid your money, you got your service. Or your servicing. Yet the vast majority of her customers took it upon themselves whether they paid up front or not to tip her after the act or acting was done.

Was is a misguided sense of wanting to help her? Or spending money to assuage guilt? Or a subliminal need to break what had just happened down to the simplest and most binary of transactions, thereby making it mean less. Or mean more, depending on your viewpoint. Maybe some felt she was selling herself too cheaply.

Richie was a strange one. His idea of furthering sexual boundaries was to fuck in the shower.

He was not interested in dirty talk, in roleplay, anal or any of that stuff.

Grace had just had a very pleasant but very normal half hour with him. Missionary, her on top, then back to missionary. Not so much as a harsh word spoken. He'd seemed pleased that she had turned up in jeans and rugby shirt. They had had comfortable and actually fairly familiar sex. Grace realised he did not respond to her moaning on the second visit and was far beyond that now, and the noises left once the mendacious moaning subsided were gasps and inhalations of exhilaration that were absolutely genuine.

It was eerily like having a boyfriend. Or a husband.

Granted, one that was twice her age probably and with whom she had precisely nothing in common with, but it had a real sense of usuality about it. Midweek-sex-after-Law-&-Order-after-a-long-day-at-work. Comfort zone.

It was so at odds with the decoration on the walls. He was, at one time, quite the rock and roll producer for a lot of underground bands she had never heard of. They were all sexual fuck-ups weren't they? Too high too often on drugs throughout the 80s and now only able to maintain an erection at the extreme and most visceral end of the sexual spectrum, right?

Richie did not look like he had ever done drugs in his life, in fairness to him. Grace watched him get dressed. He was well-spoken, polite and respectful.

Maybe that was it. He wanted a girlfriend. She remembered him soundless above her, eyes closed respectfully. Right at that moment she had been his significant other, and maybe the normality of it was not mere sexual circumstance but a very real psychological need for stability and a comfort zone that was a sure thing. She was his sure thing. She was a comfort to him. The hypothesis almost demanded some level of deep sadness and disappointment behind his warm and clear greyish eyes.

What is he going to think when I tell him I'm going to be someone else's comfort and someone else's sure thing?

Grace had been trying professionally to keep Dylan out of her mind but she let him in as Richie handed her a crisp brand new fifty pound note from his sock drawer.

She accepted Gracefully and with a minimum of fuss. Richie could not look her in the eye as he handed her the tip. Another three hundred pounds sat in the back pocket of her jeans already. He could have paid at the end but he always chose to almost open his front door holding out the money. It was as if he was trying to make her a sure thing and get it out of the way.

With the paying, the fucking and the tipping out of the way her dates with Richie usually ended soon after.

"Would you like a cup of tea?"

Grace accepted and they went into the lounge. He brought the tea over and to her amazement Richie switched on the television and began hunting through the planner for something suitable. Against all better judgement she stayed for an hour as they watched the end of some big budget film about ancient Greece. Richie said nothing for most of it, offering the odd titbit of historical information but nothing more. She was happy of the escapism and happy not to have to think about Dylan.

She left when the film ended, the tea leaving a sour taste in her mouth. The cab ride back to hers was spent psychoanalysing her customers.

Creepy Simon. Nice Bloke Peter. Sure Thing Richie. Mateyboy in Mudchute.

Perhaps there was a theme running through all this?

Maybe they wanted her. Not just sexually but as a companion for more than just a night and some release of desires?

For the first time in her life, Grace realised she was girlfriend material. It was not the overwhelmingly-positive realisation she thought it may have been. Instead all it did was remind her of how far she had gone in the last few months and how far back she had to go to get back to being anyone's girlfriend. It was a long, long way back.

But the path was defined now. She knew clearer what she had to do and maybe mentally having a picture of her destination helped. She smiled grimly in the dark clattering of the back of the black cab that she was searching for the same normality in some respects that Sure Thing Richie craved.

Maybe not quite that normal.

It was not just a social observation but a wider theme that nobody talks about, she realised sagely.

You search for your normal. That's all dating is. Then you meet someone, you set up normal. for some it works, for others normal is a little too comfortable and it doesn't work. So you find someone who wants the same normal as you.

The thoughts and ruminations came and went idly as the traffic lights changed in the darkness around her and the light reflections flashed across the glass. It was rare for her to allow herself to delve too deep into her thoughts where companionship, love, sex and her profession were concerned. It was normally not something anyone wanted to over-think.

Why would you?

Daydreaming them to their conclusion she observed a niche

within a niche of being a girlfriend-for-hire.

Wondering idly of ways in which she could monetise it without having to actually do the sex part or have to do the tell the boyfriend part, Grace was pleased to let Dylan slip out of her mind.

Out of sight but always in the back of the mind.

*****

"Sixty five fucking quid!"

Dylan was raging under his breath as the cab pulled away from outside Claridge's place in Wapping. He could not fault the route he had taken yet it seemed much more expensive than it needed to be. He wished he was having a night in with Grace instead of having to drop fucking drugs off to cunts who he did not even fucking like.

Bean buzzed him up. The flat was not busy yet but a smattering of shadowy people drifted around. Claridge was deep in conversation with some tough football hooligan looking types by his kitchen island but winked at Dylan as he walked in. As always the music was too loud and the smoke persistent and acrid. It even stank when he had been there when there was no party on.

Bean pulled him to one side.

"Alright fellla."

"Right geezer. How's it going?"

"Cladge wants the pills."

"What, now?" Dylan was a little insulted.

"Yeah. Finchy and his mates are taking them."

Dylan knew Claridge was making his broker's commission on the deal and that he could probably make an extra hundred quid if he went to Finchy direct.

But he did not know which of the threatening shaven-headed lads he was and even if he did he did not trust Bean or Claridge not to tell them he was Chelsea, and a regular away bod as well.

99% of the time it would be good banter, some jokes and a laugh at a bygone era. But you never really knew for sure with that sort of bloke. Some didn't have a sense of humour about footballing rivalries even decades after there was any real needle. It was not like Dylan had even been going to football in the early 80s when the real rivalry was on, yet somehow being a regular away face made confrontations - even over huge quantities of The Love Drug - something to be feared and if possible avoided.

Contrary to popular media, the top boys of yesteryear buying loads of E's just meant they liked taking drugs. It was by no means a green light to go over and start taking the piss imagining they would return with hugs and questions about his night.

And he certainly could not risk upsetting Claridge. He was not affiliated to any footballing club Dylan knew of but somehow that made him more unpredictable. Years and years of gear abuse at levels Dylan could only wincingly guess at had to play some serious and lasting tricks on the mind. Claridge had been on about doing cage fighting at one point… He would think nothing of giving him a proper slapping in front of everyone if Dylan merited one, he knew for sure. So it was harsh but fair.

Dylan pulled out the gear with as much subtlety as someone can from a messenger bag at an open-plan houseparty.

"There's some 2CI and some acid in there as well… different bag obviously like. A present from me to him, but..."

"Go easy yeah I know." Bean was gesturing with his hand, looking over his shoulder at Claridge. He was keen to finish the deal as quickly as possible.

The bags disappeared with Bean and Dylan stood there looking very alone. He hated dealing with other people.

Bean returned after five minutes.

"Clad's gonna sort you out later."

It sounded oddly portentous. Something began to chime in Dylan's head.

"OK. When?"

"Finchy is off in a minute, he's going to owe Clad for the gear Clad is going to pay you."

Dylan shrugged. This was most unlike Claridge. A bacon-faced fuckhead he may have been, but he did not fuck around.

Dylan nursed one and then another can of Stella for an hour before he saw Finchy and his boys leave. They did not acknowledge him as they left. Claridge disappeared.

He gave him the fright of his life when he loomed up behind him.

"There you are." There was a crushing, smothering bear hug.

"How's it going youth?" Claridge had a strange way of pronouncing the word. It came out as "Youuuf" - Dylan thought it made him sound like some Senegalese footballer.

Dylan decided to play it cool.

"Not so bad mate. Sorry about earlier, all sorted now?"

Claridge frowned.

"Yeah, let's talk in the bedroom."

Fucking hell....

Dylan obediently followed the huge man into the bedroom. The door closed behind them. Before Dylan could react Claridge had pulled out a (monogrammed) silver cocaine straw and was noisily tidying away a huge, Jason-esque line of powder from a mirror on his bedroom table. He passed it over his shoulder to Dylan without asking.

Dylan accepted and walked over. The mirror was the right size for the sideboard. He looked around. One huge mirror on the wall and one floor to ceiling job next to the wardrobe.

This mirror never goes up on the wall. It is condemned to sit here and just proffer gack to idiots, totally away from its intended use which is showing people what they look like. And yet somehow still doing it, just in a different way.

Just like me.

Shaking his head gently at his rather uncomfortable personal juxtaposition with an item of Claridge's household furniture, Dylan almost apologetically hoovered up a line. It was not his gear. It was duller somehow, not as pure. But quantity has a quality all of its own, and he found himself fighting mild nausea with his knees bent rubbing his eyes with the balls of his hands just a few seconds afterwards.

Breathless, he sat down on the bed as Claridge began to line up another one.

Comparing yourself to a dirty mirror in Claridge's bedroom Dylan. Oh dear, oh dear.

"So. Finchy enjoyed the little fellas from the other day and reckons he wants to buy a weight. So I've given him all but a few of the ones I bought off you the other day and also the lot you just gave him."

Dylan was a little uncomfortable with Claridge's red faced use of the word "gave".

"...so he wants another three hundred."

Claridge stared at him in the dim light.

"I was planning to front him up the pills you sorted today but I've not got the cash on me. Normally you know it's no problem but..."

Dylan was already shaking his head but answering in the pained affirmative.

"Alright. You're good for it. When can you get me the money?"

"Bring the other three hundred, I'll buy those off you and give you the cash lump sum then. Fair?"

Dylan's heart sank.

Another three hundred. Another trip to Tufnell Park. Fuck. Sake.

He had an unmovable picture on his mind of an empty and battered box floating in the post-tsunami debris in the surf on a far away beach, with a broken mirror lying desolate next to it.

You absolute cunt.

"When do you need them?" he asked testily.

"Wednesday. He needs them by next Wednesday." Claridge's eyes had grown huge and he was not sure whether it was the coke or the prospect of something very lucrative with Finchy.

"I'll have to let you know mate. Short notice and I dunno if I can arrange it in time."

Claridge had already taken his answer as done and dusted and was busily finishing another dusty line.

"And again?" came his muffled enquiry, waving the straw daintily at him like a teaspoon at tea party.

Dylan did the line, left the party shortly afterwards to barely a reaction from his hosts and then spent the rest of the evening wishing he had said no to the cocaine.

THIRTY-EIGHT

Soundtrack

Maor Levi – 'Chasing Love'

The week cascaded by. Tuesday shuddered to a halt as Dylan arranged to meet Grace in a bar on Wednesday after work. Thoughts and ideas rattled ceaselessly inside him as the hours ticked by on Wednesday afternoon.

Grace showed just after 7 and seemed nonplussed by Dylan having already got her a gin and tonic. Dylan wondered if he had overstepped. She swigged it in four mouthfuls as if trying to get rid of a bad taste, relief evident on her features in the half-light.

The booming Euro-techno did nothing for the conversation despite Dylan's best efforts and he sensed a hurriedness from Grace to get out and get back to hers. They did not discuss it. It never even came up. Dylan went with her, cherishing the lift the beer gave him, melting the nerves.

They regarded each other from opposite seats on a packed tube train. Dylan tried not to stare for half a minute before giving his seat up for an older lady.

Grace beamed at him.

Dylan watched the happiness in her eyes. It seemed to tell him she placed some imponderable value on his battered sense of decency and manners, enduring from childhood.

What have you seen? What do you know?

What scumbags must you have dated before me to find a simple gesture so charming?

*****

Grace started the evening off feeling a little uncomfortable. Another midday no-show had put her in a bad mood and a very mundane afternoon booking with Old Street Guy had done little to stimulate her. He on the other hand, still welted from her last trip, seemed more animated than usual. He had squirmed and begged, propped up on two pillows on the end of his bed, without using the safe word. She recalled his heavy breathing, seemingly on the edge of sobbing as she rubbed Nivea into his well-leathered and blistered rear end afterwards.

It had been so strange in his dark little apartment with the curtains closed. But for his begging and pleading to some brutal, ethereal mistress or mother figure she certainly was not but he preferred to pretend she was, there had been almost no talking.

She had asked him to fetch the strap and then present himself for correction, and that had been that. The money was on the dresser. He didn't move. He never did, not any more.

Walking away toward Moorgate and her meeting with Dylan after work she wondered whether his neighbours had heard the rhythmic loud snapping noises and pained groans. He certainly did not seem to care. As the beating went on his moans became more tormented. Grace watched him slap his wrinkled palms onto the duvet cover, clenching fists and then by the end grabbing the bed for dear life.

His feet had remained planted to the carpet until the last set of twelve, toes crunched up in agony. The beating had continued for longer this time. He hadn't told her to, neither had she decided to, it just came to and end when it came to an end. He'd counted out several dozen strokes, hoarse and rattling with breath by the end. Grace sensed she was taking him to something close to a node point for him. Some barrier to be pushed and broken when he felt safe enough with her. That it was important for him somehow, although she could not fathom how or why. The last had landed with a thud that reverted around the room and all the way up her arm, met only by a gratified, broken whimper from the agonised man on the bed.

What had gone on with him? What nightmarish psychological position had taken hold to engender such a primal need to be abused? Was it his childhood? Grace was no psychologist but reckoned so.

She raised her hand to scratch her nose. Her fingers smelt delicately of moisturizer and faintly of leather. She smiled as she remembered the banknotes in her coat pocket.

Money for old leather. Money for old memories.

The drinks were a waste of time.

She couldn't hear a word Dylan was saying and did not know why he had bought her a gin and tonic. She downed it as fast as she could and ordered a bottle of wine. Bored of the rigmarole, she was just keen to get back to her home and did not remember making a decision that Dylan should come back with her. He just was. That was it. That was what boyfriends and girlfriends did wasn't it?

The tube home was packed. The harsh light did little for Dylan's features but his half-shark, half-clown smile charmed nonetheless. To her delight he stood up for a woman, giving up his seat. Nobody did that any more.

It had been some time since she had seen such a small token of chivalry. It was old fashioned and a bit sexist but there was something nice about it. A comforting feeling that Dylan was not like the other men she saw every day. He was nice. He was decent. She reasoned he was not the type of guy who would ever degrade a woman by paying to have sex with her. And that she was not the type of woman who slept with men like that out of choice.

The sex was a release. Grace was delighted in a weird way her lunchtime booking had not showed.

Dylan was a bolder and more confident creature than the previous Saturday and was certainly a fast learner. It was businesslike in a way. The clothes came off, the talking stopped. It was humourless, just easy. Comfortable, but in a nice way.

She felt as though Dylan had been a lover of hers for a long time. It felt like that. He came quickly but stayed hard with some professional encouragement from Grace and the second round was slower and easier again. He sat up in bed and she sat in his lap facing him, his belly touching hers. The kissing seemed to last forever, and she had no desire for it to end. Kissing had become a taboo for her of late and the release of being able to kiss someone she wanted to kiss, for it to mean whatever she fucking well wanted it to mean, was liberating.

She felt herself smile as she kissed him.

You're a decent man, Dylan. And I am definitely feeling things for you.

THIRTY-NINE

Soundtrack

Harry J. Allstars – 'Liquidator'

"Fucking hell, you don't waste any time."

Dylan stood with his hands on his hips staring in mild disapproval at the coffee table in the middle of an unfamiliar room.

Rush was already on hands and knees in front of him, ministering to some white powder poured onto a CD case. He ignored him.

It was barely lunchtime, and Dylan had dropped in to see Rush before they met up with Mox and Fat James. Chelsea were away at Crystal Palace and it was one of those rare Saturday 3pm kick-offs. A proper football day. Dylan would have preferred to meet in the pub but Rush was insistent. He knew it was about the gear.

Three huge lines appeared from the white chaos on the CD cover. One and then another disappeared up either side of Rush's nose before Dylan realised they were even ready. There was a long, contended sigh from the heap on the floor as Rush spread out like a carpet angel.

"Thaaaaaats better." Dylan was at once reminded of those cartoon tea folk characters on those tea adverts. Screwing his nose up, he felt his knees crack in complaint as he knelt down to see off the other remaining line. He did not even want it. He did it anyway, almost resenting the rush of the powder. Saturday 3pm kick offs and London aways were all about days out on the piss not doing gear in people's smelly lounges. Dylan had no sooner handed over the two grammes to Rush as the other man was straight into it like a starved convict. It offended Dylan somehow. That he could be pushed aside in favour of the powder. Or was it that someone else had a proper honest-to-God gack problem that was so unedifying that even Dylan had to feel somewhat disapproving, thereby validating his own opinion that his own was neither addiction nor problem?

As if reading his mind Rush knelt up, head raised to the heavens, eyes closed and pointed a mock-accusatory figure in his direction.

"It is what it is mate."

Dylan stopped mid-utterance, remembering how pointless it was to have a conversation about gear or any drugs for that matter with Rush. Rush was one of those fringe mates who seemed to know everyone but was not in anyone's close circle of adhesive mates. Everybody knew him. They had met at a houseparty many moons ago. He was seeing a girl that Jason used to work with, and when they split up he stayed sort-of-mates with Jason and came to a couple of the houseparties they had back in the day. Dylan had got talking to him and in one of those weird London coincidences it turned out Rush sat in the block next to him in the Matthew Harding Stand at Chelsea. His real name was Simon Rushmore but everyone just called him Rush or CokeRush. Ever since he and Jason had known him, Rush had had a voracious appetite for South America's favourite export.

There was no doubt he had a proper habit. Yet Dylan only saw him semi-regularly and thus could not possibly be his only supplier, despite the obvious relief flooding across the man's face implying he had gone without for some period of time.

"You look like you enjoyed that." Dylan observed drily. "Been a while?"

"Yes, usual guy has fucked off to Benidorm for a week. Absolute cunt."

Rush looked at Dylan with a look of disgust on his face as if he were talking about a Paedophile or mugger-of-old-ladies.

"Farkin' liberty. Never gave me no warning or nothing, just left. I texted him he said he was at the fucking airport. Like, sorry and all that, see you later pal."

Dylan nodded slowly, mentally taking notes.

Rush rushed to his feet, a sunny disposition rapidly returning as the gear began to work.

"Still, you're here now. Fancy another?"

Dylan looked affronted. I'm your mate you know, not some fucking two bob drug dealer.

"Rack 'em up then fella. I'll stick the kettle on."

Dylan lost himself for a few minutes in the meticulous scraping and straightening on the CD cover. Two decent sized lines. Beautifully straight and a uniform distance apart, the exact same width and length. Correct in doseage he reckoned to the milligram.

The cocaine was in full effect now. He could feel it washing down the back of his sinuses and throat, imagining it like one of those waterfalls off the Bounty adverts, impossibly fresh and natural and pristine. Dylan closed his eyes for a second as it spread up his cortex and behind his eyes. He imagined what the cocaine would say if it could talk to him. It would have a voice made up of thousands of people whispering. Right in his ear but actually inside his head. What would it say?

You never had a doubt Dylan. Neither did we. There was no doubt. It is a special thing we do, you and us. Rush doesn't understand...

Dylan opened his eyes, credit card mid-sweep. Rush was holding out a mug of tea.

"Let's smash these away and we'll go. How much do I owe you?"

It took him a second to snap out of his reverie and remember how much.

"Eighty matey."

Rush handed him seventy pounds in grubby, stinking tenners.

"I'll sort you the other one later on." Rush said hopefully.

No you fucking won't. You're hoping I agree to let it slide because I've done one and very shortly will do a second of your gear that I very kindly brought you, and when I don't you'll just forget to pay it to me later anyway.

Dylan smiled.

"Don't worry about it mate. Just buy us a pint later yeah?"

Fuck's sake. You are soft as shit sometimes, you really are.

The tea was terrible as always but it took the taste away, which of course was exactly why Rush had made it.

With a blast of welcome fresh air the two emerged from the gloom of Rush's dingy front room onto the Wandsworth street. The cocaine put a confident bounce in their step and the conversation seemed to energise from the daylight as they walked laughing and joking down toward the East Hill crossroads. Mox and Fat James were waiting in the pub and to Dylan's delight James had brought his little brother Sweary Ed. Wraps were passed out and money not very surreptitiously handed over. Beers appeared. Beers disappeared. They piled into two black cabs and made their way to Clapham Junction to get the next train to Selhurst Park.

Chelsea were everywhere. The singing started in earnest on the train much to the horror of the rest of the passengers. Mox chanced a key bump of gear when he thought nobody was looking and got away with it. Dylan stopped Fat James from doing likewise as he knew the mountain of a man was incapable of doing it as stealthily as the slight and chancey-looking Mox. James winked at Dylan and went to the train toilet. Shortly afterwards he came back looking rather green around the gills in obvious disgust at the stench and state of the facilities.

"Couldn't do it, involved sniffing, involves fucking smelling. Don't want to do that. What the hell is wrong with people?" he muttered.

Without thinking, Dylan stood up on the seat and began to bellow "Carefree" to the packed carriage. All the Chelsea stood up off their seats, hands aloft as the luggage racks would allow and joined in.

The train pulled into Selhurst Park station and the atmosphere completely changed. Police were everywhere. As they got off the platform there was a sound of a smashing pint glass and everyone flinched. The Chelsea around them took up a loud rendition of a song, then the many more Palace fans immediately drowned them out.

Dylan leant in and asked a policeman where the Chelsea pub was. The police always had one pub all the away fans had to go to.

The policeman's face was one of fear initially, eyes wide in shock as he clearly was not expecting one of the away fans to speak to him. The question did not register so Dylan repeated himself.

"Move along! Keep moving. Fuck off!" came the response as the policeman's face twisted into a snarl of pure hatred.

"Leave it out mate, I was only asking!"

"FUCKING MOVE ALONG!" Two of the policeman's companions were moving up behind him ready for Dylan to say something abusive back.

James pulled him away before he could say what he thought.

"Looking for an excuse mate. Fucking wankers. Just leave it yeah."

Dylan shot the policeman a poisonous look and moved into a gap in the crowd on front of him. The cocaine boiled inside him, fraying his tolerances and grating his temper. Another pint glass exploded on the pavement in front of Ed as they walked out of the station, showering him with glass.

"You alright mate?" Mox was over like a shot.

The 16 year old Ed raised himself to his full 5 foot 2 stature, stuck out his chin and began to scream abuse at some Palace Ultras up ahead. Wanker signs were batted back and forth. The police saw the exchange but made no effort to apprehend the glass thrower.

The tension ratcheted up. They closed up, walking in each other's shadows toward the Chelsea pub. Hundreds of Chelsea were spilling out of the front garden and onto the road. Metropolitan Police with video cameras were filming every move. Emboldened Palace youths were walking in close, taking the piss and willing Chelsea to leap the short wall and get stuck in, knowing the van-loads of police nearby would save them from any harm. By and large the Chelsea in the garden returned the insults and gestures, sporadically breaking out into song, but showed no interest in getting arrested. The Palace youths recognized this so got braver and braver. Ed, being underage and very obviously so, kept out of sight amongst the crowd by the picnic tables. Mox and James disappeared into the pub, coming out a little later rubbing their noses and carrying pints. Rush conveniently disappeared to the toilet once the pints were drunk so Dylan headed in to the get the round in. The pub was heaving with Chelsea, a seething mass of blue testosterone. The noise from the singing was overwhelming, muddied by the roar of laughter and shouting. The air was thick and humid, stinking of stale beer and too much aftershave. The floor was slick with muddy liquid. Dylan joined in a coruscating "Fuck 'em all" and pushed up to the bar.

All around was a cross section of the Chelsea support. The younger guys all had immaculate quiffs and crisply ironed designer shirts and smart trousers, not caring about the damage being done to their unfeasibly expensive slipons by the murk on the floor. The older guys were a mixture of Stone Island-clad shaven-headed hardcases and replica shirt-wearing loyalists, tight breathable nylon fabric stretched taut over rippling beer guts and floppy man breasts. A number of women were stood around singing even louder and more passionately than the men.

Dylan looked along the back wall of the pub. Some Rangers fans he had seen many times before had brought a huge Loyalists banner and somehow managed to cover one wall with it. A scattering of

Rangers blue mingled with the almost-identical Chelsea blue. Dylan said hello to two lads he last saw at Blackburn away in the cup who he did not know the names of, but who weirdly knew his ex-girlfriend Kimberley's name. They seemed genuinely disappointed they had split up. One swung a treetrunk arm onto the bar and produced a Jaager shot from a crowd of glasses, almost throwing it over Dylan in his haste. Grinning, Dylan accepted, downed it and then roared with laughter as the older of the two snatched the weeping shot glass from his grip and then daintily lobbed it a full 20 feet right bang on target into a glass bin. This drew rapturous applause from the Chelsea all around and a toxic glance from a very flustered looking barmaid. She fired a stream of invective to which he blew her a kiss. The barmaid threw up her hands in impotent rage, and the gesture produced a deafening chorus of "Celery!" from the whole pub.

Dylan was grinning all over his face by the time he emerged into the beer garden with the beers. The doubt and negativity was gone. Chelsea did that to you. No matter who you were or what sort of God-awful miserable week you had had, Chelsea was always there for you. The tribalism and camaraderie of it all was like a warm hug, a pick-me-up for all five senses. It didn't even matter if they lost. That was not what it was about. People who were not into football like that could never understand. Mox was mid-bump as Ed stood guard and Fat James and Rush were chatting to Sophie and Samantha from Hillingdon, two well-known Chelsea faces who went home and away, every game.

Samantha saw Dylan come over and grabbed him, almost spilling the beer. She stank of cigarettes and late nights.

"'wight Sam" Dylan grinned. He daintily kissed her on both cheeks and did the same for her companion Sophie.

"Hows it going Soph, you alright?"

"Not so bad Dylan yeah, work very busy and all that."

"What you do for a living again?" Dylan asked. Sophie did not look upset he did not remember.

"We're both trauma nurses at Hammersmith."

Immediately Dylan remembered.

"Oh God yeah, I remember!" Dylan laughed. Sophie asked him back.

"What do you do again, sorry memory like a sieve!" she enquired.

"Fucking good question Soph! Did you want a drink?" Dylan asked.

Sophie laughed.

"No we're alright thanks mate. Although…." She leant in close. Dylan already knew what was coming.

Dylan smiled and held out a hand, wrap already ready to go.

"Help yourself."

Sophie and Sam came back from the toilets, returned the wrap and winked at Dylan before going back to their little group. Dylan knew it was unlikely they would speak to him again that day. That was just how it went.

The pints were hurried down as the pub began to empty. It was almost kick-off time.

FORTY

Soundtrack

Sneaker Pimps – 'Six Underground'

The call had come a little too early in the day not to be from the previous night. Grace answered her phone and almost hung up.

The guy had a flat in Kennington and had been out clubbing or something the previous night. Whoever he had had back to the flat had left and the customer was, judging by his pupils and endless gum-chewing not going to be able to sleep any time soon. He was a new customer and had asked her to come in a long coat with nice underwear on underneath. Grace usually enjoyed this particular request more than most so agreed to meet him at his place. The money was passed over and the conversation was perfunctory. It was too early in the day for a glass of anything but Grace accepted and downed the champagne while the customer closed the curtains. He rounded on her in the half light, hands grabbing and grasping.

Grace allowed him to disrobe her.

He seemed impressed to the point of heavy-breathing silence at her stockings and suspenders and lacy bra. Immediately he was nuzzling her neck and undoing the clasp. What was the point in requesting someone wear nice underwear just to take it off immediately, she wondered.

"I want to lick you everywhere." He informed her between muffled snuffles.

"Please be my guest. It's been soooooo long since…" she let her whore voice tail off coquettishly.

Hands startled her. He yanked at her undergarments and boding lifted her toward the bed. Panic rose inside her and then subsided. She was knelt forward on all fours, knickers pulled down to mid-thigh as he buried his face in her from behind, stroking and touching her stocking tops as he did so.

It wasn't really what she had in mind but she resolved to go with it. He was actually pretty good at it. Before long she was arching her back and thrusting her sex into his nose and lips in exaggeration with the moans to go with it, but she knew that if he kept up the pressure and light strokes of his tongue, the noises would be real soon. She wondered whether he could tell that she was into it. She bit her lip and implored him in her best breathless whore patter not to stop.

I might actually come here!

Something rose in her, she could feel the man's saliva drip carry down her belly. It was happening. She was actually going to…

Then he stopped suddenly.

The frustration rose in her throat but was abruptly and surprisingly cut short when the customer with a animalistic groan moved her buttocks apart and plunged his tongue deep into her most intimate of places. Grace froze, all at once very self-conscious and afraid. Her muscles stood taut, unable to move. Still the man's fingers and tongue probed. She was uncomfortable so moved a hand to her forlorn clit and straight away began fake moaning to hurry things up. She "came" within seconds, buzz totally gone. Without stopping, the man pushed past her and got on all fours in front of her. A horrible realization began to dawn on Grace.

"Now me. Do me."

Oh for fuck's sake.

Fuck.

Grace hesitated. She honestly did not know what to do. The idea of returning the favour for the man repulsed her. There were only a reasonable few things she was absolutely not willing to do. This was one of those things. Instinctively she ran her hands back to her wet and streaked behind.

"That is a special favour. Special favours cost extra." The silken voice sounded absolutely nothing like her.

"I'll give you five hundred quid more." Came a muffled voice from the pillow area.

Grace almost laughed out loud.

"Well then. That is a VERY special favour." She knelt behind him. It occurred right at that moment that she had never done it before nor had the slightest idea what was involved. Certainly it seemed like a sex act laden with expectation. Of what? And would it be horrible?

Oh fuck please God be nice and clean and not stinky. Please. I'll do anything.

He was evidently freshly showered and so it was not as bad as Grace was expecting. Even so, to say she enjoyed it was a stretch. The customer on the other hand seemed enraptured to levels that impressed even Grace.

She closed her eyes and imagined she was licking an envelope.

To hurry things along she wrapped a hand around his thigh and began to stroke his well-below-average sized member. He came very shortly after that with a shriek she was worried the neighbours might hear.

It was not that bad at all actually, she mused. As long as she visualized licking something other than some random stranger's pucker it was tolerable. She did not have to do it for very long.

A sudden abrupt image from nowhere of her fishing her hard-earned five hundred quid out of the place she had just been licking made her giggle out loud and caused the man's head to appear from the pillows at the head of the bed.

She shook a mock finger at him and smiled sardonically.

"You are a naughty puppy aren't you?" she purred.

"Yes. Are you going to spit on me? Or humiliate me?" the man asked hopefully, eyes wide and revitalised. The smile dropped off Grace's face.

"I think that's enough fun for one day don't you think."

The man looked disappointed but agreed. He handed her five hundred pounds to go with the two hundred and fifty he had given her at the start of the visit, less than ten minutes before. Grace could only stuff the money into her coat pocket, worried she might gape at it in incredulity if she held it for too long. If the man felt short-changed or under-serviced he did not show it.

"Would you like to come over next weekend? Same again?" he asked.

Grace agreed and nodded, hugged him and kissed his forehead and promised him in whispers an amazing time, resolving simultaneously never to answer calls from him again. She was absolutely sure she was only aware of his more vanilla turn-ons and although the money was a real boon, the shock of it and the lack of time to think about it made her uneasy.

She left and went straight to a small Boots store a couple of doors down to buy some mouthwash and gargle into a rubbish bin outside. Nobody batted an eyelid as she did so as if whores in macs and high heels gargling Listerine into stinking bins in South London early on a weekend morning was the most natural thing in the world.

She was almost home when the Batphone went again with a text. She hated it when that happened. It was from a new number. She scrolled down, ready to get off the train and go back in the opposite direction, back to work.

"Hello Kenneth. Nice to meet you." She breathed as she read the rest of the text.

An eyebrow shot up.

"Do I do watersports?"

The phone snapped shut.

That's a no from me.

What happened to one man, one woman, a cock, a fanny and a good time?

I think I am too vanilla for this game.

FORTY-ONE

Soundtrack

The Smiths – 'Panic'

Chelsea had scored first, a scrappy finish from six yards by one of the club's Brazilian contingent. A succession of chances went begging and the frustration set in. The team could not afford to drop points. Then one of Palace's forwards tried a speculative lob from 30 yards that wrongfooted the static Chelsea keeper via a wicked deflection and in it went. Selhurst Park erupted into a cataclysm of noise and abuse. The home fans sensed a valuable point was in the offing and were roaring their team on to take the point from Chelsea. Chelsea for their part seemed to retreat into themselves, unsure of what to do with the flying tackles and physicality. Chelsea's end responded, screaming and chanting.

Dylan was fuzzy headed with the effort of singing and yelling as the beer and cocaine dulled his senses. Ed in front of him was lolling from side to side after downing at least two pints during half time. Mox was off with Sam and Sophie apparently trying to pull at least one of them. Next to Dylan, Fat James was beetroot-faced, pumping his fist in the air with spumes of spittle cascading from his mouth from the sheer power of the ejection of the words.

There were two minutes left. A Palace player went right through the back of Fabregas in the centre circle and Chelsea had a free kick. It was floated over and knocked down by one of the towering centrebacks. The ball cannoned off someone. A Chelsea player had a drive at goal but the ball was blocked. There was a melee of players. Someone hacked at the ball. It arrowed toward goal.

The intake of breath seemed to last an eternity. Dylan felt like he was seeing it in slow-motion. Looking around in real time at the open mouths and wild eyes around him. Something huge seemed to rise from the very crust of the earth underneath them. Dylan was reminded of a documentary he once saw about a reservoir of lava underneath the Yellowstone culdera that the National Park sits in. A foretelling of increasing pressure and a numbing release. The ball carried on. The Palace keeper was not going to get there.

Dylan watched his white-gloved hand arc close to the ball but fall short.

Would it go over the bar though?

*****

Chelsea won at Palace and he had gone out with Mox and Sutton Dave after the game. He had got very drunk and done huge quantities of powder in various pubs around Wandsworth and Putney before heading back to Bounds Green via Pizza Hut feeling sorry for himself at his lack of discipline and lack of Grace.

Many hours after going to bed, Dylan got up to meet his Sunday. The Sunday passed by without incident.

Ostensibly as severe punishment for his previous evening's transgressions he went out for a traumatic, heart-whirling run around Alexandra Palace and then a "healthy" frozen ready meal, whilst Grace had a customer in the mid-afternoon and then went to the gym in the evening. Both felt drained not from the alcohol consumed over the past 48 hours or even the late nights but more from the emotional effort of growing and nurturing feelings for each other, and also lying to each other and at the same time realising they had been lying to themselves for much longer.

In Dylan's case the realisation came after a very terse two minute conversation with a mono-syllabic Luca. It was hard to gauge with him. You never really knew if he was upset or not. Dylan did not really care either way, but recent strengthening of things with Grace meant he was compelled to feel more cautious than normal. Two broken legs and his front teeth pulverised would be tough to explain.

After work on Monday he zipped up for battle and headed up to Tufnell Park for what would, he hoped, be the last time he would see Luca.

And that weird cunt Antonio.

It had started to rain properly mid afternoon and carried on into the evening so much so that by the time he stepped off the tube and up to street level water was cascading down the gutters as the drains were unable to deal with the deluge. The very brisk walk up the hill was long enough for the self-counselling to begin in earnest.

Luca's just a bloke. He wanted to do business with you, he still does and you are one of his best customers. He isn't interested in hurting you even if he is a cunt most of the time. He isn't going to fuckin' behead you. Its all an act. So you go in there, you keep yourself to yourself, you don't fucking breathe a word about Claridge or Finchy and you don't...

Well what business is it of his anyway if even if you do tell him? What, he's the only Billy Big Bollocks in London who can sell weights now? Fuck off.

No, go in there. Relax. Do the deal, hand him the cash, look him in the eye and be nice, then you walk out and you go home. That's all you do.

The doorbell rang and to Dylan's surprise Luca opened it. He did not say anything but ushered him into the darkness.

What was it with these people and darkness?

The gloom outside was blinding in comparison to the almost total dark inside. Dylan hesitated. This is not right. Something's up.

Luca, naked from the waist up walked into the lounge and Dylan followed him uncertainly. Antonio was playing another very dark sci-fi shooter game on the X-Box and seemed oblivious to his presence. The game looked at a tense moment so Dylan thought it best not to lean over and offer to shake his hand. Instead, he slowly took one of the two armchairs. Luca settled in soundlessly on the one close by.

"So you sellin' weights now." There was not inquisitive edge in his voice. It was not a question. It never was with Luca. Dylan was momentarily thrown off guard.

"No, not really geezer. A mate of mine knows someone who is putting on some party or rave or something... I didn't ask really. But he was after a batch so here I am."

Luca remained passive.

"It's not a regular thing mate."

Luca began to nod slowly. Dylan at once noticed he was likely extremely stoned. A huge and very well worn bong was sat on the coffee table and Dylan had been so worried about the dark that he had not noticed the air thick with what smelt like high end green.

"I don't care mate. You sell to who you fuckin' sell to youhaahmean."

Dylan tried not to look relieved.

"Are they the same pills?"

"Same yeah. But only I have five hundred left. You take them all right?"

Dylan's mind flashed. "Uh...no I only need three hundred."

"But you're be back in a couple of weeks inni? Usual thing."

There was a moment.

Dylan had no option but to say yes. If he had said no Luca would know he was getting out and block the sale, then he would have to go back to Claridge and say he could not get the pills.

That would go down… poorly.

Finchy would likely not pay him and Dylan doubted whether

Claridge would therefore follow up on his promise to pay Dylan for the first batch. He'd seen it too often. It was the curse of dealing to your mates. The "I'll sort you out next week/on payday/next time I see you" thing. It rarely ended well. Dylan had started out extending small credit lines for a tenner here or twenty quid there but as his short-term memory carried on taking a battering so too did the integrity of some of his friends. They would just forget hoping he would too. It could easily shave 15-20% off his overall cut from a month's dealing...

Dealing. I am a drug dealer. I'm sat here in a dark fucking room with this fucking psycho about to buy hundreds of fucking E's.

How is that not "proper dealing"?

Fuck's sake.

Dylan fixed his eyes on the very stoned Luca. His eyes glinted in the darkness. Dylan found it very uneasy to look into his eyes in the darkness. There was something predatory about it. It was probably why Luca did it. Trying to look hard and scare people. Dylan wondered how hard he was, really.

He was an inch shorter than Dylan and probably a stone lighter but had substantial upper body strength judging from his arms and chest. A huge multi gym hulked in the near-pitch darkness in the corner. He was probably on it every day. It wasn't like he had a job to do.

Did he? Dylan had never thought to ask.

"Apart from being my favourite drug dealer and an all round bang up bloke, what do you actually do all day Luca? Do you have a job?"

Fuck me. That's brave.

To his surprise, Luca smiled. It was a sweet smile, not sharkish at all. Dylan had genuinely caught him off guard.

"I use to be in the Aeronautica Militaire back when I was at 'ome." Luca showed him a faded tattoo on his upper left arm, depicting a tiger, an F16 and a NATO badge.

"My unit flew combat jets in Kosovo. I was a head flight engineer.

Aviano mostly."

"Fucking hell..." Dylan was impressed.

"I work now for a charity."

Dylan was beyond impressed.

"...looking after the 'omeless peoples you know? Only part time but it keeps me busy, allows me time to concentrate on other things."

"Fair play mate. Worthy stuff."

Luca snapped back into sinister drug dealer mode.

"You have the cash? You need powder too?"

Dylan did the sums in his head and realised that luckily he did. The money from Claridge's midweek batch was still in his bag. He declined Luca's gracious invitation to buy anything else.

He studiously counted it out and handed it to Luca who wrapped an elastic band around it and hurled it at Antonio who almost jumped out of his skin when it slapped him in the back of the head.

Luca chuckled. Antonio paused his game and shot Dylan a poisonous look. Presently he came back from the bedroom with a huge bag of pills. It was easily the biggest Dylan had ever seen. It would not let him look away.

How is that not being a fucking drug dealer Dylan you idiot?

Luca sensed Dylan's unease at handling such a large contingent and muttered something in very fast and guttural Italian to Antonio who darted obediently into the kitchen. He came back with a plastic icecream box with some instant coffee grains rattling about in the bottom.

"Use this."

Dylan put his head to one side, unsure.

"Coffee it smell very strong. The dog he cannot smell anything. Is easy."

Antonio wrapped the cellophane bag in tin foil and then nestled it into the icecream box, scattering some more instant coffee over the top from a sachet.

The box closed and it was done.

"As long as you don' get stopped and searched you be ok." Luca sounded surer than Dylan felt.

"Catch you later." Dylan was up and moving toward the door.

"Ciao." Luca did not get up.

The comparative brightness of the rainy night outside was a blessing. The water ran down off his head as he walked down the hill seeming to streak off the layer of filth that permeated his skin.

The change of plans created a problem for Dylan. The plan had been to straight to Claridge's but now he had to count out the pills and that meant a trip home. He debated the usual tube vs black cab issue and decided on the basis that he probably did have enough on his Oystercard to get back to Bounds Green but that Luca had wiped out his cash reserves and there did not appear to be a cash machine nearby. Tension rose as he plugged in his headphones and bleeped through the barrier.

The train was all but empty. Dylan sank into the seat trying his best to look as un-guilty as possible. A lot more people got on at Kings Cross.

To his horror he saw a reflection in the glass of a two man dog handling team. They were about to get on his carriage.

The doors were still open. He could make a break for it, but that probably meant walking right past them. The realisation hit like a donkey punch to the gut.

Luca's bong smoke was certainly in his clothes and a person could probably smell it so a dog would have no issue.

Breaking for another carriage would also certainly get him lifted as there were not quite enough people in the carriage to mask a dash to his left or right. And didn't they work in pairs anyway? Where was the other team?

Dylan screwed his eyes shut. His music boomed in his ears. Morrissey crooned out the story of his impending demise on 'Panic' from a The Smiths best of compilation.

At any moment he would feel rough hands on his arms, holding, catching and imprisoning.

He opened his eyes.

The doors had closed. The train was moving.

He chanced a look sideways. The dog and his handler had not got on the train. Craning his neck round he saw the two officers sharing an evidently very hilarious joke as the spaniel padded alongside oblivious.

How many more times you stupid, stupid bastard?

Dylan allowed himself an expulsion of all the air in his body.

That was close. That was too close. That was pure dumb luck. If he gets on the train as he was about to, you are done. Jesus Christ. How lucky do you want to be? Don't bother doing the lottery again in your life because you just won it twice back to back Dylan.

He got off at Old Street with extreme caution, ready to walk very quickly in the opposite direction if he saw another dog team. The overground to Bounds Green seemed to go on for hours.

Fuck. That. Was. Close.

The front door slammed shut behind him and the terrors of the London night outside were finally banished. Dylan ran upstairs and to his room, symbolically locking the door behind him. The adrenalin that coursed through him on the tube train was ragged now, his stomach sour. There was the nausea again.

Some fucking drug dealer you are.

Dylan stood up from sitting on the bed and took off his coat. The pill counting took longer than expected because his hands were shaking. A long time later he pulled out the brown box from under his bed and emptied the couple of hundred left over into it. The sight of it shocked him all over again. It was supposed to be just a box now!

Two hundred pills to go again.

*****

Grace was in a noisy bar.

Her evening appointment had failed to show and at a loose end in the West End she called Abi and Rebekah for a post-work glass of wine. Both worked near Russell Square so it had been an easy choice. These things usually depended on logistical ease during the week. It if wasn't close by mostly people could not be bothered.

They were busily grilling Grace on her new boyfriend.

"It's about time." Rebekah observed.

"He's a nice bloke. I don't know him that well, more of a mate of a mate. Carla says he is sound though. Funny guy." Abi chimed in.

Grace smiled. "Yes he is. We went for a date and I don't think he... you should have seen this pub. Honestly!" Grace laughed.

"So have you two... you know?" Abi asked with a mischief in her little dark eyes.

Grace realised if she said yes she would have to make full disclosure to the girls and that meant having to tell them about his premature accident. She thought it was sweet but remembering the look of absolute desolation on his face at the exact moment she decided on discretion.

She smiled and lifted her eyebrows to heaven.

Both girls exploded with a noise that was not quite laughter.

"So???? Fuck's sake Gracey. We need to know!" Rebekeh demanded.

Grace took a moment, choosing her words.

"He's a very nice bloke. A gentleman. And he's very funny. I really like him."

"That calls for another bottle in celebration of our friend Gracey defrosting her fanny and coming back to the land of normal people who actually have sex." Abi was making a voice as if she was attempting to sound like a movie voiceover.

"Concurred!" Rebekah giggled.

Grace smile-glared at Abi and held her glass aloft in symobolic acceptance.

If only they knew! Defrosted my fanny? Seriously?

Abi dashed for the toilet at the exact right moment and Rebekah, knowing when she was outwitted, headed to the bar to buy another Pinot.

Grace looked around her. Office worker types and couples everywhere. Kasabian. Laughter. Cheer. Amusement. Normality.

Comfort.

"The Land of the Living." she said to herself, doing a far better movie voiceover impression than Abi had managed.

*****

Dylan did not feel much like eating so switched on the TV and smoked the rest of one of Jason's joints.

He was texting Grace before he realised he was doing it, rolling another spliff with his other hand, inwardly debating sprinkling some of the good coke into it for good measure.

The paper dropped to the floor.

Multi-tasking wasn't going to happen. Texting was more important.

Hiya how are you doing? Having a nice evening? DSx

No. Too stalky. Delete.

Hiya, I'm just chilling at home, what you up to? DSx

No. You sound like a boring bastard. Delete.

Hiya. Thought about you today. :) DSx

Just. No. Delete.

Hiya, I very nearly got busted with four hundred and three pills on the tube this evening by a sniffer dog. I'm a drug dealer, I pay for sex, I go down on randoms who want gear off me - and I'm a liar and scumbag you see. Hope you are having a nice evening. DSx

Dylan laughed out loud.

Perhaps not!

The fear he had felt earlier came back to him again and he knew he would probably have a nightmare that evening. A melatonin would fix that.

Massive joint, couple of a beers AND a Melatonin Dylan? Really?

Dylan reflected as he picked up the bottle from the bathroom cabinet that it was getting lighter and lighter. It suggested that the nightmares were becoming too frequent and soon herbal remedy sleeping agents would not be able to stop them.

*****

Dylan awoke with a start. He was fully clothed on his bed and his alarm had just gone off. Tuesday morning. He could not decide if he had just had nine hours deep deep sleep, or just drifted off for a minute or two. Melatonin's ability to put him under - deep under - never failed to impress. Maybe it had been the weed too, but it had been a dreamless sleep. A successful sleep.

Then he realised he had wet the bed.

*****

Grace awoke with a sore head. The three girls had carried on until closing time and she was sure they would be feeling worse than her, but even so they had got through four bottles between the them before the rum and Cokes had started.

She stiffly rose and walked into the kitchen. Barney greeted her with an open eye from his spot on the sofa. Her phones were sat on the kitchen counter.

Oh fuck.

Did she text him last night?

She stumbled over still with eyes full of sleep and flicked through the messages.

There was one from her Clapham North guy about that evening, an enquiry about that afternoon from a new guy in Dulwich and nothing about her no-show from the previous evening. She picked up the other one.

Nothing from Dylan.

Just to make sure she flicked through to her sent messages.

There it was.

Hi Dylan. Just wanted to say hi, hope you are doing ok looking forward to seeing you on Weds. Hope you are good. Grace xx

It wasn't as bad as she feared, to be fair. It did sound like she was complaining at his lack of contact by asking twice how he was, which if she was absolutely honest was more or less the truth. But apart from that it was ok. Nothing to get upset about. He had not texted back but that was fair enough given that she had sent it at almost half past twelve. She was quite impressed it had made any sense!

*****

Dylan had uttered a long stream of nothing but the vilest profanities for a solid twenty minutes. All his clothes and the bed sheets and mattress protector had gone into the washing machine. It had not really soaked through to the mattress much but the room stank unmistakably.

He was more than twenty five minutes late for work when he finally barged through the double doors and stomped to his desk.

He did not check his phone until mid-morning and was surprised and a little cornered to find a text from Grace.

Fuck.

Did she want to come over to his on Wednesday? He could not get a new mattress in 24 hours and in any case could not afford a decent one. He could afford some chemicals though so resolved to Febreze the piss out of the mattress when he got home from Claridge's.

You grimy bastard.

The afternoon finally ground to its conclusion without Dylan having done even a tiny bit of work all day. He skipped out of the office with a lot more gusto than he had entered and almost sprinted past the security guys and into the London late afternoon. The rain from the previous day had gone but it had not got warm enough to dry the roads and pavements so under clear and cold skies it remained damp. Dylan could not get the reflection of the dog and the handler out of his head as he walked fast toward Liverpool Street.

It had occurred to him in a mid-afternoon moment of caffeine-driven enlightenment that there had been another possibility. He had only seen a reflection. Had it even existed? Or had he imagined it?

It was a fairly common thing wasn't it? To imagine your own fears so much that now and again you might actually see them when they weren't there?

Dylan was sure he had read a pamphlet once warning about side effects of prolonged gear usage. It can make you paranoid. Especially if you are smoking a little bit of dope, not sleeping enough, drinking too much and taking herbal sleep remedies to try to circumvent the dreams...

It had just been a fleeting glimpse reflected in the glass. What had they been laughing at? In his mind he could smell the dog, smell the policeman, almost feel the hands and the grasping.

Dylan wrestled with it all the way to Wapping.

*****

Grace opened her phone in the back of the cab. There was a response from Dylan. Her heart rose and she found herself smiling.

Hiya. Quiet night, sorry I missed your text. All cool here. Can't wait to see you tomorrow. DSx

He can't wait to see me!

*****

Dylan had been worried about the shift in Claridge, the new shiftiness from a hitherto reasonably straight shooter. But as it turned out Claridge was cool.

His flat was cool and quiet. The faint smell of the weekend still lingered in the air. Perhaps it would never leave, Dylan wondered.

Claridge had given him all the money from both batches plus fifty quid for his cab. He had seemed very eager to make Dylan seem as comfortable as possible and seemed on rare clarity. In fact he was still in his suit from work.

He and Dylan had chatted for a little while over a bottle of ice cold Sol before Claridge rose to his feet.

"Sorry matey, I have to get back to work. Look, thank you ever so much for sorting this out. I'm sorry it was so complicated. Finchy's a complicated geezer, d'ya know what I mean?"

Dylan drained the bitter ends of his bottle and stood up.

"No dramas mate. Pleased we could get it done." Dylan considered at that moment telling Claridge while he was straight up about him stopping the dealing but in then end being ushered toward the door made his mind up for him.

"Really appreciate it mate. Give my love to Carla."

"Will do squeezer."

The door closed. Dylan started off down the corridor unable to shift the small brown box lurking under his bed from his mind.

Three hundred gone to Claridge. Finchy sorted. Cashed up.

Two hundred to go.

FORTY-TWO

Soundtrack

Kasabian – 'Ladies And Gentlemen (Roll The Dice)'

Joyfully, Wednesday dawned and Dylan could not get to Grace quick enough.

Luckily she did not seem interested in going to his.

They went back to hers after a decent but expensive steak and they settled on her sofa. Barney came up to say hello while Grace fiddled with her phone and placed it down on the coffee table next to Dylan's. She produced a bottle of Shiraz and two glasses, and then disappeared to the bathroom. Barney lost interest shortly afterwards and leaped down onto the floor striding for the kitchen.

Then Dylan heard it.

It took a second to realise what it was. Then it beyond question. The sound of a phone vibrating.

Grace came back into the lounge just as it stopped.

Dylan poured the wine.

"Your work phone was ringing." he looked up.

Grace looked like a rabbit in headlights. Without saying anything she darted for her coat and pulled out the cheap Nokia Dylan recognised from the previous Saturday in the pub.

It was more her reaction that aroused Dylan to give it more than a passing thought. Her face was a mask of pure fear. Not unlike what he imagined his looked like on the Monday night at the real or imagined prospect of a close encounter with the Met Police canine sniffer unit. The fear in her face paused him.

Something was not right.

He finished pouring the wine and sank back onto the sofa watching her.

The Nokia was one of those cheap disposable ones they sell at petrol stations. Luca had one just like it weirdly.

Dylan laughed inwardly at the notion of Grace as a drug dealer.

Not a drug dealer. But...

"How come your work doesn't give you a Blackberry or something?" he asked, watching Grace's face.

"No idea. Cheapo bastards don't want to spend the money I guess."

It may have been enough for Dylan were it not for the look on her face when he told her about the phone ringing.

But the look was one of fear, of being caught.

He knew it well.

The look would not drop from his mind as they drank. Dylan changed the subject and they carried on drinking the wine. She snuggled in close to him as they chatted. The warmth of her body against his almost made him forget about the question in his mind. Almost.

Grace got up to go to the toilet again and something switched inside Dylan.

He was up and moving across the carpet as soon as the bathroom light went on and the door closed. Her handbag lay on the kitchen counter. It was open.

Dylan looked inside.

Tampons. Makeup. A pen. An iPod. Headphones. A little can of bodyspray. Condoms. More makeup. Some breathmints. Some tissues. More tissues. Wetwipes. A can of something, some sort of spray.

Pepper spray!

A small notepad. Some chewing gum. A sanitary towel in its wrapper. More condoms!

In the back compartment.

Leather.

Some sort of leather strap. And... a little baggy of blue Viagra pills!

In the front compartment. Some cards.

Call girl cards.

Dylan stared. The woman on the pic gurning back at him did not look anything like Grace save for the hair colour. But there were what, six? Seven cards? All the same?

FUCK.

SHE'S A FUCKING PROSTITUTE.

He closed the bag silently and instead sidestepped to Grace's winerack as she switched off the bathroom light, utterly oblivious to his indiscretion.

They drank half the second bottle and Dylan carried Grace to bed, helping her with her clothes. She was incredibly tired. Her limbs seemed floppy like a ragdoll. She was asleep before her head hit the pillow and Dylan let her sleep, stroking her hair gently.

No sex was fine.

It all fit. Even in the semi-drunk haze and post-date tiredness Dylan was sure.

The-Girl-In-The-Pink-Overcoat, his girl, his Grace - was a prostitute.

Was she his girl though?

Was she his Grace?

Dylan lay in the darkness unable to sleep. He wished he had a Melatonin because his mind was racing in directions and in tangents he could not control.

Maybe she was but she was only an escort, she did not actually have sex? No, then what were the Viagra and the condoms for if not for sex?

Maybe she was a sex therapist?

Maybe she was a drug addict? She didn't look like a drug addict. There were no track marks on her arms. What could have happened to her to make her into a prostitute? What terrible misfortune?

What else was a lie though? The stuff about the British Museum? Does Abi know? Fucking hell - does Carla?

No, they couldn't. They couldn't possibly know. Dylan was sure of that.

Was he blowing it out of proportion?

Was it just a part time effort? Maybe. A very occasional thing?

Was she just seeing someone else? Dylan could not see it. Maybe it was a trust thing, but he could not reconcile the contents of her handbag, the beautiful, wonderful and amazing woman herself and the tawdry idea of her seeing someone else. Someone with some very varied sexual tastes by the look of it. No, it was not that. It could not be that. The calling cards ruled it out utterly.

Maybe it was just a part-time thing? Maybe she was giving it up?

How did he feel about that?

Being a drug dealer is far worse than being a hooker.

Dylan slipped out early and let her sleep.

She heard him go but was too comfortable to stir. He left the door open and Barney came in to see her, curling up warmly against her head and going to sleep. Dylan had obviously fed him from the half open can in the fridge otherwise he would be all over her and not letting her rest. She drifted back off to sleep.

*****

Dylan did even less work during the day than for the previous day. The thoughts and questions would not stop. He had awoken with a sense of dread in his stomach that repressed his appetite. The wine and steak from the previous evening boiled inside him and coffee seemed to do little but turn the mix sour.

The questions would not stop.

The dread would not go away. It was like a terrible foreboding. Dylan allowed himself to think on it further on a bench outside the office at lunchtime. The scene was as depressingly familiar as Dylan could imagine. Grey clouds skated across the sky in a fresh spring breeze. He watched the planes bank over the little hexagon of sky he could see on their way into Heathrow. Food singularly un-appealed so he nibbled a banana.

What was he dreading? What was he so afraid of? What was haunting his thoughts?

At once it seemed to dawn on him as a cloud moved aside and the square was bathed in weak yellow sunshine.

He was afraid of losing Grace. It was disappointment.

Maybe he already had. Maybe she was never destined to be with him. Maybe he should take the date and the sex and move on, learn the life lesson whatever that professed to be and get on with being him.

The idea made him sick to his stomach. She was perfect.

The emotion of remembering her as if she was already lost seemed wildly out of kilter. It threatened to topple him like some freakish fairground ride. He could not catch his breath. The banana in his mouth smothered him.

They had only had a couple of dates. But he liked her. The prospect of losing or even having lost her already was not something he could entertain. It was like those romantic movies, he wondered. Boy meets girl, girl agrees to date boy, boy loses girl.

Ok so you don't want to let her go, fine.

But how are you going to keep her, genius?

Like a Polaroid his plan began to form.

Boy keeps girl.

How the fuck was he supposed to do that, he wondered. He surely wasn't emasculated enough to be fine with other blokes screwing his girlfriend for money, whether it was on her terms or not. The question was stark.

Have her but share her or not have her at all.

Astonished at his own lack of macho backbone he searched inside himself and came up empty. No, he wanted to keep her and any cost would be worth it.

Boy keeps girl at any cost.

FORTY-THREE

Soundtrack

Echobelly – 'Dark Therapy'

Grace watched the huge plane hum quietly across the sky. She was making her way to a set of waterfront flats near Battersea. She stood and watched it as it came directly over. It made a curious low noise that sounded almost other-worldly as vapour flashed across the backs of its enormous wingspan. The bright logo of a well-known Middle Eastern airline was clearly visible across its whale-like belly. She immediately remembered the TV advert about flying this or that airline to far-flung exotic lands.

Was it too early to want to go on holiday with Dylan?

Somewhere amazing.

She imagined spending a week on an exotic island with Dylan, him looking after her. It seemed so far away but just tantalisingly within reach.

She had little moments of panic when she wanted to get out. To run and not stop. London was all things to all men and women but it had a way of preying on people's fears and suspicions. It was an emotionally draining place to be at times, she knew all too well.

She would stop the hooking. The battery was coming out of the Batphone. This would be her last visit. It was a shame it was not with one of her regulars but maybe that was a good thing, lest she be tempted to say something. She had got off the train in The City first to go see an employment agency. The job hunt would not take too long. She was ready for a professional challenge after six months charity work in Tajikistan, or so the lie to the agent went. They seemed impressed. The kindly plump woman had said there and then she had some things that would be suitable. She would go for some interviews soon, she was sure. Dylan would never know.

The little adjoining pub to the flats was already open and she walked in. There was a happy feel to it, as the strains of nostalgia made the previous tawdry six months better in hindsight. Certainly her bank balance would miss the sex work. But it was time.

Just one more party.

It was quite a nice pub, actually. Far nicer than some of the meeting places she had disgraced herself at over the previous few months. There were a few people dotted around but none made eye-contact as she entered. A Britpop song was playing in the background: it was one of those places that had a jukebox that had not been updated since it was put in, circa 1995. The place smelt of freshly cleaned floors and something rich and garlicky cooking in the kitchen, managing almost to cover up the stale beer aroma. Almost.

A man was beckoning her over from a corner. She went over. The guy was balding. Strands of hair were draped across his head seemingly stuck as if he had been caught in the rain. Grace did not immediately make eye-contact with him but sat down.

"Pink overcoat." he gestured to her. His voice was whiney and had an odd clipped pitch to it. She caught his eye and something stopped her. His eyes. He had angry eyes.

Grace gave a mock laugh. "Not many of them about. Shall we have a drink?"

The man seemed affronted. "No, I'd... let's go…"

With that he was off. Grace pulled her coat back on and followed him out of the pub.

He was wearing a dark bottle green sweater from the 70s and a pair of badly-fitted supermarket own-brand jeans with a pair of smartish but faded black brogues. Something deep inside her started to speak but she was in too much of a hurry to listen.

This is your last one Gracey. Say goodbye to Nadia.

They walked very fast down a sidestreet and before she could object, he had disappeared down a side alley. She followed.

"...erm...?" she started in a sense of building urgency. The voice inside was speaking clearly now.

He turned back towards her, eyes blazing. Moving right up to her, inside her personal space immediately.

Too late.

She saw the darting rabbit punch coming but could not get her arm up fast enough to block it. A jarring impact hammered into the side of her face. Dazed, she could do nothing about the follow-up right to her left eye that knocked the ground out from under her.

She fell limply.

Her head cracked off the slimy concrete and her head exploded in pain. White light flashed in front of her eyes. Pavement filth and grit rubbed against her temple.

Instinctively Grace tried to pull her arms in and curled up tightly into a defensive ball as the first kick came. The air was smashed savagely from her body as the shoe powered into her chest below her chin. A second immediately glanced off her shoulder.

A vicious stamp smashed into her calf, followed immediately by another. Her leg felt as though it had shattered.

A scream stifled to a pitiful squeak, she could not breathe. The pain smothered her, ripping the oxygen from her lungs and bulging her eyes from their sockets in shock.

“Dirty! Filthy disease-ridden whore!" His hissed accusations dripped venom.

When opened her eyes he was gone, though she had not heard him run off. How long had it been? A second? Or a minute? Or longer?

Something warm dribbled down her ear. He had spat on her.

He had had angry eyes.

She tried to raise her head but something heavy inside her stopped her. Blood pounded in her head, behind her eyes. She could not rise, or pull up an arm to wipe her face. Her leg ached. Her eyes rolled.

Then it all went dark. Grace's head impacted off the pavement again and stopped with a sickening thud.

Goodnight Nadia.

FORTY-FOUR

Soundtrack

Joris Voorn – 'Incident'

Dylan was at his desk about to actually do some work when his phone began to vibrate in his pocket.

He pulled it out. It was Grace.

He answered, happy but quizzical. Maybe she had realised he had been rummaging and wanted a word? Maybe she was going to tell him?

Maybe she was going to dump him?

FUCK.

"Hi!"

There was a noise on the line. Lots of things happening in the background. There was a breath and then a man's voice.

"Hello, is this Dylan Short?"

Dylan froze. It was her boyfriend. She had told him and he was calling him from her phone to tell him stay away and fuck off and it was all over and...

FUCK.

"Yeah. Who's this?"

"Afternoon mate. My name is Miles, I'm a paramedic doctor with London Ambulance Service. I've got Grace here with me, she's had an accident.... She.... She's been attacked..."

Vomit rose in Dylan's throat. The breath was kicked out of him so hard he almost fell out of his chair.

"Where... what hospital mate?"

"Chelsea Royal Infirmary, not sure if you were the right one to call you were just the last person on her phone so I..."

"Yeah, great mate. I'm coming down, tell her.... tell her I'm...I'm on my way. Is she ok?"

"She's had a crack on the head. Come down and we'll talk more then ok?"

The phone was in the pocket and the chair spinning across the floor. Dylan was up and running. He nimbly sidestepped Geeta doing some photocopying and increased the sprint toward the door. People crossed his path. For a second it looked as though he might make it.

The new IT manager guy did not dodge him in time and the two men collided hard.

Sturrock stayed on his feet but Dylan fell sideways and into a pedestal drawer unit. The impact echoed across the office, as stationary flew in all directions. A loud crack echoed inside Dylan. He was on his feet before the last of the papers and stationary items fell to the carpet.

"Fucking hell! Watch it, retard!"

Sturrock screamed after him, coffee dripping off his fingers. The breath would not come. He staggered out of the stairwell and through the emergency doors. An alarm began to scream. Dylan was not interested.

One of the Indian lads tried to stop him as he turned hard right almost slipping on the greasy floor and ran full pelt into the car park. Mercifully a black cab was driving past and Dylan leapt in front of it almost bouncing off its bonnet. Dylan threw the door open and jumped inside.

He could barely get the words out to an incredulous taxi driver.

"Fuck me pal. You must have really fucking upset someone. Who the fuck's chasing you?" the driver asked.

Dylan could not properly articulate so concentrated on wiping the blood from his split lip on the corner of his shirt.

"Chelsea Royal hospital mate. Please hurry. Please." he managed between snatched breaths.

The driver got the idea and nodded. The taxi picked up speed.

Dylan sprawled across the backseat and pulled out his phone.

Who you going to call Dylan?

Who?

Who are you going to call?

Dylan felt so alone he thought he might sob in solitude. The enormity of the events sank in and continued to sink. The questions overwhelmed him. The fact that Grace was selling her body to guys she did not know for money was neither here nor there. A small detail. It genuinely did not bother him.

All he wanted was for her to be ok.

Breath returning, the words began to spill out. Ones and twos at first then like a London rain shower there was no stopping it. The driver just nodded as he listened for several miles.

"...and she's fucking perfect mate. In all the ways someone can be perfect. She's fucking beautiful mate. She's so beautiful it makes me want to cry do you ever get like that mate? When you just can't cope?"

The driver nodded as another amber light flashed past.

"...mate she's amazing. I found out yeah... she's a brass. No, not like... not like a brass but like a..."

Dylan couldn't find the word.

"Like a prostitute?" The driver offered.

"No! No! But yeah.. I mean... sort of yeah. Like a… like a… a special one.... like a good one not a wrongun… do you know what I mean? Like…."

The driver shook his head but did not ask any more questions.

"Well she don't know that I know mate. Can you fucking believe that? She doesn't even know that I know. But I'm that into her I honestly don't fucking care. She's perfect mate. SHE'S FUCKING PERFECT!!!" he screamed out loud, unable to control the adrenalin.

The driver's wide eyes regarded him from the mirror with a mixture of concern and fear.

It was the antithesis to the Hugh Grant Richard Gere films, a mad and violent dash for an exit and a damp and bleeding cab ride. A cinema audience would not think it was in any way romantic.

Neither did the driver. He regarded the shabby, chubby and dishevelled man in his mirror further, almost hitting a scaffolding lorry on his way onto the Embankment. He was high on something, he was sure. His eyes were bulging!

"And she's in the hospital???" he asked cautiously.

"Yes! Fuck!! Yes! Some cunt fucking attacked her!!"

Dylan looked properly traumatised, the driver wondered if it was all some weird psychotic episode and he had been the one who had been attacked. He certainly looked as though he had been beaten up. The driver thought about warning Dylan not to get blood on his cab seats but decided against it as Dylan had begun to snivel quietly, eyes wide.

They pulled up at the hospital and Dylan overpaid the cab fare by twenty pounds. The driver got out of his door to give him his note back but Dylan was just gone.

Dylan clattered flat footed into the reception of the Accident and Emergency and was directed to a set of curtains. An ambulance guy in green overalls stepped in front of him and gestured for him to talk to Dylan but he was not to be denied.

The sidestep was not as successful as Dylan wanted and his footing went again.

FORTY-FIVE

Soundtrack

Magnetic Man – 'Anthemic'

Grace just been awake a couple of minutes and was groggy. The pain in her head was just a thud as they had given her something for it. She had a mild concussion but there was no swelling so she would just have a sore head for a few days. The massive bruise on her sternum and even larger one on her calf would take longer to heal. The doctor guy had told her they thought she had cracked a rib as well.

Something was rushing outside her little curtained cubicle.

The curtains slashed off the ceiling in a deafening crash, scaring her. Light blue material rolled everywhere as a huge mass shot from left to right, dragging the plastic and scattering nurses everywhere.

Grace took a second to process that the mass the doctors and nurses were tending to on the floor covered in curtains was a person.

A nurse stood back as the curtains were thrown aside and the man got up in considerable apparent pain.

The nurses and curtains parted and Dylan rushed over, his face a mass of pain and relief.

She threw her arms painfully around him and began to cry.

"You look like shit." she murmured.

Dylan began to laugh, utterly ignoring the accusative Tagalog yapping of the nurses behind him.

"You look beautiful." he beamed.

"What happened to your face?"

"I fell over. I may have cracked a rib. It's cool."

Grace began to laugh then grimaced in pain.

"Same here actually."

"Listen! I have to tell you something..."

Dylan was leaning in close. Behind him a hospital porter had appeared almost instantly with a small stepladder and was reattaching the curtain rail to holders in the roof. The nurses lost interest in Dylan and began to disperse.

Grace nodded.

"Listen. I know. About the sex thing, the call girl escort thing. I know."

Grace's eyes widened and tears began to form.

Her heart fell out of the bottom of her stomach.

Cold water rushed over her skin as her mouth ran utterly dry.

Dylan was sure he saw her world explode in her eyes.

Her heart pounded. The horror!

HE KNOWS!

Dylan began to tap her arm insistently, not letting her form a defence. Some plaintive excuse or justification. Anything. The words would not form anyway as the crying began to build. She could not talk and anyway Dylan would not let her. He was desperate to tell her something. He began to talk. A big blob of spittle flew out and landed on her robed stomach. Grace watched it helplessly soak into the gown before daring to meet his wild eyes.

She was astonished to find tenderness and care in the manic expression.

"It's ok! It's ok. I don't mind. I don't mind! Its cool. We'll work through it. Important thing is you are ok and I've got you in my life."

Grace's mind struggled to process the enormity of it all. How could he have found out?

Could she deny it?

Judging by the look on Dylan's face, definitely not.

How did he know?

And how could he possibly be alright with it?

"How?" was all she could give. The effort was Herculean. Merely forming the word exhausted her as the tears started in earnest.

"Don't worry about it, ok? Main thing is you are ok." Dylan looked so relieved.

Grace began to cry again, quietly this time.

Overwhelming relief of ages began to flood out.

*****

Dylan went to get some cups of tea after a while and when he came back he found the bed missing.

She was having an X-ray according to a kindly Asian nurse. Dylan volunteered himself for the same procedure more to be with Grace than anything else, but lifting up his shirt and hissing at the touch of a biro from the doctor, he realised perhaps his self-diagnosis was right.

The news was good. Both had a cracked rib but in both cases it would heal on its own.

The doctor promised to prescribe some really strong painkillers. Dylan nodded in guilty approval.

Grace pulled him in close.

"I'm going to stop. After today I can't not really. I've got some temping application forms in my bag. I was going to stop... even before today. You must believe me." her eyes implored Dylan.

"I'm done. I was going to before I met you but now I've met you… well I want to and I will. You are amazing." She continued, on the edge of tears once more.

Dylan started speaking and the words came out without him

telling them to.

"I believe you."

He hesitated.

Grace became aware through instinct alone that what he was about to say was incredibly important to him. And maybe to her as well.

Then the words spilled out.

"Look… I have to tell you."

Tell me what?

"…I used to be a fucking….. a fucking…. fucking scumbag drug dealer and now I have met you I don't want to any more. I'm properly into you. You make me want to do better. To be better you know? That means no dealing…"

Grace did not even look angry.

"Dealer? Like, actual dealing?"

Dylan carried on uncertainly without answering her question. The hospital noise reduced to uncomfortable whispering silence behind them.

"Was just small fry though, you know...just a couple of pills and stuff you know? Party stuff not crack and shit."

There was a long, long pause.

Grace nodded. It was clear to Dylan the distinction was easy for her to form.

She did not even look surprised.

"You understand that right?" Dylan asked uncertainly.

"Yeah. As long as you are stopping it now, it's no issue. I mean, lots of people do, don't they? And… well…Carla is a bit of a wild child isn't she? I kind of figured with you living in a party house with party people that you probably were... well…. well not dealing.... but.... I mean it's just a little bit of gear right?"

"Right. And I'm not doing it any more. Done. Finished. Finito. " Dylan agreed with a ostentatious sweeping gesture of finality with both palms.

Grace nodded with a serene smile of peace on her face.

He had got away with it.

He was sure his knees were going to go from under him with relief. The warm comfort gently pushed the trauma away and he bizarrely felt as if he might wet himself.

He felt his heart and soul go soaring through the sky to a far off exotic land.

"The truth sets you free." he observed wryly.

"I'm glad we.... you know?" Grace whispered.

“Coming clean.” Dylan nodded slowly.

"And you don’t hate me?" Dylan asked, evidently unable to believe his good providence.

"Why would I?" Grace asked, her face utterly clear. There was no doubt there.

Dylan mumbled a half-hearted self-deprecating protest.

"Dyl, you could be the second coming of Pablo Escobar I wouldn’t care. You are the best thing that's happened to me for years. Honestly, I..."

"Thank fuck for that." Dylan announced flatly, not letting her finish.

"Let's agree just not to mention it again. Our little secret. Have you got any gear left?"

Dylan was not sure he followed.

"Maybe we could go down to the river, I’ll dump the Batphone and the pepper spray and that horrible spanking paddle thing and the Viagra... you dump your.... your things? Your stuff? All of it, all of mine. We could do it together?"

Dylan did the maths. 200 pills.

North of £250.

Don’t be a total idiot.

He realised that a net loss on the rest of the pills was a small price to pay. And he mused, to be honest it would be a good penance.

"Sounds good to me. Sounds perfect." Dylan agreed.

FORTY-SIX

Soundtrack

Envio – 'For You' (Blizzard Mix)

Four hours later they were stood by the Thames.

It was cold outside even though it was mid-April. Grace wore a knitted hat to cover her bandage. Another black cab rattled expectantly in the background, its door ajar imploring them to hurry up and get back into the warm.

"Do you think we should like... say something?" Dylan asked.

"Well... like what?" Grace asked as she examined the ornate black box. The lid slid away.

"I dunno. End of an era though, isn't it?" Dylan observed.

Grace said nothing.

Into the box went two mobile phones, all of Grace's Viagra, the spanking leather, some lubricant, some fairly natty red underwear, both pepper sprays and north of forty condoms.

Dylan and Grace stared at it in the open. The brown wood shape seemed to take on a character of something else, almost making a sound as it seemed to bulge and pulse in the night air. The truth echoed across the Thames from the Box of Lies.

The drugs were, for some time, the only connection between Dylan and the truth. They were the thing he was most dishonest about yet they held the most truth for him. The coke. The pills. The Ketamine. They were merely windows on his soul, rendering his mind incapable of lying. Requiring truth.

Grace watched the box in deep though about exactly this.

With a shudder she realised that, in their moments of climax and in the moments leading up to it, her clients were the truest thing in her life. Apart from Barney. They didn't care who she was, they just wanted what they wanted. Usually this was their truth to hide from their significant other, if any. How ironic then that the biggest and most authentic truth in her life for months and indeed of Dylan's, was the very thing they had needed to be the most dishonest about. A requirement of truth. It sounded like a Depeche Mode record.

The inky blackness of the river seemed to invite the box and all its lies and stark truths.

Dylan was right. It was an end of an era.

The box seemed to be pregnant with circumstance and memories.

Dylan tugged futilely at the packet of two hundred pills.

"Couldn't we just... like… you know?..."

"No. Fuck's sake Dylan. No!" Grace laughed.

Dylan began to laugh.

You are fucking unbelievable, you are.

"Absolutely, yeah. Sorry." Dylan nodded in sheepish acceptance, all at once embarrassed to have even said it.

Grace pulled out a wodge of what looked like some letters and stuffed them into the box.

"What's that?"

"Letters from Fraser. He was a cunt." Grace's words sounded like the best eulogy Dylan had ever heard.

"Then he goes in the box!" declared Dylan as the cab beeped behind.

The lid closed.

The two of them hurled the box awkwardly into the river. It hit with a splash lost against the London night and sank like a stone.

The box of lies was gone.

Dylan and Grace watched the disturbed water for a long minute before she tugged at his coat to get back into the cab.

"That's that then." Dylan said philosophically.

"That's that. Shall we go back to mine?" Grace offered with a tenderness in her voice.

The cab doors closed and they moved off.

"Sounds good to me. If you've got anything in I'll cook you something? Or we can get a take out?"

"I have no idea." Grace laughed then grimaced in pain in her side.

Dylan threw a meaty arm around Grace.

"Do you still have any more of that underwear?"

"You'll see."

11798588R00223

Printed in Great Britain
by Amazon.co.uk, Ltd.,
Marston Gate.